IT STARTED WITH NO STRINGS…

BY
KATE HARDY

ONE MORE NIGHT WITH HER DESERT PRINCE…

BY
JENNIFER TAYLOR

MILLS & BOON

Kate Hardy lives in Norwich, in the east of England, with her husband, two young children, one bouncy spaniel and too many books to count! When she's not busy writing romance or researching local history she helps out at her children's schools. She also loves cooking—spot the recipes sneaked into her books! (They're also on her website, along with extracts and stories behind the books.) Writing for Mills & Boon® has been a dream come true for Kate—something she wanted to do ever since she was twelve. She's been writing Medical Romances™ for over ten years now. She says it's the best of both worlds, because she gets to learn lots of new things when she's researching the background to a book: add a touch of passion, drama and danger, a new gorgeous hero every time, and it's the perfect job!

Kate's always delighted to hear from readers, so do drop in to her website at www.katehardy.com

**BOUND BY A BABY by Kate Hardy
won the 2014 RoNA
(Romantic Novelists' Association) Rose award!**

Jennifer Taylor lives in the north-west of England, in a small village surrounded by some really beautiful countryside. She has written for several different Mills & Boon® series in the past, but it wasn't until she read her first Medical Romance™ that she truly found her niche. She was so captivated by these heart-warming stories that she set out to write them herself! When she's not writing, or doing research for her latest book, Jennifer's hobbies include reading, gardening, travel, and chatting to friends both on and off-line. She is always delighted to hear from readers, so do visit her website at www.jennifer-taylor.com

IT STARTED WITH NO STRINGS…

BY
KATE HARDY

MILLS
BOON

Published in Great Britain 2014
by Mills & Boon, an imprint of Harlequin (UK) Limited,
Eton House, 18-24 Paradise Road, Richmond, Surrey, TW9 1SR

© 2014 Pamela Brooks

ISBN: 978-0-263-90793-3

Harlequin (UK) Limited's policy is to use papers that are natural, renewable and recyclable products and made from wood grown in sustainable forests. The logging and manufacturing processes conform to the legal environmental regulations of the country of origin.

Printed and bound in Spain
by Blackprint CPI, Barcelona

Dear Reader

This book actually started life about five years ago, when the late author Maggie Kingsley and I were chatting about how interesting it would be to have a shaman as a hero.

I haven't gone quite that far in this book—my heroine is the daughter of an American Indian healer—but I did enjoy the research. And, given that my heroine has been wrapped in cotton wool for her entire life, it makes sense for her to want to work in an area where she gets to do exciting things vicariously, through her patients—hence she works in the department of tropical medicine and infectious diseases.

Then there's my poor hero, from a family who doesn't just have a stiff upper lip—they're practically encased in permafrost. When he ends up falling for my heroine, who has a close family which adores her, he's like a fish out of water. How is he going to learn to cope with it and get a happy ending?

You'll have to read on to find out :) And I hope you enjoy their journey.

I'm always delighted to hear from readers, so do come and visit me at www.katehardy.com

With love

Kate Hardy

IT STARTED WITH NO STRINGS...
is Kate Hardy's 60th Mills & Boon® romance

Recent titles by Kate Hardy:

Mills & Boon® Medical Romance™

200 HARLEY STREET: THE SOLDIER PRINCE*
HER REAL FAMILY CHRISTMAS
A DATE WITH THE ICE PRINCESS
THE BROODING DOC'S REDEMPTION
ONCE A PLAYBOY…
DR CINDERELLA'S MIDNIGHT FLING
ITALIAN DOCTOR, NO STRINGS ATTACHED

*200 Harley Street

Mills & Boon® Cherish™

BEHIND THE FILM STAR'S SMILE
BOUND BY A BABY
BALLROOM TO BRIDE AND GROOM

**These books are also available in eBook format
from www.millsandboon.co.uk**

**Praise for
Kate Hardy:**

'BOUND BY A BABY moved me to tears many times.
It is a full-on emotional drama. Author Kate Hardy
brought this tale shimmering with emotions.
Highly recommended for all lovers of romance.'
—*Contemporary Romance Reviews*

CHAPTER ONE

'WELCOME TO LONDON.' Aaron lifted his pint in a wry toast to himself.

It was his own fault that he was sitting here on his own at the bar in a salsa club. When Tim had suggested going out to celebrate Aaron's first weekend in London and catch up, of course he hadn't meant just going out for a quiet pint. Aaron should've remembered their student days: Tim had always been the life and soul of the party, and always ended up surrounded by a crowd of pretty girls. He was still the same in his thirties as he'd been in his late teens; right now, Aaron couldn't even see him in the crowded club.

So when he'd finished his pint, Aaron decided, he'd try and find Tim, say a quiet goodbye, and go back to the impersonal flat he'd rented near the hospital.

Or maybe he wouldn't even bother with the rest of the pint. He set the still half-full glass back on the bar and turned away, looking for Tim.

And that was when he saw her.

The woman with the most amazing hair: dark as midnight, flowing down almost to her waist, perfectly straight and shiny. She was wearing a short scarlet dress that set her hair off to perfection and showcased long, beautifully shaped legs. And somehow she was managing to salsa in a pair of seriously high heels.

Aaron blew out a breath. This wasn't why he was here. He wasn't looking for any kind of relationship right now, even a temporary one. Not when he was about to start a new job and all his time was going to be taken up with work.

Yet there was something about the woman that drew him.

As he watched her dance, she turned slightly and he saw her face properly for the first time. She was stunning, with a heart-shaped face, dark eyes and the most beautiful mouth he'd ever seen.

Her friend said something to her and she tipped her head back and laughed, revealing even white teeth.

Aaron forgot all about Tim. Forgot why he was here. Forgot about everything except the woman in the red dress. Instead of being the staid, sensible workaholic he'd always been, he found himself walking across the dance floor towards her. Moth to a flame.

And, right at that moment, he didn't care if he got burned.

'You are the best friend *ever*.' Joni hugged Bailey. 'And I love you.'

'I love you, too, sweetie.' Bailey hugged her right back.

'You were so right. Dancing and champagne. That's just what I need tonight.' It was pretty much what Joni had originally planned to be doing tonight—except it would've been a different sort of dancing. A slow, elegant waltz in a floaty, frothy bridal dress to a romantic song; whereas right now the dancing was hot, sweaty, endorphin-boosting salsa and the dress she was wearing had the shortest skirt she'd ever owned, thanks to Bailey's encouragement.

'Of course I'm right. I'm a doctor,' Bailey teased. 'And exercise is one of the best medicines ever.'

Joni laughed. 'Says the specialist in sports medicine who's just a teensy bit biased.'

'It's true. I can quote tons of studies.' Bailey spread her hands. 'There are links to reduction in the risk of cancer and dementia, it works as well as drugs in curing depression, and it boosts academic progress in teenagers. Wins all round.'

'So salsa's the cure for everything?' Even a broken heart? Though Joni didn't quite understand why her heart should still feel broken when she'd been the one to call off the wedding, six months before.

'Endorphins rock. Plus salsa's fun.' Bailey grinned. 'Now, *shimmy*!'

Joni couldn't help laughing. And trust her irrepressible best friend to stop her moping on the day she'd been dreading for months: the day of the wedding-that-wasn't. Bailey specialised in sports medicine and Joni in tropical and infectious diseases; but even though they didn't actually work together they'd been best friends ever since they'd met on their first day at university. They'd supported each other through the dark times and celebrated the bright ones.

'Don't look round,' Bailey said, 'but there's a hot guy who was sitting at the bar. Right now he's heading in our direction, and he's looking straight at you.'

'He's probably wondering what on earth someone as coordinated as you is doing dancing with someone who keeps doing the steps totally wrong,' Joni said with a smile.

'I don't think so. Try "wow, who's the hot babe?" Especially as your hair's down.' Bailey wound the end of Joni's hair briefly round her fingertips. 'You know, every woman in this room would kill for your hair. Including me.'

Hair that Marty had wanted her to cut. Her ex was the latest in a string of men who'd made Joni feel that she wasn't quite good enough. And she'd vowed after Marty that she'd never make that mistake again—she wouldn't sacrifice her career or her self-esteem just to please someone else. From now on, it was equal or nothing.

'Earth to Joni.' Bailey waved both hands in front of her face. 'We agreed. No brooding and absolutely no thinking about Marty the Maggot. And I think Hot Guy is about to ask you to dance.'

Joni shook her head. 'Even if he does—'

'Then you're going to say yes,' Bailey cut in. 'Doctor's orders. Dancing with a hot guy is good for you.'

'So if he asks *you* to dance—' Joni began.

'He's not going to ask me, sweetie.' Bailey winked at her. 'He's only got eyes for you.'

Aaron stood close enough that she'd be able to hear him over the music, but not close enough to be creepy. 'Would you like to dance?' he asked.

'I, um...'

The blush made her look even prettier. And he liked the fact that she clearly wasn't aware of how gorgeous she was.

Even though his head told him this was insane, the

rest of him most definitely wasn't listening. And then her friend smiled and said, 'Dancing's a great idea. My feet are feeling a bit sore right now and I really need to sit down for a few minutes.'

Aaron knew she was fibbing, because she'd been dancing without even the slightest wince as he'd walked over to them, but he appreciated her tact.

'Bailey!' There was the tiniest hint of panic in Ms Drop Dead Gorgeous's eyes as her friend waved and did a theatrical limp in the direction of the chairs at the bar.

Yeah. There was a fair bit of panic going on inside him, too, right now. He knew from experience that getting involved was a bad idea—emotions just led to pain—but he'd asked her to dance and it was too late to go back. Too late for doubts.

'Hello. I'm Aaron,' he said, extending a hand.

'I'm Joni.' She took his hand and shook it nervously. 'Look, I'm sorry about my friend. I—'

'There's no need to apologise,' he said with a smile. 'Though I might have to apologise to you in advance, as I'm not exactly the world's best dancer.'

'Neither am I. Bailey's the one who can dance, not me,' she said ruefully. 'Though I'll try not to tread on your feet.'

'Let's make that a mutual pact,' he said, and took her hand to dance with her.

Somehow, they muddled through the first half of the next track together; then the awkwardness between them seemed to vanish and the panic seeped away. And Aaron found himself really enjoying the throbbing Latin beat of the music.

Especially when the next song came on and everything slowed down. And then she was in his arms, right where he wanted her to be, all warm and soft and sweet. They swayed together, moving in time to the music; his arms were wrapped round her waist and her arms were wrapped round his neck.

He smiled down at her. Her dark eyes were gorgeous; up close, he could see that she wasn't wearing much make-up. She didn't need it. Just the tiniest bit of mascara to emphasise those long, long lashes, and soft red lipstick that made him want to kiss it all off. Even as the thought went through his head, he found himself dipping his head down towards hers. When his mouth brushed against hers, it felt like electricity prickling through every nerve end. Then she kissed him back, and the rest of the room seemed to vanish; there was only the two of them and the music.

But the next track was one with a much faster beat, and they were forced to pull apart. They stood there, just looking at each other, and Aaron wondered if Joni felt as dazed as he did.

This really shouldn't be happening. He didn't do this sort of thing.

And yet...

'Hey. I'm going to get a taxi home,' her friend said as she joined them.

'I guess I'd better go, too,' Joni said.

But Aaron wasn't ready to let her go. Not yet. 'Stay just a little bit longer?' he asked. 'I'll make sure you get home safely.'

Bailey leaned in closer so that her mouth was hidden from view and her words were for Joni's ears only. 'Stay and have some fun,' she said. 'Don't start thinking or analysing.' She squeezed Joni's hand. 'Just enjoy it for what it is: a bit of a dance with a seriously hot guy. And, before you ask, no, your lipstick isn't all over your face—even though you were snogging like teenagers just now.'

Joni felt the colour flood through her skin. 'Oh, God. I'm behaving like a tart,' she muttered.

'No, you're not. You're just having some fun on a night that would've been difficult for you otherwise. Nothing serious, no consequences. Just live for the moment and enjoy it. And, actually, snogging Hot Guy there will be very good for you. It'll produce more endorphins. We like endorphins. Endorphins are *good*.'

Trust Bailey to take that tack. Joni couldn't help smiling. 'Are you sure you don't want me to come with you?'

'I'm sure,' Bailey confirmed. 'Stay and have some fun. Call me tomorrow, OK?'

'I will.' Joni hugged her goodbye, then carried on dancing with Aaron until her feet were sore.

'Shall we have a break and get a drink?' she suggested.

'Great idea,' he said.

She liked the way he walked with her towards the bar, with a hand protectively at her back and yet not making her feel helpless and pathetic, the way her exes had always ended up making her feel. Aaron had beautiful manners, and he didn't seem the sort who would put a woman down to make himself feel better. Not that she trusted her own judgement on that score any more. She'd got it wrong so many times in the past, thanks to the rose-tinted glasses she couldn't seem to remove.

'My shout,' she said as they reached the bar. 'Bailey and I were drinking champagne, earlier. Would you like to join me?'

'Are you celebrating something?' he asked.

She certainly was. The luckiest escape of her life. Though, at the same time, part of her mourned the wreckage of her future plans. It should've been so good...

For a second Joni looked sad, and then Aaron wondered if it had just been his imagination because she gave him a broad, broad smile. 'It's Saturday night, and that's always worth celebrating, isn't it?'

He had a feeling that she didn't mean anything like that at all, but he didn't push her to elaborate. He simply smiled and accepted the glass of champagne she'd offered.

Then they danced until most people had either drifted home or gone elsewhere, and the dance floor was almost empty. Aaron noticed that Tim hadn't bothered trying to find him or say goodnight when he left. But that was Tim all over—a good-time guy who didn't think too deeply. Maybe he ought to take a leaf out of his old friend's book.

And he wasn't quite ready to see Joni home just yet.

'There probably aren't any cafés open nearby, so would you like to come back to my place for a coffee?' he asked.

She looked wary. 'Thanks for the offer, but—'

'Hey,' he cut in softly, 'when I said coffee, I meant *just* coffee. I'm not expecting anything else.'

She bit her lip. 'Sorry, I'm not used to...well...'

She had to be kidding. That gorgeous, and she didn't date?

Or maybe she'd just come out of a relationship, one that had left her confidence shaky. Making him

Rebound Man. Which was fine, because that meant she wouldn't want forever from him. 'It's OK,' he said. 'Me, neither.' He didn't date much. In between work, studying, work and more work, he simply didn't have time.

Wanting to lighten the atmosphere, he said, 'Though I can tell you that my coffee-making skills are a lot better than my dancing.' He'd worked as a barista to help put himself through university, and his expensive Italian coffee machine was the one gadget he'd never part with.

'Then thank you,' she said. 'I'd love a coffee.'

As they left the club, they were lucky enough to see an empty taxi passing. He hailed the cab, gave the driver his address, and held the door open for her to get in.

Joni was quiet in the back of the cab and Aaron didn't push her to talk; he simply curled his fingers round hers, and eventually the pressure was returned.

How long was it since he'd held hands with someone in the back of a taxi?

He reminded himself not to think. This relationship wasn't going anywhere. This was just for tonight; he didn't do 'for always'. Never had and never would.

When the taxi stopped outside his flat, he paid the driver and ushered her across to his front door.

She removed her shoes as soon as they were inside the front door. 'Um, may I borrow your bathroom, please?'

'Sure.' He indicated the bathroom door. 'I'll be through here in the kitchen when you're ready.'

She was a while in the bathroom. When she joined him in the kitchen, she said, 'Can I be immensely rude and cheeky and ask for a glass of orange juice and a sandwich as well as the coffee, please?'

Oh, help. He'd come across this before. Someone

who was suddenly hungry and thirsty after going club-
bing and then going to the bathroom. If he looked closer,
he'd just bet her pupils would be pinpoints.

His thoughts must have shown in his face because
she said, 'Actually, yes, a needle was involved.'

Uh-oh.

'But not drugs,' she said crisply.

'Not drugs.' He really wasn't following.

She took something out of her bag to show him. 'I'm
a diabetic and this is a blood glucose monitor. I prick my
finger and test the blood on a strip to check my blood
sugar levels. Right now, my blood sugar's a bit out of
whack—probably because I had a couple of glasses of
champagne tonight and I don't usually drink very much,
plus I've spent all night dancing. So right now I could
do with some carbs to get my blood sugar stable. I'm
not going to pass out on you or anything like that,' she
reassured him swiftly. 'This just happens sometimes,
and a sandwich and some orange juice will sort me out
pretty quickly.'

He relaxed, then. Diabetes explained a lot. Joni might
still be trouble with a capital T, but at least it wasn't
going to get complicated and he wouldn't feel responsible for someone else making a bad lifestyle choice.
And clearly Joni was very used to looking after herself properly because she'd explained exactly why her
blood sugar was a problem right now and how it could
be fixed.

He almost told her he was a doctor, but he didn't want
to make her feel awkward. Instead, he poured a glass
of juice and handed it to her.

'Thank you.'

He rummaged in the fridge. It had been years since

he'd done a stint on the endocrine ward, but he remembered that a protein and carbohydrate snack was good for someone whose blood sugar was a bit low but not in the unmanageable range. 'Would a bacon sandwich be OK?' he asked. And please don't let him have offended her because she was a vegetarian. He'd already made enough of an idiot of himself.

'A bacon sandwich would be absolutely fantastic. Thank you so much.' She gave him another of those sweet, sweet smiles. 'Is there anything I can do to help?'

'No, it's fine. You can sit and chat to me, if you like.'

He put bacon under the grill and grabbed the bread, then turned to face her. 'What kind of coffee would you like? Cappuccino, latte, flat white?'

She looked surprised. 'You can really do all those sorts of coffees?'

He gestured to his coffee machine. 'Yup. My one bit of self-indulgence.'

'Impressive.' She smiled. 'A cappuccino would be lovely—but no chocolate on the top for me, please.'

'You don't like chocolate? Or is that a diabetic thing?'

'A bit of both,' she said. 'I'm probably the only woman in the world who doesn't really like chocolate. My best friend says I'm weird.'

He laughed, and made her a cappuccino.

She took a sip and her eyes widened. 'This is fabulous. What coffee do you use?'

'It's a blend from a deli in Manchester,' he explained. 'I'm hoping I'll find somewhere like it in London.'

'So you've just moved here?'

He nodded. 'I'm starting a new job.' Moving on. Moving upwards. Making a difference. The one thing he hadn't been able to do when it really counted, and he'd vowed to spend the rest of his life making up for it. Not that he wanted to talk about why he'd always been so driven in his career. Especially to someone he'd only just met. So he concentrated on making them both a bacon sandwich, then handed a plate to her.

She took a bite. 'You are *perfect*.' Then she blushed. 'Sorry.'

Aaron couldn't resist teasing her. 'Were you talking to me or the sandwich?'

'The sandwich,' she confessed. 'Though I guess that, as you made it, you're perfect by association.' She grimaced. 'Sorry, my social skills are usually a bit better than this. Blame it on the champagne.'

'No problem.' He smiled at her. He couldn't remember the last time he'd met someone so cute; her warmth and sweetness made him like her instinctively.

And that made Joni exactly the wrong kind of woman for him. The more he talked to her, the more he could tell that she wasn't the sort who kept relationships short and sweet and didn't let them get in the way of her life, the way he did. He didn't want something permanent— and it wouldn't be fair to lead her on and let her think that he could offer her something he knew he just wasn't capable of giving.

He managed to make small talk until she'd finished her coffee. 'I'll drive you home.'

She looked nervous. 'That's very nice of you to offer, but you were drinking at the club.'

'I had half a pint of beer, plus one glass of champagne with you, and we've just eaten. I'm safely under the alcohol limit for driving, but I can call you a taxi if you'd rather.'

'Thank you, but I think I've impinged enough on you. I'll call one myself.'

He knew he should just let her go—it would be the sensible option. But something made him want to keep her close, just for a last few moments.

'Dance with me again first?' he asked.

She looked at him. For a moment he thought she was going to say no; then she nodded. 'OK.'

He put on an album by a jazz singer with a soft, smoky voice and held out his arms. She walked into them and rested her head against his shoulder. He rested his cheek against her hair; it was as soft and silky against his skin as he'd expected it to be.

This was a bad, bad idea.

But he couldn't help himself. There was just something about her. Something different. Something that drew him. Something he couldn't put his finger on.

As they swayed together, he gave in and closed his eyes, letting himself focus on holding her and dancing with her.

He wasn't sure which of them moved first, but then he was kissing her—*really* kissing her—and she was kissing him all the way back.

He dragged his mouth from hers. 'Joni,' he whispered.

She stroked his face, and he ended up pressing a kiss into her palm. 'I honestly didn't ask you back here for anything more than coffee.'

'I know,' she said softly.

He was finding it hard to breathe. 'But now... Will you stay?' he asked, his voice hoarse.

CHAPTER TWO

WOULD SHE STAY or would she go?

Aaron didn't have a clue.

Joni was silent for a long, long time. And then she said, 'I, um, don't usually do this sort of thing.'

'I'd already guessed that,' he said softly. 'Sorry. I shouldn't have asked you.'

'It's not that,' she said. 'I'm flattered. But I'm not looking for a relationship right now.'

'Neither am I,' he said. 'Which makes it even more unforgivable of me to have asked you to stay. It's totally dishonourable.'

He was about to turn away and grab the phone to call her a taxi when she slid her hand over his and squeezed it. 'The answer's yes.'

He knew he ought to give her a chance to change her mind. But right now he wanted this so badly. *Needed* this so badly. And he had the strongest feeling it was the same for her.

In answer, he kissed her.

Then he lifted her up and carried her to his bedroom. He stood by the bed and let her slide down his body so she was left in no doubt about how much he wanted her.

She looked him in the eye and licked her lower lip.

He took the invitation and kissed her, then lifted her hair so it fell over her shoulder towards the front of her body, turned her round and undid the zip very, very slowly. He caressed her skin as he uncovered it; it was so soft, he couldn't resist touching his mouth to it and kissing his way down her spine. She made a tiny noise of pleasure, so he unsnapped her bra and continued kissing his way downwards. When he eased the dress over her shoulders so it could slide to the floor, she stepped out of it. Then, once he'd dealt with her bra, he turned her to face him.

'You're so beautiful,' he said softly. She was still wearing her knickers and, with her hair falling to cover her breasts, she looked almost as modest as she would've done wearing a bikini at a beach. Yet, at the same time, she was sexy as hell. The ultimate temptress.

'I need to see you, Joni,' he said hoarsely. 'Lift your hair.'

Just as he'd hoped, she pushed her hair back with both hands and lifted them to the back of her head.

'Like a goddess,' he whispered.

She blushed. 'Hardly. I'm just an ordinary woman.'

Did she really have no idea? 'You're gorgeous,' he said. 'Everything about you. Your hair, your smile, your eyes—just gorgeous.'

This time, she actually smiled. 'And I'm feeling just a little bit vulnerable here, because you're wearing an awful lot more than I am.'

It took him less than ten seconds to get naked. 'Better?'

'Much better.' And this time it was his turn to blush as she surveyed him.

She leaned forward and traced a line from his rib-cage to his belly button. 'Very nice abs.'

'Thank you. But I'm just ord—' He caught himself as she laughed.

'You're not very good at taking compliments,' she said.

'That makes two of us,' he said wryly.

She swallowed. 'I forgot to ask—do you have, um, protection?'

'Yeah. Though I guess I ought to check it's in date.'

She blinked. 'You're seriously telling me that a hot guy like you…' She stopped and clapped her hand over her mouth. 'Sorry. None of my business. No questions.'

Meaning, he thought, that she didn't want him to ask questions, either. That moment when she'd looked sad in the salsa club and then claimed that she was celebrating… Whatever the reason, she clearly didn't want to talk about it.

And it suited him just fine—because he didn't want to talk about emotional stuff, either.

'Thank you for the compliment,' he said, focusing on the bit that wasn't going to rake across any raw edges. 'I guess I ought to let you know that I don't normally invite women I've only just met back to my flat.' He stroked her face. 'And I'm pretty sure you don't normally accept invitations from men you've only just met.'

'I don't.' She shook her head.

So why him? Why tonight?

No questions.

Ask nothing, and you'll hear no lies. And you won't be expected to answer anything, either, he reminded himself.

He rummaged in his bedside drawer and checked the

date on the packet of condoms. 'We're safe.' He paused. 'Though if you'd rather I left the room so you could get dressed while I call you a taxi, that's fine—I'm not the kind of man who'd ever force a woman to do something she didn't want to do.'

'I know,' she said softly. 'Or I wouldn't have agreed to come here with you.'

Funny how her confidence in him warmed him. It almost felt as if something had cracked around the region of his heart. Though he was pretty sure the permafrost would be too deep for that. This was about pleasure, not emotions. He'd make this good for her. Good for himself, too. And then he'd drive her home, they'd say goodbye, and the chances of their paths crossing again in a city of nearly eight million people were pretty remote. They'd just get on with their lives. And he could go back to doing what he always did: getting on just fine with people, fitting in with the crowd on the surface, and not letting himself get too close to anyone.

'Don't think,' she said softly.

Meaning that she didn't want to think, either? He was pretty sure that she was running from something; and he appreciated that she didn't want to discuss it. Because he sure as hell didn't want to discuss what was ricocheting round his head.

'No thinking,' he agreed, and kissed her.

And it was easier not to think when he was touching her. Easier just to feel, to lose himself in pleasure.

He pushed the duvet aside, then lifted her up and laid her against the pillows.

She stroked his cheek and smiled at him. 'Aaron.'

He kissed her again, then hooked his thumbs into the

sides of her knickers and drew them down. She lifted her bottom slightly so he could remove them easily.

'You're beautiful,' he said again. 'And I really want to touch you.'

'Then do it,' she commanded softly.

He dipped his head and nuzzled the hollows of her collar bones. She arched back against the bed and he moved lower, taking one nipple into his mouth and sucking hard. She slid her hands into his hair, urging him on.

He kissed his way down over her abdomen, then shifted to kneel between her legs. She dragged in a breath as he took one ankle and slowly stroked his way upwards, letting his mouth follow the path of his fingers; and she was almost hyperventilating when he kissed his way along her inner thigh. Which was just what he wanted; right now he wanted to make them both forget everything except this.

'Aaron, yes,' she whispered as his tongue stroked along her sex.

He teased her, flicking the tip of her clitoris with the tip of his tongue, taking it harder and faster until she was almost whimpering in need, then slowing it right down again and letting it build up and up again. He could feel the second that she climaxed, her body tightening beneath his mouth; he held her there for a long, glorious moment, and then ripped open the foil packet, slid on the condom, and pushed into her.

He could still feel the aftershocks of her climax rippling through her. He loved the idea that he'd managed to turn this gorgeous woman to complete mush.

'Aaron,' she whispered, and he held still, letting her body adjust to the feel of him inside her.

'I wanted the first time to be for you,' he said softly.

Her eyes filled with tears, as if she wasn't used to being considered like that, and he wanted to punch the guy who'd made her think her feelings weren't important. Right at that moment he had a pretty good idea what she'd been running from and why her confidence in herself was so low.

Well, he could make her feel better. And at the same time he could make himself feel better, too.

'No thinking,' he said, and began to move.

She wrapped her legs round him to draw him deeper and tensed her muscles round him.

'That's so good,' he groaned.

She smiled, and did it again.

'Do you know what I really want?' he asked.

'What?'

'You on top of me. With that glorious hair falling over both of us.'

She looked slightly shocked. 'You like my hair?'

How could she not know how glorious her hair was? 'I *love* your hair.'

She smiled, and let him roll with her so that he was lying on his back and she was straddling him. Then she moved over him and tipped her head forward so her hair fell over them, just as he'd asked.

And the reality was even better than his fantasy.

'You're gorgeous,' he said. 'Totally gorgeous.'

She seemed to like being the one in control; she teased him the way he'd teased her earlier, letting the pressure build to almost fever pitch and then easing off just a little, then letting it build again.

By the time he climaxed, he was near to hyperventilating.

He felt her hit the peak again at the same time, so he

wrapped his arms round her and held her tightly until it had all ebbed away.

'I'd better deal with the condom,' he said finally.

She nodded. 'And I guess I ought to get dressed and call a cab.'

He glanced at his bedside clock. 'At this time of the morning?'

She looked at the time, too, and grimaced. 'I suppose it's a little late.'

'Stay,' he said softly. 'No pressure. Unless you have to be somewhere?'

'I can be anywhere I choose,' she said.

'Then stay,' he said, shocking himself. What the hell was he doing? He should be getting dressed and offering to drive her home, not asking her to stay. This was the first step on a very slippery slope towards letting someone into his life. Bad move. He was rubbish at being close to people. Work was fine, but anything emotional made him back off. Every single one of his girlfriends had complained that they needed more emotional commitment than Aaron could give them. But not one of them had made him feel strongly enough to want to change or keep the relationship going—and that reinforced what he'd always known, deep down. Love wasn't for him.

So he needed to stop this. Right now.

But his mouth clearly wasn't working with the plan. 'I can make you breakfast. There's a patisserie round the corner that does fantastic croissants.'

'And would that mean more of your coffee?' she asked.

'Definitely more of my coffee.'

Where was his common sense? Why wasn't he pushing her out of here as quickly as he could?

He made a last-ditch effort to put an obstacle in the way. 'Do you need—well, insulin or anything?'

'I'm sorted,' she said.

He could hardly say now that he'd changed his mind and ask her to leave, could he?

OK. This was just for tonight. Spending one night with someone wasn't the same as a declaration of everlasting love, was it? So it wasn't as if he was going to screw things up totally. Even he couldn't manage to do that with a one-night fling.

He went to the bathroom, dealt with the condom and came back to the bedroom. 'There are fresh towels in the bathroom. Help yourself to whatever you need.'

She gave him an embarrassed smile. 'I know this is going to sound crazy after what we've just done, but do you, um, have a bathrobe or something I could borrow?'

'Sure.' He took his bathroom from the hook behind the door and handed it to her. 'And I'll close my eyes.'

'Thank you.'

She returned a few minutes later, smelling of his citrus shower gel and with her skin still slightly damp.

'Do you want me to close my eyes again?' he asked when she stood beside the bed.

She nodded. 'It's a bit pathetic, I know.'

No. It just meant she really wasn't used to having a one-night fling.

But maybe this was what both of them needed, right now.

He waited until she'd got into bed and he'd felt the duvet being pulled up on her side, then leaned over and kissed the tip of her nose. 'Just for the record, it's not pathetic,' he said. 'It's kind of cute. And I'm very flat-tered that you chose me to—um, well. Be with you.'

'Hmm,' she said, but her eyes crinkled at the corners.

'Let's get some sleep,' he said, and switched off the light.

It had been a long, long time since he'd spent the night with someone. He knew it wasn't the most sensible decision he'd ever made; but right now it felt good to fall asleep curled round a warm body. So he'd go with it. And tomorrow—tomorrow, they'd have breakfast, they'd smile, they'd say goodbye and they'd walk away.

Joni was warm and comfortable, the body wrapped round hers holding her close.

Then she opened her eyes as the realisation hit her. *The body wrapped round hers.*

She'd stayed overnight with Aaron.

Uh-oh.

This could be awkward.

Last night was—well, last night. A crazy impulse, one she really shouldn't have acted on.

Why had she stayed for that last dance? Why had she let him kiss her stupid and then made love with him? Why hadn't she taken the chances he'd offered her to back away and flee to the safety of her own flat?

Panic seeped through her. What would Aaron expect of her this morning? Last night he'd talked about having breakfast. But would he think that they were now officially a couple because she'd stayed the night? Or would he, too, be having these doubts and panicking that she'd want much more from him than he was prepared to give?

She took a deep breath, held it, and listened.

He was breathing deeply and evenly. OK, so he could be faking it—but his body didn't feel tense against hers, which it would do if he really was faking it, Joni told herself. His body felt relaxed; so it was pretty safe to assume that he was still asleep, and she might just have a chance of salvaging the situation.

Leaving without saying goodbye was taking the coward's way out, she knew, but right at that moment she could live with that. All she had to do was get out of the bed without waking him, collect her clothes, dress as quickly as she could, and then let herself quietly out of his flat and out of his life. The chances of them bumping into each other again in a city as big as London were pretty remote, especially as she had no intention of going back to the salsa club. And this way they'd both be left with some good memories and no disappointed expectations.

Tentatively, she lifted the fingers of his hand away from her waist. His breathing remained deep and even, to her relief. Clearly Aaron was one of those people who slept like the dead and it would take a really loud alarm to wake him in the morning.

She hoped.

Moving slowly, she managed to wriggle out of his hold and slide out of the bed.

There was enough light coming through the curtains for her to locate her clothes, and she remembered that she'd left her shoes by the front door. She crept out of the room, hoping that she wouldn't accidentally stand on a squeaky floorboard and wake him, and closed the door very gently behind her.

From there, it was a matter of seconds to drag her

clothes on and find her handbag where she'd left it on the worktop in his kitchen.

Leaving without a word seemed a little harsh. But there was a memo block and a pen next to the phone in his kitchen. She scribbled a brief note and left it pinned down in the corner by one of the clean mugs. Then she collected her shoes and let herself quietly out of his flat.

A passer-by in the street gave her a knowing look; it was Sunday morning, and she was dressed for a Saturday night, so it was obvious that she hadn't gone back to her own place. She ignored the passer-by and straightened her spine. OK, so her behaviour last night hadn't been the way she normally acted. But it had been exactly what she'd needed. Aaron, unlike Marty, had made her feel good about herself. He'd taken away the lingering sadness of a day she'd been dreading. So she had no regrets. And now she'd find a taxi, go home, and get on with the rest of her life.

Aaron woke to find the bed beside him stone cold.

Joni had clearly left without waking him.

He knew he ought to feel relieved; he really didn't want the complication of getting involved with someone. And yet he was shocked to discover that what he actually felt was disappointment. He'd actually been looking forward to waking up beside Joni and having a leisurely breakfast together.

Was he totally crazy?

He shook his head to clear it. He knew nothing about Joni other than her first name. The chances of finding her in a city like London were next to nothing. And that, he reminded himself sharply, was probably for the best.

He showered, dressed, and went to make himself a

coffee. Which was when he saw her note: *Thank you for everything. J.*

Cute. Good manners.

But he also noticed that she hadn't left him her phone number or any way of contacting her. Which meant that, as far as she was concerned, last night had been a total one-off. She didn't want to see him again.

'It's for the best,' he said—out loud, this time, to convince himself properly. Though his voice sounded a little bit hollow.

Still, he didn't have time to brood. He started his new job tomorrow. And that would keep him busy enough to stop him thinking about the gorgeous woman with amazing hair who'd made him see stars and spent the night curled in his arms.

New job. New responsibilities. Part of a new team.

And on his own. Which was the only way that really worked for him.

CHAPTER THREE

'SO HAVE YOU met our new consultant?' Nancy, the ward sister, asked as Joni made herself a coffee in the ward kitchen.

'Not yet. I've been in the travel medicine clinic all morning, and this is the first break I've had today,' Joni said. 'What's he like?'

'Here he is now, so you can take a look for yourself,' Nancy said as the door opened.

Joni turned towards the newcomer, all ready to be friendly and welcoming to a new colleague—then looked at his face and stopped dead.

Of all the wards, in all the hospitals, in all the world, he had to walk into hers.

She could see the immediate recognition in his face, too.

Oh, great. The one and only time in her life when she had a mad, crazy fling with a handsome stranger, and he turned out to be someone who was going to be working with her for the foreseeable future.

How come life ended up being this complicated and awkward?

Eric Flinders, the head of the department, introduced them. 'This is Mr Hughes, our new consultant—Aaron, you've already met Sister Meadows. This is Dr Parker, our specialty reg. She's going to be working closely with you.'

Awkwarder and awkwarder. If only the ground would open and swallow her now, she thought.

But it didn't.

She had no choice but to face him.

'Mr Hughes. Very nice to meet you,' Joni said politely, and held her hand out to him.

To her relief, he didn't mention that they'd met before and simply shook her hand. 'Nice to meet you, too, Dr Parker.'

So much for never seeing his beautiful stranger again, Aaron thought. And now he'd just been told that he was going to be working closely with her.

The high heels, short skirt and amazing hair of Saturday night were all gone. Today, she was wearing trousers and a white coat, teamed with flat shoes, and her hair was neatly plaited into a single braid.

And he also noticed that there was a name tag on her coat. Dr N. Parker. And yet she'd called herself 'Joni' on Saturday night. It didn't stack up. Had the name she'd used been an extra layer of disguise?

She was smiling, but the smile didn't quite reach her eyes. It wasn't lack of friendliness he saw there, though, but sheer unadulterated panic. Clearly she was worrying that he was going to mention Saturday night.

Well, he wasn't going to tell any tales if she didn't. Because this was just as awkward for him as it was for her. Saturday night had been a moment of craziness; the last thing he wanted right now was to start a new relationship. And he really, really hoped it was the same for her.

'You'll be doing the TB clinic together this afternoon,' Eric Flinders said. He smiled at Joni. 'Perhaps you'd like to brief Mr Hughes on the clinic and how things work around here?'

'Of course, Mr Flinders,' she said.

So they worked on formal terms in the department? Aaron wondered. Or was it just Eric Flinders who insisted on formality?

Joni glanced at her watch. 'Um, perhaps I could brief you over lunch, Mr Hughes?'

'That works for me, Dr Parker,' he said with a smile.

She returned his smile. 'Good, because then I can show you where the cafeteria is and what have you. A new hospital always feels a bit like a rabbit warren until you get to know where everything is, doesn't it?'

Now he understood why the head of the department had asked his junior colleague to do the briefing rather than doing it himself. Joni Parker was clearly the sort who took new people under her wing and made them feel part of the team. Which meant she was a sweetheart, as well as being utterly gorgeous. And that made her even more off limits, as far as Aaron was concerned.

'Thank you,' he said politely.

'I'm actually due on ward rounds now,' she said. 'So shall I meet you here at half past twelve?'

'Half past twelve will be fine,' he said. And the frightening thing was that he was actually looking forward to it. Hell. He had to stop this. Right now. Joni—Dr N. Parker—was his colleague first, last and everything in between. And he'd better keep that in mind.

* * *

She was ten minutes late meeting him. 'I'm so sorry. The ward round took a bit longer than I th—'

'That's fine,' he cut in gently. 'I know we have targets for treatment times, but if a patient needs a bit of extra time you can't just tell them they've already had their allotted few minutes and they'll just have to wait for the next appointment.'

She shot him a grateful glance. 'Thanks for understanding. I guess we ought to head to the cafeteria right now, or we'll be late for the TB clinic this afternoon. I'm really sorry to cut your lunch break short.'

'It's not a problem,' he said.

It would've taken him twice as long to find the place without her showing him the way, Aaron thought as they reached the hospital café. He wasn't surprised when Joni chose a super-healthy balanced meal rather than grabbing the nearest sandwich and a chocolate bar, and she was drinking plain water rather than a sugary drink; she was clearly very careful about her blood sugar. Saturday night really had been out of the norm for her, then.

And he really had to stop thinking about Saturday night. About how her skin had felt against his. Any relationship with her other than a working one was completely out of the question.

'The coffee here isn't too bad,' she said—and then blushed, as if remembering the coffee he'd made her. 'Um. Anyway. I guess our ward works the same as wherever you were before.'

'Manchester.'

'OK.' She smiled at him. 'So we have the usual ward work and ward rounds, referral meetings, case reviews and research meetings. Then we have the regular clinics—TB, travel medicine, parasitology and general tropical diseases. There's also a daily walk-in clinic for people who've just come back from abroad, so they don't have to be referred by their GP first. That one tends to be the usual stuff—tummy bugs, rashes and fever. Sometimes we have something a bit rarer, but for the most part it's gastro symptoms.'

Pretty much what he'd done in Manchester. Though he noticed that Joni went through the entire run-through without actually looking him in the eye. Which didn't leave him much choice; he was going to have to broach the subject, and they were going to have to deal with it and get it out of the way.

'Dr Parker,' he said softly.

She looked nervous. 'Ye-es.'

'It might be a good idea if we dealt with the elephant in the room.'

She blew out a breath. 'I'm sorry. I don't usually...' She buried her face in her hands. 'Arrgh. I said I'd stop apologising all the time, too. Bailey would fine me for that one.'

He knew who Bailey was—the friend who'd been at the salsa club with her—but he really didn't follow the rest of it. 'Fine you? Why?'

'For apologising when I don't need to.' She gave him a wry smile. 'You know how people sometimes have a swear jar if they're trying to give up swearing, and they put money in it every time they swear? Well, I have a sorry jar. I'm banned from using the s-word more than once a day.' She bit her lip. 'And I bet I've apologised to you twice already today.'

'Try three.' He just about managed to hide a grin. 'I won't tell if you won't,' he said. 'And, actually, that was what I was going to say. No telling. What happened at the weekend is just between us and has nothing to do with anyone else.'

'Thank you.' She looked relieved. 'I couldn't believe it when I saw you. I mean, in a city the size of London— what are the chances of even bumping into you again, let alone finding out that we're working together?'

'Pretty small,' he agreed. 'Though I guess, given what we both do for a living, we would've met again at some point—maybe through a friend of a friend of a friend.'

'It's not even as if infectious and tropical diseases is a common speciality,' she protested.

'True. But I bet you know everyone in the emergency department.'

'I guess I do,' she admitted. 'If we haven't worked together on a case, we've met at an inter-departmental do.'

'As I said. Friend of a friend of a friend.' He shrugged. 'Maybe we should start again, as if we've just met for the first time. Hello. I'm Aaron Hughes, tropical medical specialist. Pleased to meet you.' He held out his hand.

She shook it, and his skin tingled where she'd touched him. Not good. He really didn't want to react to her like this. He couldn't afford any emotional ties.

'I'm Joni Parker. Also a tropical medical specialist. Pleased to meet you,' she said.

So she'd been telling the truth about her name on Saturday, then. But 'Joni' didn't start with N, and he was curious. He glanced at her name tag. 'What does the N stand for?'

'Nizhoni,' she said. 'But my first name's a bit of a mouthful, so people tend to call me Joni for short.'

'It's an unusual name,' he remarked. Not one he'd ever heard before.

She nodded. 'It's a bit exotic.'

'I guess it goes with your speciality. Also exotic,' he said. 'And now I'm going to shut up before I dig myself another hole.'

'I can't argue with that. And thank you. For not—well—making a big deal out of it.' She rewarded him with a real smile. One that made those gorgeous dark eyes light up—and that, in turn, made his blood tingle. Which was a seriously bad idea. He couldn't afford to let himself get emotionally involved with Joni Parker, no matter how attractive he found her. He'd learned at a young age that keeping his distance was the safe way. The way not to get hurt. Loving someone just led to loss and heartbreak. Keeping your distance was the only way to survive with your heart intact.

'I guess we both acted out of character,' he said. 'And now we're colleagues. Making a big deal out of what happened is going to make work awkward.'

'Which is the last thing you need, especially in a new job.'

'Exactly. And I'm sure you could do without it, too. So today's the first time we met, OK?'

'OK,' she agreed.

'I think the only difference between here and Manchester,' he said, 'is that everyone's more formal here. I'm used to working on first-name terms with my colleagues.'

'We do here, too,' she said. 'Except for Mr Flinders—he's a bit of a stickler for formality.'

'So it's first-name terms most of the time, and formal around the head of department?' Aaron asked.

'Pretty much,' she said. 'Nancy's lovely—she's the senior sister. Most of the team's been here longer than I have, but we've got a couple of others just started—there's Mikey, our F1 doctor, who's not sure if he wants to do tropical medicine or emergency for his specialty, so he's doing a six-month rotation with us to help him make his mind up, and two newly qualified nurses.' She filled him in on the rest of the team. 'Actually, we're a fairly close bunch. We try to get a team night out at least once a month. We take turns in organising it, and there's a bit of a competition about who can find the most unusual thing to do.' She gave him the most mischievous grin. 'I win, at the moment.'

'What did you do?' he asked, intrigued.

'Pizza night,' she said.

'And that's unusual *how* exactly?' he asked, not understanding in the slightest. There was practically a pizzeria on every street.

Her grin broadened. 'It's unusual if you have to walk through a rainstorm without getting wet first.'

He looked at her, understanding even less. 'How does that work? You're telling me you can predict the weather?'

She took pity on him. 'No, it was an art installation. It's finished now, or I'd suggest you go, because it was utterly brilliant and I went four times. Basically there were sensors that picked up your movements and stopped the "rain" falling on you. Though that depended on how you moved and how quickly you moved.'

'That sounds like fun,' he said.

'It was. We were like a bunch of kids, trying to get the sensors to rain on us. We tried hopping through the room, waltzing, moonwalking, doing the samba...'

She laughed, and again Aaron felt his blood heat. Hell. Get with the programme, he reminded his head. She's off limits.

'We've done ice-skating, had a tango lesson—oh, and there's always food afterwards, whether it's fish and chips or pizza or a curry. And then there's the quarterly quiz night with the emergency department. The losing team keeps the winners in chocolate biscuits for a week. I hope you're good at general knowledge, because we lost the last three.' She gave him another of those mischievous grins that made him want to pull her into his arms and kiss her. 'We could really do with a win this time, just to stop them gloating quite so much.'

'I'm reasonable at general knowledge, but don't bet the biscuits on me,' he said, returning the grin. 'It's nice that you're close to other departments.'

'We are.' She sighed. 'But the new hospital director doesn't quite see it like that. He's sending a group of us on a team-building exercise in a couple of weeks, to one of those outdoor course places.'

'It sounds as if you don't approve,' he remarked.

'I think we do a good enough job on our own. If we really need expert help in building a relationship with our colleagues in other departments, that'd make us a pretty sad bunch. And if we really have to have the experts in, then I'd rather get someone to come in for a morning to do a team-building thing in one of the hospital meeting rooms, and spend the rest of the money on the patients, rather than spend all that cash sending teams of staff out to some expensive place.' She shrugged. 'But it's not my call and I guess we have to do what the hospital director says.'

'I guess,' he said. 'Can I buy you a coffee?'

She looked wary. 'Why?'

'Just to say thank you for showing me around and telling me pretty much everything I need to know about how the department works,' he added swiftly.

She smiled, looking relieved; Joni Parker really was an open book, Aaron thought. What you saw was exactly what you got. Clearly she wasn't used to hiding her emotions, the way he was.

'You really don't have to—I'm always happy to show people round—but thank you, a coffee would be lovely. Cappuccino, please, but no chocolate on the top.'

Yeah. He remembered. And he was glad of the excuse to leave their table before he did something reckless. Like asking her out to dinner. Because that would be a really stupid thing to do. They were colleagues. They didn't need complications like being attracted to each other. Even if she was the most gorgeous woman he'd ever met. He needed to resist these wild, utterly ridiculous urges.

He had to hide a grimace when he brought their coffee back to their table and took a sip of his espresso. And for once he clearly wasn't that successful in hiding his thoughts because she said, 'You hate it, don't you?'

'I'm a bit of a coffee geek,' he said. 'So I'm not answering that one.'

She smiled. 'In that case, I should warn you that the stuff in the ward kitchen is instant, and it's not that posh barista-style instant coffee either. It's whatever happens to be on special offer in the supermarket when Nancy takes the kitty and tops us up on tea and coffee. And the tea's usually worse than the coffee.'

'Warning heeded,' he said.

'So how did you get to be a coffee geek?'

It was a personal question, but not an emotional one, so he didn't mind answering. 'I worked as a barista while I was a student. And it was at an indie coffee house, not a chain. My boss was a super-geek—the coffee equivalent of a wine buff. I learned a lot from him.'

'Hence your posh coffee machine.' Joni blushed. 'Um. The one I'm only guessing about, that is. I wouldn't know anything about your kitchen.'

He couldn't help smiling. 'Of course.'

She glanced at her watch. 'We'd better go. Clinic's in fifteen minutes.'

A convenient excuse, he thought. And one that suited him, too. Because he'd discovered that the more time he spent with Joni Parker, the more he liked her. Which wasn't what was supposed to happen. And it could be seriously dangerous to his peace of mind.

Bailey had called Aaron 'Hot Guy' at the salsa club. But at the hospital Aaron was even more gorgeous, Joni thought. She'd always had a soft spot for geeky guys— she would've picked Clark Kent over Superman any day—and, in his white coat and with those narrow-rimmed glasses, Aaron would definitely count as geeky.

Though he was also way, way out of her league.

So remembering the way he'd made her feel on Saturday night was totally stupid. He'd been the one to bring up the subject in the hospital cafeteria, and he'd made it very clear that he had no intention of repeating what had happened between them. And she knew he was making the right call: any kind of relationship between colleagues who worked together, apart from a professional one, could make life way too awkward for the rest of the team.

It would be much more sensible to keep her distance. And she'd focus on being professional.

Their third patient in the TB clinic that afternoon was a nineteen-year-old girl who'd taken a gap year before starting university and had worked at a school in Borneo.

'I've been home a couple of months,' Cara said, 'but for the last month I've been coughing a lot. I've tried about ten different sorts of cough mixture but none of them works and I just can't get rid of it.' She bit her lip. 'Then last week I started coughing up icky stuff, and there was blood in it. I panicked a bit and Mum dragged me off to the family doctor. He...' She caught her breath. 'Mum looked it up on the Internet. It's a sign of cancer. And so's losing weight without trying. And I've been really hot and sweaty at night.'

'Have you been eating normally?' Joni asked, thinking about the weight loss.

'I haven't been feeling that hungry,' Cara admitted. 'And I'm tired all the time. Mum says that's a symptom of cancer, too.'

'Losing your appetite and being tired can be symptoms of a lot of other things, not just cancer,' Aaron said gently, reaching out to take her hand. 'It's good that the Internet is making people aware of their health, but sometimes you can really scare yourself with what you read, so it's always a good idea to go and check with your doctor to stop yourself worrying unnecessarily.'

'The doctor sent me for an X-ray. I think he thought it might be cancer, too.' She shivered. 'I'm nineteen. I'm too young for this.'

'As Mr Hughes said, there could be lots of things causing your symptoms,' Joni said gently. 'Your family doctor sent you for that X-ray so he could start to rule things out, not because he was sure it was cancer. And I can tell you that as a doctor I normally start by ruling out the nasty stuff, because I don't want my patients worrying any longer than they need to.'

Cara nodded. 'The guy who did the X-ray said there weren't any signs of a tumour. But he said there were white patches on my lungs and it might be TB.'

'That's why he sent you to us for the next lot of tests—TB comes under tropical medicine and infectious diseases,' Joni explained.

Aaron brought up the X-ray file and turned the screen so Cara could see it, too. 'There is some scarring on your lungs, here and here, and those white patches are a classic symptom of TB. Plus you mentioned those other symptoms—night sweats, loss of appetite and losing weight. That's all adding up to a picture for me.' He looked at the screen. 'I see that your family doctor also sent you for a skin test.'

'Last week.' She frowned. 'But I don't see how it can be TB. I don't even know anyone who's ever had TB. I mean, I didn't think people even got it any more. How could I get it?'

'TB is a bacterial infection, and it's still pretty prevalent in parts of the world,' Aaron explained. 'It's spread by droplets—coughs, sneezes, that sort of thing. It can affect the lungs, which is why it makes people cough and why your doctor sent you for an X-ray to check your lungs, but it can also affect other parts of the body. That's why we need to check you out here. Not everyone who has TB is infectious, so you won't catch it by just sitting next to someone on a train—but if you share a room with someone who has TB then there's much more of a chance of you picking it up. And you said you've spent a few months in Borneo, yes?'

She nodded. 'Three months, working as a teacher.'

'Borneo has quite a high rate of infection, so if your skin test is positive then I'd guess that's where you picked it up.'

Cara looked worried. 'I shared a room with some of the other students working out there. Does that mean they might be infected, too?'

'Either one of them infected you, or if you picked it up from somewhere else then you might have infected them,' Joni said. 'So it would be a good idea to get in touch with them and ask them to go and see their doctor to get themselves checked out.'

'I don't have everyone's number,' Cara said. 'But I can call the agency that did the placements and ask them to pass on an urgent message to everyone.' She bit her lip. 'Oh, God. I feel so bad that I might've passed this on to other people.'

'It's not your fault,' Joni said. 'You didn't know you were ill, and TB takes a while to show up.'

'So you had the skin test on Friday?' Aaron asked, double-checking her notes. At Cara's nod, he examined her lower arm. 'There's definitely a hard red lump there, so the skin test is positive.' He measured the lump and Joni updated Cara's notes with the details. 'I'll need you to do a sputum test for me as well, but we have to culture the bacteria so it'll take a couple of weeks to get the results back.'

'So what happens while we wait for the results?' Cara asked.

'I'm pretty sure from the results of the skin test, plus what I can see on the X-ray and the symptoms you've described, that you have TB. So I'd like to start treatment now,' Aaron said.

'The good news is that you can be treated at home—you don't have to stay in hospital,' Joni added, seeing the flicker of dread on Cara's face. 'We'll give you a course of antibiotics. You need to take two different types to make sure the infection clears up.'

'You'll start to feel better after a couple of weeks,' Aaron said, 'but it's really important for you to keep taking the medication for the next six months and don't stop taking it just because you're feeling better.'

'Six months?' Cara looked shocked.

'Six months,' Aaron confirmed. 'Otherwise the infection won't clear up and the bacteria might become resistant to the antibiotics we give you. If that happens, it will take even longer to clear up.'

'OK. I promise I'll take the medication, even after I feel better,' Cara said.

'Good. Sometimes people get side effects from the antibiotics,' Joni told her. 'If you do, you need to come back and see us so we can change the medication you're on to something that will deal with the TB but won't give you the side effects.'

'So that's if you feel nauseous or you're actually sick, if you get a rash or itching, or you have any numbness or tingling in your hands or feet,' Aaron said. 'And I'd want you to come straight back and see us if your skin goes a bit yellow and your urine's dark, or you start getting blurred vision.'

Cara looked worried. 'Blurred vision?'

'It's one side effect, but we can sort it out. I know it's a lot to take in, but we'll give you a leaflet with all this information so you can talk it over with your mum,' Joni

said. 'As well as a leaflet with advice on how to stop
TB spreading to your family, friends or anyone you're
in contact with at work or college. You need to cover
your mouth when you cough or sneeze or laugh, and
put any used tissues in a sealed plastic bag. And don't
sleep in the same room as anyone else, as you might
cough or sneeze in your sleep.'

'Because that's how it spreads,' Cara said.

'Exactly. For now, you need to stay at home—we'll
see you once a fortnight and keep an eye on you, and
we'll tell you when it's safe to go back to work or college,' Aaron said. 'If you're worried at any time, just
come and see us or give us a call.' He wrote the prescription while Joni printed off the patient information
notes for Cara.

He was good with patients, Joni thought. Clear and
thorough—and kind, too, like the way he'd squeezed
the girl's hand to reassure her through her worries about
cancer. And the way he worked so easily with her made
the clinic a pleasure. This was teamwork at its best. She
had no intention of jeopardising that with a ridiculous
crush on the guy. Give it a few days and it would go
away anyway.

She hoped.

The clinic was soon over, leaving them both with
notes to write up.

'Thanks for making my first clinic here a good one,'
he said.

'Pleasure.' Had it not been for Saturday night, she
would've invited him out for a drink with a couple of
the others after the end of their shift tonight or tomorrow, to help him settle in. But Saturday night *had* happened; and she didn't want him to take any invitation

the wrong way, especially as he'd made it very clear that he didn't want to take up where they'd left off.

So the attraction wasn't mutual—and Joni wasn't going to start yet another relationship with a man who'd make her put most of the effort in. Been there, done that, and finally learned her lesson. 'I guess I'll see you tomorrow, then.'

'Sure. See you tomorrow,' he said, and left for his office.

CHAPTER FOUR

'YOU'RE KIDDING. MR HOT from the salsa club is your new consultant?' Bailey whispered from her yoga mat as the class moved into the downward dog position.

'Yup.' Joni groaned softly. 'And it gets worse.'

'Jenna's glaring at us, so we'd better stop talking. Tell me after class and get in the plank position,' Bailey whispered back.

'I hate the plank,' Joni said feelingly, but did it anyway.

After the yoga class, they went to the bistro round the corner.

'Two glasses of sparkling water with a slice of lime, please, two chicken superfood salads,' Joni said to the waitress, 'and please can we swap the dough sticks—?'

'For extra avocado? Sure. I'll bring them right over,' the waitress said.

Bailey smiled at her best friend. 'Now we've hit thirty, we're so predictable that the staff here know exactly what we're going to order even before we look at the menu.'

'Though we have actually tried everything on the menu here,' Joni reminded her. 'The chicken salad's your favourite as well as mine. And swapping out the dough sticks means we can have dessert.'

'Talking about food isn't going to get you out of telling me about Mr Hot. And I take it he's Mr rather than Dr, since he's a consultant?'

'Yes.' Joni blew out a breath. '*And* he's rostered on with me.'

Bailey gave her a wicked grin. 'Then I hope he's a better doctor than he is a dancer.'

Joni couldn't help smiling. 'He is. He's kind, he listens and he's got good patient skills.'

'But?'

She wriggled uncomfortably on her seat. 'I had a *fling* with him on Saturday night, Bailey. I went home with him and I spent the night with him. And he was a complete stranger!'

Bailey flapped a dismissive hand. 'It's not as if you make a habit of it, Joni. It's the first time you've ever had a one-night stand in all the years I've known you. You're the poster child for "good girl", so lighten up and don't be so hard on yourself. Besides, Saturday was a tough day for you. I think you needed something to take your mind off it.' She looked her friend straight in the eye. 'So is he as hot in a white coat as he was in that shirt on Saturday?'

Joni felt the betraying colour seep into her skin.

Bailey grinned. 'Ah. Don't tell me he wears glasses.'

Joni could only nod. Busted. Big time. Bailey knew exactly what made up Joni's perfect man.

Bailey's grin broadened. 'And he looks as hot as Robert Downey Jr in said glasses?'

Joni put her face in her hands. 'I'm not answering that one.'

'You don't have to, sweetie.' Bailey reached over to squeeze her shoulder. 'This is good. You've met a guy who's actually nice—not like Marty the Maggot. Bonus, he's hot as well and he ticks all your boxes. I know he likes you, because of the way he was looking at you on the dance floor. And you've got stuff in common because of your job. Wins all round. So when are you going out on a date?'

'We're not.'

'Ah. The sticking point. Don't tell me—his pride's still hurting that you walked out on him without a word?'

Joni rolled her eyes. 'I didn't walk out on him without a word. I left him a note.'

'A short one,' Bailey agreed. 'So what's the problem, then?'

Joni grimaced. 'We're colleagues and it'd be way too awkward. He brought it up, actually. When we had lunch.'

Bailey blinked. 'You had lunch with him?'

'Because I was briefing him on the department, in between ward rounds and the TB clinic. Lunch was the only gap I had, so don't get ideas,' Joni said swiftly. 'Anyway, we agreed that today was the first time we met. Just so it's not awkward in the future.'

'Hmm.' Bailey turned to the waitress and thanked her for bringing their drinks and salads. 'OK, Joni, I get that you're both worried that things might be awkward at work. Fair point. But is there still chemistry between you?'

Joni sighed. 'He's out of my league, Bailey.'

'I've met him, so I'm qualified to argue with that

statement,' Bailey pointed out. 'And I notice you didn't answer my question, which means the answer's yes.'

'It's one-sided.' Joni grimaced. 'And I'm never going to put myself in another situation where I'm the one who puts in most of the emotional effort.'

'Marty the Maggot,' Bailey said, 'has an awful lot to answer for.'

'Not just Marty,' Joni said ruefully. 'We both know how good I am at picking Mr Wrong. The one who starts off as a sweetie but ends up being more and more distant the longer we're together, or wants to change me once he really gets to know me.'

'And makes you feel that you're not good enough, so you apologise all the time when you really don't need to. But you've given that up now—or, at least, you're trying to,' Bailey said. 'Anyway, how do you know it's one-sided between you and Mr Hot?'

'I just do.'

'Hmm,' was all Bailey said. 'It didn't look one-sided on Saturday night.'

'Well, it is. He's made it very clear that he's not interested.'

'Maybe,' Bailey said thoughtfully, 'he dated the female version of Marty the Maggot. Someone who stomped all over his heart. Maybe you'd be good for each other.'

'We're colleagues, and that's all,' Joni said. 'And you're one to talk. When was the last time you dated?'

'Not long enough ago,' Bailey said, 'and we're not talking about me.'

Joni, remembering the way her best friend's life had imploded two years ago, reached over and squeezed her hand. 'Sorry—I didn't mean it like that. Just that maybe it's time you took your life off hold and let yourself meet someone and be happy again.'

'I appreciate the concern, but I'm perfectly fine as I am,' Bailey said, returning the pressure on her hand. 'Besides, this isn't about me. It's about you and Mr Hot.'

'Not going to happen,' Joni said. 'Now, shut up, or you get no pudding *and* I'll tell Jenna that you want to do extra warrior poses in the next class.'

'That's mean. OK. I'll shut up,' Bailey said.

'And no thinking either,' Joni warned.

Bailey gave her an innocent look that didn't have Joni fooled in the slightest.

It was just because he'd been celibate for months. Stupid physical feelings that he could tame in the gym, Aaron told himself.

Well, celibate except for Saturday night.

He couldn't even blame that one on alcohol, because half a glass of beer and a glass of champagne weren't enough to make him let down all his barriers. He'd been in full control of his actions.

He'd just been stupid and let desire out-talk his common sense when he'd seen Joni on the dance floor.

He added more weights to the bar, just so he'd have to concentrate on what he was doing and wouldn't be able to think about emotional stuff. About sex. About Joni Parker.

She was his colleague. And, even if she weren't, there were a hundred other reasons why she should be off limits. He didn't want emotional stuff messing up his focus on his new job. He'd just been promoted to consultant. He didn't have time to be distracted.

But the weights weren't working. They weren't diverting his thoughts from her.

The rowing machine didn't help either.

And neither did the treadmill, even though he pushed himself to his limit.

Aaron's shirt was soaked by the time he'd finished his workout at the gym, but working his muscles to fatigue hadn't gone anywhere near making him too tired to think.

'She's off limits,' he told himself firmly. Out loud. In an attempt to make his head listen.

Except it wasn't working. Because he couldn't stop thinking about her. Wanting her. Wondering, *what if...?*

On Thursday, a teenage girl came in to the walk-in clinic with her stepmother and younger sister. Mrs Stone looked worried sick, but managed to give Joni a run-down that tallied with the notes their family doctor had sent. 'She's had a temperature for a couple of days but she feels cold all the time, she's been sick, and she's got a headache. None of the painkillers the doctor gave us has done anything to help it.' She bit her lip. 'I was worried it might be meningitis, but I couldn't see a rash. And the doctor said to come and see you because it might be Lyme disease.'

'Have you been staying in an area that's prone to ticks?' Joni asked.

The girl said nothing—clearly she was feeling too ill to talk—and Mrs Stone shrugged helplessly. 'I don't know, really. We went camping in Colorado. You know, hiking, that sort of thing. Our doctor thinks she might've been bitten by a tick.'

It was a possibility. 'I need to examine you, Josie,'

Joni said gently to the girl. 'I know it's a bit embarrassing, but I'm going to have to ask you to take your clothes off. If I step outside the cubicle, can you take your clothes off for me?'

The girl nodded, and Joni stepped outside with Mrs Stone and the little girl, to give Josie some privacy.

'If she's been bitten and the tick was a carrier of Lyme disease, I'd expect to see a rash,' Joni said. 'How long ago were you there?'

'We've been back four days, and we went for a fortnight,' Mrs Stone said.

'OK. If the bite happened just before you came back, then the rash might not be visible yet and antibodies to the bacteria might not show up in the blood tests—we might have to do another blood test in a couple of weeks,' Joni warned. 'But you're in the right place. We'll find out what's wrong with her.'

She stepped back into the cubicle, followed by Mrs Stone and the little girl, and examined the girl gently. There was absolutely no sign of a rash. So it could be Lyme disease, or it could be something completely different. 'Does anything hurt, apart from your head?' she asked.

Josie shook her head very slightly.

'OK. You've definitely got an infection, but I'm going to need to do some blood tests to find out exactly what's causing the infection,' Joni said. 'In the meantime I'm going to start on you some broad-spectrum antibiotics to start dealing with the bugs that are making you ill. And I want to admit you to the ward, because I want to keep an eye on your temperature. It's up to you if you want to get dressed again, or if you'd rather I can get you a hospital gown to wear until your mum can bring you some pyjamas in.'

'She's not my mum,' Josie muttered, and Mrs Stone looked as if she'd been slapped.

Clearly there were family tensions here on top of what could turn out to be a serious illness, and that wasn't a good mix. Out of Josie's sight, Joni patted Mrs Stone's hand and mouthed, 'We'll talk in a minute.'

'OK, Josie. I'll leave you to get dressed,' she said to the teenager, 'and then I'm going to take some blood samples from you and send you for a chest X-ray.'

'Whatever,' Josie muttered.

'I'm sorry,' Mrs Stone said quietly when they'd stepped away from the cubicle again. 'I'm her stepmother.' Her eyes filled with tears. 'She makes that very clear, even though her mum left years and years ago and hasn't bothered with her ever since. We used to get on, when I first married her dad, and it was even OK when I had Ruby, because we really tried to make Josie feel included and important as a big sister. But it hasn't been good for us as a family for a while.' She sighed. 'I guess because she's a teenager and she's trying to find out where she fits in the world. That's why we went on a family hiking trip. We thought it would give her a chance to chill out a bit, away from all the influences of social media, and maybe then she'd go back to being the sweet kid I first met.'

'Teenagers are hard and families are complicated.' Joni squeezed her hand. 'Don't blame yourself.'

'But if she got bitten by something that's made her sick, then it's my fault. I should've pulled rank and *made* her use the insect repellent spray instead of letting her get away with having a strop and refusing to do it.' Mrs

Stone looked anguished. 'She said the smell made her feel sick and she wasn't going to use it. At the time, it just seemed like an extra battle I was going to lose and it wasn't worth the effort. I wish—I just *wish*…' Her words were cut off by a sob.

'Apart from the fact that you can't force a teenager to do something they really don't want to do, insect repellents aren't a hundred per cent effective in any case—so this *isn't* your fault,' Joni said. 'Right now I don't know what's causing the infection, but the chest X-ray and the blood tests might give me more of a clue. In the meantime, I'm going to give her some antibiotics—something broad-spectrum that will kill most bugs, and if the blood tests show that we can give her a better, more specific antibiotic, we'll switch over to that. Try not to worry.'

Later that afternoon, the test results showed that Josie's chest X-ray was clear, but her white blood cell count was slightly elevated. It would be another couple of days before the blood tests for Lyme disease came back, so it was a matter of being patient and hoping that the antibiotics would start to make a difference to the infection.

Joni was in the middle of seeing another patient when Nancy stepped into the cubicle. 'I'm really sorry to interrupt, Dr Parker. I need an urgent word.'

This didn't sound good. Joni apologised to her patient, and stepped into the corridor with Nancy. 'What is it?'

'Josie Stone. I think she's going into shock.'

Oh, no. Please don't let it be septic shock, Joni begged silently. With septic shock, chemicals released into the blood by the body's immune system to fight an infection triggered inflammation throughout the body. This led to blood clotting in the veins and arteries, which reduced the blood supply to the body's organs; once deprived of oxygen and nutrients, the organs could begin to fail.

Joni went straight to the ward and examined the girl swiftly. Josie's blood pressure was low, her temperature had spiked despite the medication Joni had given her, and although the girl was talking she sounded rambling and confused.

This wasn't looking good. All the symptoms pointed to septic shock, so they needed to act fast.

'Is Aaron around?' she asked Nancy quietly.

'I'll get him,' she said.

Josie was already on antibiotics; Joni quickly put her on intravenous fluids to deal with any potential blood-clotting problem and keep her blood pressure stable. 'I'm going to put a mask on you now, Josie,' she said, 'with oxygen, to help you breathe more easily, OK?'

Aaron came on to the ward. 'Nancy said you needed me.'

And his cool, calm demeanour was just what she needed to stem the panic rising through her. She filled him in on Josie's case history and the treatment regime she'd started.

'That's everything I would've done,' he said.

Meaning that the treatment would work? Because she had a bad, bad feeling about this. Nothing she could put her finger on, but something wasn't right. Josie had had a second dose of antibiotics and they should be starting to work by now. Her symptoms shouldn't be getting worse.

As if Aaron could read her mind, he said, 'We can run a couple more blood tests, but all we can do now really is wait for the antibiotics to work on that infection, and wait for the other test results to come back. Hang on in there.' He touched her shoulder briefly in a gesture of solidarity. 'And call me if you need me, OK?'

Joni took more blood samples; as she left Josie's bedside, she noticed that little Ruby was sobbing quietly next to her mother. Poor kid. She was clearly worried sick. Joni took a tissue out of her pocket, crouched down to Ruby's level and handed her the tissue. 'Here you go,' she said softly.

Ruby rubbed it across her nose. 'Thank you,' she said between tears.

'I know this is scary, but don't worry,' Joni said. 'We're doing our best to make your big sister better. She's in the right place and we're looking after her.'

'But it's my fault she's sick,' Ruby sobbed.

'It's not your fault, sweetie. Sometimes these things just happen,' Joni reassured her.

'But it *is* my fault. I wished she'd get sick, and she did.' She gulped. 'Josie's always so mean to me. And I wanted her to be sick so then she'd be sorry about the squirrel.'

A memory stirred in the back of Joni's head about an article she'd read recently about Colorado and diseases in rodents. 'What happened with the squirrel?' she asked gently.

'It died. I wanted to bury it, but Mummy said I couldn't and I had to leave it. I sneaked back because I knew if you didn't bury the squirrel then it wouldn't get to heaven. I made a cross and a flower crown for it. I was going to bury it and say a prayer, but Josie followed me and she picked it up and threw it down the ravine. Stuff came out of the squirrel and went all over her—it was horrible!' Her face grew anguished. 'And she said—' Her breath hitched. 'Josie said if I told anyone about it I'd be in real trouble.'

Joni squeezed Ruby's hand reassuringly. 'You're not in trouble, sweetie, not at all. Actually, you might have told me something that will help her get better. Can you tell me when this happened?'

'It was the last day of our holiday. That's why Mummy said she didn't want me to bury the squirrel, because there wasn't enough time and I was supposed to go and pack my stuff.'

'That's really helpful, Ruby,' Joni said softly. 'Thank you. I'll be back really soon to see you all, but I need to get these blood samples off for testing and check out a few other things.'

The little girl gave her a watery smile. 'Is Josie going to be all right?'

Until they knew for sure what was wrong, that wasn't a promise Joni wanted to make. 'I'll try my very best to make her better. And she's in absolutely the right place.'

CHAPTER FIVE

JONI WENT BACK to her office and checked the computer swiftly for the article she remembered seeing, printed it out, and went to find Aaron.

'I'm pretty sure Josie Stone doesn't have Lyme disease,' she said. She told him what Ruby had confided to her about the squirrel. 'I read an article a couple of months ago about rodents in Colorado and the bubonic plague.'

'And you really think it's that?' He looked sceptical. 'I don't want to burst your bubble, but I've never come across a case of plague yet, not in all the years I've worked in tropical medicine.'

'Neither have I, but look at this.' She showed him the printout. 'This is all about a teenager with sudden, severe septic shock in the chest, and the diagnosis turned out to be bubonic plague.'

He frowned. 'But aren't plague bacteria spread through flea bites?'

'Josie picked up the squirrel. If there were any fleas on the carcass, they could've bitten her—and it only takes one infected flea for the bacteria to spread,' Joni pointed out. 'I was looking for the bull's-eye rash of Lyme disease somewhere around her wrists and ankles, but there wasn't a rash of any kind when I examined her.'

'What about buboes?'

'None. No swelling at all on her lymph nodes in her armpits, and she said she didn't have any pain anywhere except her head. But, apart from the fact that plague doesn't always present with buboes,' she reminded him, 'the thing with the squirrel happened on the last day of their holiday. They've been back for four days, and the incubation period for plague is two to six days. She's been ill for a couple of days. It all fits, Aaron.'

'You've started her on a broad-spectrum antibiotic, yes?'

'But it might not be the right one.' She bit her lip. 'There's a very good chance it might already have moved from bubonic to septicaemic plague. We need more blood tests. And I think we need to give the whole family prophylactic antibiotics.'

'Good call,' he said, looking grim. 'Just as well Ruby told you.'

'Apart from the fact that she's blaming herself, poor kid.'

Aaron knew how that felt. He'd been a couple of years older than little Ruby when Ned had died, but he could remember it as clearly as if it had been yesterday. Knowing that his older brother's death was his fault. Knowing that the rest of the family blamed him, too—because if Ned hadn't thrown himself over Aaron to protect him from the blast, he wouldn't have been injured and gone to hospital. And if Ned hadn't gone to hospital, he wouldn't have caught malaria. And if he hadn't caught malaria and developed complications, he wouldn't have died. The chain of blame dragged on and on and on.

Even though part of Aaron knew that he'd been a child at the time and of course it hadn't all been his fault, he still couldn't rid himself of the guilt. He'd made it through the fallout from the bomb with a couple of tiny scratches and a bit of claustrophobia. Ned—who'd had so much to give the world—hadn't made it at all.

He shook himself. *Not now.* 'OK. Let's go and examine her.'

When Joni and Aaron examined Josie again, they discovered a couple of tiny bites on her arms, so tiny that they would've been easy to miss during the first examination. Aaron agreed that they looked like flea bites. There was still no sign of any swelling in the girl's lymph glands, but Joni was sure that it was plague.

'I think you're right. The infection's already moved from Josie's lymph nodes to her blood vessels,' Aaron said quietly. 'I agree. We need to get the lab to add an extra test into the blood they already have. For now we'll start her on different antibiotics and put her in isolation—and I want all nursing staff to be gowned and masked when they come in to her room to treat her.'

'OK. I'll let the public health department know, too,' Joni said. The plague—incredibly rare as it was—was a notifiable disease. 'And we'll keep an eye out for any sign of a rash. If she goes into DIC…'

Disseminated intravascular coagulation caused tiny blood clots to form throughout the body and depleted the blood's clotting resources, so the body could no longer control bleeding. One of the classic signs was a dark purple rash. And if Josie went into DIC and they couldn't get her blood clotting back under control, the girl wouldn't make it.

Aaron rested his hand briefly on Joni's shoulder. 'Hey. You spotted what it was, and we'll keep her under very close observation.'

'Uh-huh.' But Joni had a bad, bad feeling about this. The teenager wasn't out of the woods, not by a very long way. The later that treatment started, the less likely it was that the outcome would be good. Even with treatment, if it had already turned to septicaemic plague then there was a fifty-fifty chance that Josie wouldn't make it.

When Josie's stepmother came in to visit, Joni took her to one side for a quiet word first.

'There isn't an easy way to say this, Mrs Stone,' she said, 'so I'll go for the straight option, and I'm happy to answer any questions you might have. We're waiting on test results, but we're pretty sure we know what the infection is now. Josie has the plague.'

'The *plague*?' Mrs Stone looked shocked. 'What, you mean, like the thing that killed loads of people just before the Great Fire of London?'

'Yes.'

Mrs Stone shook her head as if trying to clear it. 'But I thought—I thought that had all died out years and years ago.'

'No. The plague's still around in some parts of the world,' Josie said. 'We need to give your whole family antibiotics, just in case Josie has passed the infection to any of you.'

Mrs Stone looked perplexed. 'But she didn't say she'd been bitten by anything, and I thought the plague was spread by rats?'

'It's actually spread by the fleas on the rats,' Joni said. 'Ruby told me something in confidence, and that's what made me connect Josie's condition with the plague.' She paused. 'I promised Ruby she wouldn't get into trouble.'

'Of course she won't get into trouble. What did she say?'

Joni explained what the little girl had told her about the squirrel and what Josie had done.

Mrs Stone looked horrified. 'Oh, my God. So both my girls could be infected?'

'I don't think Ruby actually touched the squirrel, and she isn't showing any of the symptoms that Josie has, so it's very unlikely that she was bitten by one of the fleas,' Joni said. She took Mrs Stone's hands. 'But I won't lie to you. It's not going to be an easy road ahead.'

'Could Josie d—?' Mrs Stone bit off the word, shuddered and stared at Joni in dismay. 'No. No. She can't. She just *can't*.'

'We're doing our best,' Joni told her. 'But she is very sick right now.'

Josie didn't seem to respond to the new antibiotic treatment, and the next morning Joni was in the middle of a clinic when Nancy sent Shelley, one of the newly qualified nurses, to fetch her. 'Josie Stone's arrested,' Shelley said. 'Mikey's there, but Nancy needs you, too.'

'I'll go straight there. Can you let Aaron know, please, Shelley, and ask Reception to explain to my patients that I've been called to an emergency so there will be a delay, and ask them to sort out cover for me? And then if you can ring Mrs Stone and ask her to come straight in, I'd really appreciate it,' Joni said.

'Yes, of course.'

'Thanks, Shelley.' Joni pulled on gloves, a gown and a mask as she headed to the isolation room, where Mikey and Nancy had already intubated the girl and were alternately doing chest compressions and ventilating her with the bag and mask.

The defibrillator was already charging. Joni applied the gel pads to Josie's chest. 'OK. Clear and ready to shock at two hundred,' she said, checking that everyone had taken their hands off the patient before she pressed down with the paddles to make sure Josie didn't arch off the bed, and delivered the first shock.

'No change,' Nancy called, looking at the monitor.

'OK. Charging to two hundred again. And clear!'

The second shock did nothing either. Hell, hell, hell. This *had* to work.

'Charging to three-sixty,' Joni said. 'And clear!'

Again, nothing.

'Administering adrenaline,' she said, taking the ampoule from Shelley, who'd come in to say that she'd left a message on Mrs Stone's answering machine and her voicemail, asking her to contact the hospital straight away. 'Mikey, are you still OK to do compressions?'

'I think we should switch over again—Mikey, take over the bagging,' Nancy said, and took over doing the compressions.

After a minute of CPR, there was still no change.

Joni changed the gel pads. 'OK. Round two. Charging to three-sixty. And clear!'

Still no response.

Aaron strode in to the room. 'Shelley got me up to speed. What do you need me to do?'

'Help with the CPR protocol. We're *not* going to lose her,' Joni said, and kept going with the defibrillator.

They kept checking the monitor for output after every shock, and they worked on Joni as a team for the next half an hour—all to no avail.

Finally Aaron put his hand on Joni's shoulder. 'She's gone, Joni. Do you want to call it, or do you want me to do it?'

Joni took in a gulp of air. 'One more round. Please. Just one more round.'

'She's gone,' he said gently. 'It's been half an hour. You know as well as I do it's not going to work now. Her heart stopped and, although we've been breathing for her and doing chest compressions, there will have been too much damage.'

Joni squeezed her eyes tightly shut to keep the tears back. Losing a patient was always hard—and it was rare in her department, so she'd never become even slightly accustomed to it happening. 'OK.' She took a deep breath and looked at the team. 'Does everyone else agree that I should call it?'

Mikey, Shelley and Nancy all gave her grim-faced nods.

'Time of death ten forty-five,' she said. 'Thanks for your efforts, everyone. It's…' She gulped hard, unable to continue. What could you say when a teenage girl had died? All that promise, all that bright future wiped out. How would her family ever get over it?

'We all did what we could,' Aaron said gently.

But it hadn't been enough. 'Are the Stones here yet?' Joni asked.

'I don't think so, or someone would've come in to tell us,' Nancy said.

Joni bit her lip. 'OK. I'll try calling Mrs Stone again.'

Except there was still no answer. This wasn't the

kind of news Joni wanted to break remotely, so she simply left a message.

'Do you want me to tell them when they get here?' Aaron asked.

She shook her head. 'Josie is—*was*—my patient. And you've got people waiting in clinic.' As had she.

He gave her a searching look. 'Call me if you need me, OK?'

'Thanks.' She kept her words to a minimum, not trusting herself not to break down into tears. She wasn't going to be that unprofessional in front of him. 'Shelley, can you keep an eye out for the Stones and put them in the side room for me when they arrive, please?'

'Of course.' Shelley gave her a hug. 'Hang on in there, kiddo.'

Considering that she was actually a few years older than the nurse, the irony made Joni smile. 'You, too. And thanks.'

She'd just finished getting Josie ready for her family to see her and written up the paperwork when Shelley came in. 'They're here.' Her eyes were full of sympathy. 'Mrs Stone and the little girl.'

Oh, help. It was bad enough having to tell adults this kind of news. Telling a child that they'd just lost someone close...that was going to be really hard.

Joni took a deep breath and walked to the side room.

'How is she?' Mrs Stone stood up, looking anxious. 'When the nurse asked us to wait in here... She's worse, isn't she?'

Joni took her hand. 'I'm so sorry.' This was the bit of her job she really, really hated. It didn't happen very often, but she hated punching an unfillable hole in people's lives.

'She—she's not…?' Shock filled Mrs Stone's face.

'Her heart stopped working this morning,' Joni said gently. 'We did everything we could to get her heart started again, but she was just too sick. I'm so sorry.'

Both Mrs Stone and Ruby were devastated by the news; Joni spent the next few minutes comforting them, feeling utterly helpless and wishing that she'd found a way to save Josie.

Later that afternoon, Aaron walked in to the office where Joni was writing up her notes from the afternoon clinic. He could see that she'd been crying, because her eyes were still red and slightly puffy. And he knew exactly what had upset her.

'Are you OK?' he asked gently.

She bit her lip. 'Not really. We don't lose many patients here and it always hits me for six. Especially when it's a child. I…' She gulped. 'That's why I could never work in the emergency department. I don't think I'd be able to cope with losing patients in those kinds of numbers.'

'It wasn't your fault. You followed all the right protocols and you put all the pieces together to see what we'd all missed,' Aaron said.

'And it still wasn't enough.' She lifted her chin. 'I'm sorry. I shouldn't be burdening you with this. Anyway, I rang my mum and I'm going home when I've finished my paperwork. I'll be better after an evening of TLC with my family.'

TLC.

From your family.

Aaron stood there, feeling awkward. He knew he should at least offer her a hug—it was what you'd do to comfort a colleague—but he could still remember what it felt like to hold Joni close, and he didn't trust himself not to do something stupid. Like trying to kiss away her sadness. And, at the same time, part of him felt wistful and a tiny bit envious. How good it must be to have a family that supportive—to know that when you'd had a bad day you could call and they'd make everything better, and they wouldn't despise you for showing the least sign of weakness.

His own family was much more distant—and not just geographically. Ever since Ned's death… He pushed the thought away. *Not now.* He wasn't going to let all the misery seep through him now. 'Well, if there's anything I can do,' he said, hoping that she wasn't actually going to take him up on the offer because he hated dealing with emotional stuff, 'you know where I am.'

She nodded. 'Yes. And thank you.'

'No problem.'

'Aaron, are you OK?' she asked, shocking him. Nobody ever asked him how he felt.

'I'm fine,' he said.

'Josie was your patient, too, so you must be feeling as bad as I am. Why don't you come to my parents' place with me after you finish your shift?' she asked.

He was tempted.

But that would be a huge step towards getting involved with her. Involvement led to pain and misery. So keeping his distance would be the sensible way of dealing with it. 'Thanks for the offer,' he said, 'but I'm fine. I'll probably go and take it out in the gym.'

'My friend Bailey would approve of that. Endorphins are good,' she said with an attempt at a smile.

'They certainly are.' He forced himself to smile back. 'See you later.'

The department felt subdued for the following week. Even the beginning of the departmental evening out on the following Saturday night was quiet, until the demands of the climbing wall made everyone concentrate on the physical movements instead of the ache in their hearts.

It was the first time that Joni had seen Aaron wearing jeans. It made him look younger and less remote. And she loved the T-shirt he was wearing—a *pi* sign with six extra 'legs' and the word 'octopi' written above it. It was the kind of geek joke she'd always enjoyed.

'He hasn't mentioned a partner to me,' Nancy said softly.

'Who hasn't?' Josie asked.

Nancy rolled her eyes. 'Love, I could see you watching him just now. You know exactly who I mean. Why don't you ask him out?'

Because he'd already made it clear that he didn't want to repeat what had happened between them at the salsa club. Not that Joni wanted any of her colleagues to know about that night. It made her feel too ashamed. She fell back on a safe excuse. 'Because we work together. It'll make things too embarrassing and awkward at work when he turns me down.'

'Sweetie, what makes you think he'd turn you down?' Nancy asked.

Joni grimaced. Wasn't it obvious?

'I could strangle that Marty—except I wouldn't be first in the queue,' Nancy said. 'He was never good enough for you and he knew it—that's why he did a hatchet job on your self-esteem. Ending your engagement was the best thing you ever did. And you really need to take that extra step and start seeing someone else, to let you finish getting over him.'

Joni gave her a wry smile. 'You've been talking to Bailey.'

'No, love, I'm just saying what everyone thinks. You're a lovely girl and you have so much to give, and…' Nancy smiled at her. 'And I bet your mum's already said all that to you, hasn't she?'

'Well, yes,' Joni admitted. 'And so have my brothers, and my dad, and my grandmothers…'

'There you are, then.'

'It's not going to happen, Nancy. It's best to be just colleagues.' And Joni spent the rest of the evening trying not to think about that other Saturday night. Because she knew she'd be a fool to think that it could happen again.

CHAPTER SIX

THE FOLLOWING WEEK, the day of the team-building exercises arrived. Joni, Aaron and the new F1 doctor Mikey were sent to the outdoor adventure centre, together with medical staff from the emergency department, the children's ward and the maternity department.

After a briefing meeting, the course leader sent them on an outdoor obstacle course where they had to work as a team. At each obstacle one team member had to trust the others to lift them over the obstacle or guide them blindfold through part of the course.

'Third place. That isn't bad,' Aaron said as their team reached the finish line.

'You worked well together,' the course leader said with a smile. 'It's a great start.'

And, oh, please let it all be over soon, so we can get back to the hospital and look after our patients again, Joni thought.

'The next challenge,' the course leader said after they'd had a short break for tea and biscuits, 'is a treasure hunt, in pairs. We'll give each pair a map and the first clue, which will lead to you the next clue, and so on. The final clue will lead you to a box with a message inside. The first pair to call us with the message is the winner, and we'll brief you on the next activity over lunch.'

And they'd get a chance to dry out a bit, Joni hoped. It had rained for the last five days solid, so the obstacle course had left them all covered in mud.

'And the pairs are...'

She waited while the course leader divided everyone into groups. Maybe this time the leader would mix up the different departments so they were working as part of a bigger team instead of a group within their own wards.

Then, halfway through, she heard him say, 'Joni Parker and Aaron Hughes.'

Oh, great. Aaron had been quiet enough so far today. And she'd made it worse by blushing when he'd lifted her up during the first activity, remembering how he'd carried her to his bed that night after the salsa club. She'd caught his eye and the heat in his expression had told her that he was remembering, too—which was a complication they could both do without.

'So. You and me,' Aaron said, his voice neutral.

Was he embarrassed, disappointed—wary, even? She didn't have a clue. Normally, Joni was reasonably good at reading people, but she found Aaron a puzzle. 'Uh-huh.' She looked at the map and the clue; pretending to study them was a lot easier than facing Aaron. 'I think we should be heading here.' She pointed at location on the map.

He read the clue and nodded. 'Agreed.'

It didn't take them long to reach their first location and discover their next clue. It was an easy anagram, and they both said the word at the same time.

'Teamwork,' Aaron said softly. 'We think along the same lines.'

Maybe in a work situation, Joni thought, but definitely not on a personal level. Although Aaron was perfectly friendly and polite to everyone in the department, she could sense that he was keeping just a little bit of distance between himself and everyone else. He fitted in very well, on the surface; but he didn't really connect with anyone on a deeper level. He kept himself in reserve.

Which made her wonder even more why he'd asked her back to his flat the night they'd met at the salsa club. It just wasn't Aaron-like behaviour.

Not that she could ask him. That was way, way too personal. She'd learned over the last couple of weeks that Aaron didn't do personal. He was a good doctor, brilliant with patients, and he worked incredibly hard—even staying on past the end of his shift to coach some of the younger members of the team—but she still knew practically no more about him than she had on the day they'd first met.

He deflected any personal question, usually by smiling and asking the other person about something so they were distracted away from the subject. Which intrigued her—what was he hiding?—but at the same time it made her wary of him. Emotional distance was what had wrecked all her past relationships. She'd be crazy to get involved with yet another man who was emotionally distant. Yet still something about him drew her. Who was the man behind the barriers? She'd glimpsed him a couple of times and she'd liked what she'd seen.

She shook herself. Tough? This was meant to be a professional team-building day, not a time to start fantasising about a man who'd already made it clear that their fling had been just that. A one-off. Finished.

The final clue took them to a tunnel at the edge of the woodland.

'You take the left hand of the tunnel and I'll take the right, and whoever finds the clue calls the other?' Aaron asked.

'Fine by me,' she said, and switched on her torch to help her see in the gloom.

Joni had just found the box containing their message when there was a roar and a crash, and the dim light in the tunnel went out completely.

'Aaron, are you all right?' she called.

'Yes. I'm over here.'

She saw a patch of light shining on the floor, showing her where he was in the tunnel.

'Are you OK?' he asked.

'Yes. What just happened?' she asked.

'Given that it's been so wet this month, I'd guess part of the roof got over-saturated and fell in,' he said.

'And it's blocked our exit—that's why it just got darker?'

'That's the most likely answer,' he said.

'OK. I'm coming over to you and then we can check it out together.' She shoved the small box in her pocket, then picked her way over to him carefully, keeping the beam of her torch on the floor so she could see where she was walking and stopping every so often to check that she was still heading towards him; in the complete darkness it was easy to get disorientated.

Together, they made their way carefully to where the entrance of the tunnel had been and shone their torches around. All Joni could see was a pile of rubble. 'Maybe we can dig ourselves out,' she suggested.

He bent to take a closer look and rubbed some of the soil between his fingers. 'Better not. It's sandstone and the roof needs stabilising. If we try tunnelling out, we could trigger another roof fall and end up getting buried in the middle of it.'

'That sounds as if you're talking from experience,' she said.

'You could say that.' His voice was dry.

'I'll ring back to base and let them know what's happened.' She took her mobile phone from her pocket. 'Oh, great—no signal.' She rolled her eyes.

'Probably because we're underground,' he said.

She knew what he meant. 'My phone's like that sometimes in the middle of a shopping precinct—it just can't pick up a signal. So we're not even going to be able to send a text to tell anyone that we're stuck here.'

'I'll try my phone, just in case I can get a signal.' There was a pause, then a sigh. 'No. It's the same with mine.'

'So what do we do? Take turns trying to dig ourselves out—but being *really* careful?'

'Apart from the fact we don't have anything we can use as a shovel to move the earth, it's really not safe to try digging out,' he said. 'Not with a fragile rock like sandstone.'

Just to back him up, there was another rumble and more earth fell from the ceiling.

'I guess if the organisers haven't heard from us by lunchtime, they'll realise something's wrong. If they try to call us they'll guess that we don't have a signal, and then they'll start looking for us and get us out of here safely,' he said. 'Right now we need to find a safe spot where the roof isn't likely to collapse on us, and we'll just have to wait it out until they come to find us.'

'Right,' she said. Great. Trapped in a tunnel with a man who wasn't keen on small talk—and who seemed to avoid deeper, personal stuff as much as he could. The time was going to go very slowly indeed.

He sounded concerned as he asked, 'Are you OK insulin-wise?'

'I'm fine,' she said, though she appreciated the fact that he'd actually asked. 'I take it twice a day so I'm not actually due to take it again until this evening. Though I always have a supply with me as well as fast-acting carbs, so I can deal with a blood sugar problem either way.' She paused. 'How do we know if there's a safe spot to wait? Or could the whole roof fall in on us?' Even the idea of it made her feel suddenly nervous.

'We listen to find out if we can hear anything, then shine our torches round to see if there are any other areas where rubble's fallen,' he said. 'Oh, and keep the beam on the ground. In this environment, it'll hurt if a torch shines in your eyes because your pupils are at maximum dilation.'

They were both silent. Joni could hear nothing; and when she shone her torch around she couldn't see any new-looking piles of rubble or earth. Hopefully that meant the rest of the roof of the tunnel was stable.

'I think we'll be safe over here,' Aaron said, and found them a spot near the wall. 'But we'd better not sit directly on the ground or we'll lose too much body heat.' He took off his jacket and spread it on the ground.

'Let's sit on this. My jacket's waterproof, so we won't get wet.'

'Aren't you going to be cold without a jacket?' she asked.

He shrugged. 'I'll be fine.'

'How do you know all this stuff?' she asked. 'Did you used to do rock-climbing or something?'

'Manchester's very near the Peak District. Some of the people I knew in the emergency department were in the local mountain rescue team, working with climbers and cavers,' he explained.

He'd said 'people I knew', not 'friends', she noted. 'And you were part of that, too?' she asked.

'Not me,' he said. 'Caving's never been my thing.'

'That sounded a bit heartfelt,' she said.

'I guess.' Though she noticed that he didn't offer any further information, and she didn't push him. It felt too intrusive to ask anything more.

And then he surprised her by filling the silence. 'I got buried in rubble when I was about eight. So I don't tend to do underground stuff by choice,' he said.

'That's understandable. What happened?' Then she caught herself. 'Sorry. I'm being nosey.'

'Strike one for your sorry jar,' he said. 'I pretty much invited the question.'

She wasn't sure whether to be more shocked that he'd remembered she was trying to break her apology habit, or that he was actually volunteering information about himself. And her silence lasted long enough for him to fill it again.

'Bomb,' he said economically. 'My parents were in

the armed forces. We were in a war zone at the time. I was at home after school when our house was hit.'

'Did it take the rescue party long to get you out?' she asked.

'It felt like hours,' he said. 'It probably wasn't anywhere near that long, but when you're young and scared and in the dark under a pile of rubble, you tend to lose all sense of time.' His voice went decidedly neutral, as if he was picking his words carefully and taking out all the emotional stuff. 'My parents sent me back to boarding school in England so I'd be safe, well away from the war zone.'

Safe but lonely, she thought, sent away from his family; no doubt he'd felt as if he'd been punished for being scared. Even though people much older and more experienced in life than an eight-year-old boy would be terrified and have nightmares about it if they'd been caught under a pile of rubble after an explosion. For a young child, it must have been an incredibly scary experience. 'That must've been hard on you,' she said softly.

He shrugged again. 'I survived. What about you? Have you ever gone caving?'

She laughed. 'No, that's way too dangerous for me. I'm afraid I'm a bit of a wuss. I've spent most of my life wrapped in cotton wool.'

'Because you're diabetic?'

'Partly.' She wrinkled her nose. 'It's a long story. I guess, like you said, we just have to sit tight and wait it out.'

He nodded. 'I don't know how long we're going to be here, so we ought to conserve our light. Are you OK with being in the dark if we switch the torches off?'

She had a feeling that he might not be, after his experiences as a child. And that he'd never admit it. If she took his hand to offer him comfort, she was pretty sure he'd pull away. Whereas if he thought he was giving *her* comfort and strength, maybe he'd feel less awkward about it. 'I don't mind the dark, so much,' she said. 'But don't let me think about spiders, OK?'

He switched off the light. 'Spiders are far more scared of you than you are of them, you know.'

'I wouldn't bet on that.' She guessed that he might not want the headspace to remember how it felt to be buried in rubble, alone and in the dark. 'Talk to me about something else to take my mind off the spiders,' she invited.

'Like what?'

She knew it was a personal question and he'd probably deflect it, but she asked anyway. 'What made you decide to specialise in tropical medicine and infectious diseases?'

Of all the things she could have asked. Aaron groaned inwardly.

Maybe he should make something up. Say he'd had a mad crush on the tropical medicine lecturer at university, something like that. But the words just wouldn't come. The silence stretched longer and longer and longer, and he still couldn't think of a decent reason. Finally, he mumbled the truth. 'My brother had malaria.'

'So you wanted to work in the specialty that saved him—like a kind of payback?' she asked.

Far, far worse than that. And it felt as if he was choking as the words forced their way out. 'It didn't save him.'

He heard her shocked gasp. Soft. Guilty.

Though no amount of guilt could ever match the amount that had built up on his soul over the years.

He felt her hand fumbling for his, squeezing his fingers. 'I'm sorry. That must have been so hard for you. For all your family.'

Yeah. His parents had never been the same, after. Third-generation armed forces, they'd always had a fairly stiff upper lip—but after Ned's death it had been permafrosted as well. And they'd sent him away. So he'd be safe—but he knew that it had also been so his presence wouldn't remind them of what they'd lost.

'It was my fault.'

Oh, hell. He hadn't meant to tell her that. But the words had slipped out when he wasn't paying attention.

Her fingers were still wrapped round his. How? How could she bear to be anywhere near him, now she knew the ugly truth about him?

'What happened?' she asked, her voice gentle. So sweet. So soft.

His first instinct was to pull away. His second was to hold her close and take comfort from her. Torn between the two, he was frozen.

'Aaron?'

She clearly wasn't going to let this go. She wasn't letting his hand go either. Hating himself, but not seeing any other option—because they were stuck here together alone in the dark and he had no idea how long it would be until they were rescued—he gave in. 'The bomb... I wasn't on my own in the house. My brother had come home early from sixth form. I was hungry, and he was making me a sandwich.' Easy-going, sweet-tempered Ned—the one person in the family who hadn't minded Aaron trailing along behind him or seen him as a nuisance. Aaron had always known he was an accidental baby—eight years younger than Ned, ten years younger than his sister, twelve years younger than his oldest brother. With an age gap like that, of course he hadn't been planned. But Ned hadn't made him feel like an unwanted nuisance. He'd built model planes with Aaron, taught him to play cricket. Aaron had adored him.

And his death weighed so heavily on Aaron's shoulders. Even now, nearly a quarter of a century later, the guilt hadn't lessened one bit.

'When the first blast hit, he threw me to the floor and covered me, to keep me safe. Except he was injured by the rubble. I couldn't do anything to help him—just talk to him and tell him stupid jokes, anything to make the time pass until someone came to dig us out.' He dragged in a breath. Why the hell was he telling Joni all this? He never spoke about Ned. Never.

But being trapped in a tunnel with falling rubble had brought it all back so clearly that he couldn't stop the words tumbling out.

'They dug us out eventually. Took Ned to hospital. But someone slipped up with the malaria tablets. You know how it happens. Even if you take the tablets all the time, they're not a hundred per cent protection. And if you miss a couple and you get bitten by a mosquito…' He closed his eyes, but he could still see Ned's face. 'He caught malaria.'

'*Falciparum?*' she asked.

The most serious type of malaria. The one that caused complications. The fatal kind.

'Yes.' The word was ripped from him.

'I'm sorry. That must've been hard on you.'

Particularly as he'd hardly ever been allowed to visit Ned. It had been made very clear to Aaron that he mustn't be a nuisance—the baby of the family who always got in the way. He gave a soft huff of agreement.

'But, Aaron—you were only eight when it happened. A child. It wasn't your fault.'

Could she really not see it? The chain of causality was so simple. 'If Ned hadn't thrown himself over me, he wouldn't have been injured by the rubble, so he wouldn't have gone to hospital, and then he wouldn't have caught malaria.'

'I have two younger brothers,' she said. 'And if you were eight when your brother was in sixth form, then there's pretty much the same gap between us as there was between you and Ned. I'm six years older than Olly, and eight years older than Luke. And I can assure you that if we'd been in those circumstances, I would've done exactly the same as Ned did.'

It didn't help. At all.

'If I'd been hurt in the rubble, I wouldn't have blamed my brothers,' she added softly. 'They weren't the ones who launched the bombs.'

Intellectually, Aaron knew that Joni was speaking the truth. But, in his heart, he'd never forgive himself for Ned's loss. Never forgive himself for being the one who'd survived.

As if she'd read his thoughts, she said, 'I know I'm speaking out of turn, but it sounds to me as if you've got survivor guilt.'

He didn't answer.

'And I bet your parents blame themselves just as much,' she said. 'Because they weren't there when it happened.'

'That's ridiculous. It wasn't their fault.'

'And it definitely wasn't yours.'

He wasn't going to bother arguing that one with her. 'Ned had so much to give. He was going to be a doctor. And he would've been a really good one.'

'Is that why you became a doctor? Because he didn't have the chance and you wanted to make up for that?' she asked.

'Partly,' Aaron admitted. 'And I guess part of me wanted to be like him. But I'm a doctor for me, too. So I can help people.' Save them. Make a difference. And not feel as helpless as he had during Ned's final decline.

'Did anyone give you counselling after he died?'

'No.' A family who believed in stiff upper lips most definitely didn't believe in counselling. You never, ever talked to people about things. You just got on with it and ignored how you were feeling. And he really shouldn't be talking to her about this now.

'Maybe it's worth talking to someone,' she suggested. 'Someone who can help you to see for yourself that it really wasn't your fault.'

'I know it wasn't, and I'm fine,' he lied. He needed to get her off the subject. Now. And there was only one way he could think of to do it, even though it felt like scraping the scabs off his own wounds. 'Tell me about your brothers.'

It was the first time Aaron had asked her anything really personal, Joni thought. And she was just beginning to understand what made him tick. The youngest child of an armed forces family, having to go wherever they were posted and never really having the chance to settle and make friends. In some ways, she thought, that would tend to draw a family closer together, because they'd be the only constant thing in each other's life. Or maybe instead they'd had to grow hard shells and not let themselves get too attached to anyone, including each other. Especially given his older brother's death. It explained why Aaron was always polite and fitted in with everyone, but at the same time he kept that bit of distance between himself and other people. Because he was scared of getting close to someone and then risk losing them, the way he'd lost his brother.

'Luke's a trainee architect and Olly's a music teacher—by day, anyway,' she said. 'By night and at weekends, he's the lead guitarist in a rock band.'

'You sound proud of him,' Aaron said.

'I am. He's brilliant and I always go to see him play when he has a gig. So does Luke—they both live in London. And we often get to have dinner together first and catch up on everything. I love both my brothers to bits.' She laughed. 'Even if they do boss me about.'

'But you're the oldest—shouldn't you be the bossy one?' he asked, sounding surprised.

She laughed again. 'I've tried telling them that, but they don't listen to a word of it. I guess they're a bit overprotective because of the diabetes.'

'Lots of people live with diabetes,' Aaron said. 'It sounds as if there's more of a story to it than that.'

'I guess the way we found out about it was a bit dramatic,' she said. 'We didn't actually know I was diabetic. Then I went round Europe with Bailey in the summer holidays at the end of our first year as medical students. You know, that thing where your ticket means you can travel on any train throughout Europe for a whole month. We tried to explore as many places as we could. I hadn't been feeling brilliant, but no way was I going to spoil our trip by moaning about feeling ill. We'd just travelled from Rome to Venice, and that's where I collapsed. I ended up being rushed to hospital on a water ambulance. Not that I remember any of it.' She shrugged. 'It turned out that I had DKA, so I was kept in for a couple of days.'

Joni had spoken lightly, but Aaron knew as well as she did that diabetic ketoacidosis could have been fatal. A collapse like that meant hospital treatment; the medics would've needed to resuscitate her, clear the ketones from her blood, correct her electrolyte imbalance and then start insulin treatment to stabilise her. No wonder her family had gone super-protective. They must've been terrified that they'd lose her. 'You'd really had no idea that you might be diabetic?'

'None at all. I'd been feeling tired and a bit sick for a few days, but I assumed that was because we were doing a lot of walking in the midday sun. I'd lost my hat a couple of days before, and hadn't quite got round to replacing it—I thought maybe I had slight sunstroke, and that was why I was thirsty all the time and needed to drink a lot.'

The symptoms were similar to those of undiagnosed diabetes, he knew, so it had been a fair call. Especially to a first-year medical student. 'It must've been pretty scary for your friend, being in the middle of a medical emergency in a foreign country.'

'Luckily for us, Bailey's mum is Italian, so Bailey can speak the language really well. She was able to translate for me when the doctors came round, and also for Mum and Dad,' Joni explained. 'They came rushing straight out to Venice when Bailey rang them from the hospital. 'So that's mostly why my family's a bit over-protective.' He could hear the wry smile in Joni's voice as she added, 'I never did get to have that gondola ride Bailey and I were planning.'

'Maybe one day,' he said. 'So you've travelled a lot?'

'Not really. When I was young, we always used to hire a cottage in England for a couple of weeks, some-where by the sea. Dad wasn't really that keen on going abroad. It was only when Mum got in touch with my grandparents, when I was about eight, that we went to visit them in Arizona.'

'Arizona?'

She blew out a breath. 'Um, that's the other reason Dad's a bit overprotective of me. Mum's not actually my birth mother—she met him when I was three and I was in her class at nursery school.'

'So your dad was a single parent?' he asked.

'My birth mother didn't abandon me, if that's what you're thinking. Not from choice, anyway.' She bit her lip. 'Ajei died from complications the day after I was born.'

'Ah-heh?' The name wasn't familiar to him at all.

'Ajei. My birth mother.' She swallowed hard. 'She had a pulmonary embolism. There was nothing they could do.'

He realised that their fingers were still linked—how had that happened?—and he squeezed her hand. 'Sorry. That's tough on you, and I'm being intrusive.'

'No, it's fine. I'm OK talking about it. Obviously I never knew Ajei, but I've seen pictures of her, and in every single one she's smiling and looking happy. She's the one who named me Nizhoni.'

'I'd never even heard the name before I met you,' he said.

'You probably wouldn't, outside a certain area of America,' she said. 'It's Navajo—my mum's family's language. It means "beautiful". It's the first thing she said when she saw me, and she wanted it to be my name.'

'That's lovely.' He squeezed her hand again. 'So your mother was a Navajo?'

'The tribe's actually known as Diné, meaning "the people",' she said. 'But yes. She was an art student, training to be a silversmith. The jewellery she made was just gorgeous, all turquoise and silver. Dad was studying for a year in America after graduating from art school over here, and he met my mum at art college in LA. They fell in love, and then I came along.' She blew out a breath. 'I wasn't planned, and my grandparents weren't too pleased. But Ajei was their only child and they wanted her to be happy.'

Her fingers tightened round his. 'When she died, there was a huge row between my grandparents and my dad. Dad blamed them for encouraging my mum to have a home birth because they might've saved her in hospital; and my grandparents blamed him for getting my mum pregnant in the first place. They were all grieving, all angry about their loss, and they just couldn't see each other's point of view.'

'It must've been hard for all of them,' Aaron said.

'It was. Dad decided he'd had enough of the fighting and walked out—he left America and brought me straight home to England. And, until Mum persuaded him to try building a few bridges, he had no contact with my grandparents at all after he walked out.'

'Your mum sounds like a very special person. Both of your mothers, that is,' he said.

'They are. Ajei—her name means "my heart", and it's the first thing my grandmother said when she held her baby for the very first time—was special. Dad said there was something about her that always made him feel as if the sun had just risen. And Marianna's brilliant. She's always treated me as her daughter—she's never made me feel like the unwanted stepkid, not even when she had the boys,' Joni said.

'That's why Josie Stone's death hit you so hard,' he said. 'Because she was the stepchild, like you.'

She sighed. 'Yes. The sad thing is, I think Mrs Stone wanted to love Josie like her own—the way Mum loves me and I love her—but being a teenage girl is hard at the best of times. I guess it was easier for Josie to push her away.' She paused. 'And, with Ruby blaming herself for Josie getting the plague—that must've hit a sore spot for you, too.'

It had. And he didn't want to talk about it. 'You were telling me about your grandparents,' he said, hoping to distract her further. 'So how did your mum get them talking to your dad again?'

'She convinced Dad that I really needed to know where I came from, and that my grandparents needed to know me. They'd already lost their only child and it wasn't fair to keep their only grandchild from them, too. I guess he felt a bit guilty, because he agreed. So she tracked them down from the last address he had for them, managed to find someone on the Internet who could get in touch with them, and sent them a picture of me. They asked if I could come to meet them—if all of us would come to Arizona. Dad was worried that they'd end up fighting again, but in the end they apologised to each other and made it up.' He could hear the smile in her voice. 'So I spend a couple of weeks in Arizona every year to catch up with my other family. *Shimá sání* has the Internet now, so we can Skype once a week and send emails, too.'

'Shimma what?' he asked.

'Shih-mah tsah-nih,' Joni said slowly. 'Basically that means my maternal grandmother.'

'In Navajo?' he guessed. 'You actually speak Navajo?'

'Only a little bit. I probably couldn't translate a whole conversation between English and Navajo, but I know the important stuff. My family's names, "I love you", that sort of thing.' She paused. 'Actually, one of my great-great-uncles was a Navajo code talker in the Second World War.'

'What's a code talker?' he asked.

'They were the people who encoded messages. They created a code that was never broken by the enemy. And they were really fast—it took them about twenty seconds to encode, transmit and decode a three-line message in English, whereas the code machines of the time would take about thirty minutes to do the same thing,' she said, sounding immensely proud.

He was stunned. 'That's amazing to have something like that in your family.'

'The Diné are amazing,' she said. 'And I'm really proud of my family.'

'I would be, too, in your shoes.' He paused. 'And your heritage explains your incredible hair.'

'You actually like my hair?'

'Yes. Why do you sound so surprised?'

'Because…' She sighed. 'It's complicated. And I owe you an apology.'

'For what?' He was mystified.

'About that night. The salsa club. I'm a bit ashamed about it because I, um, kind of used you.'

He really wasn't following. 'Used me? How?'

'To block out my wedding day.'

CHAPTER SEVEN

'YOU CAME HOME with me the night you got *married*?'
Aaron began to think that he was in some kind of par-
allel universe. No way would someone like Joni Parker
get married, dump her new husband and go off with a
complete stranger that very evening. She just wouldn't.

Then again, she *had* told him that she was celebrating something, when he'd asked why she was drinking
champagne...

He shook his head to clear it. 'No. That's just not the
sort of thing you'd do. And I can't see you jilting someone at the altar, either.'

'I didn't jilt him or get married. It was just the day,'
she explained. 'The one when I was supposed to get
married, except it didn't happen.'

'And you were trying to block it out?'

'Yes.'

He could hear in her voice that she was upset. And if
your colleague was upset, the kind thing to do would be
to put your arms round her and give her a hug, wouldn't
it? It didn't mean he was getting *involved*. He ignored
the fact that when she'd been upset after Josie Stone's
death on the ward, he hadn't hugged her then.

Besides, it was cold in the damp, dark tunnel, so

pulling Joni onto his lap and wrapping his arms round her was also the sensible thing to do, he told himself. Sharing body heat. It had everything to do with being practical and nothing at all with emotions. Nothing at all. Nothing at all to do with the fact that her warmth and sweetness drew him to her, made him want things he'd never wanted before. And he really wasn't sure whether it scared or thrilled him most.

She leaned her head against his shoulder, and he automatically stroked her hair. Her gorgeous, silky hair. Hair that he could remember falling across his face as she'd straddled him...

Though it really wasn't a good idea to let himself remember that. Or the way she'd made him feel. Because he couldn't afford to let himself feel things. Hadn't he learned from Ned's death that getting close to someone just led to pain and loneliness? 'For what it's worth, I think he was an idiot for dumping you,' he said.

She gave a mirthless laugh. 'He didn't dump me. I was the one who broke it off.'

He winced. 'Sorry. I didn't meant to put my foot in it.'

'But you assumed that I was the dumpee.'

'Joni, I know I've worked with you for less than a month, but I've seen the way you are with people. You're not the sort who'd trample over someone's feelings or be selfish,' he said. 'That's why I assumed that you were the one who got hurt.'

'Thank you for the vote of confidence,' she said dryly.

He knew he shouldn't ask. Especially as he had no intention of sharing his own situation. But it was as if his mouth wasn't in step with the programme. 'What happened?'

'He was offered a job. It meant moving to the other end of the country, so I wouldn't get to see much of my family.'

'And you might've had to change specialty,' Aaron said, 'if the local hospital didn't have a tropical medicine department.'

'The firm he worked for had branches all over the country. I asked if he could negotiate, find out if he could do the same job in a branch within London instead of at the other end of the country,' Joni said. 'I wouldn't have minded a longer commute here every day.'

As long as she'd still been near her family, he guessed. 'And they couldn't do it?'

'He said not, though I wonder now if he ever even asked. According to Marty, it was his dream job. If I'd said that I didn't want to leave London—I didn't want to leave my family, my friends and my job—then he would've accused me of putting my family before him.'

'But he was asking you to put him before your family and your career. To put his needs before yours.'

'Yes. And I didn't think marriage was supposed to be like that. I thought it was supposed to be about compromise, about working together and finding something that works for both of you. Being a team,' she said. 'But Marty didn't like compromise. He liked things his way. And I was pretty spineless. I normally just went along with what he wanted. It seemed a bit—well—pointless and petty to make a fuss about all the little things.'

'What about the big things?' he asked softly.

'I agreed to go,' she said, and he noticed that she

hadn't answered his question. 'I agreed to leave London and everyone here.'

He waited, knowing there was more and sure that she would fill the silence.

'And then,' she continued softly, 'he said that I should cut my hair. That it would look more professional and give me a better chance of getting a good job.'

'Apart from the fact you already have a good job, how on earth would cutting your hair make you look more professional?' Aaron asked, not understanding. 'Anyway, you always wear it back for work.'

'I think,' she said, 'it was just another hoop he wanted me to jump through. And I realised I didn't want to do that, only for him to want me to change something else. I wanted…' She sighed. 'It's going to sound wet, and I don't mean to complain. But I always manage to pick the wrong guy. I do my best to make it work, but eventually I realise that I'm the one making all the compromises and all the effort and he's really not that bothered. And I'm just not prepared to do that any more.'

'That sounds entirely reasonable,' Aaron said. And it was yet another reminder that he was wrong for her. She needed someone who could do the emotional stuff. Not him. 'I can't believe your ex actually expected you to cut your hair just because he wanted you to do it. It's your hair, and it's up to you how you wear it.'

'Exactly. I know it sounds petty, but there had been so many other little things. I guess that one was the last straw. It made me think about what I wanted from life—and I didn't want the life I saw opening up in front of me. I didn't want to marry Marty and get more and more miserable. So I called off the wedding.'

'That takes a lot of courage,' Aaron said. 'Once everything's set in motion and everyone's expecting the big day to happen, it's really hard to say that you've made a mistake and you've changed your mind. It's easier to go along with it and do what everyone expects you to do.'

'I almost did,' she said. 'We'd booked the church and the reception venue, ordered the flowers and the cars, chosen the food. We'd paid all the deposits.'

'Sometimes,' he said, 'there are more important things to think about than money. Sometimes it's more important to do the right thing.'

'That's what all my family and friends said, when I called it off. That I was doing the right thing,' Joni said. 'Marty didn't get along with Bailey, either, so I only ever got to see her for lunch in the hospital cafeteria towards the end. And even then I'd tell him I had lunch with friends and not be specific about who, to avoid a row. He didn't want her to be my bridesmaid—he wanted his sister to be my only bridesmaid.'

'Your ex sounds like a total control freak,' Aaron said.

'He wasn't, at first. He was a sweetheart when I met him. But then he changed, little by little.'

Little things leading to bigger things. 'Maybe he got confident enough to stop hiding who he really was,' Aaron suggested.

'That's what Bailey said.'

'Wise,' he said. He'd only exchanged a couple of words with Joni's best friend at the salsa club, but the more he heard about her the more he liked her.

'It was Bailey's idea to go to the salsa club to celebrate my lucky escape. She said we could either stay at home and eat our body weight in junk food and ice cream and then feel gross the next morning—and it would seriously mess up my blood sugar, so she didn't recommend it—or we could go and dance ourselves happy.' Joni laughed. 'She's a sports medicine specialist, so she's a great believer in endorphins. According to her, exercise makes *everything* better.'

He couldn't help smiling. 'She has a point. When I've had a tough shift, going for a run always makes me feel better.'

'I wasn't actually looking to start something with someone that night,' Joni said. 'But I'd had a glass of champagne, and because of my diabetes I don't drink very often, so the bubbles went to my head. I guess it makes me a bit of a cheap date.'

Aaron laughed. 'There's absolutely nothing cheap about you, Joni Parker. I wasn't looking to start something with anyone, either. You and me...it just happened.'

'And we've agreed it was a one-off,' she said quickly.

'Absolutely.' So why did that make him feel disappointed? He should've felt relieved. Happy, even. His head really wasn't in the right place for a relationship. And sitting here with her on his lap and his arms wrapped round her was a really bad idea. Except he couldn't think of a way to back off without hurting her—and he didn't want to do that. Plus, if he was honest with himself, he *liked* sitting here with his arms wrapped round her. He liked holding her close.

'I'm not good at relationships,' he said. 'I don't do emotional stuff. So it never lasts beyond a few dates.'

'Maybe,' she said, 'you just haven't yet found the right person for you.'

'Do you actually believe that? That there's a Mr or Miss Right for everyone?' he asked.

'A soul mate, you mean?'

'Yes.'

She was silent for a while, obviously thinking about it. 'Yes. Though it isn't necessarily the person you think it's going to be, and it isn't necessarily just one person for the whole of your life. I mean, look at my dad—he was so young when my mum died. I don't think Ajei would've wanted him to be alone for the rest of his life, mourning her for the next fifty years or more. I think she would've wanted him to find someone who'd make him happy and who'd love me as her own. Which he did, when he met Marianna, and I'm really glad.'

'And that's what you're looking for?' he asked. 'Mr Right?'

'Right now,' she said, 'I'm not looking for anyone at all. And I'm sorry I used you to block out my wedding day.'

'Don't apologise.' He kept his arms round her. 'I think what happened was down to both of us.'

'It wasn't meant to happen. I planned just to have a glass or two of champagne and dance myself silly.'

But then he'd asked her to dance. And the moment of attraction across a crowded floor had suddenly got a whole lot more complex.

Just as right now had suddenly got a whole lot more complex. She was in his arms, sitting on his lap, and her face was only centimetres away from his. All he had to do was turn very slightly, dip his head very slightly, and his mouth would connect with hers.

He knew it would be the wrong thing to do. Joni wanted someone who'd make her happy—and he was rubbish at emotional stuff. He'd end up hurting her just as much as her ex had.

But, even as the thought bloomed in his head, he found himself moving closer. Touching his mouth to hers, brushing so lightly across it that his skin tingled.

Once wasn't enough.

He did it again, and his mouth tingled some more.

'Aaron,' she said, her voice sweet and soft and inviting.

The next thing he knew, her hands were in his hair, his arms were wrapped tightly round her, and she was kissing him back. Hot, urgent, desperate.

Hell. This had to stop.

He broke the kiss. 'Joni,' he said hoarsely, 'I'm sorry. I shouldn't have done that.'

'Uh-huh.' Her voice went all cool, and she wriggled on his lap, clearly trying to put some space between them.

'I didn't...' Oh, hell. 'I've never been inarticulate in my life,' he said, 'but I am with you, and I'm making a total mess of this.'

She stopped wriggling. 'So what are you saying, Aaron?'

'I'm saying I wish I was different,' he said. 'There's a big part of me that wants to ask you to see where this thing between us goes. But that wouldn't be fair to you. As I said, I'm not good at emotional stuff. And I don't want to hurt you, Joni. Just as I'm betting that you've already been hurt enough and you don't want to risk it, either.'

'Hey. I've picked myself up and dusted myself down,' she said. 'I'm not letting what happened with Marty affect the rest of my life. Well, I'm trying not to,' she said. 'And when I meet the right person, I'll learn to trust again.'

'Good.' And how sad was it that part of him really wished he could be that right person?

'You know, *shimá sání* always told me that I could be whoever I wanted to be,' she said.

Where was she going with this?

'You just said, you wished you were different. Which means you want to be.' She paused. 'Which means you *could* be.'

Was she suggesting that they could see where this thing between them was going? That they could take the risk—together?

The tightness across Aaron's shoulders eased a little. And, even though they were sitting in the pitch dark, weirdly everything seemed a tiny bit brighter.

'I like you, Aaron,' she said.

He liked her, too, but he wouldn't say it. Because how could he ask her to take a huge emotional risk on someone who was such a mess inside?

'You're a good doctor,' she continued. 'From what I've seen you're kind to the patients, you're easy to work with, and you're good at teaching the junior staff and giving them confidence in their abilities.'

'Thank you. So are you,' he said, meaning it.

'Thank you.' She paused. 'And you're hot.'

He didn't quite believe she'd said that. 'I'm what?'

'You heard. I'm not repeating it.'

'Are you propositioning me, Joni Parker?'

'That's your flaw, Mr Hughes,' she said. 'You're just a tiny bit slow on the uptake.' But there was laughter in her voice. She was teasing him, not criticising or condemning.

'So you *are* propositioning me.'

'Right now, I'm sitting on your lap and your arms are wrapped around me,' she pointed out.

'Because we're in a damp, cold place and this is the most efficient way for us both to keep warm.'

She'd obviously worked out that it was all an excuse—little more than bravado—because she asked, 'So you'd be sitting here exactly like this if you were stuck here with another colleague from the department?'

'Sure,' he lied.

'Even if it was Mikey or Mr Flinders?'

He pressed his cheek against hers. 'OK. Maybe not if it was Mikey or Mr Flinders.'

She laughed. 'Well, then. I'm just saying, you could be that different person.' She paused. 'If you wanted to.'

Could he?

The temptation was so strong.

'So you'd take a risk on me if I asked you out? Even though I don't have a good track record with relationships?'

She kissed the very corner of his mouth. 'There's only one way to find out, isn't there?'

CHAPTER EIGHT

JONI KNEW SHE was taking a huge risk and this could all blow up in her face. If she'd got this wrong…well, it would be awkward and embarrassing at work for a couple of weeks, but eventually they'd move past it, she told herself. And if she'd got it right…

Oh, please let her have got this right.

'Be the person I want to be,' Aaron said, as if mulling it over. 'Joni, I need to be fair with you. I'm not good at relationships, apart from professional ones with my patients and colleagues. I'm not even that good at having friends. I never have been. I get on fine with people and I fit in OK, but I don't know how to be close to people. And I'm a total disaster area when it comes to emotional stuff.' He blew out a breath. 'But, despite all that, would you consider having dinner with me some time?'

'Just to be clear—you're asking me out on a date?' she asked.

'Yes. I'm asking you out on a date,' he said softly.

'We've both been hurt in the past, made mistakes,' she said, equally softly. 'I'm probably just as much a disaster area as you when it comes to relationships. But, yes, I'd like to go on a proper date with you. I'd love to have dinner with you.'

'Good.' He kissed the corner of her mouth, and it made her feel hot all over. All she could concentrate on was the warmth of his arms around her and the softness of his lips. A couple of minutes ago, they'd been kissing each other desperately, everything happening at a rate of knots. Now the pace had shifted to slow and unbearably sweet. And the possibility of how good it could be between them left her breathless.

'So we'll take it slowly,' she said.

She could feel him smiling against her mouth. 'I guess we started with things rather the wrong way round.'

Joni was really glad that they were in complete darkness, otherwise she knew her face would be beetroot red to betray her shame. 'Just so you know, I don't normally get drunk and go off with complete strangers I've only just met on the dance floor.'

'I know I'm a little slow on the uptake,' he said, 'but I'd already worked that one out for myself. And, just so *you* know, I don't normally go dancing and take complete strangers home with me, either.'

'I'm glad to hear it.'

'Though,' he said, his voice deepening, 'I don't regret taking you home with me at all. Except for one thing.'

Joni went very still, thinking of the way Marty had started to change once they'd begun dating. All her doubts came rushing back. Was she just about to make the same stupid mistake all over again and start a relationship with someone who wouldn't put as much effort in as she did? He'd practically warned her off. She'd been an idiot, refusing to listen. Would she never learn?

'What's that?' she asked carefully.

'That I sleep like the dead—otherwise I would've

heard you get up in the morning. I would've made you a coffee before you left, and hopefully persuaded you to stay for breakfast.'

She relaxed again. 'Oh.'

'And,' he said, 'about that dinner date...I think I'd like a breakfast date some time, too.'

'Breakfast,' she said, 'isn't exactly taking things slowly.'

'It is if we don't spend the night together first—say if we meet somewhere for breakfast,' he pointed out. 'And I'd like that. To spend a whole day with you, getting to know you better. Finding out what makes you tick.'

In answer, she kissed him.

By the time she broke the kiss, they were both shaking.

'And this is just between you and me, right?' she asked. 'As far as work's concerned, we're just colleagues—not because I'm ashamed of dating you or anything like that, but because it stops things getting complicated.'

'Agreed,' he said. 'Though I reserve the right to sneak a kiss in the corridor when nobody's looking.'

She laughed. 'Aaron, you make me feel like a teenager again. And I'm thirty years old.'

'Snap. On the teenager bit,' he said. 'Though you have a few years on me. I'm thirty-three.'

'That's quite young, for a consultant.' She stroked his face. 'Which means you're clever. Geeky, even.' She stole another kiss. 'And that T-shirt you were wearing when we went rock-climbing on the departmental night out gives you extra points. I like your sense of humour.'

'Good.' He paused. 'Speaking of the departmental

night out...I hope you realise I had a bad time that evening. All because of your jeans.'

'Because of my jeans?' She didn't understand. 'Why?'

'Because I wanted to be on my own with you in a very private place so I could peel them off you. Very, very slowly,' he said. 'So if I was a bit offish with anyone that evening, now you know why. I was trying to keep my imagination and my libido under control.'

'Uh-huh.' And now he'd put ideas into her imagination. Ideas that were rapidly spiralling out of control. So much for taking this slowly. Aaron Hughes made her temperature and her pulse spike.

He kissed her again. 'So. You and me. For now, until we know where it's going, it's just between us. And I think we need to change the subject and talk about something really serious and work-related, because otherwise it could be really embarrassing when they dig us out of here and we look as if we've been kissing each other stupid.'

He was right. She knew that. It would be sensible to put some distance between them. Even though she didn't want to move because she liked being in his arms. 'I guess I'd better, um, move.'

His arms stayed wrapped right round her. 'I didn't quite mean that. Besides, this is efficient sharing of body heat.'

Oh. So he didn't want her to move, either. 'Uh-huh,' she said.

'Talk to me about work. You know why I went into tropical medicine. What about you?'

'Because that way I get to hear about all the exciting places where my patients have visited,' she said, laughing. 'Which is horribly shallow of me. But I also like the research side, and I really love the idea of helping to eradicate a disease or find a vaccine to help prevent it in the first place.' She paused. 'Funnily enough, *shimá sání* is a bit—well, fey, I guess you'd say. She said when my mum was pregnant with me, she knew I'd be a healer.'

'You mean, like a shaman?' he asked.

'Maybe, if I'd grown up on the reservation in Arizona. Though in my mum's language it's not shaman, it's *hatałii*.'

'Ha'atathli,' he said, trying to copy her pronunciation. 'Could you still be one now?'

'No,' she said. 'You need to be apprenticed at a really young age because there's so much to learn and it's not written down—everything's passed down orally from one generation to the next, and it's obviously all in Navajo and I don't speak enough of it. Though I would've had someone to be apprenticed to. *Shi cheii*—my grandfather—is a *hatałii*,' she said.

'Your grandfather's a healer? So what happened to your mum…' He blew out a breath. 'That must've made things even harder for your family to handle.'

'Yes. That's why the row was so bad,' she said. 'Dad and *shi cheii* both felt guilty that their way had failed, and it made them really lash out at each other.'

'So, as a qualified doctor, you're caught in the middle between them?'

'Actually, no,' she said. '*Shi cheii* is really proud that I've followed in his footsteps—only obviously in my father's culture rather than my mother's. And I have great discussions with him about medicine and how he'd treat someone compared with the way I would. I think we've learned a lot from each other. In Diné culture, it's very much holistic medicine—it's about restoring *hózhǫ́* to the patient.'

'What's ho-joh?' Aaron asked.

'*Hózhǫ́* means harmony—I guess you could call it order, because it's about putting everything in balance, not just curing the symptoms. Holistic medicine, really. So the *hatałii* will spend time talking to the patient, finding out everything that's wrong and that's worrying them.'

'And if a patient talks, and feels they're being listened to, that's a good thing,' Aaron said. 'It reduces a lot of the worry and stress.'

'Exactly. And think how many illnesses have stress as their root cause,' Joni continued. 'Teaching people to restore the balance in their life can help with that, too.'

'So it's all psychological?'

'No, there's some herbal medicine, too. Apprentices start by making up medicine bundles, mainly herbs. Some are made into tinctures, some are burned.'

'And I'm guessing that if you broke them down into their chemical composition, there would be similarities with Western medicines?' Aaron asked.

'Yes. Actually, I've got a research proposal with Mr Flinders at the moment, looking into alternatives to antibiotics that might exist in Native American medicine.'

'That sounds really interesting,' Aaron said. 'With more bacteria becoming resistant to the antibiotics we have now, we really need to look at alternatives because we only have a few more years left while they'll still work, and then we'll be right back to where we started in the years before penicillin was discovered, where people can die from scratching themselves on a thorn. Tell me more.'

Joni found herself telling him all about her pet project.

'For what it's worth, you've got my backing,' he said when she'd finished. 'And if I can do anything to help, I'd love to be involved. It sounds fascinating.'

'Thank you. I might well take you up on that,' Joni said.

Right then, Aaron's stomach growled. 'Sorry. It feels like a long time since we had that tea and biscuits,' he said.

'What's the time?'

'I'll check my phone.' Light glowed in the tunnel, giving Aaron's face a ghostly air as he checked the time on his phone. 'It's nearly lunchtime.'

'Because of the diabetes, I always carry snacks with me,' she said. 'I have a couple of cereal bars and a bag of jelly babies in my pocket. We can share them.'

'No, you need to eat them,' he said. 'Don't worry about me. I can live with being a bit hungry, but I don't want your blood sugar crashing. Do you need to check your blood glucose? I can put the torch on for a bit, so you can see what you're doing.'

'Thanks. I have to admit, I'm starting to feel as if my blood sugar's getting a bit low.' She tested herself while he held the torch steady. 'Yes, it's dropping a bit. I could do with some carbs.' She fished the jelly babies out of her pocket and offered the bag to him.

'Thanks, but, honestly, I'm fine,' he said, and stroked her face. 'You need them more than I do. Although the rest of the group must have worked out that we're missing by now, they still have to find us and we don't know how long we're going to be stuck in here.'

'I'm on insulin twice a day,' she said, 'but I don't need to take any until this evening. These and the cereal bar will keep me going for a few more hours. Though I still feel bad about eating and you not having anything.'

He kissed her lightly. 'There's a medical reason for it, so don't feel bad. Put it this way, I'd feel an awful lot worse if I ate your food and you had a hypo while we're trapped in a tunnel and I couldn't do anything to help you. So will you please stop stressing and just eat?'

'Point taken,' she said, and ate a handful of the jelly babies and one of the cereal bars. Though she was relieved that Aaron did at least accept a couple of mouthfuls from the bottle of water she also carried with her.

'Did you hear that?' Aaron asked a while later. 'Someone's shouting outside.'

'You think they've worked out where we are?' Joni asked.

'I hope so. After three, if we both yell "hello" as loud as we can, they've got more chance of hearing us. And they'll know it's a voice making the noise rather than just a stone falling or something.'

'Agreed,' Joni said.

He counted them in, and they both yelled, 'Hello!'

There was a yell back from outside.

'We're in here,' Aaron called. 'The roof fell in.'

The words from outside were muffled, but he could just about work them out: 'We're making it safe and digging you out.'

'We need to move back a bit further,' he said to Joni, 'in case their digging triggers another roof fall.'

'Do we get some light, this time?' she asked.

'Good idea,' he said.

It took their rescuers another hour to build a stable tunnel to get them out, and just as Aaron had feared there were a couple more roof falls in the meantime, but finally they could see daylight coming in from the outside.

'Come out one at a time, and try not to dislodge anything on your way out,' a voice Aaron recognised as that of the team leader called.

'You first,' he told Joni. 'And don't argue.'

Waiting in the tunnel, knowing that the entrance could easily fall in again and trap him alone in the dark—just as he'd been all those years ago when the house had been bombed—stretched his nerves to the limit. But at last Joni was through, and it was his turn to crawl through the makeshift tunnel.

'We were so worried when you didn't get back,' Nancy said. 'We tried ringing your mobile, Joni, but it kept saying you were unavailable. We thought one or both of you might have fallen and been hurt.'

'Just a roof fall blocking our way out. We're fine,' Aaron said lightly. 'No injuries of any description, and Joni had some carbs on her so her blood sugar's OK, too.'

'We couldn't call anyone from the tunnel because we didn't have a signal on our phones,' Joni said. 'We just hoped you'd realise something was wrong when we didn't come back and would come and find us.'

'We searched for you for an hour before we found you,' the team leader said. Joni produced the small box from her pocket. 'We did get the final clue, by the way. We just couldn't call it in because of the signal problem.'

'I think you can be forgiven,' the team leader said. 'Come on, let's get you back to base and get you warmed up. It must have been freezing in there.'

'Just a tad,' Joni said with a smile.

And was it his imagination, Aaron wondered, or was she blushing ever so slightly? Because there had been quite a few moments when neither of them had been aware of the temperature...

Back at base, they had hot drinks and a cooked meal, and then there was a final set of team-building exercises.

'I think,' Mikey said when they were on the way back to the hospital at the end of the day, 'we can definitely say we all bonded today. We were that worried about you two.'

'We were just lucky that the tunnel entrance collapsed when we were nowhere near it,' Joni said.

'All the same, we'll be raising a glass to you both at the next departmental night out,' Nancy said. 'Actually, that reminds me, Aaron—the next one's already organised, but can I put you down to organise the one after that?'

'Sure,' he said with a smile.

Maybe here in London it would be different.

And he could be different, too. Learn to do emotional stuff.

CHAPTER NINE

LATER THAT EVENING, Aaron called Joni. 'Hi.'

'Hi.'

Help. What did he say now? His social skills seemed to have completely deserted him. Which was utterly ridiculous. 'I, um, was just wondering how you were.'

'I'm fine,' she said. 'All the lights in my flat are on and I've checked everywhere for spiders.'

'That's good.' He paused. Oh, for pity's sake. This was worse than being a teenager again, asking out the girl you didn't think you had a chance with. Though he'd already done that bit, hadn't he? In principle. And this call was meant to be about specifics. He pulled himself together and made an effort. 'You know we talked about having dinner—I was wondering when you might be free.'

'How about Friday?' she suggested.

'That works for me, too. OK. I'll book something.' And now he was back in his comfort zone. 'Is there any food you really hate, or do you have any allergies?'

'No allergies, and I like just about everything except offal and chocolate,' she said. 'I really don't mind where we go, as long as I know the dress code.'

'Sure. I'll find something and text you later, OK?'

'OK. And, Aaron?'

'Yes,' he said warily.

'I'm really glad you called.'

Funny how that made him feel all warm inside. He wasn't used to feeling like this, and it scared him as much as it made him feel good. 'Yeah. See you tomorrow,' he mumbled, and ended the call.

He spent a while browsing the Internet, trying to find a restaurant he thought Joni would enjoy. Nothing too casual, because he wanted to her feel that he'd thought about it and was trying to make the evening special for her; but nothing too fussy where they wouldn't get a chance to talk.

In the end, he chanced upon something a little bit different.

It would be a risk. Especially for an official first date.

He rang to see if there were any spaces left. They were full, but they'd just had a cancellation so two places had become free. This was fate, he told himself, and booked it.

Then he texted Joni.

Booked for Friday. Meet at the tube station near your flat, six p.m. Dressy, but wear shoes you can walk in.

She texted back within moments.

OK. Where are we going?

Surprise, he texted back. She didn't need to know that it was going to be a surprise for him, too—did she?

Dressy, but wear shoes you can walk in. Which told

her absolutely nothing, other than that they were going to have to walk from the tube station to the restaurant. But shoes she could walk in just didn't go with her dress. So did she wear flats until they got to the restaurant, and change her shoes then? Or…

She texted Aaron.

I could book us a taxi, if you like.

And then he'd have to tell her where they were going instead of keeping it as a 'surprise', right?

No. We have to take the tube, he replied.

What? Why? She had absolutely no idea, and if she texted him she knew he wouldn't give her a proper answer, so she gave up and rang him. 'Why do we have to take the tube?'

'I'll explain on Friday.'

She sighed. 'You like playing the Man of Mystery, don't you?'

'Maybe.'

'Arrgh,' she said in frustration, and he laughed.

'By the way—do you prefer red or white wine?' he asked.

'Either. Why?'

'More Man of Mystery stuff,' he said, and she groaned again.

Aaron refused to be drawn about what was really happening on Friday night when she asked him at work, too, so Joni was none the wiser by the time Friday evening arrived.

Dressy.

So that would be her little black dress—demure, knee-length and very plain. Flats to walk in, the red high heels she'd worn at the salsa club to change into when they got there—wherever 'there' was—and her mother's turquoise choker, she decided. Hair most definitely down, and her usual bare minimum of make-up teamed with a spritz of her favourite perfume; and she was at the tube station near to her flat at exactly six o'clock.

Aaron was waiting outside, leaning against the wall, and he was attracting second glances from just about every woman who passed. Which was hardly surprising, she thought; in a dark suit, white shirt and a plain deep red silk tie, he looked stunning.

And he was all hers.

It made her feel like a teenage girl on her first date with the coolest boy in school. Except she and Aaron had already gone way beyond the first date. Before they'd even been dating.

And now they'd agreed to take it slowly. Get to know each other better outside work. Tonight was their first date. Just the thought of it made her tingle all over with anticipation and excitement. Yet, at the same time, it scared her witless. Given the mess her last relationship had become, and the fact that Aaron had been very frank with her about being hopeless with emotional stuff, was she doing the right thing? Was she setting herself up for yet another fall?

To cover her doubts, she walked over to him and gave him her brightest smile. 'Hi,' she said, and kissed him on the cheek. And then she grimaced. 'Sorry. I've just covered you in lipstick.' She grabbed a tissue from her handbag and dabbed the lipstick off his skin.

He just smiled. 'You look gorgeous. And I'm glad you wore your hair down.'

'Thank you.' She felt the colour seeping into her face. To cover her embarrassment, she asked, 'So now I'm here, where are we actually going, oh Man of Mystery?'

'Right at this moment,' he said, 'I don't actually know.'

She blinked, surprised. 'But you said you'd booked somewhere.'

'I have.'

She still didn't understand. 'So why don't you know where we're going?'

'Because it's a surprise supper club,' he explained. 'The venue changes every week—we've booked for tonight and I should get a text any minute now to tell us where to go.'

Now she understood why he'd asked her to wear shoes she could walk in. 'So it's like a pop-up restaurant crossed with a magical mystery tour?' She smiled. 'What a fabulous idea.'

He looked visibly relieved. 'It's a bit of a risk—especially for a first date—because I have absolutely no clue what the venue's going to be like. But apparently the food's fantastic. The only thing is, there's a set menu so you don't get a choice, and you have to bring your own wine because they don't have a licence to sell alcohol.'

'Which is why you asked me if I preferred red or white wine.'

He gestured to the carrier bag he was holding. 'I played it safe. I hope you like Sauvignon Blanc.'

'I do.' She smiled. 'This is so exciting. I've always wanted to go to a pop-up restaurant.'

'We were really lucky. Someone had cancelled just before I called, so we managed to get the last two places.'

'Obviously it was meant to be,' she said.

His phone beeped, and he read the text. 'We get off the train three stops from here, and then we'll get more directions.'

'And at least this treasure hunt isn't going to end in a tunnel that collapses on us,' she said, laughing.

He frowned. 'Actually, for all I know we *might* end up in a tunnel. Would that be a problem?'

'No, because it wouldn't be like the one on the team-building day.'

The guarded look left his face. 'Let's go, then.'

They took the train as directed, and then followed the directions in a series of texts. The last one sent them down a flight of narrow stairs to a basement room, where a waiter in a burgundy bow tie and black tail-coat handed them a glass of something sparkling and directed them through to the next room.

'It's a wine cellar,' she said as they passed rack upon rack of dusty bottles. She took a sip from her glass. 'Elderflower cordial. That's lovely—really summery.'

The next room took her breath away; there were tiny bistro tables laid out in the wine cellar, with white dam-ask tablecloths, sparkling silverware and fresh flowers. The whole place was lit by candlelight alone.

'This so romantic,' she said softly. 'Thank you for booking this, Aaron. I've never been anywhere so lovely.'

Joni didn't think it could get better than that but, just after the waitress had seated them and uncorked their wine, a group of four musicians—all in tailcoats and white bow ties and carrying a cello, a violin or a viola—came in and sat down in the corner. As soon as they started playing, she recognised the melody.

'Oh, I love this—Pachelbel's *Canon*,' she said. 'So

we get great live music as well as great food? Aaron, this is utterly perfect.'

'I'm glad you like it.'

He still seemed a little tense, so she lifted her wine-glass. 'To us,' she said, 'and seeing where this takes us—whether it ends up being a good friendship or something more.'

For a moment, she didn't think he was going to respond. And then he smiled—a smile that actually reached his eyes. Clearly he was as nervous about this whole thing as she was. 'To us,' he echoed.

'Given that you're a coffee geek, would I be right in thinking you're a foodie, too?' she asked.

'A bit,' he admitted. 'I know my way round a kitchen, and I'm comfortable experimenting. You?'

'The same—though I'm very boring on Monday nights. Bailey and I always go out for dinner to the same restaurant after our yoga class—and, although we've worked our way through the entire menu over the last year or so, we're a bit, um, predictable with our order nowadays,' she confessed.

He smiled. 'There's nothing wrong with having favourites.'

The food turned out to be as fabulous as Aaron had hoped—beetroot risotto, followed by salmon served on a bed of puy lentils with finely shredded Savoy cabbage.

'Definitely cooked in butter, lemon and chilli,' Joni said after she'd tasted the greens. 'What a fabulous mix-ture.'

'I agree,' Aaron said.

The Eton mess with raspberries served with the thin-nest, lightest shortbread rounds were perfect, and then finally coffee—which lived up to Aaron's standards—

and petits fours, including the thinnest slice of orange Joni had ever seen. 'That must have been cut with a mandolin,' she said.

Aaron took a bite of his. 'And it's been caramelised.'

'Without changing the colour? That's amazing,' she said, and tried hers. 'That's seriously impressive. Thank you, Aaron,' she said. 'This is the nicest meal I've had in a very long time.' She looked thoughtful. 'Do you think the organisers would do a one-off pop-up for a group?'

'They might do. Are you thinking I could book them for the departmental night out Nancy wants me to organise?' he asked.

'I think the team would love it. And if the organisers can find somewhere really different, you might just beat my rainstorm as the most unusual night out ever.'

'That sounds like a challenge,' Aaron said.

She raised an eyebrow. 'It might be.'

'So, if I meet your challenge, what are the stakes?'

'We can start at a kiss,' she said.

'Start at a kiss—and finish where?'

Even the thought left her breathless. 'Um—Woman of Mystery stuff?' she suggested, and he laughed.

They chatted to the organiser after the event. 'We really enjoyed ourselves tonight,' Aaron said, 'and we were wondering if you would be able to organise an event for a team night out?'

'How many people?' the organiser asked.

Aaron looked at Joni.

'About fifteen,' Joni said.

'That's doable,' the organiser said. 'I'll need to check my diary so I can give you a date—is that OK?'

'That's great. We tend to organise it for the middle

of the week so most of us can make it,' Joni explained, 'and usually we do something before we eat.'

'Or you could include the entertainment as part of the night,' the organiser suggested. 'One of my clients runs a circus school, so maybe we could serve the meal in a marquee and you and your colleagues could do a bit of tightrope walking and juggling beforehand. And my client could ask some of his troupe to do an act in between the main course and pudding.'

Aaron and Joni looked at each other.

'That,' Aaron said, 'would be absolutely perfect.'

When they'd finished making arrangements, Aaron called a taxi. Joni's flat was on the way to his, so he dropped her there first, asking the taxi driver to wait while he saw her safely inside.

'You're very welcome to come in for a cup of tea,' Joni said, 'but no way am I going to dare to offer you a coffee.'

He laughed. 'I'm not that picky.'

Her expression said that she begged to differ.

And he wasn't quite ready for the evening to end yet. 'A cup of tea would be lovely,' he said. 'I'll just pay the taxi driver.'

'I'll put the kettle on,' she said.

Joni's flat was pretty much what Aaron had expected. Like her, the decor was warm and vibrant. The kitchen was painted a bright sunshiny yellow, with maple cupboards and worktops; there was a shelf full of cookery books, and there were lots of photographs and postcards held to the fridge with magnets.

Clearly she'd seen his glance because she smiled. 'Knock yourself out.' She poured boiling water into the two mugs, then came back to talk him through the photographs. 'Bailey, you already know. That's Olly on stage with his band, Luke in Rome because he says the Pantheon roof is the most perfect piece of architectural engineering ever and he has to visit it at least once a year so he can drool over it, and Mum and Dad.'

He could see the resemblance between Joni and her father, and between her brothers.

'This is *shi cheii* and *shimá sání*—my grandparents.' Both were wearing jeans and checked shirts, which surprised him, and clearly it showed in his face because Joni gave him a sidelong look. 'American Indians don't wear traditional clothes all the time, you know.'

'No. Of course not. Sorry.'

'And this is *shimá*—my mother, Ajei.'

The photograph was of a young woman with long dark hair, sitting on a rock against a bright blue sky, clearly pregnant and looking absolutely radiant. The picture of happiness, Aaron thought. 'She's beautiful. She looks so much like you.'

Joni inclined her head in acknowledgement. 'Thank you. Though I'm ten years older now than she is in that picture.'

He could see the sadness in her eyes. Not knowing what else to do, he gave her a hug.

She leaned against him briefly. 'Thank you,' she said softly. 'Come and sit down.'

Her living room was also painted a sunshiny yellow. There was a burnt-orange sofa with deep red cushions; the rug in the middle of floor was the same deep red as the cushions, with geometric designs woven into it. Again she clearly saw where he was looking. 'That rug was woven by one of my cousins. I brought it back from Arizona a couple of years ago.'

'Your cousin's a very talented weaver,' he said.

Joni smiled. 'I'll tell her that, the next time I talk to her.'

There were lots of family photographs on the mantelpiece, Aaron noticed, including Joni's graduation and those of her brothers, and a photograph of her parents' wedding with Joni cuddled between them as the bridesmaid. There was so much love in her family and everyone seemed so close. How could he ever be enough for her?

He pushed the panic away. Later. Not now. 'I meant to say earlier, I really like your necklace.'

She looked pleased. 'My mother made it.'

'It's beautiful—like you, Nizhoni.'

She blushed. *'Ahéhee.'*

'I'm guessing that's Navajo,' he said, 'but what does it mean?'

'Thank you,' she said with a smile.

'You're welcome,' he said, smiling back. 'Do you have much of your mother's jewellery?'

'I have another necklace, two bracelets and a ring,' she said. 'I gave some of the pieces to *shimá sání*, because I thought she really ought to have some of her daughter's work.'

'That's kind,' he said.

'Not really.' She shrugged. 'She's my grandmother and I love her.'

So easy. Aaron thought of his own grandparents—remote, on both sides. He'd stayed with them sometimes during school holidays, and he'd felt as much of a nuisance to them as he'd been to his parents. What must it be like to have such an easy relationship—to be close despite the geographical distance? His own family might as well have been in another solar system. And he hated the idea that it could hurt her.

'What are you thinking?' she asked softly.

No way was he admitting to any of that. 'The tunnel. The best thing about that day was holding you. And there's the fact that I met your challenge, earlier—the stakes, I believe, were a kiss.' And even the idea of it melted his self-control. Almost. He just about managed to let himself pause. 'May I?'

She stroked his face. 'Aaron, you're so sweet. I like the fact that you ask, you don't just assume.'

Well, good. But he needed to kiss her. Right now. Before he imploded. He coughed. 'Was that a yes or a no?'

'A definite yes.'

'Good.' He set her mug of tea on the floor next to his, and scooped her onto his lap. Funny how holding her made him feel so much better.

'I really had a great time tonight,' she said. 'Thank you for organising it.'

'It was a bit of a risk,' he admitted. 'If the venue or food had been awful...'

'Actually, it wouldn't have mattered,' she said, 'because you put a lot of thought into it and tried to make it a special evening, and that's the important thing.'

'So you've forgiven me for all the Man of Mystery stuff?' he asked.

'Ask me nicely, and I'll tell you,' she said with a teasing smile.

'All right. Please will you forgive me for the Man of Mystery stuff?'

She laughed. 'That's not quite what I meant by "nicely".'

'So I'm being slow on the uptake again?'

She grinned. 'Just a tad. Think about the stakes I owe you.'

He kissed her, long and slow and tender. Dragging it out, just because he really liked kissing her. And even though his head was yelling a warning that he shouldn't let his guard down, shouldn't let himself get involved, he couldn't stop himself. The feel of her skin against his. The soft floral scent she wore. The sound of his blood thrumming through his veins. The way she tasted.

And how incredibly hot she looked when he broke the kiss—her eyes all huge, her lips reddened and parted, and her head tipped back slightly in offering. It made him want to do it all over again. And again. And take it further, until she was falling apart under the touch of his hands and his mouth.

He'd never felt this kind of temptation before. It scared the hell out of him; and yet at the same time he wanted more, too.

'Now, that's what I call a kiss,' she said, and laughed up at him.

God, she was gorgeous. And he wanted her more than he'd ever wanted anyone in his life. 'So am I forgiven?' Or did he get to kiss her some more, until hopefully she was in as stupid a state as he was?

'You're forgiven,' she said. 'Just.'

'*Ahéhee*,' he said, and she laughed and kissed him until he was dizzy.

'So do you like other music apart from classical?' she asked.

'I like a pretty wide range of music,' he said, 'except maybe boy-band stuff.'

She smiled. 'That's because you're not a teenage girl. My brother's band is playing on Wednesday night. A few of us from the department are going, as well as my family and Bailey—so I was wondering, would you like to come?'

It wasn't a 'meet the family' thing, then—more like a mini departmental night out. OK. He could cope with that. 'I'd like that very much,' he said, then paused. 'Um, would this be an exception to my "I don't really like boy bands" stance?'

'Absolutely not,' she said. 'Olly's band is a cross between rock and blues. They do some cover versions, but he writes a lot of their own songs.'

'Rock and blues? Now, that,' he said, 'so happens to be my favourite kind of music.' He named a few of the bands he liked.

'Olly loves them. Have you seen any of them live?'

'Manchester has a good music scene,' he said. 'So, yes—several times.'

'Then I think you and Olly are going to get on really, really well,' she said with a smile.

Although she didn't spell it out, he knew from what she'd said before that Marty hadn't got on that well with her family. Family wasn't everything—though he had a feeling it might be, to Joni. There were so many places where this could all go wrong and hurt them both. And that made him antsy.

He finished his mug of tea and kissed her lingeringly. 'I'd better let you get some sleep. Thanks for this evening.'

'No, thank *you*—you're the one who sorted it all out and it was fantastic.' She paused. 'Um, are you busy tomorrow?'

'Not particularly.'

'Give me a call if you fancy going for a walk or something. It might be nice to have a wander round Chelsea Physic Garden,' she said.

'That sounds good. I'll call you tomorrow.' He kissed her again. 'Goodnight, Nizhoni who most definitely lives up to her name.'

And her face turned a very gratifying shade of pink.

The weather the next morning was awful. So much for their planned walk around the medicinal botanical garden at Chelsea, Aaron thought. But he called Joni anyway. 'I've got waterproofs if you're game for walking round a garden in all this rain,' he said, 'but I guess we're not going to see that much.'

'I guess not,' she agreed. 'Unless we switch the venue to somewhere indoors. How about a wander around an art gallery or museum?'

'That works for me,' he said.

'Great. Where do you want to go?'

'I don't know London that well. Surprise me,' he suggested.

Half an hour later, he met her at her flat. Last night she'd been dressed to the nines; today, her face was scrubbed clean and she was wearing jeans and a T-shirt teamed with flat canvas shoes. But she was still utterly beautiful, and even looking at her made his heart skip a beat.

He kissed her hello. 'You're wearing your hair back.'

She shrugged. 'I can loosen it, if you want.'

'It's up to you how you wear your hair,' he said, remembering that her ex had been a control freak. 'But I think it's too gorgeous to hide in a ponytail.'

She blushed prettily and smiled. 'Thank you.' She took the scrunchie out of her hair and stuffed it into her pocket, then shook her hair loose. 'Are you ready to go?'

'Sure. Where are we going?'

'You told me to surprise you. I can't do that if I tell you where we're going,' she pointed out.

He laughed. 'You're just trying to get your own back for me doing the Man of Mystery stuff last night.'

She grinned. 'Just a little bit. Though you set the bar a bit on the high side. I need a bit of time to research somewhere different.'

'Or maybe we could make a list together,' he said.

Her smile warmed him all the way through. 'Now, that,' she said, 'is an excellent idea. We'll make a list of quirky stuff we want to do, together. Today we're going to somewhere that's pretty well known, but I still think it's worth a visit.'

'That works for me,' he said. Particularly because it meant he was spending time with her.

Walking in the rain with her to the tube station was fun, because it meant being tucked under an umbrella together and it was a great excuse to put his arm round her.

Before Joni, Aaron had never really thought of himself as the tactile type. But he liked being close to her. Liked being able to smell her floral scent. Liked the warmth of her skin next to his hand. It made him feel as if he was in same kind of brave new world—one that was full of wonder and brightness. Joni made all his senses feel hyper-alert—and he was really starting to like that feeling.

They left the train at Charing Cross. Aaron still wasn't quite sure where she had in mind until they reached the church of St Martin in the Fields and she stopped and indicated a poster that was advertising a concert that afternoon. 'I love Bach.' Then she looked worried, as if she was being too demanding. Was that how her ex had made her feel? Her next words confirmed exactly what she was worrying about. 'Do you have time to go to that as well as where we're going now?'

He wanted to reassure her—but, at the same time, he didn't want her to feel stifled or as if he was just humouring her. It was a fine line to walk, and he could still get it so very wrong. 'I have time and it's a great idea,' he said. 'Let's get the tickets now, so we don't have to worry about queuing later.'

Once they'd bought the tickets, she led him round the corner to Trafalgar Square and he recognised the building instantly. 'The National Gallery?'

'It's such a nice way to spend a Saturday morning,' she said. 'And I love their Van Goghs—it's the brightness and the light in the paintings.'

Aaron thoroughly enjoyed wandering around with her, hand in hand, looking at the paintings. After they'd grabbed a quick sandwich and a drink, Joni noticed that it had stopped raining. 'Let's go and see the lions,' she said. 'I know it's touristy, but I've always loved them. I've got a picture with me and the boys posing by the lions when we were really small, and it's one of my favourites.'

Family again.

Would she be able to cope with the fact that his family wasn't close at all, or would it be a deal-breaker?

He pushed the thought away and walked round the fountain with her, then admired Nelson's Column.

'We have to do the touristy thing,' she said, and drew him over to one of the Landseer lions guarding the column. She held out her phone at arm's length to take a selfie of them with his arms wrapped round her and her cheek pressed against his; it made him feel as young and unencumbered as the teenagers around them who were doing exactly the same thing. Which was weird, because he'd always been a serious and nerdy teen, throwing his energies into studying rather than partying.

And he enjoyed holding her hand all the way through the concert that afternoon: perfect music in a perfect environment and with perfect company,

Back at the tube station, he had a pretty good idea of how she'd felt when she'd asked him to go to the concert. Pretty much the way he was feeling now—worried that he was wanting too much, moving things too fast. But he asked anyway. 'I know I'm being greedy, but I'm not quite ready for today to end. Do you have time to have dinner with me?'

'I'd love to.' He realised that she actually had dimples when she smiled, dimples that made him want to sweep her off her feet, spin her round and kiss her until they were both dizzy, regardless of who could see them—and he'd never been that reckless.

Not good.

What had happened to his self-control? But he didn't have time to think about that when she added,

'And I know a very nice little Italian trattoria just round the corner.'

'That sounds perfect.'

And it was. Aaron really enjoyed talking to Joni about films and books, especially when he discovered that she liked the same kind of art-house films that he did. He also found himself sharing much more information about himself than he normally would. Which should have made him feel wary; yet with her he could relax.

He kissed her goodbye on her doorstep.

'Do you want to come in for a drink or something?' she asked.

Or something, he thought. He wanted to carry her to her bed. Peel her clothes off, exceedingly slowly. Find out just where and how she liked being touched—by both his hands and his mouth—and then keep doing it until she cried out his name in release.

But this wasn't the deal.

'Better not.'

She looked wary, and he remembered what she'd said about always being the one to put in all the effort. He needed to explain and take that wariness out of her eyes. 'Not because I don't want to, but because I don't want to rush things.'

'You don't want to rush things.'

She still looked wary, so he knew he had to make a little more effort. Even though he wasn't used to spilling his guts like this, she needed to hear it. 'I had a fabulous time with you today.'

His reward was her smile. A heartfelt one. 'Me, too.' She stroked his face. 'I'll see you at work on Monday. And thank you for a lovely day.'

All the way home, Aaron was smiling. And then he realised why. He was actually *happy*. He couldn't ever remember feeling this kind of lightness in his soul.

Joni had definitely changed his life for the better. Yet a part of him wondered could it really stay like this? Or was he hoping for too much—from himself, as well as from her?

CHAPTER TEN

MONDAY MORNING SAW Aaron and Joni both rostered to the walk-in clinic. In the staff kitchen they exchanged a glance that made Joni feel hot all over, but she knew this wasn't the place to do what she really wanted and kiss him until his eyes grew dark and desire slashed colour through his cheeks. It was still early days, and they'd agreed to keep this just between them. Right now, they were colleagues—and, as far as everyone else was concerned, *just* colleagues. She gave him a professional smile. 'Did you have a good weekend?' she asked.

'Very nice. You?' he replied.

'One of the nicest I've had in ages,' she said. 'A bit of culture, seeing friends and my family. It doesn't get any better than that.'

And the warmth in his eyes told her that he knew exactly what she was saying.

Joni's first case that morning was a man who'd been seriously grumpy with the receptionist and had almost fallen foul of the hospital's zero-tolerance policy. But Joni knew that sometimes feeling ill could make people act out of character, so she decided to give him the benefit of the doubt.

'What seems to be the problem, Mr Gillespie?'
she asked.

'I couldn't get in to see my GP so I've been to the
emergency department and they were rubbish. They
wouldn't let me talk and they kept interrupting me.' He
scowled. 'They told me it was a summer cold or mild flu
and to go and see a pharmacist to get something over
the counter. The stuff the pharmacist gave me hasn't
touched my headache, and I'm hot all over, and now I've
got a rash. My back aches and my legs hurt.' He glared
at her. 'And I'm fed up with people not listening to me.'

Feeling really rough and as if nobody would listen to
him or help him—no wonder he'd been grumpy. 'Well,
I'm definitely listening,' she said. 'As you're feeling hot,
would you mind if I took your temperature?'

'It's about time someone did,' he complained, but he
let her check his temperature with the ear thermometer.

'Your temperature's definitely too high,' she said,
'and I can see that your eyes are red as well. Do they
hurt?'

'They itch,' he said.

'OK. I can give you something for that. May I see
the rash?'

He lifted his T-shirt to reveal a purpuric rash on
his torso.

'Given that this is the walk-in clinic for tropical medicine and infectious diseases, I know you've probably
already been asked this, so I'm sorry to repeat it and ask
you again,' she said gently, 'but have you been abroad
at all recently?'

'I went to France two weeks ago,' he said.

'OK.' Hardly tropical, but Mr Gillespie's symptoms

were definitely starting to look like those of a notifiable disease.

'On the first day I was in a kayak,' he said, 'on a river. And I capsized. I swallowed a lot of water. I started feeling ill a few days later—I've been sick and I had the runs, so I'm sure it was something in the water I swallowed.'

'I think you're right,' she said. 'Given that you have that rash, your eyes are red and sore and you have a high temperature, plus the fact that you've swallowed water from a river, I think there's a strong possibility that you have leptospirosis.'

'I *knew* I was ill,' he said. 'I'm going to complain about that other lot.'

'To be fair,' she said gently, 'the symptoms in the early stages of leptospirosis are really similar to those of flu, so it's a tricky one to diagnose. When did you first notice the rash?'

'Yesterday,' he said.

'I need to take a blood sample from you to confirm my diagnosis,' she said, 'but I'm going to start you on a week's course of antibiotics. Have you ever had any kind of allergic reaction to antibiotics in the past—a rash, swelling or nausea?'

'No.'

'Good—then you can take them at home,' she said. 'Leptospirosis is a bacterium, and it can survive for several months in water or damp soil. You're most likely to come into contact with the bacteria in canals or rivers, so you were right about that river making you ill.'

'Can anyone catch it from me?' he asked.

'No. It's not spread from person to person. It's spread by water or soil containing the bacteria entering a cut

in your skin, or through your mucous membranes—
your eyes or your mouth. I'm afraid this bit isn't very
nice—usually it's spread by infected rats excreting the
bacteria in their urine.'

'Infected rat pee?' He gagged.

'Sorry,' she said, 'but they don't necessarily look ill
when they're infected so you wouldn't know that the
water was full of spirochaetes.'

'I wish I'd never gone on that sailing trip. It was my
brother's idea. I only went because he said we'd go to
some vineyards and chateaux.' He grimaced. 'And my
brother's fine. He didn't capsize.'

'Rotten luck for you,' she said sympathetically.
'Would you mind me taking a blood sample now?'

'I hate needles,' Mr Gillespie grumbled, but he let
her take the sample.

She wrote out a prescription. 'You can take this into
any pharmacy, and I want you to start taking them now.
The bad news is that you'll probably still feel rough for
the next couple of days, but the good news is that you
should feel a lot better within a week.'

'Huh,' he said, and grimaced.

'But,' she said, 'sometimes the symptoms of leptospirosis can develop into something a bit more serious.
So if you start to feel more unwell than you do now, or
your skin and the whites of your eyes turn yellow, or
your ankles swell up or you don't pass as much urine
as usual, then I want you to come straight in and we'll
admit you because you'll need more treatment.' She
printed out a patient information leaflet for him. 'This
is so you don't have to try and remember everything I
said. And if you find that the rash and your high tem-

perature and headache go for a little while but come back again, then I want you straight back here, OK? Don't go to your family doctor or the emergency department—come straight here.'

'OK,' he said.

'I'll call you with the results of the blood test and let you know if I want you to come back and change your treatment, but these antibiotics should clear it up.'

'Thank you,' he said. 'And I'm never going sailing, *ever* again.'

'I don't blame you,' she said.

Joni was rushed off her feet for the rest of the morning, but she managed to meet Aaron for a snatched sandwich during their lunch break. 'How was your morning?'

'Full of gastro problems—things that probably aren't the right things to discuss at this moment,' he said, indicating their lunch. 'How was yours?'

'I had a case of leptospirosis.'

'Unusual,' he said. 'Local?'

'No. He capsized a kayak in a river in France,' she explained. 'The poor guy swallowed a lot of water.'

'And unless you'd been warned about the area, you wouldn't necessarily know that there was leptospirosis around.'

'Not until you started getting the gastro problems, then the high temperature, the conjunctivitis and the rash appeared,' she agreed.

'Does he have jaundice?' he asked.

'Not right now, and I'm keeping my fingers crossed it doesn't develop that far.'

And how good it was to be able to sit with him and

chat easily about work. Marty had always been bored by her work, though he'd been very happy to talk about his own. Aaron actually listened.

And life, Joni thought, was good. Really good.

That evening, as usual Joni met Bailey for their yoga class and dinner afterwards.

'You're glowing,' Bailey said when they'd sat down in the restaurant and had ordered their meal.

'We did a lot of downward dogs in class, so it must be all that blood rushing to my head,' Joni said.

Bailey grinned. 'Yeah, right. It wouldn't have anything to do with a certain tropical medicine doctor who wears glasses, would it?'

Joni blushed.

'So you're dating officially?' Bailey asked. At Joni's nod, she said, 'Good. I think he might be just what you need after Marty the Maggot.'

'We're just seeing how it goes,' Joni said. 'He's coming to Olly's gig on Wednesday. But that's as part of the team, not as my date—we're keeping it just between us for now. So don't say anything to Mum and Dad, will you?'

'Of course not.' Bailey patted her hand. 'It's nice to see you looking happy.'

'I am.' Joni smiled. 'But we'll see how it goes.'

On the Wednesday evening. a group from the tropical medicine department went for a meal straight after work, and then headed to the pub where Joni's brother's band was playing.

Her family was already there and greeted her with a hug and kiss.

'Everyone, this is Aaron, our new consultant,' she said.

So she was introducing him to her family as her colleague rather than her date. Aaron knew why she'd said it—it was still early days between them—but it still stung a bit.

He had to make an effort to follow the rest of her conversation.

'Aaron, these are my parents, Sam and Marianna Parker, and my brothers, Luke and Olly. Aaron's a blues fan, so that's why I dragged him out with us all tonight,' she explained.

'Olly's band is amazing,' Marianna said, and then she grinned. 'Not that I'm at *all* biased, as his mother.'

Aaron smiled. 'Joni said almost exactly the same thing. I'm looking forward to this.'

'She's already told me that we like the same kind of music—and that you've seen my favourite band four times,' Olly said, giving him a high five. 'I'm going to have to be boring and rush off now and set up stuff on stage, but I'll see you later, OK, and we'll catch up then?'

'Sure,' Aaron said.

'So how are you settling into London?' Sam asked.

'Fine, thanks—it's a great department and they're a good bunch of people to work with.'

'They certainly are,' Sam said.

'Where are you from?' Marianna asked.

'Manchester.'

'That's quite a way from here—do you have family in London at all?' she asked.

Yes, but that would open a can of worms. 'My family's a bit scattered around the globe,' he said. 'They're all in the armed forces, except me.' And he was the only one in four generations who'd turned his back on that way of life. It hadn't gone down well.

'You didn't want to be an army doctor?' Sam asked, unintentionally rubbing a sore spot.

'Battlefield medicine isn't for me. I wanted to do something a bit different,' Aaron said.

'And tropical medicine's such an interesting area,' Marianna said. 'Has Joni told you about her research proposal?'

'Yes, and it's fascinating,' Aaron said.

Marianna and Sam both looked pleased, and Luke talked to him about football and beer and his favourite buildings until the support act came on. Aaron could understand now why Joni was so warm. Her family was just like her—sweet and kind and making everyone feel included.

Joni's friend Bailey arrived just when the support act had finished and gave Joni a hug. 'Sorry I'm late. The game went on a bit and I had to strap up a knee. Hopefully my patient isn't going to end up with cartilage damage.'

Joni introduced them swiftly. 'Bailey, this is Aaron Hughes, our new consultant. Aaron, this is Bailey Randall, my best friend.'

'The sports medicine specialist and endorphin fiend, right?' he said with a smile, shaking Bailey's hand.

Bailey smiled back at him and he knew that she recognised him; he also had the strongest feeling that she knew exactly what was happening between him and Joni, but she wasn't going to blow their cover.

He chatted to her until Olly's band came on.

He enjoyed the gig, but there was one blues song in particular where he really wanted to wrap his arms round Joni and hold her close. He knew he couldn't do that or it would make things awkward for her; but he was disappointed that he didn't even get the chance to walk her home and kiss her goodnight on her doorstep.

Aaron managed to have a quick coffee with her between clinics the next day, on the pretext of talking through a case.

'I enjoyed the gig last night,' he said. 'Your brother's very talented.'

She looked proud. 'Yes, he is.'

'I noticed you introduced me to your family as your colleague.'

She spread her hands. 'Aaron, half of the department was with us and we agreed this is just between us for now. If I'd told Mum and Dad we were seeing each other, someone would've overheard us and we'd be the hottest topic on the hospital grapevine right now.'

'Fair point,' he said. It wasn't nice to think that everyone was talking about you.

'Plus,' she added, 'if I'd told my family who you really are, they would've grilled you, and I'm not sure you're ready for that.'

'Probably not,' he agreed. 'Sorry, I shouldn't have called you on it.'

'It's OK—though, actually, it's nice that you minded,' she said. 'Just so you know, I minded, too.'

'Bailey knows, though?' he asked.

She wrinkled her nose. 'Bailey's my best friend—as close as if she were my sister. She's not going to tell anyone.'

'Thank you,' he said quietly. And he was glad she had someone fighting her corner for her. 'What do you want to do at the weekend?'

'I was thinking,' she said, 'it might be fun to see the pelicans being fed in St James's Park on Saturday afternoon. Dad used to take me there when I was tiny and I always loved it.'

'Sounds good to me. Let me know where and when you want me to meet you.' He finished his coffee. 'I've got clinic. I'd better run. Catch you later.'

He thought about her family's warmth all the way home. Maybe if he made a bit more effort, his own family could be like that. Then again, it had never been their style. He was expecting too much from them, and that wasn't fair.

And it also gave Aaron pause for thought. He couldn't offer Joni anything near what she could offer him. His family would be distant with her and he knew it would hurt her. Given that her own family was so close, he didn't have a clue how to explain it to her. How could she possibly understand their stiff upper lip stance when she'd never grown up with it? So maybe he ought to back off a little and give her the space to cool things down between them.

The only problem was, he didn't want to.

But maybe he ought to stop being selfish and put her needs before his own.

On Friday morning, a worried-looking couple walked in with a letter of referral from their family doctor.

'Pete thinks it's a summer virus and I'm making a fuss over nothing,' Mrs Kirby said, 'but I've got a bad feeling about this.'

And so did the GP, from the look of the referral. *Suspected EBLV from bat bite.*

European Bat Lyssavirus—also known as bat rabies —was a rabies-like virus transmitted by bats, which could kill if symptoms developed. And there was nothing in the letter about any rabies vaccination being administered. Classic rabies, transmitted by dogs, cats and other animals, was almost unknown in the UK. Joni had dealt with a couple of precautionary cases when a local zookeeper had been bitten or scratched by an imported exotic animal with suspected rabies, but all the zookeepers had been vaccinated against rabies, and all of them had come in as soon as they'd been infected and well before any symptoms had started. The usual procedure—cleaning the wound thoroughly and administering vaccination post-exposure to stop the infection spreading—had worked.

But a case where symptoms had already started... Joni knew exactly why Mrs Kirby was panicking. She'd be panicking, too, in the other woman's shoes because, once the patient started having symptoms, bat rabies could be fatal and the only treatment you could give was to sedate the patient and keep them comfortable until they fell into a coma and died from heart failure.

'Would you like to tell me about your symptoms and a bit of the background as to what happened?' Joni asked gently.

Mr Kirby grimaced. 'I'm an art restorer and I conserve wall paintings. I was working in a church—there are bats in the tower, but normally they don't bother

me when I'm working. Something must've spooked
them last week, because they all rushed out past me in
a flock. I was up a ladder at the time and it caught me
by surprise, and I banged my hand. I didn't feel as if
I'd been bitten—if anything, I probably just caught my
hand on a nail or something—but Debs here reckons
I was bitten, because I've been feeling a bit off for the
last couple of days.'

'He's got a sore throat, a headache and a high temperature, but he's shivering and says he feels chilly,'
Mrs Kirby said.

'It's just a summer flu,' her husband said. 'There's a
nasty bug doing the rounds.'

'But you've been irritable. You're not normally like
that. And you said your hand was tingling.'

'Probably an allergic reaction to something I've been
using in the church. You spill stuff and it gets on your
skin,' he said, flapping a dismissive hand.

'But bats can spread rabies, or something that's like
it,' Mrs Kirby said, looking anxious.

'European Bat Lyssavirus,' Joni confirmed. 'It's
often called bat rabies.'

'Supposing one of them did bite you and you just
didn't feel it?' Mrs Kirby asked.

'We can do some blood tests to check,' Joni said, 'and
test your saliva as well. If there are EBLV antibodies,
then we know what we're dealing with.'

'And you can treat it?' Mrs Kirby asked.

Not if it developed into full-blown bat rabies. And the
sad thing was that if he'd come into the department on
the day he'd been bitten, even though he hadn't had any
previous vaccinations against rabies, the immunoglobulin and post-exposure vaccine would've been enough to

deal with the virus. 'I'll be able to tell you more when I see the results of the blood tests,' Joni said, not wanting to worry the Kirbys further. 'Mr Kirby, can I ask you, did you notice any unusual behaviour among the bats?'

'They were just a bit spooked. There were a lot of them and they rushed about in the church for a few minutes. The poor verger had a hell of a job cleaning up when they finally went back to their roost. There was guano everywhere.' He shrugged. 'I can't really tell you anything more than that.'

'OK.' Now for the hard questions. The ones she didn't want to worry them with, but she needed to know the answers. 'Have you had any difficulty swallowing, or sweated more than normal, or have you felt unusually anxious?'

'No. Debs is worrying about nothing,' Mr Kirby insisted, but he allowed Joni to take blood and saliva samples.

Once she'd taken the samples and sent them to the lab, she went in search of Aaron. 'I need to pick your brains. Have you come across many cases of EBLV?'

'It's pretty rare, though I've had two or three back in Manchester,' Aaron said. 'A couple were zookeepers who got bitten, and one was a bat handler. Luckily they'd all had vaccinations and they all came in pretty much as soon as they'd been bitten, so I could treat them promptly enough to avoid them developing the full-blown virus.' He raised an eyebrow. 'Is that what you've had this morning? A zookeeper who's been bitten?'

'No, my patient's a restoration specialist—but he was working in a church and he *might* have been bitten by a bat. Before you ask, no, he hasn't ever been vaccinated.'

'Clean the wound with hydrogen peroxide, give him

rabies immunoglobulin and start him on a course of the rabies vaccine,' Aaron advised. 'That should stop the virus developing.'

'There's one teensy, teensy problem,' Joni said. 'It happened a week ago, and he isn't sure if he was bitten—he says the bats were spooked and came round him in a flock, and he banged his hand. He thinks he's just got summer flu, and the symptoms he describes are the same as flu.'

Aaron grimaced. 'And as early bat rabies.'

She nodded. 'His wife is convinced he was bitten, and his GP's clearly working on the safe side and referred him to us.'

'Have you taken bloods?' Aaron asked.

'And saliva samples. I've sent everything off to the lab.' She bit her lip. 'But if the results show he has the antibodies as well as the early symptoms, there's nothing we can do, is there?'

'All we'll be able to do for him then is to give him sedatives, to protect him from the pain and the emotional upset.' Aaron looked thoughtful. 'Though there is maybe something. My boss in Manchester went to a conference a couple of years back and there was a session about the Milwaukee protocol.'

'A cure?' she asked.

'It's pretty experimental and has a very low success rate,' he warned. 'They think it might not actually be the treatment that makes the patient survive—instead, it might be because of something in their immune systems, or they were infected with a weak strain of the virus.'

'But it's worked on some people?' At his nod, Joni continued, 'Then it's better than the alternative—which is doing nothing and just letting him die.' She blew out a breath. 'I'm getting ahead of myself. I'll wait and see what the tests show before I start panicking. But, if it's bat rabies, can I come and grab you?'

'Of course. Unless you'd rather ask Mr Flinders, because he might have more experience in the area.'

She shook her head. 'I'm happy to take advice from you. You're a consultant—even if you are barely out of nappies.'

He rolled his eyes at her. 'Hardly. I'm three years older than you are.'

'And you're still the youngest consultant I know. To get this far, this soon, you're seriously good at your job. Plus you have more experience than I do.'

'Well, thanks for the compliment,' he said, sounding a little awkward and yet a little pleased at the same time. 'Come and get me if you need me.'

Aaron was writing up some notes later that afternoon when Joni rapped on his door.

'You got the tests back?' he asked.

'Yup. Just now.' She blew out a breath. 'It's not good news. It's definitely bat rabies.'

'Right. You need to talk to your patient.'

'And his wife.'

'I'll come with you. We'll have to tell them what the options are and see what they want us to do,' Aaron said. 'I can't promise the Milwaukee protocol will work.'

'But at least it gives them a chance,' Joni said softly. 'Which is better than nothing. I'd take it—wouldn't you?'

A few months ago, Aaron wouldn't have been that fussed either way. He did his job—and that was who

and what he was. But since Joni had come into his life...
'Yes. Let's go and see them.'

Joni introduced Aaron to the Kirbys.

'It's bad news, isn't it?' Mrs Kirby asked. 'Otherwise
you wouldn't have brought another doctor in with you.'

'I'm sorry,' Joni said. 'The test results show you were
infected by one of the bats.'

'So I have bat rabies?' Mr Kirby asked.

She nodded.

'And there isn't a cure for it,' Mrs Kirby said.

'I'm so sorry,' Joni said again.

'So I'm going to die?' Mr Kirby looked shocked.
'Oh, my God. I'm going to run around, foaming at the
mouth and being afraid of water and biting people?'

'It's not a fear of water and you won't bite anyone.
Though you will produce a lot more saliva,' Joni said,
'and you'll find it harder and harder to swallow.'

He shook his head. 'I can't take it in.'

'There is an alternative,' Aaron said. 'I need to tell
you that we can't guarantee it will definitely work. It's
an experimental treatment with a low success rate so
far.'

'But at least it gives me a chance of surviving,' Mr
Kirby said. 'From what you've just said, it's my only
chance, so I'll take it. What do you have to do?'

'We think that the way the rabies virus works is
that it affects your brain before your body can fight
the infection,' Aaron explained. 'So if we put you into
a medically induced coma to protect your brain, we
can give you antiviral medication to help your body
fight the disease.'

'A bit like that bloke who had the skiing accident

and hit his head—they kept him in a coma until they'd treated him, didn't they?' Mr Kirby asked.

'A bit like that, yes,' Aaron said. 'We can give you fluids and electrolytes on a drip, so we can keep your body functioning—and you won't know anything about it.'

'And if it doesn't work, then I don't get the thing where I can't swallow,' Mr Kirby said.

'We wouldn't let you go through that anyway,' Joni said. 'If you'd rather not give this a try—and as my senior colleague said, it *is* an experimental procedure and it might not work—then we'd give you some medication to keep you comfortable and also so you wouldn't be aware of what was happening to you.'

Mr Kirby looked at his wife. 'So it's die, or give it a go and it probably won't work, but there's a tiny outside chance it might and I'll be back to normal.'

'If it does work, there might still be some damage from the virus and you might need some rehab before you get back to normal,' Aaron said. 'But you've summed it up pretty well.'

Mr Kirby blew out a breath. 'OK. I'll do it. But I want to see the kids first. I want to say goodbye to them, just in case it doesn't work.'

'We can arrange that. And if there's anything either of you need, anything at all, you just ask,' Joni said.

Saying goodbye to the kids.

Aaron hadn't really had the chance to say goodbye to Ned. His brother had been in a coma because of the malaria. And, even though doctors thought that patients in a coma might be able to hear, Aaron would never know if Ned had heard his last words. Saying that he loved him, he was going to be a doctor like Ned planned to be, and he'd make his brother proud of him. Do his best to save people, the way the doctors hadn't been able to save Ned.

And he'd kept his promise. He'd worked hard, and he'd saved most of his patients. He might not be able to do that for Mr Kirby, but he'd try his very hardest. And by his side there would be the one person he was beginning to realise he could rely on—Joni. Working with him. Keeping him going through the tough times with the sweetness of her smile.

Under the table, he reached for her hand and squeezed it.

As if she guessed what he was thinking, she returned the pressure.

They'd do their best. Together.

On Saturday afternoon, Joni and Aaron walked hand in hand through St James's Park to find the rock on the lake where the pelicans were spreading their wings and basking in the sun. The second that the wildlife officer appeared by the lake with his bucket of fish, they came over and crowded around him, eager to be fed—just as the children in the park crowded around, eager to see.

'The pelicans have been here in the park since 1664, when the very first one was a gift from the Russian Ambassador,' the wildlife officer explained. 'They eat the fish in the lake, but they also like the mackerel and herring I bring them.' He tossed a fish to each bird, which caught it deftly. 'We did have a pelican who used to fly over to London Zoo and steal their fish for his lunch, but these ones are all happy to wait for me to turn up.'

Joni enjoyed the show, but she noticed that Aaron had gone quiet. Maybe seeing the pelicans wasn't his kind of thing; after all, they hadn't got round to doing their list of places they wanted to go and see together.

But as the afternoon went on he became quieter and quieter, and she knew she was going to have to broach the subject because she hated this awkwardness between them.

'Aaron, is something wrong?' she asked.

'No.'

His expression was absolutely unreadable. It was obvious to her that something was wrong, but she didn't have a clue what it was. Or maybe he was seeing what Marty saw in her, so this relationship was going to be just as much of a failure as her broken engagement—and it was all her fault for not being good enough.

'I'm sorry,' she said miserably.

He frowned. 'What for?'

'Obviously I've said something wrong.' She spread her hands. 'Or done something wrong. Or not done or said something that I should've done or said.'

'No, of course you haven't.' His frown deepened. 'Joni, why are you apologising to me?'

'I...' She didn't want to explain that.

'Is this what used to happen with Marty?' he asked.

Yes. Way too often.

She couldn't bring herself to answer, too ashamed to admit the truth, and looked away.

Gently, he cupped her face. 'Look at me, Joni,' he said softly.

Warily, not sure what she'd see in his expression, she did so.

'You've done nothing wrong. *Nothing*,' he emphasised.

'I just...' How could she explain?

He kissed the tip of her nose. 'It's not you. It's me. I'm sorry. It's stupid stuff in my head—and I promise you it's nothing to do with you.' He sighed. 'I did warn you I'm not very good at relationships. But promise me you'll never apologise to me again.'

'I'm sor—' she began, and stopped herself. She grimaced. 'Um.'

He smiled. 'I think that one was fineable—and I bet Bailey would agree with me if I asked her.'

The tightness between her shoulders eased. 'You're going to fine me for using the s-word?'

'Yup. I was thinking about making you buy me an ice cream as a fine, but I've just had a better idea—instead, it means you have to have dinner with me tonight. I'll cook for us.' He paused. 'If you're not busy, that is. Otherwise we can do it some other time.'

No, she wasn't busy. 'Does that mean I get fabulous coffee from your flashy machine?' she asked, not wanting to appear *too* available.

'It might do. If you ask me very nicely,' he teased.

Relief flooded through her. This was going to be all right.

She stood on tiptoe. 'Pretty please with sugar on it?' She kissed him lightly on the lips.

He wrapped his arms around her. 'That'll do very nicely.'

Back at Aaron's flat, she noticed all kinds of things that she hadn't had time to notice on the night of the salsa club. She hadn't seen his living room before; it was all very neat, but there was only one shelf of medical textbooks, and there were no films or music or fiction.

'I thought you liked music,' she said.

'I do.'

'But you don't have any.'

He smiled. 'It's all digital. The same with my films—I stream them. It saves all the clutter.'

'And your books?'

'Also digital,' he said, 'apart from those medical textbooks. Weirdly, I prefer the old-fashioned way when it comes to work.'

There were no family photographs, either, and nothing personal that really told her anything about who he was. Maybe he'd learned to live in such a pared-down world because he'd had to pack up everything very quickly, either to move on to a new posting with his family in the army, or to move between their home and boarding school at either end of term. Though she wasn't going to ask him, because she didn't want to make him feel uncomfortable.

She followed him into the kitchen, where he was rummaging in his fridge.

'Is there anything I can do to help?' she asked.

'No, just sit and chat to me,' he said, and made her a frothy cappuccino just the way she liked it.

'This is fabulous,' she said. 'I feel very spoiled.'

He kissed her lightly. 'Good. That's my intention—and hopefully the spinach and chicken risotto will be a little bit better than a bacon sandwich.'

She grinned. 'I'll have you know that bacon sandwich was awesome. The only thing missing was avocado.'

'So that's your weakness?'

'One of them.' She noticed he wasn't using a recipe book. 'So this is one of your staples?'

He shrugged. 'It's a fairly basic recipe. I just tweak it depending on my mood.'

Marty had never cooked for Joni. He'd always expected her to do the cooking—and she'd been spineless enough to let him get away with it, instead of pointing out that her job was just as demanding as his and asking him to do his share of the chores.

'Thanks,' she said. 'Just so you know, I really appreciate it.'

'Good.' He stole a kiss, then went back to cooking for them.

After dinner, they watched a film in his living room, curled up on his sofa together. Wrapped in his arms, Joni felt warm and safe, and happier than she'd felt in a very long time.

As if he could guess at her thoughts, Aaron drew her just that little bit closer. He pushed her hair over one shoulder, and she felt his mouth against the nape of her neck—soft, sweet, enticing kisses. She closed her eyes and tipped her head to one side, giving him better access, and his lips grazed the side of her neck, finding the sensitive spot that made her quiver.

His hands slid beneath the hem of her T-shirt and he splayed his fingers over her midriff.

'Aaron,' she murmured, and shifted in his arms to face him.

He took full advantage of her new position and kissed her, his lips teasing and coaxing hers into a response. In turn, she untucked his shirt and slid her hands under the material, running her fingers across the hard wall of his abdomen. 'You feel so good,' she whispered.

He let his hands slide further up under her T-shirt, unclipping her bra and then cupping her breasts in his hands. 'So do you,' he said hoarsely. 'So soft. I need to see you, Joni.'

She kissed him. 'Yes.'

It didn't take him long to remove her T-shirt.

She coughed. 'Equals, remember.'

He laughed, and stripped off his own shirt. 'As you wish.'

Catching the movie reference, she laughed back, and let her fingers stray over his pectoral muscles. 'For a geek, you're in amazing shape. I love just looking at you,' she said.

He stole a kiss. 'Looking isn't enough for me right now.'

'Then touch me. Kiss me,' she said, and closed her eyes, and he kissed a path down her throat, meandering across her collarbones to linger in the hollows for a moment, then nuzzled his way down her sternum and took one nipple into his mouth.

'That's so good,' she whispered.

'Yes.' His voice was husky with need. 'Have I told you how gorgeous you are?'

'Keep talking,' she invited.

And then she wished she'd kept her mouth shut when he stopped touching her and pulled back.

'This was meant to be taking things slowly,' he said. 'Getting to know each other.'

She felt the colour staining her face. 'And I'm acting like a tart.'

'No.' He leaned over to kiss her lightly. 'Just I find you very hard to resist. It's never been like this for me. I've always been in control. But, with you, it's different.'

'Different good or different bad?' The words slipped out, needy and embarrassing, before she could stop them. Annoyed with herself, she crossed her arms across her breasts. 'You don't have to answer that.'

'Yes, I do. Definitely different good. Scary,' he said, 'but good.' He laid one palm against her cheek. 'Joni. Much as I'd like to carry you to my bed right now and spend the rest of the night making love with you, I'm not going to.'

Because she wasn't enough? Just as she hadn't been enough for Marty?

Either it showed in her face or he knew her well enough to guess what she was thinking, because he said softly, 'I don't want to rush this or take you for granted. I want to cherish you.' He kissed her. 'We have all the time in the world, and I want this to be a proper courtship.'

From Aaron, that was tantamount to a declaration of intent. She sat up and kissed him back. 'That's the sweetest thing anyone's ever said to me.'

'It comes from the heart.' He took her hand and placed it over his heart. She could feel how strong his heartbeat was, how fast. And all for her.

'From the heart,' she echoed. 'Then, if you wouldn't mind turning your back or closing your eyes, I'll get dressed again.'

He smiled. 'This time, Nizhoni who lives up to her name, I will. Next time...'

And the very idea of what he was implying sent a thrill all the way through her.

CHAPTER ELEVEN

OVER THE NEXT couple of weeks, Joni was really happy. She was in tune with Aaron at work, and she felt they were getting closer as they continued dating. They had similar tastes, and they'd enjoyed compiling a list together of all the quirky places they really wanted to visit. Best of all, Joni felt that both of them were losing the fear that this thing between them was all going to go pear-shaped. She still knew next to nothing about his family and he hadn't suggested meeting hers again, but she was sure that all they needed was a little time.

And, incredibly, they'd managed to pull off the one thing they hadn't quite dared to hope for. Mr Kirby, their patient with bat rabies, had been in a coma for ten days—long enough for the antiviral medication and the immunoglobulin to work. They'd brought him out of his coma very gradually, but it seemed that the virus had been the weaker strain often found in bats, or the experimental treatment really did work because he'd actually survived his ordeal. There was some damage to his speech and motor systems, but she knew that rehab would help with that.

'And it's all thanks to you,' she said to Aaron when they'd managed to sneak off to lunch.

He shrugged it off. 'I just knew about the treatment. You're the one who put everything into place.'

'Then it's down to great teamwork,' she said, giving him her sunniest smile.

'I'll drink to that,' Aaron said, raising his mug of coffee. 'So how was your morning?'

'Mostly OK, apart from my poor man from the other week with leptospirosis—he came back in today and I had to admit him.'

'He's developed jaundice?' Aaron guessed.

She nodded. 'I think he might need dialysis in the next couple of days.'

'Even if he does, the damage to his kidneys should repair itself over the next couple of months,' Aaron said.

'That's what I told him, though the poor man's worried sick.'

'If you want me to come and support you next time you talk to him, give me a yell,' he said.

She smiled at him. 'Thanks. I might just take you up on that. Not because I doubt my diagnosis, but I think Mr Gillespie could just do with a bit of extra reassurance, and you're senior to me.'

'Your skills are as good as mine,' Aaron said, 'but I know what you mean about a patient's point of view. Consider it done.'

On Saturday morning, they met at Joni's flat. 'I thought we could do something really foodie today,' she told Aaron. 'How do you fancy going to one of the oldest markets in London, right next to London Bridge?'

'Sounds good to me,' he said.

They caught the tube to Borough Market and spent an hour browsing through the stalls. Joni was pleased to discover a stall selling granola suitable for diabetics, and Aaron was thrilled to discover a coffee stall selling some of the blends he'd bought back in Manchester. He ended up having a very geeky conversation with the barista about brewing coffee, much to Joni's amusement.

'So you're telling me that there are floral notes in coffee?' she asked.

'There is in this one. And I'll prove it,' Aaron said and ordered them both a cappuccino without chocolate on the top.

It was a much lighter roast than Joni was used to, but she could see what he meant. 'It's nice,' she said.

'Good. I'm glad you like it.' Aaron bought two bags of beans. 'So how far are we from St Paul's?' he asked.

'You want to have a look round the cathedral and do the Whispering Gallery?' she asked.

'No. There's a park on our list that's nearby. It has a really interesting memorial.'

'I know the one you mean,' she said. 'It's not that far. We could take the tube—or, as it's a nice day, we could just walk over the bridge. You can see St Paul's from here on the other side of the river. It's less than half an hour's walk.'

'So we could have a picnic in the park,' he suggested.

'Great idea.'

They bought artisan bread, ham, tomatoes and artisan cheese for lunch, along with a punnet of peaches and some bottles of water, then walked over the bridge, hand in hand. It took them a little while to find the park, and the space was almost empty when they walked in, apart from a scattering of pigeons.

'That's it,' he said, gesturing to a wall with a tiled

roof above it to protect it from the weather. 'The Watts Memorial to Heroic Self Sacrifice—named after the Victorian painter who set it up. He wanted to tell the stories of ordinary people who died saving others. Apparently it was meant to be for Queen Victoria's Golden Jubilee, but the committee rejected the idea. He eventually set it up with the vicar of the nearby church. After his death, his widow continued the gallery for a while, but then she was busy with other things and it was abandoned halfway through.'

They went over to take a closer look.

'Dr Alexander Stewart Brown,' she read. '"Though suffering from severe spinal injury the result of a recent accident died from his brave efforts to rescue a drowning man and to restore his life." I wonder what happened?'

'I did find a website with more information about the stories behind the plaques. Hang on.' Aaron looked it up on his phone. 'Apparently he was convalescing in Boulogne after a carriage accident that damaged his back. He was walking on the pier when he saw a man drowning in the sea. He jumped in to rescue the man, worked on him for two hours and saved his life—but ended up catching a bad cold, which turned to pneumonia.'

'Poor man,' Joni said. 'And this one's tragic— "George Lee, fireman. At a fire in Clerkenwell carried an unconscious girl to the escape falling six times and died of his injuries."'

'And this one,' he said. '"Samuel Rabbeth, medical officer of the Royal Free Hospital, who tried to save a child suffering from diphtheria at the cost of his own life."' He looked it up. 'The little boy was only four. They gave him a tracheotomy, but a membrane was still obstructing his breathing. Rabbeth put a tube in and tried to suck the membrane out—and he ended up getting diphtheria himself.'

They looked at each other. 'Nowadays we have a lot more protection,' she said, 'with barrier nursing and prophylactic medicine and what have you—but I guess we'd still take risks if we thought we could save someone and it was the only way.' She shivered. 'It's kind of nice that these people have been commemorated— saving people from drowning and fires and the like— but how sad.'

Aaron held her close. 'Sorry. I didn't mean to make you unhappy.'

'Not unhappy, exactly—just realising how lucky we are,' she said. 'I guess you need to enjoy every moment of life, because you never know what's just round the corner.'

'"Gather ye rosebuds while ye may."' He kissed her lightly. 'Come on. Let's have our picnic and enjoy the sunshine.'

Just being with him made her feel relaxed and happy, and she enjoyed sharing the food they'd bought from the deli stalls.

'I was going to ask you,' he said, 'what traditional Diné food was like.'

And he'd used the right term, she thought with a smile. He'd paid attention. He was interested in her heritage and respected it. And it felt so good to be accepted for who she was—to feel as if she was *enough*. 'It's fairly simple stuff—bread, vegetables, meat and fish. The Diné are basically farmers,' she said. 'I could cook something traditional for you tonight, if you like.

We'll need to go to the supermarket on the way home to pick up a couple of things.'

'Sounds good to me,' he said. 'I'd really like that. If I'm not imposing.'

She laughed. ''Course you're not. And you can help with the washing up. I'm not proud.'

He laughed back. 'You're on.'

Joni was as comfortable with him sitting in her kitchen while she cooked as he seemed to be with her. 'So this is Navajo stew—sweet potatoes, bell peppers and onions. You just roast the lot in the oven, add it to a tomato and dried smoked chilli sauce along with black beans, let it bubble for a bit, and serve it with grilled fish.' She smiled. 'And fried bread. I love it when *shimá sání* makes this. It's a real treat.'

'Fried bread?'

'It isn't quite as artery-clogging as it sounds,' she said with a grin. 'It's a bit like an Indian paratha—you make bread, roll it out until it's really thin like a French pancake, and then fry it on both sides.'

'This is fantastic,' Aaron said when she'd finished cooking dinner and he'd set the table.

'It's very simple, but it's a good combination of flavours,' she said with a smile.

Afterwards, they curled up on her sofa together.

'I haven't been this happy in a long while,' he said softly. 'You've made my world a brighter place.'

Her eyes filled with tears.

'Joni? Why are you crying?'

'That's just such a nice thing to say.' She swallowed hard. 'Sorry, I'm being wet.'

'No, you're not.' He kissed away the single tear that had spilled over her lashes.

'You've made my world a brighter place, too,' she said softly.

'I'm glad. I like you, Joni. I like you a lot.'

'I like you a lot, too.' More than a lot, but she wasn't quite ready to voice it. 'Stay tonight?' she asked softly. 'I can't promise you good coffee, but I can promise you the best bacon sandwich for breakfast.'

He kissed her. 'Are you sure about this?'

She nodded. 'Slowly isn't enough for me any more.'

'Me neither.' He looked at her. 'So what do you want, Joni?'

'You,' she said simply. 'In my bed. Naked.' She paused. 'Inside me.'

It was as if she'd flipped a switch, because his eyes widened, and he scooped her up in his arms. 'Where's your bedroom?' His voice had dropped an octave; clearly he was picturing exactly what she'd just suggested, and he liked the idea as much as she did.

'Down the corridor, second on the right,' she said, and thoroughly enjoyed the fact that Aaron had turned into a caveman.

He set her down gently on her feet, pulled the curtains and switched the bedside light on. 'Are you sure about this?' he asked.

'Very sure,' she said.

He drew the hem of her T-shirt slowly upwards, and excitement began to fizz through her veins. They were going to be skin to skin again. At last. And this time he wasn't going to stop. She lifted her arms so he could pull her T-shirt over her head. And then he held her at arm's length, just looking at her.

'You're beautiful,' he said softly. 'So beautiful that you drive me out of my mind.'

That made two of them.

He drew one finger along the lacy edge of her bra. 'I like this,' he said. And then he unsnapped it and let the garment fall to the floor. 'But I like this even more.' His eyes were dark and intense as he cupped her breasts, rubbing the pad of his thumb across her hardened nipples.

'So do I,' she whispered. 'But I need more.'

'Good.' He gave her another of those intense looks, then dropped to his knees in front of her, took one nipple into his mouth and sucked. She slid her fingers into his hair, urging him on.

His hands stroked down over her back, curved over her bottom. Her jeans were in the way, and she wriggled against him in frustration. 'More,' she said.

He rocked back then, and gave her an insolent grin. 'More?'

'I need to be naked with you. Right now.'

He inclined his head, and undid the button of her jeans. She dragged in a breath; he was taking his sweet time about this, and it was exquisite torture.

At last, he lowered the zip. Eased the denim over her hips and peeled it down her legs. Slow, slow, slow.

She wriggled again. 'You're driving me crazy.'

'Good,' he said, with another of those insolent grins, and refused to hurry.

She whimpered. 'Aaron.'

'Slow and easy,' he said, completely inexorable.

She'd go insane if he kept this up.

But he still took it slowly, and her desire stoked higher and higher as he took his time undressing her, stroking every bit of skin he uncovered, teasing her with his mouth.

Definitely insane, she thought. 'Aaron. Please.' She was begging now. She couldn't help herself. 'Touch me.'

'Here?' He stroked the hollows of her ankles.

'North,' she said.

'North.' He paused, as if pondering, and stroked the backs of her knees.

Since when had the backs of her knees been an erogenous zone? Knees weren't sexy. At all. And yet her temperature was climbing and she was wet, so wet and ready for him.

'More north,' she whispered.

'More north.' He paused again, and she quivered in anticipation of his next move. Which was to kiss her inner thigh.

'Warmer,' she said.

'Warmer. Hmm.'

She closed her eyes, knowing what he was going to do next, and wanting it so badly. And then she opened her eyes again in disbelief as he rubbed his cheek against her midriff.

'North, you said.'

'Too far.' And she actually whimpered, to her shame.

And then, at last, he slid his hand between her thighs. 'Warmer?' he asked with a grin.

As if he didn't know. And she was going to kill him if he teased her much more.

But then his thumb circled her clitoris.

'Better?' he asked softly.

'Almost.'

He did it again. And again. Until her body hit climax and her knees buckled.

But he was there to hold her, to support her until she

could stand again. And then he scooped her up, laid her on the bed, and stripped in five seconds flat.

'What you said earlier,' he said. 'Naked. In your bed. And inside you.'

'Yes,' she said. 'Now.'

He paused for just long enough to slide on a condom, and then at last he knelt between her thighs and eased into her.

'Much better,' she said in satisfaction, and kissed him.

Much better, Aaron thought. He felt complete, here with her. Losing himself in her—and yet finding himself, too. With Joni, he was different. With Joni, he could be himself and the past didn't matter. And maybe, just maybe, he could do this. Do the emotional stuff. Connect with her in heart as well as in body.

She wrapped her legs round him, pulling him deeper, and he stopped thinking. All he could do was feel. The joy. The way his climax shattered through him—and made him feel re-forged, stronger than before. Looking into her eyes, Aaron thought, I could love this woman. Really, really love her. Heart and soul.

Strangely, it didn't scare him. It simply made everything come into focus. Feel *real*.

And, when Joni fell asleep in his arms, Aaron felt more at peace than he had in years.

CHAPTER TWELVE

On Tuesday, a fifteen-year-old boy came in to the walk-in clinic with his mother.

'He went to Dominica with the school a month ago,' she told them. 'He said he took the malaria tablets while he was there. But I'm not sure you remembered all the time, Nick.'

'I did, Mum,' the boy protested. 'I didn't miss a dose. The teachers were really strict about it.'

Malaria. The disease that had coloured Aaron's whole life. He forced himself to lock the emotions away, the way he usually did, and schooled his voice to be as professional as possible. 'And you think he has malaria?' Aaron asked.

'He's got a headache and fever, he's shivering and he's had the runs,' Nick's mother said, 'though he hasn't thrown up. But if he took the tablets and they used mosquito nets and sprays, he can't have malaria, can he?'

'The tablets aren't always a hundred per cent effective,' Joni said.

Aaron was aware of her looking at him, her expression slightly anxious. Clearly she was worried that the case would upset him. But he was a doctor. His patients came first and his emotions came last. This was about treating the boy, not what had happened to Ned.

'And if you have been taking the tablets and you get malaria, then the symptoms show up later than if you haven't taken any of the tablets,' Aaron added.

'Can we examine you, please, Nick?' Joni asked.

Nick nodded, and let them check his pulse, blood pressure and sats.

'We're going to take a blood sample to confirm our suspicions,' Aaron said, 'and we should have the results back in about an hour, if you want to go and get a drink and something to eat in the meantime.'

The test came back positive for malaria.

'I'm sorry to say that you're right—you do have malaria, Nick,' Joni said. 'It's caused by the parasite *Plasmodium* and you get it through the bite of an infected mosquito—it can't be passed on by humans, so you don't have to worry that anyone else in the family will get it.'

Nick's mother looked worried. 'So how does he get treated? Do I have to give him tablets?'

'Actually, we're going to need to admit him to the ward,' Aaron said. 'The type of malaria Nick has is *Plasmodium falciparum,* which is the most serious one—we want you here so we can keep an eye on you, because sometimes you can get very ill very quickly with this type.'

Which was exactly what had happened to Ned. The parasite had destroyed his red blood cells, giving him severe anaemia. From there the infection had progressed to cerebral malaria, blocking the blood vessels to Ned's brain and finally killing him.

'The good news is that you're not showing any signs of complication at the moment,' Joni added.

'Your blood sugar is fine and the parasite count is less than two per cent, which is good—and if we do see a single sign of anything changing, we'll be able to treat it for you straight away,' Aaron explained. 'We're going to give you antimalarial medication, which will kill off the parasite, and I'm afraid you're going to get quite used to needles because we'll need to do a blood test every day to check the parasite count.'

'But try not to worry,' Joni said, 'because we'll keep a very close eye on you and you should get better, though you might feel rough for a few days yet.'

At the end of the clinic, after they'd admitted the boy to the ward, Joni looked at Aaron. 'Are you OK?'

'Sure.'

But clearly his sangfroid didn't fool her. 'It's the same type of malaria your brother had, and Nick's only a year younger than Ned was. The case must be bringing it back to you.'

It was. He shrugged. 'I'm fine. But thank you for asking.'

'I guess,' she said softly. 'Aaron, I know you hate talking about things. But sometimes it helps to unload to someone else instead of bottling it up. If you ever want to talk, I'm here. Even if it's stupid o'clock in the morning.'

She'd do that for him? He was stunned. Nobody had ever offered him that before.

But, then, nobody in his life had been anything like Joni. And he also hadn't let anyone as close as her, not since Ned's death. 'Thank you,' he said.

'I mean it. I'm not going to pressure you to talk,

because that isn't fair. But I'm here if you need me.' Her eyes were full of sincerity, and he knew she really meant it. She really was there for him.

Suddenly not caring who saw, he slid his arms round her and hugged her. 'Thank you, Joni. I appreciate it.'

She looked utterly shocked by his unexpected display of emotion—but then she smiled and stroked his face. 'I know.' And the expression in her eyes told him that she was warmed all the way through by the fact that he'd hugged her in public.

The more time Aaron spent with Joni, the more he realised that he was falling for her. She complemented him, filled all his empty spaces. And he knew she could give him everything he'd always wanted: a close family and someone to love, who'd also love him all the way back.

Was he going to be good enough for her, though? Or would he end up disappointing her, the way he'd disappointed everyone else in his life—including himself?

He wanted to make the effort. So, the following weekend, he called over to her flat. They'd both been on duty the previous day, and hadn't had a chance to go out; he knew that she spent Sunday afternoons with her family, but he thought he might be able to snatch a few minutes with her in the morning before she had to leave to see them.

She answered the doorbell at first ring and smiled when she saw him. 'Aaron! I wasn't expecting to see you today. Come in and have a cup of tea.'

'Thanks. I'd like that.' He brought his hands from

behind his back and presented her with the bouquet he'd bought. 'For you.'

'Sunflowers—how lovely!' She smiled and kissed him. 'Thank you so much.'

'I hoped you'd like them. I remembered what you said about the Van Gogh paintings.'

'And the real things are even better. I love the colour. They're so cheerful.' She beamed at him. 'I'll just put them in water. Come in.'

But as he stepped inside the door he could hear people talking. 'You have company?'

'My family,' she said. 'We take it in turns to host lunch. It's my turn today.'

It hadn't even occurred to him that they'd meet at her flat. On the rare occasions he saw his family, it was always at his parents' home. He took a step back. 'Sorry. I'm intruding on your time with your family.'

'Of course you're not. Come and join us,' she said. 'And you're very welcome to stay for lunch, if you're free—because my flat's so small, I tend to do a buffet rather than a Sunday roast, and there's more than enough food to go round.'

The wariness must have shown in his expression because she reached up and kissed him again. 'Stop thinking and come in. If you want to make yourself useful, you can make some coffee.'

He was relieved to have a job to do—and to have a respite from facing her family, even though it was only a small one. It wasn't that he disliked them—he'd responded to their warmth and friendliness when he'd met them at the concert—but this was way outside his comfort zone. And even having Joni by his side wasn't enough to stem the panic that this was all going to go horribly wrong.

'Something smells nice,' he said, trying to distract himself.

'Nothing too exciting, I'm afraid,' she said. 'I made ratatouille earlier, the jacket potatoes are doing now, and I'll put the salmon and chicken in the oven a bit later.'

'I feel bad about not contributing.'

'That's my fault for inviting you at the very last second—anyway, you brought me flowers. That counts as a contribution.' She kissed him again. 'Stop fussing and make the coffee.'

'Yes, ma'am,' he said, wishing he was a hundred miles away right now. He didn't feel anywhere near ready for this. To meet her family as her partner, not just as her colleague.

He made a pot of coffee, then followed her in to the living room. Sam and Marianna were there, along with Luke and Olly and their girlfriends; they all greeted him warmly.

Aaron did his best to be friendly and polite and fit in, the way he always did, but inside he felt such a fake. These people were all such a close unit, and he just didn't belong here—just as he didn't really belong in his own family. And he knew the fault was in him, not them.

So he had the answer to his question after all. He couldn't be enough for Joni. She deserved more than he could give her. And, even though he was willing to try his best, he knew that you couldn't be more than the sum of your parts. He couldn't be someone he wasn't. Someone who was good at emotional stuff, who could connect on a deeper level with her family and her friends, who could make her feel that she was the centre of the universe.

He couldn't do any of that.

Yes, the physical attraction between them was strong. Yes, he liked her—more than liked her. This was as close as he'd ever got to falling in love. But he couldn't be the man she needed. And the longer he let their relationship go on, the more hurt both of them would be when it ended. So he needed to stop it now. He wouldn't break up with her in front of her family—he wasn't that crass—but he'd find a quiet moment tomorrow. And then he'd do the right thing. For both their sakes.

Later that evening, after Aaron had left, Marianna said, 'He's quite cagey, isn't he, your Aaron?'

'How do you mean, Mum?' Joni asked.

'He doesn't give away anything about himself, does he? Don't get me wrong, he seems a sweetie and he's polite and charming, but...' She shook her head. 'Every time I asked him something personal, he changed the subject. I mean, I work with young children. I know all the distraction techniques. And he was definitely using them on me.'

'Mum, we haven't been together long, and he didn't know you were all going to be here today—I did rather drop him in at the deep end,' Joni said. 'Meeting you as my partner isn't quite the same as meeting you as my colleague.'

'Even so. I can't put my finger on it, but something isn't quite right,' Marianna said, sounding concerned. 'It worries me.'

Joni hugged her. 'That's because you're my mum and you're *supposed* to worry. It's fine. Just early days, that's all. His family are all in the army, so I guess he's used to not getting too close to people because he was never in one place for that long when he was younger. And he went to boarding school when he was quite young. I guess that would make anyone a bit reserved.'

'Maybe.' But Marianna didn't look convinced.

'He's not like Marty.' Joni smiled at her. 'Don't worry, Mum. It's all going to be just fine.'

On Monday morning, Aaron caught up with Joni in the staff kitchen just before clinic. 'We need to talk,' he said quietly. 'Can we meet in the canteen after clinic?'

'Sure,' Joni said.

But he looked grim, and she had a nasty feeling that things were just about to go completely pear-shaped. Especially as Aaron had made an excuse to leave before her family had, the day before—and he hadn't called her or texted her later that evening. She'd thought maybe he was panicking a bit about meeting her family and needed some space to come to terms with it; or maybe she'd done completely the wrong thing and given him too much time to brood and come to the wrong conclusion.

But her clinic was totally full that morning and she was so rushed off her feet that she didn't have time to think about the situation and work out how to fix things.

When she met Aaron in the canteen, he said, 'Maybe we can grab a sandwich and head to the park?'

'Sure,' she said, giving him a bright smile, but she was feeling worse and worse about this. As if there was a black hole in her heart, sucking everything in and leaving a vacuum.

He waited until they were out of earshot of everyone in the park before he spoke. 'Joni, I'm sorry. This thing between us…'

He was ending it. Which she'd half expected, but it still hurt. They'd been getting on so well. Everything had been fine.

Until yesterday, when he'd gone really quiet on her.

When he'd spent the afternoon with her family.

So it looked as if she'd made the same mistake all over again: she'd let herself fall for a man who wasn't comfortable with his family and was even less comfortable with the fact that she was close to hers.

What an idiot she'd been, thinking that at last she'd found someone who cared about her for who she was, not for who he wanted her to be. So much for taking off her rose-tinted glasses. She hadn't done that at all; if anything, she'd let them become blinkers.

OK. She could let him end it—or she could keep her pride intact and be the one to end it. Either way it would hurt like hell, but at least being the one to call a halt would make her feel slightly less inferior. She lifted her chin. 'You're right,' she said, trying to sound and cool and breezy and professional as she could. 'It's too complicated, with us being colleagues. It's probably best to stick to just working with each other. Take out the personal stuff.'

He looked relieved that she wasn't going to make a fuss. 'I'm sorry.'

That was her line. Not that she could quite bear to make a joke about it.

But he shouldn't be apologising because it wasn't just his fault, was it? It was hers, too, for being so stupid. For thinking that maybe they could have a future. For thinking that he might feel the same way about her as she felt about him. For not learning from her past mistakes. 'Not a problem.' She gave him her brightest smile. 'Actually—I don't really have time for lunch. I have a horrendous amount of paperwork that I really should catch up with. So I'll see you later, OK?'

And she left before he could say another word. Before her smile stopped being able to mask how hurt and miserable she felt. And she was never, ever going to let herself fall in love again.

Aaron felt hideously guilty as Joni walked away from him, knowing that he'd hurt her. But he was absolutely sure that he'd done the right thing, for her sake. Even though it hurt him, too. Right at the start, he'd said to her that if he were different he'd ask her out. Although she'd believed that he could be different, it turned out that he couldn't after all. So it was definitely better to end it now.

Though having Joni at arm's length in his life, a colleague rather than his lover, meant that everything felt faded. All the brightness was gone. For the first time ever, Aaron recognised exactly what he'd been feeling all those years—a feeling that had gone away while he'd been seeing Joni, but now was firmly back in place.

Loneliness.

Well, tough. He'd just have to live with it. Because feeling miserable and lonely was a damn sight better than making *her* feel miserable and lonely. And he'd done the right thing. He really had. He'd given her the chance to find someone who deserved her.

CHAPTER THIRTEEN

FOR THE NEXT week, work was grim. Aaron just kept out of Joni's way as much as possible, and buried himself in paperwork in between clinics and ward rounds. And he most definitely didn't go on the next team night out. He knew he'd have to show up at the one after that, because he'd organised it, but he just couldn't face seeing Joni outside work. Not until he'd got his feelings completely under control and had managed to stop himself wanting to hold her every time he saw her. Not until he'd forced himself to stop missing her.

The whole thing was ridiculous. He knew it wasn't going to work out between them and he'd just make her miserable. So why couldn't he stop being so selfish? Why couldn't he stop wanting her? And why couldn't he ignore the growing urge to tell her that he'd just made the biggest mistake of his life and ask her to give him another chance?

Luckily she had a couple of days off that didn't coincide with his own off-duty. Having a bit of space between them was good. It might even help his head get with the programme.

Except it didn't.

He missed her more than ever.

And the only thing that saved him was the fact that they were really, really busy in the department. Although he was rostered onto the same clinics as Joni, she didn't ask for his advice with any of her cases, and he didn't need to consult her about any of his. Even though he did think about it when Mrs Moore came in.

'So you've been having flu-like symptoms for a few days,' he said, making notes.

'I've been hot and cold, and then I got this annoying dry cough and I started bringing up this disgusting greeny-yellow stuff. And it's really hard to breathe.' She bit her lip. 'I wouldn't have bothered a doctor with it, but there was a bit of blood whenever I brought something up, so I panicked a bit.'

'Sometimes coughing can burst some of the tiny blood vessels, and that's why you see blood when you have a productive cough. It's very common,' Aaron reassured her. 'You've obviously got an infection, so if you don't mind me taking a blood sample I can do some tests to pin it down and give you the right treatment for it.'

'Thank you, Doctor. It's so *stupid* getting the flu when you've been away in the sun,' Mrs Moore said.

'Where did you go?' Aaron asked, partly to be polite and partly to help distract his patient while he took the blood sample.

'Spain. Though it wasn't quite what we were hoping for—the food wasn't so good, and the air-conditioning at the hotel was on the blink half the time.'

Alarm bells rang in the back of Aaron's head. 'Did you go on your own, or with friends?'

'With friends—there were a couple dozen of us. We went for a wedding, and we all stayed on together.'

'Do you know if any of the others have come down with the same kind of symptoms?'

She thought about it. 'Yes, actually, a couple of them have.'

'There's a possibility,' Aaron said, 'that you have Legionnaires' disease.'

'Legionnaires' disease?' Mrs Moore asked.

'It's caused by a bacterium that spreads in water.'

'So I might have caught it and given it to my friends?'

He shook his head. 'It doesn't spread between people and you don't get it by drinking contaminated water— you get it from breathing in drops of contaminated water in the air. Air-conditioning's one of the main causes—often the system's got a bit of limescale or rust in it, and that gives the bacteria the chance to grow.'

'Oh, my God.' She blew out a breath. 'We all thought the hotel wasn't brilliant. And now it's made us ill.'

'I'd like you to give me a urine sample,' he said, 'so I can test you for Legionnaires'. And if it's positive, I need you to get in touch with your friends for me and ask them to come in for testing and treatment. It's a no-tifiable disease, so I'll need the hotel name as well so I can talk to the public health authority in Spain.'

'Of course,' she said.

Aaron saw Joni in the corridor in between clinics. She looked pale and drawn, so he guessed that she was doing the same as he was—throwing herself into work to try and block out how she felt about the situation, and not sleeping properly.

But did she regret their break-up as much as he did? Did she wonder if they could make it work if they gave it another chance—if they could manage to put their past behind them and try again?

There was only one way to find out.

And it scared the hell out of him, because it was taking a huge risk. Getting involved. Admitting how he really felt about her. Facing up to his emotions. Knowing that she could say no and walk away.

He just needed to find the right words.

On his break, he stayed in his office rather than grabbing a cold drink in the staff kitchen. He looked up something on the Internet that he hoped might make Joni realise that he was serious about this. As soon as their shift finished, he planned to find her. Ask her to talk. And then he'd tell her what was in his heart. If she said no...well, he'd have to live with that and know it was his own fault for messing things up. But if he had the courage to ask, then maybe, just maybe, that would give her the courage to say yes.

Mrs Moore's test came back positive.

'It's definitely Legionnaires',' Aaron told her. 'I'm going to give you some antibiotics to clear it up, but I'm also going to send you for an X-ray to check your lungs, especially as you've been coughing up blood and you've had a hard time breathing.'

'Will I have to stay in?' She looked worried. 'Only I have my diabetic review with the practice nurse on Friday.'

'That really depends on the X-rays, but as you have diabetes I'd like to keep a closer eye on you—as you probably already know, diabetes makes you a bit more vulnerable to infections,' he said. And if only Joni was here to reassure Mrs Moore, to talk to her as a fellow diabetic. Yet again he missed her, as a colleague as well as a partner. 'Legionnaires' basically makes the tissues of your lungs inflamed so they don't work as well and your oxygen levels drop a bit,' he explained, 'so I'd quite like you to stay in for a couple of days and give you some oxygen treatment as well, just so you don't have to struggle so much.' He smiled at her. 'Try not to worry. You'll start to feel better in a couple of days, once the antibiotics have started working, and the oxygen will help. It might take a couple of weeks until you're totally back to normal, and you can expect to feel really tired until then, but you'll be fine.'

Aaron left his office door open at the end of his shift while he finished off his paperwork, keeping one eye out for Joni. He'd just finished and walked into the corridor when he saw her.

'Joni, can I have a quick—?' he began—but when she turned towards him, the colour drained out of her face and she keeled over in front of him.

'Joni? Joni?'

Collapsing in a faint like that wasn't good. Especially given her medical history.

Oh, hell. Please, please don't let anything happen to her.

Trying to ignore the panic rushing through his veins, Aaron went over to her and knelt down beside her to check her airways, breathing and circulation. Be a doctor first, he reminded himself. Once Joni was safe, he could let his emotions out. But right now she needed him to be a doctor. To be the best he could be.

She was breathing and her airways didn't seem compromised, but she was definitely unconscious. Aaron knew she was usually meticulous about controlling her diabetes, but he thought it was worth checking her blood sugar. If she hadn't been sleeping properly and had been working crazy hours, she might have been too distracted to keep a proper eye on her blood-sugar levels.

Nancy came rushing over. 'What's happened?'

'She just passed out in front of me.' Aaron cradled Joni in his lap. 'We need to check her blood sugar.'

'She keeps her kit in her bag. I'm sure she won't mind me looking for it.' Nancy quickly found the blood-sugar testing kit, and Aaron pricked Joni's finger and tested the blood on the strip.

'She's having a hypo,' he said. 'Her blood sugar's way too low. She's unconscious so I can't give her oral glucose in case she chokes on it. I need to give her in-tramuscular glucagon.'

Nancy looked grim. 'There's a kit on the medication trolley. I'll get it.'

'Can you bring a cloth and some water too, please?' he asked. Then he turned to Joni. 'Hang on in there, Nizhoni who lives up to her name. We'll sort this. And then—well, then I hope you'll give me another chance.' He stroked her hair out of her eyes. She looked so fragile, so vulnerable.

'And I swear I'll never let anything hurt you again,' he said softly.

Nancy returned with the glucagon kit and water. Aaron mixed up the solution and drew it up into a syringe.

'Help me put her in the recovery position before I do this,' he said to Nancy. Administering glucagon could cause some diabetics to vomit, and the last thing Joni needed when she came round was to start choking.

Once she was safely on her side, he picked up the

syringe and injected the solution into the muscle of her upper arm. Hopefully it would take effect quickly.

'If she doesn't regain consciousness within the next ten minutes, we need to recheck her blood sugar,' he said to Nancy, 'then give her a second dose of glucagon and get her straight to the emergency department.'

'I'll get a trolley bed in case we need to take her down,' she said.

He stayed with Joni, checking her breathing and her pulse.

Please let the glucagon work quickly. Please let it be enough so she'd recover and wouldn't need emergency treatment.

Just as Nancy came back with the wheeled bed, Joni's eyes fluttered open. The next second, she threw up everywhere.

'Oh, no. I'm so sorry,' she mumbled.

'Don't apologise. It's not your fault,' he said, and cleaned her up.

'I feel terrible.' She groaned. 'What happened?'

'You passed out,' he said. 'You had a hypo.'

'But I—'

'Shh. Don't try to talk, not yet. You need to recover. And the reason you threw up is because of me—your blood sugar was way too low and you were unconscious, so I couldn't risk putting glucose gel in your mouth or anything.'

'You gave me glucagon?' she asked.

He nodded. 'Your arm might be a bit sore tomorrow. Sorry.'

'Better a sore arm than diabetic coma,' she said groggily.

'Take a sip of water. It'll make your mouth feel better.' He offered her the cup. 'Nancy, if you want to get off, I'll finish up here,' he said.

'Are you sure?' the nurse asked.

'I'm sure.' More sure than he'd been of anything else in his life.

'I'll take the trolley bed back on my way out,' she said.

'Thanks.' He got to his feet, lifted Joni in his arms, and carried her down the corridor.

'Where are we—?' she began.

'My office. So you can sit down and recover for a bit before you even think about going home,' he said. 'Doctor's orders.'

'Bossy.' But at least she was smiling. That was a good sign—wasn't it?

Once in his office, he didn't want to let her go. He wanted to keep her safely in his arms. But he knew he didn't have the right. Not yet. So he gently set her down in his chair. 'I'll get you some more water,' he said, 'and something to eat from the vending machine. Will a cereal bar do if there aren't any sandwiches left?'

'Anything with some slow-release carbs,' she said, sounding tired. 'Thank you.'

'Don't go to sleep. Don't move. If you feel faint, put your head between your knees.'

When he came back with a couple of cereal bars, some more water and some mints to make her mouth feel fresher, she was still sitting there, looking a bit dazed.

'Thank you. I think you just saved my life,' she said.

He shrugged. 'You had a hypo and I gave you glucagon.'

'I passed out. My blood sugar must've been…'

'Way too low. I know. I tested it,' he said. 'Eat, and then talk.'

She ate one of the cereal bars, sipped the water and then ate one of the mints. 'Thank you. You've really looked after me.'

Because I love you, Aaron thought, and I don't want to be without you, and seeing you unconscious brought the whole thing into sharp focus. But he wasn't going to dump that on her just yet. He needed to use the right words. 'I was hardly going to leave you on the floor, collapsed,' he said. 'You're normally meticulous about your blood sugar. What happened? Have you had some kind of bug or something?'

'I've been feeling a bit odd for a day or two,' she admitted. 'I had a couple of days off earlier in the week.'

He knew. He'd missed her. Horribly.

'I didn't rush around or anything. I'd been feeling a bit sweaty and shaky, but I thought it was just one of the summer bugs doing the rounds. I thought I was OK today.' She grimaced. 'I should've kept a closer eye on my blood sugar.'

'We've been really busy on the ward,' he said, 'so while you've been here you've been rushing around. And the stress I caused you didn't help.'

She looked wary. 'We're not talking about that. It's personal stuff.'

'Which is exactly why we need to talk about it.'

She frowned. 'You don't do personal, Aaron.'

'Past tense. It's time I learned how,' he said. 'Because, since we broke up, I've been totally miserable. And I've realised how wrong and how stupid I've been. I was going to ask you if we could talk, before you collapsed.'

'Uh-huh.' She looked wary.

'My timing's rubbish. And you already know I'm totally slow on the uptake,' he said. 'But seeing you unconscious like that really brought it home to me—it made me think of what life would be without you. And it…it's unbearable.'

'But—we agreed we'd just be colleagues.'

'That's not enough for me,' he said. 'I made the biggest mistake of my life, pushing you away like that. And there's something I really need to say to you, Joni. As well as sorry for hurting you.' He took a deep breath. 'Ay-oo—oh, hell.'

'"Ay-oo—oh, hell"?' she repeated, looking totally confused. 'Have I lost the plot or are you talking gibberish at me?'

'I'm trying… I practised this and I was so sure I'd got it. And now I can't think straight. I can't remember the words. Seeing you there, not moving—it's scrambled my brain. Wait.' He grabbed his phone and sifted through the notes he'd made earlier. 'Right. Nizhoni Parker, ah-yoh ah-nee-nish-neh,' he said slowly.

She looked at him, stunned. 'Did you just say what I think you did?'

'I hope I got the pronunciation right. I looked it up on half a dozen videos.' Navajo wasn't exactly the easiest language to learn. 'And I wrote it down to remind me.'

She smiled. '*Ayóó áníínishní.*'

It didn't sound quite the same as it had when he'd said it. 'So I got it wrong?'

'No. You got it right.' She stared at him. 'I can't believe you just said that to me. And in Navajo.'

I love you. It wasn't something he'd ever said to anyone before.

'I wanted to make the effort, and I wanted you to

know that I'm making the effort, which is why I said it in Navajo instead of English,' he said. 'Because you said that's been the problem in the past. You've always picked the wrong guy—the one who's too selfish or too lazy to try. The one who always makes you feel that he's not as into you as you are into him. And I include me in that, because I really messed up. I hurt you, and I apologise.'

He blew out a breath. 'I'm not good at emotional stuff. I've spent my whole life doing the stiff upper lip thing. I've got three generations before me who did exactly the same. So I'm probably going to need reminders to act like a normal person and actually say what I feel. But I promise you I'll try from now on. And I want to put as much effort into this as you have. I want to make you feel the same way about me as I feel about you.'

She said nothing, but he knew she was just giving him the space to talk and not crowding him—because her expression was suddenly full of hope.

'I love you,' he said. 'Ah-yoh ah-nee-nish-neh. It scares the hell out of me, but it's how I feel and I can't stop it, even though I've tried. I'm a better man when I'm with you. But my family—they're not like yours. They're not close. I make a duty call to my parents once a fortnight, but we never talk for more than a couple of minutes. If they ask me how I am, they expect the answer to be "Fine"—so in their view the question doesn't really need to be asked in the first place.'

She laid her palm against the flat of her cheek. 'That's hard for you.'

'Not really. I'm used to it. It's how I grew up.' He shrugged. 'And it's the same with my sister and my other brother.'

She blinked. 'I didn't even know you had another brother and a sister.'

'They're both older than Ned. My parents spaced their children two years apart—except for me.' He flapped a dismissive hand. 'I guess accidents happen.'

She stared at him, shocked. 'You think they didn't want you?'

'They didn't *plan* me,' he corrected. 'As for wanting...it's all to do with the stiff upper lip. You just get on with things and you don't whine about the situation.'

'Right. So your brother and your sister...?'

'Sally's in Africa and Ben's in the Middle East. They're both in the armed forces, too. And they all think I wussed out, working in a safe hospital in England instead of being a battlefield doctor.' He blew out a breath. 'We have almost nothing in common and I can't even remember the last time we were all together. We're really not close. It's not a problem for me—I've never known any different. But it worries me that it'll hurt you, because that's not how it is for you.'

'So my family must've felt really full on for you.' She looked anxious. 'Too much to cope with. That's why you left early—why you backed away the day after.'

'Your family's lovely,' he said. 'They're warm and caring and supportive. But.' He had to face it. 'I can't live up to them, Joni.'

'You don't need to live up to anyone,' she said. 'All you need to do is be yourself.'

He tried to suppress it, not wanting to sound needy, but the question burst out anyway. 'How do you know that's going to be enough for you?'

'Because I know what I need,' she said.

Hope began to bloom. 'Which is?'

'Someone who enjoys quirky stuff. Someone who makes great coffee. Someone who makes me feel that the sun's shining even when there's a storm blowing outside.'

That was how he made her feel? Or was that was she wanted him to be?

The question must have been written all over his face, because she said softly, 'I need *you*, Aaron. Just as you are.'

'There's a huge gulf between the way you are and the way I am. I'm rubbish at all the emotional stuff.'

'If you're bright enough to be a consultant at the age of thirty-three, then you're also bright enough to learn about emotional stuff. With the right teacher. Which,' she said, 'would be me.'

'I want to be different,' he said softly. 'But we've been here before. I tried. I was a disappointment.'

'Not to me, you weren't. Well.' She wrinkled her nose. 'It was pretty bad when I realised you were going to dump me.'

'I disappointed myself,' he said. 'I'm not enough for you.'

'You've spent your whole life thinking you're not enough,' she said softly. 'And yet look at you. If you weren't enough, you wouldn't have qualified as a doctor. You wouldn't be a consultant at such a young age. You wouldn't get cute little hand-drawn thank-you cards from our younger patients.'

'That's different.' He flapped a dismissive hand. 'It's work. That's fine.'

'Work is part of who you are,' she said. 'And if you weren't enough, I wouldn't feel the way I do about you.

I wouldn't feel brave enough to want to take the risk of spending my future with you.'

'You'd take that risk?' He looked at her, shocked.

'Yes. Because I love you, too, Aaron. I admit, it started out as something different, when you asked me to dance with you. It was just physical stuff. But the more I've got to know you—both in and out of work— the more I've grown to like you. And it's not just like.' She stroked his face. 'And you've told me how you feel about me. You really mean that?'

'I really mean that,' he said. 'I've never felt like this about anyone before. I've always kept myself apart. But you—you're like sunshine. Irresistible. You make my world brighter just by being there.' He paused. 'I can't promise you a perfect life.'

'Nobody can make a promise like that,' she said. 'It's just setting yourself up for failure. So we're not going to promise each other perfection. But we can promise to stand by each other. To be there when we need each other. To listen. Maybe to argue some sense into each other from time to time.'

He smiled then. 'Is that what you're doing to me right now?'

She smiled back. 'Pretty much.'

'Maybe you're right.'

She coughed.

'*Probably* you're right,' he amended. 'And you'll probably have to talk sense into me quite a bit.'

'I can live with that.'

'If you're brave enough to take the risk,' he said, 'then so am I.'

'Together.' She took his hand.

'Together,' he echoed, and folded his fingers round

hers. 'Nizhoni Parker, I can't promise you a perfect life. But I do promise to love you for the rest of my days. And, with you by my side, I'll be a better man.'

'You're already good enough for me,' she said. 'And maybe I'll just have to tell you that every single day, until you start believing it for yourself.' She paused. '*Ayóó áníínishní*.'

'Ah-yoh ah-nee-nish-neh. I love you, too,' he said.

* * * * *

ONE MORE NIGHT WITH HER DESERT PRINCE…

BY
JENNIFER TAYLOR

MILLS & BOON

Published in Great Britain 2014
by Mills & Boon, an imprint of Harlequin (UK) Limited,
Eton House, 18-24 Paradise Road, Richmond, Surrey, TW9 1SR

© 2014 Jennifer Taylor

ISBN: 978-0-263-90793-3

Harlequin (UK) Limited's policy is to use papers that are natural,
renewable and recyclable products and made from wood grown in
sustainable forests. The logging and manufacturing processes conform
to the legal environmental regulations of the country of origin.

Printed and bound in Spain
by Blackprint CPI, Barcelona

Dear Reader

The desert has fascinated me for a very long time. In fact, spending time in the desert comes in at number two on my personal bucket list! As I'm not sure yet when I shall be able to get there, writing this book was the next best thing—and I have to admit, hand on heart, that I loved every single minute of it.

Bringing Sam and Khalid back together was always going to be an emotional experience. They parted on such bad terms, and each has been left badly scarred by the experience. There are so many reasons why they can't be together, and yet they both realise from the moment they meet again that the old feelings haven't disappeared as they believed. There is still something there, something that draws them to one other, and it makes no difference whatsoever that they each know the relationship is doomed, that it can never work when they come from such vastly different backgrounds.

Helping Sam and Khalid overcome their problems was a real pleasure. They are such lovely characters—brave, strong, determined and, yes, stubborn too! I always fall a little in love with my heroes and Khalid is definitely a hero to fall in love with. As for Sam—well, she is a woman who knows her own mind, a woman who has had to fight for what she wants from life, and I admire her gutsy attitude. I hope you will agree that Sam and Khalid get the ending they so deserve.

Do visit my blog and tell me what you think of this book: Jennifertaylorauthor.wordpress.com

I have a stack of wonderful photographs of the desert to show you. And who knows? I might even get the chance to take some myself!

Love to you all

Jennifer

Dedication

For all the Medical series authors,
with thanks for your kindness and support.

We are definitely going to have that party at the Ritz
when my numbers come up!

Recent titles by Jennifer Taylor:

SAVING HIS LITTLE MIRACLE
MR RIGHT ALL ALONG
THE MOTHERHOOD MIX-UP
THE REBEL WHO LOVED HER*
THE SON THAT CHANGED HIS LIFE*
THE FAMILY WHO MADE HIM WHOLE*
GINA'S LITTLE SECRET
SMALL TOWN MARRIAGE MIRACLE
THE MIDWIFE'S CHRISTMAS MIRACLE
THE DOCTOR'S BABY BOMBSHELL**
THE GP'S MEANT-TO-BE BRIDE**
MARRYING THE RUNAWAY BRIDE**

*Bride's Bay Surgery
**Dalverston Weddings

**These books are also available in eBook format
from www.millsandboon.co.uk**

Praise for
Jennifer Taylor:

'A superbly written tale of hope, redemption and
forgiveness, THE SON WHO CHANGED HIS LIFE
is a first-class contemporary romance that plumbs deep
into the heart of the human spirit and touches the soul.'
—*cataromance.com*

'Powerful, compassionate and poignant,
THE SON WHO CHANGED HIS LIFE is a brilliant
read from an outstanding writer who always delivers!'
—*cataromance.com*

CHAPTER ONE

'No! I'm sorry, Peter, but I'm simply not prepared to take Samantha Warren along on this trip. You'll have to find someone else.'

Prince Khalid, youngest son of the ruler of the Kingdom of Azad, glared at his old friend, Peter Thompson. He took a deep breath, struggling to moderate his tone when he saw the surprise on Peter's face. His response *had* been over the top but he couldn't help that. It might be six years since he had seen Sam Warren but the memory of their last meeting was as clear as though it had happened only the previous day.

'How about Liv?' he suggested, refusing to dwell on the thought. He had done what he'd had to do and there was no point regretting it. He couldn't have taken Sam to his bed, not when he had known that it could never lead anywhere. It would have gone against everything he believed in, made a mockery of the moral code he lived by. Sam had deserved so much more than a night in his arms.

'Liv's gone back home to Stockholm.'

Peter shrugged, his thin face still mirroring surprise at the strength of Khalid's outburst. Although they had been friends since Cambridge, Khalid realised that Peter had no idea what had happened between him and Sam. He had never told Peter and neither had Sam, it seemed.

It was a small sop to his feelings to discover that nobody knew what had happened that night. He still felt guilty about it, still felt that he should never have allowed things to reach that point. The problem was he had wanted to spend as much time as possible with Sam, to enjoy her company with all that it had entailed. If truth be told, he had never known a woman he had wanted as much as he had wanted Samantha Warren.

It was unsettling to admit it. Khalid forced his mind back to their current problem. 'Phone Liv and see if she's willing to change her plans.'

'I doubt she'll do that. Apparently, her mother's ill and she's gone home to look after her,' Peter explained.

'I see.'

Khalid bit down on the oath that threatened to escape as he crossed to the window. It was the middle of May and the trees in Green Park were awash with fresh new leaves. He had flown to London straight from Azad and the contrast between the barrenness of the desert he had left behind and the lushness of the view from the hotel suite seemed to overwhelm his senses. His mind was suddenly swamped by images he'd thought he had put behind him ages ago: Sam's face smiling up at him; the way her dove-grey eyes had darkened as he had bent to kiss her...

He turned away from the view, unable to cope with thoughts like that. They needed to resolve this problem and they needed to do so soon otherwise they could forget about this venture. It had been his idea to take a team of medics into the desert. Although the Kingdom of Azad had made huge advances in the past few years and now boasted a comprehensive healthcare system that supported the needs of most of its citizens, the nomadic tribes still had little access to any proper medical facilities. TB and other such diseases were rife amongst the desert tribesmen, whilst infant mortality rates were higher than anywhere else in the world. They urgently needed help, which was why Khalid had set up this project. The thought of how much effort and planning had gone into it focused his mind as nothing else could have done.

'There must be someone else. Come on, Peter—think!'

'I've done nothing but wrack my brain ever since Abby phoned and said she couldn't go,' Peter told him. 'However, the fact is that there *isn't* anyone else. Or, at least, nobody experienced enough. We need a top-notch female obstetrician and there are very few willing to take a couple of months off from their careers to go with us.'

'So, basically, what you're saying is that it's Sam or nobody,' Khalid said darkly, trying to control the sudden tightening in his chest. He took a deep breath, realising that he was beaten. If Sam didn't go along then they would have to call off the trip and it would be madness to do that, unforgivable to allow people to suffer because *he* couldn't handle the thought of working with her. He shrugged, his handsome face betraying little of what he was feeling. Maybe he did feel raw inside but nobody would guess that; he'd make sure they didn't.

'All right. If it's got to be Sam then I'll have to accept it. Give her a call and tell her to meet us here tomorrow morning at eight a.m. prompt.'

'There's no need to do that. I'm already here.'

Khalid spun round when he recognised the cool clear voice issuing from the doorway. Just for a moment his vision blurred as the blood pounded through his veins before it suddenly cleared. He took rapid stock of the petite blonde-haired woman standing in the doorway and felt his heart sink as he was hit by a raft of emotions he had hoped never to experience again. It might be six years since he had last seen Samantha Warren but she still had the power to affect him, it seemed.

Sam fixed a smile to her lips as Peter came hurrying over to her. He kissed her on both cheeks and she responded but she was merely going through the motions. Her attention was focused on the tall dark-haired man standing by the window, not that she was surprised. From the moment she had first seen Khalid, sitting with Peter in the hospital's crowded canteen when they had all been doing their rotations, he had commanded her attention.

She and Peter had become good friends by then and she hadn't hesitated when he had invited her to sit with them. He had introduced her, explaining that he and Khalid had been at Cambridge together studying medicine and it was a stroke of luck that they had both ended up working at St Gabriel's in Central London. Sam had listened to what Peter was saying but she had been aware that he could have been speaking double Dutch for all she had cared. Her attention had seemed to be wholly captured by the man sitting beside her, and it had stayed that way throughout the time she had known Khalid. When Khalid had been around, she had found it impossible to think about anything except him.

Now her eyes ran over him with lightning speed,

almost as though she was afraid that if she allowed them to linger she would never be able to drag them away. He looked little changed from what she could tell, his jet-black hair as crisp as ever, his olive skin gleaming with good health. Her eyes skimmed down the powerful length of his body, taking stock of the hard, flat muscles in his chest, the trimness of his waist, the narrowness of his hips.

He was dressed as always in clothes that bore all the hallmarks of his wealth and status yet it wasn't the clothing that made him appear so imposing: it was Khalid himself. He possessed a natural arrogance and assurance that came from his position. As the younger son of one of the richest men in the world, Khalid had no reason to doubt himself. He knew who he was, appreciated his own worth, and didn't apologise for it either. No wonder he had rejected her that night.

The thought made her flinch and she looked away, afraid that Khalid would notice. She had thought long and hard after Peter had phoned and asked her if she would go with them. Although her initial reaction had been to refuse, Peter had been so persuasive that she had found herself agreeing to think about it. She had spent the whole week doing so, in fact. She knew that in other circumstances she would have leapt at the chance to be part of this venture. It would be good experience for her, a definite plus point to put on her CV when she applied for a consultant's post, as she was hoping to do very shortly. However, the fact that Khalid would be going too put a very different slant on things.

How did she feel about working with him after what had happened between them? *Would* she be able to work with him? As the days had passed and she'd still not made up her mind, she had realised that the only way she could do so was by seeing him. If she could see Khalid and speak to him without it causing a problem then she would go along. That was why she had travelled down from Manchester that morning. Peter had told her that Khalid was staying at the Ritz so she had decided to see for herself if they would be able to get along. If they could, fine, and if they couldn't...? Well!

'How about some tea? Or coffee perhaps?' Peter bustled around, opening cupboards to find the kettle. Sam could tell that he was nervous and couldn't help feeling sorry for him. Peter was a natural peacemaker. He hated discord and wanted everyone to be happy. However, in this instance it simply wasn't possible.

'Phone room service and tell them to bring up a tray.'

Sam looked up when Khalid spoke, feeling a little knot of resentment twist her guts. Did he have to speak to Peter that way, treat him like a lackey? It was on the tip of her tongue to say something but she managed to hold back. If she did agree to go along then there must be no emotions involved, neither anger nor anything else. She had to treat Khalid as he had treated her that night, coldly, distantly, *dismissively.*

'Ah, right. Yes. Good idea.' Peter picked up the phone, frowning when he failed to get a dial tone. 'Hmm, that's odd. It doesn't seem to be working. I'll just pop downstairs and ask Reception to sort something out.'

He hurried out of the room before Sam could say anything, not that it was her place to tell him to stay. It was Khalid's suite, his decision what to do. Walking over to the sofa, she sat down and crossed her legs neatly at the ankles, glad that she had opted to wear something stylish. Maybe her clothes weren't made by a top couturier like Khalid's were, but the black cashmere suit and pale grey silk blouse she'd chosen to wear with it were good quality, as were all her clothes these days. Nobody looking at her would guess that she came from such a humble background.

'So, you decided to come and see me?' Khalid dropped into a chair, stretching out his legs under the ornate glass and brass coffee table.

'That's right.' Sam deliberately moved her feet out of the way, making it clear that she wanted to avoid any contact with him. She had thought about how she intended to go about this on the train and had decided that the only way was to be honest. No way was she going to prevaricate, to lie; she would come straight out and tell him how she felt. She gave a little shrug, feeling a spurt of pleasure run through her when she saw his eyes darken in annoyance. Obviously, Khalid didn't appreciate her taking avoiding action. Good!

'There's no point me agreeing to go along if we can't work together, Khalid. It would be a waste of both our time.'

'I agree.' He steepled his fingers and regarded her steadily over the top. 'If we have personal issues to contend with, we won't be able to give our full attention to our patients. That is something I wish to avoid.'

'So do I.' Sam smiled politely although inside she was seething. *Personal issues*, he called them. Maybe she wasn't as experienced as him, but leading someone on, *almost* sleeping with them before rejecting them in the cruellest way possible, seemed rather more than mere personal issues to her.

'What happened between us that night is in the past

and I hope that you have put it behind you as I have done.' He shrugged. 'If you haven't then I would appreciate it if you'd say so. Hopefully, we can talk it all through and put what happened into perspective.'

Oh, he must be desperate. Desperate to retain her services as a medic if not to possess her body. Sam's smile became even more brittle. 'There's no need to talk anything through, I assure you. What happened that night is history, Khalid. It doesn't have any bearing whatsoever on my life these days.'

'Good. In that case, I can't see that we shall have a problem working together.' He stood up and held out his hand. 'Welcome aboard, Sam. It's good to have you with us.'

Sam stood up, feeling her breath catch as she placed her hand in his. His fingers felt so cool as they closed around hers, cool and strong and so achingly familiar that she had to fight the urge to drag her hand away. She took a deep breath, forcing down the momentary panic. She wasn't in love with Khalid anymore, if, indeed, she had ever been in love with him. She had thought about it a lot over the years, examined her feelings, gone over them time and time again, and gradually realised the truth.

She had been dazzled by him—by his charm, by his sophistication, by his good looks—but love? No. It hadn't been love. It couldn't have been. Maybe she would have slept with him that night but that didn't mean it would have been out of love. Men and women slept together all the time and for all sorts of reasons too. Desire, loneliness, physical need—they were all grounds for intimacy. But love was rare, love was special, love was what everyone sought and very few found. Including her.

She hadn't been in love with Khalid and he hadn't been in love with her, so why was her heart racing, aching? Why did she feel so churned up inside? Why did she suddenly not believe all the reasoned arguments she had put together because she was standing here holding Khalid's hand?

As her eyes rose to his face, Sam realised with a sick feeling in her stomach that she had no idea. What she did know was that holding Khalid's hand, touching him and having him touch her, made her feel all sorts of things she had never wanted to feel again.

CHAPTER TWO

SAM CLOSED HER eyes, shutting out the view from the plane's window. They had been flying across the desert for over an hour now and her eyes were aching from the sight of the sunlight bouncing off the undulating waves of sand. She hadn't realised just how vast the desert was, how many miles of it there would be. Although Khalid had explained when they had stopped to refuel at Zadra, the capital of Azad, that they would need to fly to their base at the summer palace, it hadn't prepared her for its enormity. Just for a second she was filled with doubts. What if she couldn't cope in such a hostile environment? What if she ended up being a liability rather than a help? It wouldn't make her feel better to know that once again Khalid must regret getting involved with her.

'Cup of tea?'

Sam jumped when someone dropped down onto the seat beside her. Opening her eyes, she summoned a smile for the pleasant-faced woman holding a cup of tea out to her. It was pointless getting hung up on ideas like that. What had happened between her and Khalid in the past had no bearing on the present. She was six years older, six years wiser, six years more *experienced* and she wouldn't allow Khalid to make her doubt herself. She didn't need to prove her worth to him or to anyone else.

'Thanks.'

Sam took the cup and placed it carefully on the table, not wanting to spill tea on the butter-soft leather seat. They were using one of Khalid's father's fleet of private jets and the luxury had been rather overwhelming at first. She had only flown on scheduled aircraft before and hadn't been prepared for the opulence of real leather upholstery and genuine wooden panelling in the cabin. There was even marble in the bathrooms, smooth and cool to the touch, a world removed from the plastic and stainless steel she was more used to. If Khalid had wanted to highlight the differences in their backgrounds then he couldn't have found a better way than by inviting her to travel on this plane.

'Nothing like a cuppa to give you a boost.' The woman—Jessica Farrell, Sam remembered, digging into her memory—grinned as she settled back in the adjoining seat. If Jessica was at all awed by the luxury of their transport it didn't show and Sam suddenly felt a little better. She was setting too much store by trivialities, she realised. Reading way too much into everything that happened. Khalid's choice of transport had nothing to do with her.

'There certainly isn't.' Sam took a sip of her tea then smiled at the other woman. 'Have you been on other aid missions like this?'

'Uh-huh.' Jess swallowed a mouthful of tea. 'This is my tenth trip, although it's the first time I've been into the desert. I usually end up in the wilds of the jungle, so this will be a big change, believe me.'

'Your tenth trip? Wow!' Sam exclaimed in genuine amazement, and Jess laughed.

'I know. I must be a glutton for punishment. Every time I get back home feeling completely knackered I swear I'll never do it again but I never manage to hold out.' Jess glanced across the cabin and her expression softened. 'Peter can be so persuasive, can't he?'

'He can,' Sam agreed, hiding her smile. It appeared that Peter had a fan, not that she was surprised. Peter was such a love, kind and caring and far too considerate for his own good. He had been involved in overseas aid work ever since they had qualified, combining his job as a specialist registrar at a hospital on the south coast with various assignments abroad. Sam wasn't the least surprised that Jess thought so highly of him. What was surprising was that he and Khalid had remained such good friends when they were such very different people.

Her gaze moved to Khalid, who was sitting by himself at the rear of the plane, working on some papers. He had been polite but distant when he had welcomed her on board that morning but as he had been exactly the same with the rest of the team, she couldn't fault him for that. She had been one of the first to board and she had made a point of watching how he had treated everyone else even though she hated the fact that she had felt it necessary. They had both agreed that they had put the past behind them so what was the point of weighing up the warmth of his greeting? Nevertheless, she hadn't been able to stop herself assessing how he had behaved and it was irritating to know that he still had any kind of a hold over her. Khalid was history. Her interest in him was dead and buried. The sooner she got that clear in her head, the better.

He suddenly looked up and Sam felt her face bloom with colour when his eyes met hers. It was obvious from his expression that he had realised she was watching him and she hated the fact that she had given herself away. Turning, she stared out of the window, watching the pale glitter of sand rushing past below. She had to stop this, had to stop thinking about Khalid or she would never be able to do her job.

'Peter told me you're an obstetrician. I imagine you'll be in great demand during this trip.'

'I hope so.' Sam fixed a smile to her lips as she turned to Jess. Out of the corner of her eye she saw Khalid return to his notes and breathed a sigh of relief. Maybe he had known that she'd been watching him but so what? He must have been watching her too if he had noticed.

The thought wasn't the best to have had, definitely not one guaranteed to soothe her. Sam hurried on, determined not to dwell on it. There was bound to be a certain level of…*awareness* between them after past events. However, that was all it was, an echo from the past and not a forerunner for the future.

'Peter emailed me a printout of the infant mortality rates and I was shocked, to be frank. They shouldn't be so high in this day and age.'

'I know. I saw them too.' Jessica grimaced. 'The number of women who die in childbirth is almost as bad.'

'I'm not sure yet what's going wrong but I suspect a lot of the problems are caused by a lack of basic hygiene,' Sam observed. 'I'm hoping to train some of the local midwives and make sure they understand how important it is that basic issues, like cleanliness, are addressed.'

'You'll find that the women are more aware of the problems than you may think. You shouldn't assume that they're ignorant of the need for good hygiene.'

Sam looked up when she heard Khalid's deep voice. He was standing beside Jessica's seat, a frown drawing his elegant brows together. His comment had sounded very much like a rebuke to her and she reacted instinctively.

'I have no intention of assuming anything. I shall assess the situation first and then decide what can be done to rectify the problems.' Her eyes met his and she had to suppress a shiver when she saw how cold they were. Just for a moment she found herself recalling how he had looked at her that night, his liquid-dark eyes filled with passion, before she brushed the memory aside. Maybe Khalid had wanted her for a brief time but he had soon come to his senses after that article had appeared in the newspapers. After all, what would a man like him, a man who had the world at his feet, want with someone like her?

Sam bit her lip, determined not to let him know how much his rejection still hurt. It wasn't as though it had been the first time it had happened or the last but it was incredibly painful to recall what had gone on that night. Even though she had worked hard to get where she was, she had never been able to rid herself completely of her past. Oh, she might know how to dress these days, might have refined her manners and shed her accent, but she was still the girl from the rundown estate whose mother had brought home one man after another and whose brother was in prison.

She took a deep breath and used it to shore up her defences. The truth was that she hadn't been good enough for Khalid six years ago and she still wasn't good enough for him now.

Khalid inwardly cursed when he saw the shuttered expression on Sam's face. Why on earth had he said that or, at least, said it in that tone? Sam knew what she was doing. She wouldn't be here if he had any doubts about that. Peter had kept him informed of her progress over the years and Khalid knew that she was making her mark in the field of obstetrics. Sam was clever, committed, keen to learn and a lot of people in high places had recognised her potential. Rumour had it that she would be offered a consultant's post soon and it was yet more proof of her ability.

He knew how difficult it was for women to rise through the ranks. Although most people believed that equality between the sexes was the norm in modern-day Britain, it wasn't only in countries like Azad where women came off second best. It happened all over the world to a greater or lesser degree. His own field—surgery—was one of the worst for discriminating against women, in fact. Although he knew he was good at what he did, he also knew that it helped to be male. And rich. And have the right connections.

Sam had none of those things going for her but she was making her mark anyway and he admired her for it. She had guts and determination in spades, which was why he had been attracted to her in the first place. Sam had been very different from the other women he had known.

The thought hung in the air, far too tantalising to

feel comfortable with. Khalid thrust it aside, needing to focus on what really mattered. How he had felt about Sam was of little consequence these days.

'Of course. And I apologise if you thought I was criticising you,' he said smoothly. 'You are the expert in this field and, naturally, I shall be guided by you.'

She gave a small nod in acknowledgement although she didn't say anything. Khalid hesitated, wondering why he felt so unsure all of a sudden. He wasn't a man normally given to self-doubts—far from it. However, her response made him wonder if he should have been a little more effusive with his apology. He didn't want them getting off to a bad start, after all. It was on the tip of his tongue to say something else when Jess let out a yelp.

'Look! That can't *really* be what I think it is? Oh, Peter has to see this.'

Khalid moved aside as Jess shot out of her seat. Bending, he stared through the porthole, smiling faintly when he realised what had captured her attention. After the time they'd spent flying over the barren desert, he could understand why Jess had such difficulty believing her own eyes.

'It's like something out of a fairy tale. It can't possibly be real.'

The wonder in Sam's voice brought his eyes to her face and he felt a rush of tenderness envelop him. Sitting down on the recently vacated seat, he pointed to a spot a little to her right.

'Oh, it's real enough. Look over there and you'll see the lights on the runway.' He laughed deeply, feeling his chest tighten when he inhaled the lemon fragrance of her shampoo as she turned to do his bidding. It was an effort to continue when his breathing seemed to have come to a full stop. 'It looks less like a fairy-tale palace when you see the modern-day accoutrements that are needed to keep it functioning.'

'What a shame.' Sam shook her head, oblivious to the problems he was having as she studied the lights. 'It would have been nice to believe the fantasy even if it was only for a few minutes.'

She glanced round and Khalid stiffened when he saw how soft her eyes looked, their colour echoing the pale grey tones of the doves that flew over the summer palace. They had been the exact same colour that night, he recalled. A softly shimmering grey. He could picture them now, recall in perfect detail how she had looked as she had lain on the bed, waiting for him to make love to her.

The memory was too sharp, too raw even now. Khalid couldn't deal with it and had no intention of trying either. He stood up abruptly. 'We shall be landing in a few minutes. I need a word with the pilot, if you'll excuse me.'

He made his way to the cockpit and told the pilot to radio ahead and make sure the cars were standing by to meet them. There was no need for him to do so, of course. Everything had been arranged but it gave him something to do, a purpose, a reason to get away from Sam and all those memories that he'd thought he had dealt with years ago. As he made his way back to his seat, he realised with a sinking heart how wrong he had been. The memory of that night hadn't gone away, it had just been buried. He wanted to bury it again, bury it so deep this time that it would never surface, but could he?

Was it possible when Sam was here, a constant reminder of what he had given up?

Khalid glanced across the cabin and felt a chill run through him as he studied the gentle lines of her profile. He had a feeling that he might never be able to rid himself of the memory of that night. It might continue to haunt him. For ever.

By the time they were shown to their accommodation, Sam was exhausted. Maybe it was the length of time it had taken to get there but she couldn't even summon up the energy to look around. Jess had no such problems, however. She hurried from room to room, exclaiming in delight.

'A sunken marble bath! And a separate wet room!' Jess opened a huge glass-fronted cabinet and peered inside. 'Oh, wow! Look at all these lotions and potions. It's like having our very own beauty salon on tap.'

'Not quite what I was expecting,' Sam observed pithily, tossing her bag onto the bed. There were three bedrooms in the guest house they'd been allocated, each decorated in a style that could only be described as lavish. Opening her case, she tipped its contents onto the umber silk spread, which matched the draperies hanging from the bed's ornate gilt frame.

'Me too. I thought we'd be camping out in a grotty old tent in the middle of the desert but this is great.'

Jess went into one of the other bedrooms and Sam heard a thud as she threw herself down onto the bed. She sighed, wishing she could share Jess's enthusiasm. If she had to describe her feelings then she would have to say that she felt...well, *cheated*. Surely Khalid hadn't brought them all this way so they could lounge around in the lap of luxury? She'd honestly thought she would be doing valuable work, making a positive contribution towards improving the lives of the desert women, but how could she do that if she was cloistered away in here?

The thought spurred her into action. Leaving her clothes in an untidy heap on the bed, she hurried from the room, calling to Jess over her shoulder, 'I'm just going to have a word with Khalid.'

'Okey-dokey. I think I'll treat myself to a bath,' Jess replied dreamily. 'No point letting all those goodies go to waste, is there?'

Sam didn't bother replying. There was no point taking the shine off things by telling Jess how she felt. Crossing the huge marble-floored sitting room, she wrenched open the door then paused uncertainly.

Night had fallen now and she wasn't sure which way to go. The female members of the team had been shown to their accommodation by one of the servants and Sam hadn't taken much notice of the route as she had followed the woman through the grounds.

She turned slowly around, trying to get her bearings, and suddenly spotted the pale gleam of the palace's towers through the palm trees to her left. There was a path leading in that direction and she followed it until she came to a ten-foot-high wall. There was a gate set into it and she turned the handle, frowning when it failed to open. She tried again, tugging on the handle this time, but it still wouldn't budge and her temper, which was already hovering just below boiling point, peaked. If Khalid had had them locked in then pity help him!

* * *

Khalid took a deep breath, hoping the desert air would wash away the stresses of the day. He had honestly thought that he had been ready for what would happen but nothing could have prepared him for being around Sam again. He frowned, trying to put his feelings into context. It was bound to have been stressful to see her again—that was a given. However, he had never expected to feel so raw, so emotional. He was a master at controlling his feelings but he hadn't been able to control them today. Not with Sam. He had felt things he had never expected to feel, reacted in a way that shocked him.

It made him see how careful he would need to be in the coming weeks. He had to remember that he had nothing to offer Sam apart from a life that would stifle her as it had stifled his own mother. He wouldn't be responsible for doing that, for taking away everything that made Sam who she was. Sam was brave, kind, funny and determined and he couldn't bear to imagine how much she would change if he allowed his desire for her to take over.

The thought lay heavily in his heart as he strode along the path. The summer palace was built on the site of an oasis and the grounds benefited from an abundance of fresh water. The night-time scent of the flowers filled the air as he made his way through the grounds. Normally the richly, spicy aroma soothed him but tonight it failed to move him. The scent of Sam's shampoo still lingered in his nostrils and nothing seemed able to supplant it.

Khalid's mouth tightened as he nodded to the guard standing outside the entrance to the male guest quarters. He had to stop this, had to remember *why* Sam was here, which wasn't for his benefit. She was here to do a job and once it was done she would go back to her own life and he would go back to his. There was no future for them together and he'd be a fool to imagine that there was.

If he had been willing to take a chance he would have taken it six years ago, made love to her and made promises that he would have kept too. He had wanted her so much, wanted her in his arms, in his bed, in his life, but he had realised after those articles had appeared in the press the damage it would cause if he had acted upon his feelings.

Maybe he had wanted her, and maybe she had wanted him too, but it wouldn't have been enough to make up for what would have happened if news of their relationship had leaked out. Sam would have been subjected to constant scrutiny by the press, her every action commented on, her family's shortcomings discussed ad nauseam. He had seen how hurt she had been, how upset, and he had known that he couldn't bear to see her subjected to that kind of pressure on top of everything else she would have had to contend with if they had stayed together.

He sighed. Sam would have had to give up such a lot, her independence, her career; give up being who she *was,* in fact, and it had been far too much to ask. Even though he spent a lot of his time working in London, Azad was his home and he always came back here. If he had brought Sam here to live, she would have had to conform to a way of life that was completely alien to her. Although changes were taking place, women in Azad still faced many restrictions. Perhaps Sam could have handled it at first even with the added strain of all the unwelcome publicity, but eventually she would have found the life too oppressive, as his mother had done.

He couldn't have stood that, couldn't have tolerated watching her love turn to resentment, which was why he had done what he had that night. Khalid took a deep breath as he made himself face the cold hard facts. It had been better to destroy her love for him once and for all than watch it slowly wither and die.

Sam rolled over, struggling to untangle herself from the silken folds of the sheet. Reaching out, she pulled the alarm clock closer and sighed. Three a.m. and she was still wide awake. She had tried everything she could think of, counted sheep, recited poetry, thought sleep-inducing thoughts, but nothing had worked. Her body might be exhausted but her mind wouldn't slow down. It kept whizzing this way and that, yet always ending up at the same point: that moment six years ago when all her dreams had been shattered.

Tears filled her eyes but she blinked them away. She had done all the crying she intended to do and she wasn't going to start again. So Khalid had changed his mind, decided that he hadn't wanted her—so what? The world hadn't come to an end, the heavens hadn't fallen in and she had survived. If anything, it had made her stronger, made her value herself more. She had stopped apologising for her background, stopped feeling that she didn't deserve to be where she was. When it had come to breaking off her engagement last year, she hadn't hesitated. The relationship wouldn't have worked and she had known that...as Khalid must have known that *their* relationship had been doomed to failure.

Sam sighed as once again her thoughts returned to Khalid. Rolling over, she tried to get comfortable. She needed to sleep or she'd be fit for nothing tomorrow or, rather, today. Closing her eyes, she allowed her mind to drift, deciding it was easier than trying to steer it in any direction. Pictures flowed in and out of her mind: the desert they had flown over; the summer palace shimmering like a mirage in its lush green setting....

The sound of stealthy footsteps made her eyes fly open and she peered into the darkness. Was there someone in the room, Jess perhaps? Barely daring to breathe, she eased herself up against the pillows and felt her heart knock against her ribs when she saw the outline of a man silhouetted against the window. It hadn't occurred to her to close the shutters and she could feel the fear rising inside her as the figure approached the bed. Grabbing the clock off the nightstand, she held it aloft, wishing she had a more substantial weapon with which to defend herself.

'Get out or you're going to regret it!'

'Sam, it's me.'

Khalid's deep voice was the last thing she had expected to hear. The clock slid from her fingers and landed on the floor with a crash. Sam stared at him as he came closer, still not sure if he was real or a figment of her imagination.

'Khalid?' she whispered, her own voice sounding husky in the silence. 'Is it really you?'

'Yes.'

He bent so that she could see his face and her breath caught when she saw how his eyes glittered with an emotion she couldn't interpret. When he moved closer, so close that she could feel the warmth of his breath on her cheek, she almost cried out. It took every scrap of will power she could muster to lie there and not do anything, not react in any way at all. Khalid had come to her and it was up to him to tell her why.

'I'm sorry to wake you, Sam. I know how tired you must be after the journey.' His voice sounded softer, deeper, strumming her nerves like a violin bow, and she shuddered.

'What do you want?' she murmured, wishing that she sounded more certain and less unsure.

'You.' He suddenly smiled, his teeth gleaming whitely in the moonlight. 'I need *you*, Sam.'

CHAPTER THREE

'THE BABY'S BREECH. It's too late to turn it or perform a C-section so we'll have to deliver it vaginally.'

Sam turned to Jess and smiled. Although the young mother, Isra, couldn't understand what they were saying, she would soon guess how serious the situation was if they showed any signs of concern. Sam could tell that the girl was terrified and it wouldn't help if they lost her confidence at this point.

'I've not delivered a breech before,' Jess murmured, following Sam's lead and smiling broadly. 'I hope you have.'

'I've done my share,' Sam assured her, washing her hands in the basin of water on the dresser. There was no point stating the obvious, that the breech deliveries she'd been involved with had been carried out in the safety of a highly equipped maternity unit. They didn't have such luxuries on tap here so they would have to manage the best way they could.

'I need a word with Khalid,' she told Jess, refusing to dwell on the negatives. She had delivered several breech babies and every single one of them had survived. There was no reason to think that this baby wouldn't survive too. 'Our biggest problem is going to be the language barrier so we'll need an interpreter.'

'OK. Anything you want me to do?' Jess asked, sponging Isra's face.

'Not really. I'll only be a moment,' Sam assured her.

She left the bedroom, frowning when she discovered that there was nobody about. After Khalid had woken her, he had led her to the servants' quarters. Isra was the wife of one of the palace cooks and she and her husband lived in the grounds. Although their house was only small, much smaller than the one she and Jess were sharing, it was spotlessly clean and tidy.

Sam peered into a kitchen, which boasted a wood-burning stove, and a tiny but well-equipped bathroom as she made her way along the passageway. From what she could see, the staff were well catered for and it was good to know that they were treated with respect. She came to the sitting room, which was also small but very attractive with brightly coloured rugs on the tiled floor and heaps of cushions on the low couches. It all looked very comfortable but decidedly empty. Where *was* everyone?

Sam stepped out of the door, waiting for her eyes to adjust to the darkness, and heard footsteps approaching. Just for a second her mind whizzed back to those moments in the bedroom when she had spotted the silhouette of a man highlighted against the window and she felt her heart race. If she'd known it was Khalid, would she have felt more afraid or less? Would it have been better to face an intruder than to face him and have to go through those seconds when she'd thought he had wanted her for a very different reason?

'How is she doing?'

Khalid's voice cut through her thoughts, cool and clear in the silence of the night, and Sam shivered. She turned towards him, taking care to maintain a neutral expression. There was no way that she was going to let him know how she had felt, definitely no way that she was prepared to admit that she had wanted him too, although not for his skills as a surgeon. It would be foolish to do that, foolish and dangerous as well. Giving Khalid licence to toy with her emotions again was a mistake she didn't intend to make.

'The baby's breech,' she informed him crisply. 'It's too late to perform a section so we're going to have to deliver it vaginally but we'll need an interpreter. The mother's co-operation is vital in this situation.'

'Of course,' Khalid agreed, frowning.

Sam's brows rose. 'Is there a problem?'

'Unfortunately, yes. The female interpreter I've hired isn't joining us until tomorrow.'

'Surely there must be someone else here who speaks English.'

'Of course. However, they are all male.'

'So?'

'So it wouldn't be right to allow them to be present at the birth.'

'Why on earth not?' Sam exclaimed.

'Because men are not allowed to be present at the birth of a child, not even the father, let alone an outsider.'

'That's ridiculous,' Sam declared hotly.

'It may seem so to you but it's a cultural issue.' He shrugged, his face betraying little of what he was feeling. If he was annoyed by her outburst it didn't show, Sam thought, but, then, why should he feel anything? Khalid was indifferent to her, as he had made clear. The thought stung so that it was an effort to focus when he continued.

'Isra would lose the respect of her husband and her family if it were to happen. It's out of the question, I'm afraid.'

'How about if you did it? I mean, you're a doctor, Khalid, so surely that makes a difference?'

'I'm afraid not. Although views are changing in the city and there are even a few male obstetricians working in the hospital, the desert people still hold fast to the old ways.'

'Then what do you suggest?' Sam demanded, in no mood to compromise. Her feelings didn't enter into this, she reminded herself. It was her patient who mattered, not how hurt she had been when Khalid had rejected her. 'I need Isra to work with me, do what I tell her to do as and when it's necessary. It's vital if we hope to deliver this baby safely.'

'The only thing I can suggest is that we erect a screen across the window. Then I can stand outside and relay your instructions to her without actually being in the same room.'

'That sounds like a plan,' Sam agreed slowly, then nodded. 'Yes. It should work so long as you're able to hear what I'm saying.'

'Oh, that won't be a problem.' He smiled faintly, his beautiful mouth turning up at the corners. 'You have a very clear and distinctive voice, Sam. I'll have no difficulty hearing you.'

'Oh. Right.'

Sam felt a rush of heat sweep up her face and was glad of the darkness because it hid her confusion. That had sounded almost like a compliment and it was something she hadn't expected. She turned away, hurrying back into the house before the idea could take hold.

Khalid could have meant anything by the comment or he could have meant nothing and she would be a fool to get hung up on the idea. She quickly explained to Jess what was going to happen, half expecting the other woman to find it as ridiculous as she had done. However, Jess merely shrugged.

'I've come across it before. Some of the African tribes don't allow men to be present at a birth.'

'Really? I had no idea,' Sam admitted. She glanced round when she heard noises outside the window. 'It sounds as though Khalid is getting everything organised. We'd better get set up in here.'

She and Jess worked swiftly as they spread a sterile sheet under Isra and donned their gowns. Sam decided that she would need to perform an episiotomy to help ease the baby's passage. As it was presenting bottom first, it was harder for it to make its way out into the world and a small incision in the perineum would help enormously. It would also prevent the perineum becoming badly torn.

'Can you explain to Isra that I'm going to do an episiotomy?' she said clearly, glancing towards the window. A wooden screen had been erected across it so she couldn't see Khalid and could only assume he was there. 'If you can tell her why it's necessary, it should make it less scary for her.'

'Will do.'

His voice floated back to her, soft and deep and strangely reassuring. Although she couldn't understand what he was saying to Isra, Sam knew that his tone would have reassured *her* if she'd been in the young woman's position. It obviously did the trick because Isra stopped looking quite so scared.

Sam worked swiftly, administering a local anaesthetic before making the incision. The girl lay quite still, bearing the discomfort with a stoicism that filled Sam with admiration. 'Well done,' she told her, patting her hand.

She jumped when from the window came the sound of Khalid's voice repeating her comment. His voice sounded so warm that she shivered before she realised what she was doing and stopped herself. The warmth of his tone wasn't a measure of his regard for her but for Isra, she reminded herself.

She applied herself to the task, refusing to allow her thoughts to wander as she pressed gently on the top of the uterus to help ease the baby out. Isra's labour pains were extremely strong now and Sam decided that she needed to stop the girl pushing.

'I want you to take small breaths, like this,' she told her, panting so Isra would understand what she wanted her to do.

Khalid repeated her instructions, although Sam noticed that he didn't do the panting and smiled. Maybe it was expecting too much to hope he would mimic her. After all, he was a *prince* as well as a doctor! The thought made her chuckle and Jess looked at her quizzically.

'OK, give. What's tickled your funny bone?'

Sam knew that she should keep her thoughts to herself but she couldn't resist telling Jess. 'I was just wondering why our interpreter didn't repeat *all* my instructions,' she explained, raising her voice so that there'd be no chance of Khalid not hearing her. 'He missed out the panting.'

Jess giggled. 'Maybe not the done thing for a prince.'

'Like those mums who opt for a section because they're too posh to push?' Sam grinned. 'You could be right. He's just too posh to pant!'

Khalid felt a rush of heat flow through him when he heard the amusement in Sam's voice. He couldn't believe how good it felt to know that he was the reason why she was laughing. She'd been so distant towards him since they'd met again, so reserved, so cold, and he hated it.

Sam possessed a natural warmth that had drawn him to her from the moment they had met. Although he was used to women fawning over him because of his position, Sam had never treated him as someone special. Her response to him had been wholly natural and he had loved that, loved seeing her eyes light up when he had walked into a room, loved hearing her voice soften, loved knowing that she had wanted to be with him for who *he* was. He might be a prince, he might be rich, he might be many things, but he had never felt more like *himself* than when he had been with her. He had never needed to pretend with Sam. Not until that last night.

The thought filled him with pain and he sucked in his breath, afraid that she would hear an echo of it when he spoke. He could hear her talking to Isra, her voice so calm and reassuring that he knew it would soothe the young mother's fears even if the girl couldn't understand the actual words. He applied himself diligently to the task of translating, doing his best to mimic Sam's tone. He didn't want to let her down; he wanted to support her in any way he could. When the reedy sound of a baby's cry drifted out to him, his face broke into a smile.

'Is it all right?' he called through the screen.

'Fine. A little battered, as is mum, but he's in fine fettle,' Sam called back, and he could hear the elation in her voice. That she was thrilled by the birth of this child was clear and it touched him that she should care so much.

'It's a boy, then?' he said levelly, doing his best to control his emotions. He had to stop letting himself get carried away, had to remember that he had no rights where Sam was concerned. How she did or didn't feel wasn't his concern.

'Yes. Jess is just weighing him...' She broke off and then continued. 'He's almost three kilos so he's not a bad weight either.'

'That's excellent,' Khalid agreed. 'I'll go and inform the father if you don't need me anymore.'

'No, we're fine.' She paused then said quickly, 'Thank you, Khalid. We couldn't have managed nearly as well if you hadn't translated for us.'

'It was my pleasure,' he said softly, unable to keep the emotion out of his voice. Maybe it was foolish but it felt good to know that he had redeemed himself a little in her eyes.

He made his way to Isra's parents' house. Her husband, Wasim, had gone there to wait for news. He was delighted if a little overwhelmed when Khalid announced that he had a son. Having a royal prince inform him of his baby's birth obviously wasn't something he was prepared for. Khalid brushed aside the younger man's thanks and left. This was a time for family celebrations and they didn't need him there. As he made his way back to the palace, he found himself wondering if he would ever be in Wasim's position, celebrating the birth of his own child. It was what was expected of him as a royal prince and second in line to the throne. Even his father had started dropping hints that it was time he thought about settling down and starting a family, yet he had great difficulty imagining it happening. Although he had known many women—and known them in every sense of the word too—Sam was the only woman he had wanted to spend his life with.

His heart was heavy as he made his way to his suite. He had a feeling that if he did marry, whoever he chose would only ever be second best. How could it be fair to enter into marriage on that basis?

It was shortly before dawn by the time Sam left Isra's house. Jess had already left but she had stayed behind to make sure that there were no unforeseen complications. Thankfully, the baby seemed none the worse for his traumatic arrival and had taken his first feed. Isra seemed much happier as well and was being looked after by her mother and various female relatives. There was no reason for Sam to stay any longer so she smilingly accepted the family's thanks then made her way through the grounds, following the path that Khalid had taken the night before.

Everywhere looked very different now, the first pearly grey fingers of light lending a dreamlike quality to the scene. The palace's towers seemed to float in mid-air, shimmering above the hazy outline of the palm trees. When a horseman suddenly came into view, he seemed as insubstantial as everything else. It was only when he drew closer that Sam recognised Khalid beneath the flowing folds of the burnoose and realised it wasn't her imagination playing tricks after all.

'Have you only just finished?' he asked in surprise,

tossing back the hood of his cloak as he reined the horse to a halt.

'Yes.' Sam stroked the horse's velvety muzzle, keeping her gaze on the animal rather than allowing it to linger on Khalid. Her heart gave a little jolt as the horse shifted impatiently, bringing Khalid squarely into her line of sight. He looked so different dressed in the flowing robes, a world removed from the urbane and sophisticated man she knew, that it was an effort to respond naturally. 'I wanted to stay until I was sure Isra and the baby were all right.'

Khalid frowned. 'I appreciate that but you must be exhausted.'

'I'm fine. I'm used to late nights...and early mornings,' she added wryly. 'Babies seem to prefer to keep unsocial hours.'

He laughed, patting the horse's neck when it began to paw the ground. 'It makes me glad that I opted for surgery. At least there is usually *some* structure to my working day.'

'It doesn't bother me,' Sam told him truthfully. 'I've developed the knack of snatching an hour's sleep whenever I can.'

'That must help, but you were already tired after the journey. Are you going to try and get some sleep now?'

'I doubt I'll manage it. I'm far too keyed up,' she admitted, then wished she hadn't said anything when she saw his eyes narrow. She hurried on, not wanting him to read too much into the comment. 'It's being here in a strange place, I expect.'

'Probably,' he agreed, but she heard the scepticism in his voice and went hot all over.

Did Khalid think that he was the reason why she

felt so on edge? she wondered anxiously. And was he right? Was it less the unfamiliarity of her surroundings that had left her feeling so unsettled and more the fact that she was with him? She sensed it was true and it was hard not to show how disturbing she found the idea. She didn't want to feel anything for him but it appeared she had no choice.

'If you aren't going straight to bed, why don't you come with me?'

'Pardon?' Sam looked up in surprise and he shrugged.

'If you can't sleep then come and watch the sun rise over the desert. It's a sight worth seeing, believe me.'

'Oh, but I couldn't possibly...'

'Why not?' He stared arrogantly down at her and she could see the challenge in his eyes. 'What's to stop you, Sam? Unless you're afraid, of course?'

'Afraid? Of you?' Sam shook her head, refusing to admit that he was right. She was afraid—afraid of being with him, afraid of getting too close to him; afraid of becoming attracted to him all over again.

'In that case, there's no reason why you shouldn't come, is there?' He bent down and offered her his hand. 'Come.'

Sam took a deep breath as she placed her hand in his. She knew she was making a mistake but how could she refuse? Did she really want him to know that he still had a hold over her? Of course not.

Placing her foot in the stirrup as he instructed, she let him help her onto the horse. He settled her in front of him, putting his arm around her waist when the horse began to prance. 'Shh, Omar. There is nothing to fear.'

Drawing her back against him, he wrapped a fold of the burnoose around her, shaking his head when she opened her mouth to protest. 'It's still very cold. You'll be glad of the extra layer once we're out in the desert.'

Sam bit her lip as he turned the horse around. If she made a fuss then it would appear that she was over-reacting and that was the last thing she wanted, for Khalid to suspect that his nearness troubled her. She forced herself to relax as they rode towards the gates. The guard saw them approaching and opened them, then they were outside, the lush green vegetation clos-ing in around them. Khalid kept the horse to a walk as they made their way along the path and then all of a sudden they came to the perimeter of the oasis and before them lay the desert, shimmering like pewter in the pre-dawn light.

'All right?' Khalid asked, his voice rumbling softly in her ear.

Sam nodded mutely. She couldn't speak, couldn't seem to find her voice even. Between the raw beauty of the desert landscape and Khalid's nearness, she was awash with sensations and could barely deal with them. When he urged the horse into a canter, she clung to the pommel of the saddle. The wind rushed past, ruffling her hair and bringing with it the strangely elusive scent of the desert, yet all she could smell was Khalid's skin, a scent she would have recognised anywhere.

Closing her eyes, she gave herself up to the moment, uncaring if she was making a mistake. Maybe it was madness but being with him was what she wanted.

Desperately.

CHAPTER FOUR

KHALID SLOWED THE horse to a walk as they neared an outcrop of rock rising out of the desert floor. He always came to this place whenever he wanted to watch the sun rise. His parents had brought him here as soon as he had been old enough to sit astride a horse and he valued the connection it gave him to his childhood. Life had been so perfect before his parents had divorced.

Sadness filled him as he reined Omar to a halt. He'd been thirteen when his mother had left Azad and although now he understood her reasons for leaving, it had affected him deeply. She had returned to England afterwards while his father had remained in Azad, so Khalid had travelled between both countries, spending time with each of them. His older brother, Shahzad, the son of his father's first wife who had died in childbirth, had tried to make it easier for him, but the constant to-ing and fro-ing had been unsettling. In the end, Khalid had realised that he had to make a choice and had chosen to live in England.

He had won a place at Cambridge to study medicine and had thrown all his energy into making a success of his studies. Whilst he didn't regret the path he had chosen, there were times—like now—when he found himself wondering if he had made the wrong decision. If he had opted to live in Azad then he would never have met Sam and his life would be far less complicated now.

Khalid drove the thought from his mind as he dismounted. Having Sam here could only affect him if he allowed it to do so. Reaching up, he offered her his hand, determined that he wasn't going to let her know how ambivalent he felt. Sam had agreed to come on this mission for one reason and one reason alone: to help the desert women. If she could handle the situation then so could he.

'Take my hand,' he instructed, then sucked in his breath when she did as he'd asked. Her hand felt so small compared to his that he was struck by an unexpected rush of tenderness. He wanted to hold on to her hand, to hold on to *her*, he realised in dismay. And it was the last thought he should have been harbouring.

He quickly released her as she slid safely down to the ground. There were bound to be glitches, he told himself as he tethered Omar to a rock. Moments when his mind and his body were in conflict, but he would deal with them. He simply had to remember that being with Sam wasn't an option any more now than it had been six years ago. He had no intention of going down the same route his parents had taken, certainly didn't intend to put any children he might have through the kind of heartache he had suffered. If he kept that at the forefront of his mind, it shouldn't be a problem.

'Come. There's a path along here. It's not too steep and you shouldn't have any difficulty climbing it.' He gave her a cool smile, the sort of smile he utilised on a daily basis. Nobody looking at him would suspect that he felt far from cool inside. 'The view from the top is worth it, believe me.'

'I hope so.'

There was an edge to her voice that made him wonder if she had guessed he had mixed feelings about bringing her here. However, as it was too late to reconsider his invitation, he would have to make the best of it. He led the way, slowing his pace so she could keep up. They reached the top and stopped. Below them lay the desert, red-gold along the horizon where the sun's rays touched it, dark and mysterious closer to where they were standing. It was a sight he had seen many times before and it never failed to move him. However, it seemed to affect him even more that day, with Sam standing there beside him.

Khalid took a deep breath, trying to calm the panic that was twisting his guts as he watched the sun sail majestically over the horizon. A new day had begun and he, a man who was used to controlling his own destiny, had no idea what it would bring.

'It's amazing—'

Sam broke off, unable to put into words how the sight affected her. Wrapping her arms around herself, she shivered though not from cold. Although the temperature was still low, this shiver stemmed from the mixture of emotions she was experiencing. Sadness at what had happened in the past was mingled with joy at what she was experiencing right now; anger at the way Khalid had treated her was tempered by an unexpected acceptance. It was little wonder that she found it impossible to describe the scene so she didn't try. Anyway, it was doubtful if Khalid would be interested in her views.

She glanced at him, feeling pain tug at her heart. His heritage had never been more apparent than it was out here in the desert. It wasn't just the clothes he was wearing but his attitude. He looked every inch the desert prince, so completely at home in this bleak yet beautiful landscape that it simply highlighted the differences between them. Khalid's world wasn't her world. It never could be her world either. How could she, a Westerner with her background, become a desert princess?

'So, was I right?'

He turned to her and Sam struggled to clear her mind of everything except the need to convince him that she was over him. She had honestly thought she was, had truly believed that she had put her feelings for Khalid behind her years ago, but she was no longer sure when her heart was aching at the thought that they were such poles apart.

'Right?'

'About it being worth the climb.' He swept a hand towards the desert. 'The view from up here is magnificent, isn't it?'

'It is,' she replied coolly. 'I certainly can't fault it.'

'Did you want to?'

There was an edge to his voice that brought a rush of heat to her face. Had she been hoping to find fault with the view, to nitpick and discover flaws because it would have made it easier to find fault with him too? She sensed it was true and she hated the fact that she had been reduced to behaving in such a fashion.

'I'm sorry, Sam. Maybe bringing you here wasn't such a good idea after all.'

There was no doubt that the apology was sincere. Sam turned to look at him, seeing the sadness in his eyes. It struck her then that if she was finding it difficult to deal with this situation then it was equally hard for him. The thought shocked her so much that she didn't pause to consider the wisdom of what she was saying.

'Why did you bring me here, Khalid? Was it just so I could enjoy the view?'

'Of course. What other reasons could I have had?'

He shrugged, his broad shoulders moving lightly under the loose folds of the burnoose. Beneath it he was wearing more normal clothing, although they still weren't the clothes Sam was used to seeing him wear. Usually, Khalid wore immaculately tailored suits, not a loose-fitting white shirt, open at the neck so that she could see the satin gleam of his skin through the gap. White cotton trousers tucked into tan leather boots completed his outfit and made him look very different from the man she had known six years ago. Maybe that was why their relationship had foundered? Because he hadn't been the person she had thought he was. It hadn't had anything to do with her background after all.

The thought was far too tantalising. Sam knew that she needed to rid herself of it as quickly as possible. It would be foolish to imagine that Khalid's rejection hadn't had anything to do with her past when she knew for a fact that it had.

It had been exactly the same last year when she had become engaged to Adam Palmer. Everything had been fine at first; Adam's parents had seemed genuinely delighted about her joining their family. However, all that had changed when they had discovered that her brother was in prison. Although Sam had tried to make them understand that Michael's behaviour had nothing to do with her, the pointed remarks about the detrimental effect it could have on Adam's career if people found out that his future brother-in-law was in prison had been impossible to ignore.

In the end Sam had done the only thing she could have done and ended their engagement, given back the ring and wished Adam well. At the time she had believed it was the right thing to do, that it wasn't fair to expect Adam to continually have to defend her. But had that been the only reason? she wondered suddenly. Or had part of her known that she hadn't really loved Adam, that she had agreed to marry him simply because he had seemed like suitable husband material; that her feelings for Adam could never compare to how she had felt about Khalid?

'Come. We should get back.'

Khalid touched her arm, his fingers barely making contact with her flesh, and yet to Sam it felt as though every fingertip had left an imprint on her skin. Her eyes rose to his before she could stop them and she saw to the very second when he realised what was happening.

'Sam.' His voice was low, filled with an awareness that made her heart race. Khalid might give the impression of being indifferent to her but he couldn't quite match his actions to his words, it seemed.

He took a slow step towards her and Sam found herself holding her breath. All around them the world was silent, waiting to see what would happen. Sam knew that she wanted him to kiss her, wanted to feel his mouth on hers, wanted to taste him and absorb his very essence, but was it wise? Did she really want to risk subjecting herself to that kind of heartache again? When his hand rose to touch her again, she stepped back.

'No!' She gave a harsh little laugh. 'Let's not allow

the desert's magic to get to us, Khalid. There's no point creating problems, is there?'

Khalid didn't say a word, certainly didn't try to stop her as she turned and made her way down the path to where Omar was waiting patiently for them. Sam took a deep breath as she stroked the horse's neck. She was right and Khalid knew she was too. They needed to stick to the plans they had made for the future, a future that didn't entail them having another relationship. It shouldn't be that difficult. She simply had to remember that Khalid was only really interested in her skills as a doctor these days, not in *her* as a woman. Oh, maybe he had been tempted just now but it hadn't meant anything, not really. It had been merely the instinctive response of a red-blooded male finding himself in close proximity to a woman he'd once had an affair with.

They rode back to the palace in silence. Sam had nothing to say and it appeared that Khalid felt the same way. He stopped outside the female guest quarters and dismounted then turned to help her down, but this time she ignored his outstretched hand as she slid to the ground.

'Thank you for taking me with you. The view was stupendous,' she said politely, her heart aching. She was who she was and Khalid was who *he* was; they couldn't change that even if they wanted to. It was only in fairy tales that a girl like her was swept off her feet by a handsome prince and lived happily ever after.

'I'm glad you enjoyed it.' He paused and Sam found that she was holding her breath as she waited for him to continue, even though she knew it was silly.

'I used to imagine taking you there to watch the sun

rise,' he said, his deep voice grating. 'It was a dream of mine and it was good to have it come true at last.'

He touched her cheek, just the barest whisper of his fingertips across her skin, before he swung himself back into the saddle. Sam bit her lip as she watched him ride away, watched well after he had disappeared from view. Tears ran down her cheeks but she didn't even notice them. All she could see was the regret in Khalid's eyes as he had made that confession. Maybe they did intend to keep their distance but now she understood that it wasn't going to be any easier for him than it was for her.

They reached the encampment shortly before noon. Khalid told the driver to park beneath the awning that had been constructed to shelter the vehicles from the sun. He climbed out of the powerful four-by-four and waited while the other vehicles drew up alongside.

It had been a last-minute decision to travel in three cars rather than the two he had planned on using. However, he had felt the need to be on his own as they made their way to the first of their desert camps. Being with Sam that morning had unsettled him even more and he'd needed time to get himself under control. However, as he watched her climb out of the second car, he realised that he still felt as raw and as emotional as he had done when they had watched the sun rise together. Having Sam there, in the place that was dearest to his heart, had touched something deep inside him, as his subsequent actions had proved.

'Phew! I don't think I've ever been any place so hot!'

Khalid shrugged aside the thought when he heard Jess's comment. He summoned a smile, keeping his gaze on her rather than allowing it to wander in the direction it wanted to go. He had to remember that Sam was just another member of the team and treat her as such.

'This is the hottest part of the day and normally we would avoid travelling at this time. However, I wanted to get set up so we don't waste time later on. I sent a couple of men out to spread the word that the clinic will be open this afternoon.'

'Oh, right. I see. Good thinking, boss.'

Jess grinned at him and Khalid smiled back, appreciating the fact that she didn't stand on ceremony around him. He hated it when that happened, when people couldn't see beyond his position. Sam had been exactly the same. She hadn't fawned over him either. She had treated him simply as a colleague. And a man.

The thought was too near the knuckle. Khalid blanked it out as he pointed out which tents the women would use. There were four women in the team and four men, which had made it easier when it had come to their accommodation. Although he prided himself on having a more worldly view, he had no intention of alienating his fellow countrymen by ignoring the proprieties. Men and women would be strictly segregated when it came to their washing and sleeping facilities.

Khalid turned to Peter while the women went off to explore their tent. 'I'm not sure how many people will turn up this afternoon. We could get a couple of dozen or we could get no one at all.'

'It's always the same,' Peter replied easily, mopping the sweat from his brow with a crumpled handkerchief. 'It can take several days before people drum up enough confidence to visit the clinic, I find.'

'Really?' Khalid sighed. 'It could take longer than I thought it would, then. There are so many people who need treating and I was hoping to get started as soon possible. We're only here for a matter of weeks and I hate to think that we're wasting valuable time.'

'You have to be patient,' Peter advised him. 'Once a few folk have received treatment, more will follow. It's a sort of snowball effect and gathers its own momentum.'

'I'm not sure about snowballs in the desert,' Khalid said wryly, glancing at the sky. 'I rather think they'd melt before they gathered any momentum.'

Peter laughed as he wandered off to fetch his bag. The trucks were being unloaded now so Khalid went over to supervise as the crates containing their equipment were lifted out. There was a separate tent for the clinic, another for the operating theatre and a third that would house the more fragile pieces of equipment like the ECG machine and ultrasound scanner. These would run off solar-powered generators donated by his brother.

Khalid made sure everything was put in the right place then he and Han, the Thai male nurse, set about unpacking. It was a long and tedious job but it gave him something to do, took his mind off Sam and all the other issues. He sighed as he stowed a box of dressings on a shelf. Everything came back to Sam, didn't it? Every thought he had started or ended with her and it had to stop. Sam was here to do a job. If he said it often enough then maybe he would believe it...

And maybe he wouldn't.

Sam finished unpacking and stowed her bag under the bed. Although the facilities were nowhere near as luxurious as those at the summer palace, she was surprised by how comfortable their accommodation was. She, Jess, Anna, the paediatrician, and Aminah, their nurse-cum-interpreter, who had arrived that morning, each had their own little cubicle containing a bed plus a locker for their clothes. There was even a bathroom leading off from one end of the tent, which sported a toilet cubicle plus a shower and a washbasin. They had everything they needed and she found herself thinking how much planning must have gone into it. Obviously, Khalid had thought long and hard about this venture.

She sighed when once again she found herself thinking about him. It was only natural, of course, but she knew how quickly one thought could lead to another and wished she could stop. Maybe it would help if she kept busy, she decided. If her mind was fully occupied then no more stray thoughts could slip in.

'I'm going to see if I can help unpack the equipment,' she told the others.

'I'd offer to come with you only I'm bushed,' Anna said, fanning herself with a magazine. She was older than the rest of them, possibly in her late forties, with bright red hair and dozens of freckles on her face. Now she grimaced. 'It's so hot I think I'm going to melt.'

Sam laughed. 'We probably all will. Why don't you try out the shower? It might cool you down.'

'Good idea.'

Anna headed for the bathroom while Sam left. She could see some men unloading one of the trucks and made her way over to them. They were taking the crates into a tent at the far end of the camp, so she followed them. There was a double entry, two openings joined by a short tunnel, which could be zipped shut at each end. Both openings were wide open and she stepped inside, pausing in amazement as she took in the sight that greeted her. That couldn't be an ultrasound scanner, not here in the middle of the desert!

'Sam?'

She spun round so fast that she overbalanced and gasped when she felt herself pitch sideways. Khalid's hands shot out, gripping her forearms as he set her back on her feet. Sam felt a rush of heat flow through her, starting at the point where his fingers were clamped around her arms, and shuddered. Looking up, she stared into his face, wishing with all her heart that she didn't react this way whenever he touched her. It had been the same that morning when they had ridden into the desert and she hated it, hated the fact that she was so vulnerable. She didn't want to feel anything for him, but it seemed she was powerless to control her emotions where he was concerned.

'Sam.'

He said her name again yet it sounded very different this time and she had to force down the lump that came to her throat. To imagine that Khalid had regrets was more than she could bear. She needed him to be *sure*, to be certain that rejecting her had been the right thing to do. If she allowed herself to believe that he wished he hadn't done it, she would never be able to cope.

'Thanks. It wouldn't have been the best start if I'd ended up flat on my face.'

She gave a little laugh as she stepped back and Khalid didn't try to stop her. Relief washed over. Maybe he did have *some* regrets but deep down she knew that he would do the same thing again.

'Were you looking for me?' he asked, his voice devoid of emotion, and she breathed a little easier.

'Not really.' She glanced at the packing cases and shrugged. 'I just wondered if I could help. Obviously there's a lot to do if we hope to be ready in time for this afternoon's clinic.'

'It's kind of you but you must be tired after your late night,' he said courteously. 'It might be better if you tried to rest before clinic starts.'

'I'm fine.' Sam's spine stiffened. Maybe he was only trying to be considerate but she resented the fact that he thought she needed his advice. 'As I explained this morning, I'm used to functioning on very little sleep.'

'Indeed you did. I apologise.'

On the surface his tone hadn't altered and yet all of a sudden Sam felt her mind wing its way back to those moments when they had watched the sun rise. Seeing Khalid then had been a revelation. Even though she had always been aware of his heritage, she had never really thought about how different his life must be from hers. It hadn't seemed important but now she could see that it had been a key factor behind his rejection of her.

As a child, Sam had grown used to being the outsider. Parents had discouraged their children from making friends with her because she'd been the 'wrong sort'. Even at high school, she had never really fitted in. The boys had heard the rumours about her mother and had pursued her in the hope that she would be the same, while the girls had been openly hostile, disliking her for her looks and her intelligence as much as for her family's reputation.

University had been her salvation. Nobody had known about her background there and for the first time in her life Sam had been able to be herself. She had made friends and had gained confidence because of it. When the truth had surfaced during her final year of rotations, there had been some who had shunned her. However, most people had been prepared to accept her for who she was and not for what her family had done. She had thought that her background had no longer mattered but she'd been mistaken. It had mattered to Khalid.

Sadness ran through as she realised that she no longer felt angry about what he had done. She should never have got involved with him in the first place and certainly never allowed their relationship to reach the stage where they had been on the point of making love. Although she'd had boyfriends before Khalid, her mother's behaviour had made her wary of having a physical relationship with them.

She hadn't slept with anyone until her engagement, in fact, and only then because Adam had expected it when they were to be married. It had been a bitter disappointment for them both. Although Sam had tried to respond, she'd been unmoved by Adam's lovemaking and had felt relieved when it was over. If she was honest, she had never wanted any man that way...

Except Khalid.

She took a deep breath. She must never forget that in Khalid's eyes she was tainted goods. Maybe he had wanted to sleep with her, but he had realised at the very last moment that it would be a mistake. And in all honesty, she couldn't blame him. Khalid could have his pick of women, women who were far more suited to his lifestyle. What would he want with someone like her?

Maybe she had achieved a lot but she could never completely leave her past behind. Although her mother had died some years ago, she kept in touch with her brother and visited him whenever she could. Michael still had a couple of months of his sentence left to serve and she was hoping that with the right support he would make something of his life. She didn't intend to turn her back on him just because it wasn't convenient to have an ex-jailbird for a brother and anyone she met would need to understand that.

She sighed. The likelihood of her meeting a man she would fall in love with was so remote that it wasn't worth considering. There was only one man who had fulfilled that criterion and she wasn't venturing down that path again.

CHAPTER FIVE

By THREE O'CLOCK everything was ready. Khalid looked around, delighted that they had achieved so much in such a short time. The clinic looked very professional with its neat little examination cubicles and shelves bearing their equipment. Once again he had taken care to observe the proprieties. The tent was divided into two sections, one for the men and one for the women. Granted, people would need to queue up together while they waited to be seen but that was acceptable. Even among the desert people changes were occurring and it was no longer considered necessary to strictly segregate the sexes.

'It's looking good, isn't it?'

'It is,' Khalid agreed, as Tom Kennedy, their anaesthetist, came to join him. 'How about Theatre? Are you happy with it?'

'It's better than I dared hope,' Tom enthused. 'The lighting is ace and as for those extractor fans to remove any dust…well, they're brilliant!'

'You can thank my brother for them. He found a supplier and told them what we needed. They weren't sure if they could deliver them on time but Shahzad managed to *persuade* them.'

Tom grinned. 'One of the perks of having royal blood, I imagine. People are more disposed to bend over backwards and do what you want.'

Khalid sighed as Tom wandered off. There were advantages to being his father's son but there were drawbacks too. He had learned at an early age that he could never accept people at face value and that he always needed to be wary of their reasons for making friends with him. Far too many had tried to use him to their advantage. It had made him cautious about making friends. There were very few folk he trusted completely, people like Peter and Tom....

And Sam.

He frowned as he glanced over to where she was organising her desk. He had trusted Sam from the moment they had met. He had never felt wary about her motives for befriending him, never doubted her integrity, not even when his father's security team had handed him a detailed report about her background.

Checking up on the people he met was the norm for someone in his position. However, the account of her mother's numerous affairs and her brother's imprisonment for fraud hadn't fazed him. Sam possessed an innate honesty that had made him feel comfortable from the outset and he had known that he could trust her. It made him feel even worse about the way he had treated her. Even though he had done what he had for *her* benefit, he knew that he had hurt her in the cruellest way possible.

'Can you ask her if I can examine her breasts?' Sam said quietly, and then waited while Aminah translated her request. The nurse not only spoke English but a number of dialects particular to the desert tribes. Now she looked up and nodded.

'Yes, it is fine, Doctor. Please continue.'

'Thank you.'

Sam smiled reassuringly at the girl. Noor was just sixteen years of age and had recently given birth to her first child. She looked little more than a child herself with her long dark hair hanging in a thick plait to her waist. She had come to the clinic with her mother and her aunts, complaining of sore breasts, and Sam was keen to ensure that she received appropriate treatment.

Once Noor had removed her dress, Sam examined her, nodding when she discovered what she had expected to find. The girl was suffering from mastitis—inflammation of the breast tissue. Bacteria had entered her breasts while she had been feeding her baby, probably because her nipples were cracked. It was fairly common during the first month of breastfeeding but none the less painful because of that.

Sam explained that she would give Noor antibiotics to clear up the infection plus analgesics for the pain. Expressing milk would help to relieve the engorgement and make her more comfortable too. It all took time as everything needed to be translated but in the end they got there. Noor looked much happier when she left, clutching the tablets Sam had prescribed for her. Although Sam had asked her to come back so she could check on her progress, she wasn't anticipating any problems.

The time flew past and before she knew it, night was falling. Sam sighed as she flexed her shoulders after her last patient left. She had treated over a dozen women, which was pretty good considering this had been their first session. She looked up and smiled when Peter came over to her.

'We didn't do too badly, did we? How many folk did you see?'

'Six,' Peter informed her, sitting down on the edge of the desk. He frowned. 'Looks as though TB's going to be our biggest problem. Four of the men I saw were exhibiting classic symptoms of it.'

'It's difficult to treat unless you can keep on top of it,' Sam observed. 'The problem is that we're only going to be here for a limited time and it will take longer than that to clear it up.'

'I know,' Peter agreed worriedly. 'That's something I need to discuss with Khalid. I'd hate to think that we make a start on sorting people out and leave them in the lurch.'

'Difficult,' Sam said sympathetically.

She looked round when she heard footsteps and felt her heart jolt when she saw Khalid approaching them. All of a sudden she couldn't face the thought of having to speak to him. Her first clinic had gone extremely well and she wanted to focus on that, focus on the job she had come to do, rather than think about the emotional turmoil she experienced whenever he was near. She hastily gathered together her notes and stood up.

'I'd better get these filed and then I think I'll treat myself to a shower before dinner.'

'Oh, right. Good idea,' Peter agreed, looking faintly startled by the speed of her departure.

Sam made her way to the tiny office that had been set up in one corner of the tent and filed her notes. Khalid and Peter were deep in conversation when she left and she doubted if either noticed her departure. She sighed as she made her way to the women's tent. That was what she wanted, surely, that Khalid should treat her as just another member of the team, and it was ridiculous to feel ever so slightly miffed that he hadn't tried to speak to her. She showered and changed into clean jeans and a fresh T-shirt then made her way to the canteen. Jess and Anna were already there and they waved when she went in.

'Come and have a drink,' Jess instructed. 'There's no alcohol in it but it's delicious all the same. I could definitely get hooked on it.'

'Thanks.' Sam accepted a glass of straw-coloured liquid and sipped it tentatively. Her brows rose. 'It *is* good. What is it?'

'No idea,' Anna informed her cheerily. 'It's hitting the spot, though, and that's good enough for me.'

They all laughed and that seemed to set the tone for the evening. Whether by accident or design, it ended up with the women sitting together and the men sitting at the other side of the tent. The food was excellent, some sort of vegetable stew served with rice, followed by fresh figs and yoghurt. Cups of thick aromatic coffee rounded off the meal and Sam sighed appreciatively.

'That was delicious. I don't know what I was expecting but it definitely wasn't anywhere near as good as that.'

'I'm glad you enjoyed it.'

The sound of Khalid's voice brought her head up and she felt the colour rush to her cheeks when she discovered he was standing by her chair. He smiled around the table, his gaze lingering no longer on her than it did on the others and yet Sam knew that he was as aware of her as she was of him. All of a sudden the air seemed to be charged with tension, filled with a host of feelings she couldn't even begin to decipher, and her breath caught. She could lie to herself and claim that she was over him but what was the point? She wasn't over him. Maybe she never would get over him either.

Khalid could feel the tension in the air, thick and hot and disturbing. It took every scrap of will power he could muster to act as though nothing was wrong.

'We did extremely well today,' he said, focusing on the reason why he had stopped by the women's table. His only concern was making a success of this venture, making sure that his countrymen received the treatment they deserved. It had absolutely nothing to do with Sam and this need he felt to be with her. 'Between us we saw over three dozen people, which is an excellent result for our first clinic.'

'Sam must have seen at least a dozen patients,' Jess put in.

'Indeed.' He nodded, his eyes drifting to Sam before he forced them away again. He didn't want to look at her, couldn't afford to when his emotions were so raw. If he looked at her then he might be tempted to do something he must never do. He must never forget that Sam couldn't be part of his life.

'Obviously the women are in need of all the help we can give them,' he said, struggling to ignore the pain that ripped through him at the thought. 'It makes it all the more vital that we see as many as we can while we're here and even think about setting up a permanent clinic, not only for the mothers and babies but for everyone.'

'Would that be possible?' Sam interjected. 'I mean,

the people we're dealing with are nomadic and they move around a lot. It would be difficult to choose a suitable site for a clinic, surely?'

'That's true.' Khalid summoned a smile, trying not to let her see the effect she had on him. He had known many women, women who were far more beautiful than her, and yet none of them had had the effect on him that she had. It made him see how dangerous it would be to spend too much time with her while they were here.

'It will take a lot of thought before we can make any definite plans but it's something that needs to be considered.' He smiled around the table. 'Right. I'll say good-night. Thank you all for your hard work today. I'll see you in the morning.'

Khalid left the canteen and made his way to the men's tent. Peter arrived a few minutes later and they chatted for a while before Khalid switched off his lamp. He lay in the darkness, willing himself not to think about anything except what the next day might bring, but it was impossible. Closing his eyes, he let his mind drift, unsurprised when thoughts of Sam came flooding in. For the past six years he hadn't allowed himself to think about her, but now it seemed he couldn't stop. Had he been right to end their relationship? Or had he made a terrible mistake?

Even leaving aside the matter of all the publicity that would have been generated if their relationship had become common knowledge, it had appeared that he'd had no choice. But what if they could have found a compromise? He spent at least six months of every year in England so surely they could have worked around the problem. Sam could have visited Azad but not lived here all the time. Then she could have continued her career and not had to give it up. He couldn't understand why he hadn't considered the idea before. It could have worked...or it could have done until they'd had children.

He sighed. Everything would have had to change if they'd had a child. Although his brother was next in line to the throne, Shahzad and his wife had produced only girls so far and under current laws they could never succeed their father. If he and Sam had had a son, their child would have become heir to the throne. Sam would have been faced with an impossible choice then. Either she would have had to live in Azad permanently or she would have had to allow their child to be brought up here without her.

It was the same choice Khalid's own mother had had to make and look how it had turned out. Although his parents had loved one other, his mother hadn't been able to cope with the restrictions of life in Azad. Even though the status of women in the country was improving, there was a long way to go before it reflected modern-day European standards. Maybe Sam would have coped for a while but in the end she too would have found it too constraining and left.

The thought of the heartache it would have caused not only for them but for any children they might have had was more than Khalid could bear. When he married, he would choose a woman who understood the kind of life he had to offer her. And that meant that he could never choose Sam.

Sam was awake before dawn the next day. Surprisingly, she'd slept well and felt completely refreshed as she quietly made her way to the bathroom. Everyone else was fast asleep so as soon as she'd showered and dressed, she crept out of the tent. She shivered as the pre-dawn chill hit her, wishing that she had thought to put on a sweater. She was tempted to go back for one but the thought of waking the others stopped her. Hopefully a cup of coffee would warm her up.

She made her way to the canteen, sighing in relief when she spotted a fresh jug of coffee on the counter. She helped herself to a cup, nodding her thanks when one of the cooks offered her a dish of fruit and yoghurt. There were some tiny sweet pastries as well, dripping with honey and covered with almonds, and she accepted one of them too. She loaded everything onto a tray and carried it over to a table. She had just taken her first welcome sip of coffee when Khalid appeared.

He helped himself to coffee then looked around and Sam held her breath. Would he join her or would he opt to sit by himself? The sensible part of her hoped it would be the latter while another part hoped he would join her and she sighed. It would be so much easier if she could decide what she wanted and stick to it.

His gaze finally alighted on her and she saw him hesitate. Was it as difficult for him to decide what to do as it was for her? she wondered. If anyone had asked her how she'd felt about him a couple of weeks ago, the word she would have used to describe her feelings would have been indifferent. She had got over her anger, dealt with her pain, put it all behind her—or so she had thought. However, as she watched him walk towards her, Sam realised that *indifference* was the last thing she felt. So what had changed? Was it being with Khalid again that had re-awoken these feelings? Were they an echo from the past, a reflection of what she had felt all those years ago, ghost feelings but not actually real?

She bit her lip, praying it was so. Getting involved again with Khalid was out of the question. They'd had their chance and it would be foolish to rekindle their relationship. She knew that so why was her heart racing? Why was she finding it so hard to breathe? If she knew the answers to those questions then maybe she would know what to do.

'Good morning. You're up early.' Khalid sat down, feeling his heart hammering inside his chest. If there'd been any way he could have avoided speaking to Sam he would have done so, but it would have been too revealing if he had ignored her. He mustn't single her out. He must treat her exactly the same as any other member of the team. Now he smiled at her. 'Were you ready for your breakfast?'

'Uh-huh. I needed a cup of coffee to warm me up.' She glanced at her cup and grimaced. 'I'd forgotten how cold it is first thing of a morning.'

The comment immediately reminded him of what had happened the previous day. His hands clenched because he could still feel the imprint of her body where it had rested against him as they had ridden out to the desert. He had never taken anyone there before. It was such a special place, filled with so many precious memories that he had never wanted to share it, yet it had felt right to take Sam there.

'The extremes of temperature come as a surprise to lot of people,' he said quietly, his heart aching. Would he be able to visit that spot again or would it be too painful to stand there and watch the sun rise without her beside him? He drove the thought from his head, knowing that it was foolish to dwell on it. Sam was never going to be part of his life and he had to accept that.

'The contrast between the heat of the day and the bitter cold of the night catches a lot of people unawares.
It's been the cause of several potentially life-threatening
incidents in the past couple of years.'

'Really? Why? What happened?' she asked, frowning.

Khalid's hands clenched once more as he fought the
urge to smooth away the tiny furrows marring her brow.
He mustn't touch her, couldn't afford to do so when his
emotions were so raw. Look what had so nearly happened yesterday. If Sam hadn't had the sense to stop
him, he would have kissed her and heaven alone knew
what would have happened then. In his heart he knew
that if he kissed her, he would be lost.

'There's been several occasions when tourists have
found themselves stranded in the desert and ended up
spending the night out here,' he explained, confining
himself to answering her question. It was safer that way,
less stressful to focus on something other than his own
turbulent emotions. 'Although they may have made provision for the daytime heat, they hadn't thought about
how cold it gets at night. Consequently, several people
have ended up in hospital suffering from exposure.'

'Good heavens!' Sam exclaimed. 'But surely any
tourists should be discouraged from driving around
out here on their own.'

'They should.' Khalid picked up his cup and took a
fortifying sip of coffee. He had never considered himself to be an overly emotional person—just the opposite,
in fact. However, when he was with Sam he couldn't
seem to find the right balance and it was unnerving to
realise that. It was an effort to focus on the conversation.

'In fact, my brother, Shahzad, is currently working

with several of the major tour operators to make them understand how important it is that they discourage their clients from exploring on their own. Anyone wishing to drive out into the desert should do so only as part of a properly organised excursion.'

'It makes sense,' Sam agreed, picking up her pastry and nibbling off a corner. She put it back on the plate then delicately licked a smear of honey off her fingers, unaware of the havoc she was causing him.

Khalid looked away, trying to control the surge of desire that rushed through him. She hadn't done that to be provocative, he told himself sternly, but it made no difference. The vision of her pink tongue licking the sticky residue off her fingers was one that was going to stay with him for a long time to come.

He pushed back his chair, unable to cope with anything else. He needed a breathing space, time to get his emotions safely stowed away in the box where they normally resided. 'I'll leave you to enjoy your breakfast,' he said, relieved to hear that he sounded normal even though he didn't feel it. 'Clinic starts at seven this morning so I'll see you then.'

He left the canteen and made his way to Theatre. Han was already there, checking the equipment, so Khalid helped him. He had an operation scheduled for that morning, nothing too complicated, just resetting a femur that hadn't aligned properly. He and Han ran through a checklist of what he would need before the nurse left to get something to eat.

Khalid stayed on, going over the list once more even though he knew he had everything he needed. However, it was better to keep busy, better to stop his mind wandering down more dangerous paths. He would focus on his work and simply hope that one day he would be able to speak to Sam without it causing such havoc. All he needed to do was adjust the way he thought about her, see her purely as a colleague and nothing more.

He sighed as the image of her licking her fingers flooded his mind. One day. But obviously not *that* day!

CHAPTER SIX

THEY HELD TWO clinics: one early in the morning and one in the late afternoon so they could avoid the worst of the heat. Both were extremely busy. Sam was surprised by how many women turned up as well as by the variety of their complaints. Being used to the system in the UK, where separate ante- and post-natal clinics were the norm, it was a challenge to switch between both aspects of her job depending on what was required.

Several of the women were in an advanced stage of pregnancy and although they appeared healthy, she was keen to ensure that nothing happened to endanger them or their babies during or immediately after the birth. She decided that the best way to do this was by training the local midwives about the need for good hygiene. As soon as the last of her patients left, she sought out Khalid, knowing that she would need his help if she hoped to make a start on this very important task.

He was just leaving Theatre when she tracked him down and she waited while he deposited his gown in the hamper. Beneath it, he was wearing pale green scrubs and she felt her pulse leap as she took stock of the way the damp cotton had molded itself to his powerful chest. He turned, coming to an abrupt halt when he saw her standing in the doorway. Just for a moment his expression was unguarded and Sam felt a rush of confusion fill her. Why was he looking at her like that? He'd been the one to end their relationship and it didn't make sense to see that desire in his eyes.

'Were you looking for me?'

His tone was cool, so cool that she realised she must have imagined it. Khalid didn't desire her. Oh, maybe he had done so at one time, maybe he had even felt a tiny echo of it the other day too, but he had soon got over it. All it had taken was that article in the tabloid press to make him see how foolish it would be to involve her in his life on a permanent basis.

'Yes. Is this a good time? Or would you prefer me to leave it till later?' she asked as calmly as she could. There was no point thinking about the past, distant or recent. Khalid had done the only thing a man in his position could have done and had rid himself of a potential embarrassment. And he would do exactly the same again.

'Now's fine.' He led the way, sitting down on one of the empty packing cases that had been placed near the entrance of the tent for that very purpose. Glancing up, he smiled at her. 'Have a seat. My office may be somewhat informal but I hope the view makes up for it.'

'It certainly does.' Sam laughed as she sat down beside him, feeling some of her tension melt away. Shading her eyes against the glare of the lowering sun, she sighed appreciatively. 'I never expected the desert to be so beautiful. I mean, you see pictures on TV and get an impression of its vastness and its emptiness but it doesn't do it justice. There's something...well, magical about it that draws you in, isn't there?'

'Yes. That's how I've always felt about it.' He turned to look at her and she shivered when she saw the warmth in his gaze. 'It's not often that people who aren't born and raised in this environment appreciate its beauty that way, Sam.'

'No?' She shrugged, realising that she was in danger of stepping into dangerous waters. She wasn't trying to promote a bond between them, certainly wasn't trying to curry favour. She hurried on, deciding it would be safer to confine her remarks to what she wanted to speak to him about.

'Anyway, I know you're busy so I'll cut straight to the chase. I saw a lot of women today in the latter stages of pregnancy and although most of them were healthy enough, I'm keen to ensure they stay that way.'

'Of course. So what are you planning on doing?' he said smoothly.

Sam breathed a little easier when she heard nothing more than professional interest in his voice. If they could focus strictly on work, it would be so much easier. At least it would for her. The thought that Khalid might not be experiencing the same problems she was having was upsetting but she refused to think about it.

'I was wondering if it would be possible to visit some of the settlements and teach the local midwives about the need for good hygiene. I know from the research I've done that a lot of post-natal problems can be prevented if extra care is taken in the days following a birth.'

'I understand where you're coming from but I'm not sure if it's feasible,' he said slowly. 'We're aiming to hold two clinics a day and I can't see how there would be enough time to visit the camps as well, unless you worked seven days a week and that's out of the question.'

'Why?' She turned and looked at him. 'I'm more than happy to work every day, Khalid. I certainly didn't come here expecting to have a holiday!'

'I'm sure you didn't. However, you need to allow for the fact that working under these conditions is vastly different from what you are used to.' He shook his head. 'No. There's no way that I can allow you to work every day of the week without a break. It wouldn't be right, Sam.'

'So are you going to take time off?' she demanded. Her brows rose when he didn't answer. 'Well, are you?'

'It's different for me,' he said shortly, standing up. 'I'm used to the conditions out here and I don't find it as tiring as you will do. I don't need to take time off.'

'Oh, I see. You're a super-hero, are you, Khalid? You don't get tired like we mere mortals do.' She laughed bitterly as she stood up. 'It must be wonderful to know that you are immune to all the pressures that other folk have to contend with.'

'That wasn't what I meant,' he said flatly. 'I'm as susceptible to pressure as anyone else is.'

'Really? So that's why you couldn't wait to end our relationship, was it? Because you couldn't handle the pressure of having your name linked to me, a woman with a less than perfect past!'

Sam hadn't meant to say that. When the words erupted from her lips, she felt sick with embarrassment. Her eyes rose to Khalid's in horror and she felt her heart sink when she saw the anger on his face. 'I'm sorry. I should never have said that,' she began.

'No. You shouldn't.' His voice grated, anger and some other emotion vying for precedence. 'I did what I had to do, Sam. And I did it for your sake rather than mine, although I don't expect you to believe me. Now, if that's all, there are things I need to attend to.'

He walked away and the very stiffness of his posture told her that he was deeply insulted by the accusation. Why? Once that article had appeared, he had lost no time in ending their relationship. Every word she'd said had been justified, but Khalid refused to admit it. Why was that? Because he felt guilty about the way he had treated her?

She tried to tell herself that it was the answer but she didn't really believe it. There had been more to his decision to break up with her than she had thought and it was worrying to wonder if she had misread the situation. She could accept what had happened when she had believed that she understood his reasons but it was far less easy to accept it now that doubts had crept in.

Her breath caught as she recalled what Khalid had said. He had claimed that he had done it for her benefit, which implied that he hadn't wanted to break up with her for his own sake, as she had assumed. It cast a completely different slant on what had happened, made her feel edgy and unsure and that was the last thing she needed. She couldn't afford to start wondering about his motives. It would only give rise to hope and that was something she couldn't risk. She and Khalid were never going to get back together. He didn't want it to happen and neither did she…

Did she?

Khalid was aware that he had handled things very badly. Instead of keeping his cool, he had allowed his emotions to get the better of him. As he stepped into the shower, he could feel anger bubbling up inside him. He needed to maintain his control or Sam would grow suspicious. The last thing he wanted was to have to explain why he had felt it necessary to end things with her. What if she told him that he'd been wrong, that she could have handled the media interest their relationship would have attracted? It would be so tempting to believe her and even more tempting to consider trying again.

He sighed as he rinsed the lather off his body. There was no chance of them resuming their relationship. Even if Sam did believe she could handle the publicity, she would never cope with the restrictions of living in Azad. She was a modern woman who was used to living life on her terms and the fact that she would need to adhere to such archaic principles would only frustrate her.

Their relationship wouldn't last—it couldn't do. And there was no way that he was going to put himself in the position of having his heart broken. He had seen what it had done to his father, how his father had suffered after his mother had left, and he wasn't prepared to suffer the same kind of heartache. Getting back with Sam was out of the question even if it was what she wanted, which he very much doubted.

Peter had told him about her engagement last year. It had been a shock and an even bigger one when she had ended it a few months later. Although Khalid had no idea what had gone wrong, realistically he knew that she would meet someone else at some point, fall in love and settle down to start a family. It was what she deserved yet he couldn't pretend that he was happy at the thought of her loving another man and having his child. Not when it was what he had wanted so desperately. However, it proved unequivocally that Sam had moved on, put the past behind her and was looking to the future. And he certainly didn't feature in her future plans.

Dinner was a quiet affair. Sam wasn't sure if it was because everyone was tired after the busy day they'd had, but they seemed unusually subdued. Nobody lingered over coffee and by eight p.m. she and the other women were in their tent.

'I don't know about you lot but I'm bushed.' Jess gave a massive yawn. 'Oh, 'scuse me!'

'Don't apologise,' Anna told her, covering her own mouth with her hand. 'I'm shattered too. I don't know if it's the heat or what but I can't remember ever feeling so tired before. I feel like a limp rag.'

'I know what you mean.' Sam chuckled as she shimmied into her pyjama pants. 'I feel as though someone has wrung all the stuffing out of me! Maybe Khalid was right.'

'Right about what?' Jess queried, crawling into her bed. She tucked the sleeping bag around her then looked questioningly at Sam. 'Come on—give. What did Khalid say?'

'Oh, nothing much,' Sam muttered, wishing she hadn't mentioned it. She really didn't want to discuss what she and Khalid had been talking about earlier when it would only remind her of all the unanswered questions roaming around her head. However, there was no way she could avoid it when Jess was waiting for an answer. 'I had an idea about visiting the camps to teach the local midwives about the need for good hygiene.'

'Sounds like a good idea to me,' Jess interjected, and Sam sighed.

'I thought so but Khalid wasn't keen. He said it was

too much, what with all the clinics we have scheduled.'
She gave a little shrug as she wriggled into her sleeping bag. 'He didn't approve of me working seven days
a week, apparently, although what I'm supposed to do
with my free time is anyone's guess.'

'I suppose he does have a point,' Anna conceded. 'I
mean, look at us. We're absolutely knackered and we've
only done one full day!'

Everyone laughed when she pulled a wry face, Sam
included. However, she couldn't help thinking that there
had been more to Khalid's refusal to consider her proposal than mere concern for her wellbeing. Maybe he
preferred to call the shots and not be guided by anyone else. After all this was his project and he might
feel somewhat proprietorial about what happened while
they were here.

Sam tried to convince herself it was that as she settled down to sleep, but she didn't really believe it. She
had a feeling that Khalid had rejected her proposal
mainly because it had been hers. It hurt to think that he
could be so petty so she tried not to dwell on it. In a very
short time the sound of gentle snoring told her that the
others were asleep, although she was still wide awake.

Rolling over, she thumped the pillow into shape and
tried to get comfortable. However, despite her weariness, she couldn't drop off. When the sound of hooves
echoed through the tent she sat up. It sounded as though
they had a visitor and at this time of the night it could
only mean that someone needed help.

Climbing out of her sleeping bag, Sam dragged a
sweater over her pyjamas then undid the tent flap. Low
lighting had been set up around the camp and in the dim
glow from the lanterns she could see a horseman talk-

ing to Khalid and Peter. It was obvious that something had happened and she wasted no time in going to see if she could help.

'What's going on?' she asked as she joined them. Khalid was speaking to the man and he barely glanced at her. Nevertheless, Sam felt the heat of his gaze like a physical touch and was glad that she had put on a sweater over her night attire. Colour touched her cheeks as she turned to Peter. Although Khalid might feign indifference, it was obvious that he was as aware of her as she was of him.

'Has something happened?' she said, trying not to dwell on the thought. It didn't matter how aware they were of each other because nothing was going to come of it.

'From what I can gather, there's been an accident at one of the settlements close to here—a fire apparently.' Peter glanced at Khalid and grimaced. 'I don't know how many people have been injured but it doesn't look too good, does it?'

'No, it doesn't,' Sam agreed, taking note of the grim expression on Khalid's face.

Khalid finished speaking to the horseman and turned to them. 'From what I can glean, there are at least three people injured—a woman and two children. We need to see what we can do to help.'

'I'll come with you,' Sam offered immediately. She shook her head when he opened his mouth to object. All of a sudden she was determined to get her own way over this even though she didn't understand why it was so important. 'You'll need a female doctor so it may as well be me. There's no point waking the others when I'm already awake.'

'If you so wish.' Khalid gave a tiny shrug before he turned and made his way to the supply tent.

Peter frowned as he watched him go. 'He could have been a bit more gracious. What's wrong with him? I've never known him be so short with folk before.'

'Oh, he's probably anxious to get things sorted out,' Sam declared, wishing it were that simple. She sighed as she went to get ready. That Khalid didn't want her along was obvious if Peter had picked up on it, but she wasn't going to let it deter her. She had come here to do a job and do it she would. With or without Khalid's approval.

Khalid knew that he had been less than gracious but he couldn't do anything about it. As he gathered together everything they might need when they reached the encampment, he told himself that it didn't matter. He wasn't going to try and win Sam over—that was the last thing he intended to do. So what difference did it make if he had been a little...well, short with her?

He added several litre bags of saline to the growing heap then lifted a box of sterile dressings off a shelf. Details of what had happened were sketchy. All he knew was that three people had been injured when an oil lamp had exploded so he needed to make whatever provision he could. He stowed everything into a couple of cardboard boxes and headed outside, relieved to find that his driver was already waiting beside the four-by-four. He tossed the boxes into the back then looked round when Peter and Sam came to join him, doing his best to treat them both as colleagues. There was no problem about treating Peter that way, of course, but it was a different story when it came to Sam.

In a fast sweep his eyes ran over her, greedily drinking in the sight she made as she stood there in the glow from the lanterns. She hadn't stopped to brush her hair and the silky tendrils curled around her face, making his fingers itch to smooth them behind her ears. Although she was wearing trousers and a heavy knit sweater to ward off the night's chill, he could see the hem of her pyjama top peeking out below it and realised that she must have simply dragged on some clothes over her night attire. His breath caught because beneath the all-concealing layers, he knew that she would be naked…

'Right. Let's get going.' He swung round, refusing to allow his mind to go any further down that path. Thinking about Sam naked was the last thing he should be doing.

They left the camp, following the route the horseman had taken. It was pitch black, the light from the vehicle's headlamps barely enough to take the edge off the Stygian gloom. Fortunately, their driver was a local man and unfazed by the task of driving them there under such extreme conditions. However, even Khalid was relieved when he spotted a glow of light on the horizon. Far too many people had come to grief trying to cross the desert at night for him to be complacent about the potential dangers. They drew up on the edge of the settlement. People were milling about, dealing with the aftermath of the fire. He could see the remains of the tent near the centre of the compound and inwardly shuddered as he imagined how terrifying it must have been for the occupants to find themselves engulfed by flames.

'It must have been horrendous for the poor people who lived in that tent.'

Sam unwittingly reiterated his thoughts and he

sighed. He didn't need any reminders about how in tune they had always been, especially tonight when his emotions were so near the surface.

'I'll go and see where they've taken the injured,' he said shortly. 'Peter, if you and Sam could unload our supplies, it will save time.'

'Will do.'

Peter hopped out of the vehicle and set about unloading the boxes. Sam joined him, ignoring Khalid as she started dividing everything into three piles. Khalid paused but she didn't look up so he turned and made his way over to where a group of men were waiting to greet him. He couldn't have it all ways, couldn't treat her as a colleague one minute and expect her to respond as something more the next. It wasn't fair. He knew how he had to behave towards her and no matter how difficult it was proving to be, he must stick to it.

Sam finished sorting their supplies, making sure that they each had a selection of things they might need. Khalid was still talking to the men but he glanced round, lifting his hand to beckon her over. Picking up a box, she made her way over to him, trying to ignore the little ache that seemed to have lodged itself in the very centre of her heart.

So what if he had been short with her—what did it matter? She was here to help the injured and how Khalid felt about her wasn't the issue. Nevertheless, it was hard to hide how hurt she felt as she set the box on the ground. Maybe she shouldn't care how he treated her but she did even though she knew it was silly.

'I want you to deal with the woman,' he told her

briskly. 'Apparently, she isn't badly injured but she's pregnant and she's having pains.'

'How many weeks is she—do you know?' Sam asked quickly, forgetting her own feelings in her concern for her patient.

Khalid said something to the men. His expression was grave when he turned to her. 'Approximately twenty-eight.'

He didn't say anything else but he didn't need to. If Sam couldn't stop the woman's labour, the baby would be extremely premature. It would be worrying enough if the child was born in a highly equipped maternity unit but so much worse if it was born out here in the desert without the benefit of modern technology.

'I see.' She gave a little shrug. 'I'll go and see what's happening. Where is she?'

'In that tent over there.' Khalid pointed across the campsite, putting out his hand to stop her when she turned to leave. 'I'll be here with Peter. If you need me then ask one of the women to come and get me. OK?'

'Fine.' Sam nodded, doing her best not to let him see how his touch was affecting her. She took a deep breath as he released her. She had always been susceptible to his touch, always responded, and it seemed that little had changed. Not even the fact that he had treated her so harshly had managed to destroy her response to him.

Picking up the box, she made her way to the tent, her heart feeling like a lead weight inside her. She had thought she was over him, had truly believed that whatever she had felt six years ago was dead, but how could it be when just the touch of his hand could set off this kind of a reaction? It made her see how careful she needed to be. She didn't want to find herself back where she'd been six years ago. She had worked too hard to get over him to welcome that scenario. No, when she returned to England she intended to be free of any such destructive emotions. She had wanted Khalid once and had suffered for it too. She wasn't about to make the same mistake again.

It was a long night. By the time the sun started to edge above the horizon, Khalid was exhausted. Looking up from the makeshift operating table, he caught a glimpse of Peter's grey face and could tell that his friend was as weary as him.

'Another ten minutes and that should be it,' he said, turning his attention back to the child they were operating on. Four-year-old Ibrahim had suffered burns to his back and they had just excised the damaged tissue. Although his injuries weren't as severe as those of his elder brother, Jibril, he was suffering from shock. He was a very sick little boy and Khalid knew that the next twenty-four hours would be critical. He came to a swift decision.

'I'm going to have both the children airlifted to Zadra City. They need to be hospitalised if they're to have the best chance possible.'

'I agree.' Peter sighed. 'This little chap is going to need expert nursing if he's to pull through. And he won't receive that in the desert.'

'Exactly.' Khalid pulled off his mask as he stepped away from the table. 'I'll make the arrangements if you're happy to finish off here.'

'Not much more I can do,' Peter said stoically. 'Are you going to check on Sam and see how she's doing? Her patient might need to be transferred as well.'

'Yes.'

Khalid left the tent, gulping in a great lungful of cold air as he stepped out of its heated confines. It had been a long night and although they had done all they could, he wasn't sure if both boys would survive. Between their injuries and shock it would be touch and go and the thought made him feel extremely downhearted even though he was a realist and accepted that he couldn't save everyone who came under his care. Still, it would have been good to know that tonight had been a success. It might have helped make him feel better about the way he had treated Sam earlier. He *had* been short with her and, try as he may, he couldn't help feeling guilty about it, but, then, what was new? He had felt guilty about the way he had treated Sam for years.

Khalid sighed as he crossed the campsite. People were already up, lighting fires to prepare their breakfasts. The scent of wood smoke filled the air, reminding him of his childhood. His father had loved to go camping in the desert and had often taken Khalid and his mother and Shahzad with him. They had been magical times when they had been able to enjoy being together as a family and forget that his father was king, with all that it entailed.

Would he ever take his own children camping in the desert? he wondered. Ever be able to forge that special bond with them? He hoped so but it all depended on what happened in the future, if indeed he ever had a family of his own. The only woman he had ever wanted to have his children was Sam, but that was out of the question.

As though thinking about her had conjured her up, she appeared. Khalid's footsteps slowed. All of a sudden he was filled with a longing so intense that his breath caught. If he could turn back the clock then he wouldn't let her go. He would keep her with him and simply pray that somehow, *some way*, they could make their relationship work. Maybe there would have been problems, and maybe he would have suffered untold heartache, but would it have been any worse than this? Even if he had lost her in the end, at least he would have had her for part of his life. And that would have been so much better than this.

CHAPTER SEVEN

SAM TOOK A deep breath. It had been almost unbearably hot inside the tent, the smell of the camel dung used to fuel the fire filling her nostrils to the exclusion of everything else. Glancing around, she realised in surprise that people were already going about their day. Water was being boiled for coffee and some sort of grain turned into a kind of porridge. Her stomach rumbled and she realised in surprise that she was hungry.

'How's the mother?'

Sam jumped when Khalid appeared at her side, her heart racing as she fought to get a grip. She was tired after the long night attending to her patient and emotionally raw too. It took a lot of effort to maintain an outward show of composure.

'Not too bad, all things considered. The pains have stopped and I'm hopeful that she won't go into labour just yet, but she's obviously worried about her sons. How are they?'

'Not too good, I'm afraid.' He grimaced. 'The older boy has suffered quite extensive burns and the younger one, although not as badly burned, is very shocked. I've decided that they would be better off in hospital so I just need to make the necessary arrangements to get them there.'

'Surely it would be too much to drive them across the desert,' Sam said worriedly.

'It would. I'll have them transferred by helicopter. That way they should be there within the hour. Is the mother well enough to go with them or is it too risky to move her?'

Sam shook her head. 'No. I think she would be better off going with them. Not only will it stop her worrying so much about the boys but if she does go into labour then at least she will have all the facilities on hand. The baby won't stand much of a chance if it's born out here.'

'Right. That's what we'll do, then. I just wanted to know what you thought.' He gave her a quick smile. 'I didn't want to arrange for her to be moved against your wishes, Sam.'

'Thank you.' Sam returned his smile, feeling a little glow of happiness spring up inside her. It was good to know that he valued her opinion.

It was all systems go after that. Sam returned to the tent and with the aid of one of the women who spoke a little English explained to Jameela what was going to happen. It was obvious that the idea of traveling in the helicopter alarmed her but once she knew that her sons were going as well, she accepted it. Sam checked her over once more, relieved to find that her contractions hadn't started again. It seemed that the drugs she had given Jameela had worked, or they had done for now. All she could do was hope that if Jameela did go into labour, it wouldn't happen until she was safely in the hospital.

Half an hour later the helicopter arrived. It circled

the camp, looking for a place to land. Khalid and some of the men had marked out a suitable site and it set down there. As soon as the rotors stopped turning, he and Peter carried the two boys to the helicopter, where they were met by the on-board medics. Once the children were safely aboard, it was time to move Jameela. Sam held her hand while a couple of the women helped her walk to the helicopter. She could feel her trembling and squeezed her fingers.

'It will be fine, Jameela. There's no need to be scared,' she assured her, even though the poor soul couldn't understand a word she said.

Jameela smiled bravely as Sam let her go. She allowed the medics to help her on board and then the doors closed. Sam moved back out of the way, covering her face with her hands when the rotors began to turn, setting up a veritable sandstorm.

'Here.' Khalid pulled her to him, pressing her face against his shoulder as the sand swirled around them. He'd had the foresight to wrap a checked scarf around his head and he pulled it over his nose and mouth as the helicopter lifted off.

Sam clung to him, using his body as a buffer against the downdraught created by the helicopter as it rose. Her skin was stinging from the abrasive touch of the sand but at least she could breathe now that her face was pressed against his shoulder. With a final roar, the helicopter took to the skies and the air began to settle.

Sam raised her head, checking that it was safe to leave the protection of Khalid's shoulder, and found herself staring straight into his eyes. Just for a moment he stared right back at her as though frozen in time and then his head dipped as he claimed her mouth in a searing kiss that seemed to strike right to the very core of her being.

Sam knew she should push him away, knew that she should do anything necessary to stop what was happening, but she was powerless to resist the seductive taste of his mouth. It was only when she heard voices that she managed to break free but she could feel herself trembling, bone-shaking tremors that racked her body from head to toe.

Turning, she made her way to the four-by-four, afraid to stop, afraid to look back, afraid to do anything that would acknowledge what a fool she was. She had no idea why Khalid had kissed her but it didn't matter. The only thing that mattered was that she had wanted his kiss, wanted it desperately even though she knew how stupid it was. Tears filled her eyes as she climbed into the vehicle. She wasn't over him, as she had believed. She couldn't be. Not when he could make her feel like this.

Khalid was relieved when they arrived back at their camp. He got out of the vehicle, leaving Peter and Sam to sort out their supplies. Normally, he would have helped them, but he couldn't face it, couldn't face the thought of making conversation with Sam after what had happened. His mouth thinned as he strode into the men's tent. Why in the name of all that was holy had he kissed her? He hadn't planned on doing it, yet the moment he had looked into her eyes he had felt this overwhelming need to feel her mouth under his.

He cursed under his breath, aware that he had done the very thing he had sworn he wouldn't do. He had kissed Sam, held her close, tasted the sweetness of her lips, and it was going to be impossible to ignore what had happened. Even if he never mentioned it again, Sam knew how much he had wanted her and that was the last thing he needed. To know that *she* knew he was so vulnerable was more than he could bear.

Khalid went into the bathroom and stripped off his dusty clothes. Stepping into the shower, he tried to work out what he was going to say to her. He needed an excuse, a bona fide reason to explain why he had kissed her, but for the life of him he couldn't come up with anything. He could hardly admit that he had been so overcome with desire that he hadn't been able to stop himself kissing her, could he?

By the time he had dressed again, their first patients were starting to arrive. Han was sorting them out, giving everyone a number so they could be seen in turn. Khalid nodded to him as he made his way to his desk. Maybe it would be best to ignore what had happened and concentrate on the job he had come to do. Explaining his actions could cause more harm than good. He looked up as his first patient approached his desk and felt his heart grind to a halt when out of the corner of his eye he saw Sam come in. She glanced across at him then looked away when she realised he was watching her.

Khalid sighed. There was no point fooling himself. It wouldn't be possible to ignore that kiss when he and Sam had to work together. He had to think of an explanation for what had happened, one that had little bearing on the truth too.

It was another busy session. By the time clinic ended, Sam was reeling from exhaustion. She gathered up her notes, smiling her thanks when Aminah offered to file them for her.

'Thank you. I think I'll go and have a lie down before lunch,' she told the other woman. 'I feel absolutely shattered.'

'It's little wonder when you were up all night,' Aminah said solicitously. 'I shall attend to the notes and restock the shelves ready for this afternoon's clinic.'

Sam thanked her again then made her way to the women's tent. Jess was already there and she grimaced when Sam went in.

'How are you? Peter told me what happened. You must be exhausted.'

'I am rather,' Sam admitted, kicking off her shoes and lying down on her bed. She sighed. 'Has Peter heard how the children and their mother are doing?'

'No, not yet.' Jess shook her head. 'He said one of the boys was very badly injured, though. It didn't sound too hopeful to me.'

'Let's just pray for a miracle,' Sam said softly.

She closed her eyes, not wanting to discuss the night's events. She wanted to forget what had happened and especially what had gone on that morning. Heat poured through her veins as she recalled the feel of Khalid's mouth on hers. It might be six years since he had kissed her but she would have recognised the taste and feel of his lips anywhere. Why had he done it, though? What had possessed him to kiss her when they both knew it wasn't going to lead anywhere? Or did he think that he could pick up where he had left off and she wouldn't object?

The thought made anger flash through her. She wasn't going to become his plaything, if that's what he hoped. She valued herself far too highly for that. And the next time she saw him she would make it clear that if he had any ideas along those lines, he could forget them.

The day came to an end at last. Khalid gathered together his notes and took them over to the filing cabinet. He felt weary beyond belief, the busy day coming on top of the long night completely sapping his energy levels. He was the last to leave and he paused in the doorway, wondering if he could be bothered going for dinner. Although he knew that he should eat, it seemed too much of an effort, especially when he would have to face Sam.

He groaned. What on earth was he going to say to her about that kiss? The whole time he had been attending to his patients he had kept churning it over in the back of his mind, but he was no closer to finding an answer. How could he explain why he had experienced that burning need to feel her mouth under his when he didn't understand it himself?

His expression was grim as he bypassed the canteen. His tent was mercifully empty, the other occupants obviously having decided to go for dinner. Throwing himself down on his bed, Khalid stared at the canvas ceiling, wondering what to do. After all, nothing had changed. If he and Sam got involved again then she would end up getting hurt. And that was the one thing he had always wanted to avoid.

'Can I have a word?'

Khalid sat bolt upright when he recognised Sam's voice. She was standing just inside the entrance to the tent and he could tell immediately how tense she was. His heart began to race as he got to his feet because it was obvious why she had come. She wanted to know what was going on and it was up to him to find some sort of an explanation—if he could.

'Of course. Is there a problem?' he asked, stalling for time.

'I think so, yes.'

She stared back at him and Khalid felt his stomach sink when he saw the anger in her eyes. It was obvious that she had no intention of allowing him to fob her off, so he would have to come up with a really good reason to explain his actions.

'Why did you kiss me, Khalid? Was it because you thought it would be amusing to use me as your own personal plaything? Because if that's the case then you are sadly mistaken. I value myself too much to become any man's toy. Including yours.'

CHAPTER EIGHT

SAM COULD FEEL her heart racing as she waited for Khalid to answer. Maybe she could have couched the question a little more tactfully but she had no intention of tiptoeing around him. If Khalid was playing games with her then he needed to understand that she wasn't going to co-operate.

'You are getting things completely out of proportion.'

His voice was icy. Sam felt a shiver inch its way down her spine and fought to control it. She stared back at him, realising that he had never looked more unapproachable than he did at that moment as he pinned her with a look of disdain. However, if he hoped to deflect any more awkward questions by adopting that attitude, he could think again. He might be a royal prince, he might be rich and powerful beyond most people's wildest dreams, but that meant nothing as far as she was concerned. The only thing that mattered was the fact that he thought he could toy with her affections as he had toyed with them once before.

Anger surged through her and she glared at him. 'Am I indeed? So that kiss was the result of what exactly? Friendship? Lust? Old times' sake? Come on,

Khalid, you're the one with all the answers so you explain it to me.'

'I don't need to explain myself.'

He stared back at her, his handsome face looking as though it had been carved from stone. In other circumstances, Sam knew she would have found it intimidating to be on the receiving end of a look like that, but not now. Not when anger was bubbling inside her like red-hot lava. It was as though all the years of injustice she had suffered because of her background had melded together, chasing away any qualms she might have had.

'I disagree.' She laughed harshly. 'I'm sorry, Khalid, but I'm not one of your *subjects*. I have no intention of bowing and scraping before you if that's what you're hoping. I asked you a simple enough question and I expect an answer.'

'It happened, Sam, and it won't happen again. As far as I'm concerned that's the end of the matter.'

He went to step around her but she put out her hand and stopped him. 'And I'm expected to be happy with that, am I?' Tipping back her head, she glared up at him. 'I'm sorry, Khalid, but it's not good enough. I want to know why you kissed me when it's the last thing that should have happened.'

'I don't know why!'

Anger flared in his eyes yet she sensed that it wasn't directed at her but at himself. Heat flowed through her veins because it was the last thing she had expected. Khalid was always so in control, always able to harness his emotions and direct them whichever way he wanted them to go. She only had to remember that last night, when they had come so close to making love, to have all the proof she needed of that. And yet all of a sudden she realised that he wasn't in control anymore, that his emotions were leading him and not the other way round, and it scared her. If Khalid couldn't control his emotions then what hope was there of her controlling hers?

She didn't try to stop him again as he shrugged off her hand and left. Something warned her that it would be too dangerous. She could feel the echo of all those feelings swirling around her and shuddered. She left the tent but instead of going to join the others, she made her way to the very perimeter of the camp.

Crouching down, she stared out into the blackness of the desert, thinking about what had happened. Even when they had been on the point of making love, Khalid had managed to draw back—he hadn't allowed his desire to dictate his actions. She could never have done that. If he hadn't stopped that night then she would have made love with him and suffered even more afterwards because of it. Was that why he had called a halt, she wondered, because he hadn't wanted to hurt her any more?

She had never considered the idea before and yet all of a sudden she knew it was true. Khalid had been trying to protect her and it cast a wholly different light on what had happened six years ago. He hadn't been trying to protect himself and his reputation, as she had believed, but her.

Sam took a deep breath, feeling the little knot of hurt that had lain in her heart for all these years unravel. To know that Khalid had cared about her to such an extent changed everything, even though she wasn't sure why it should have done.

* * *

The rest of the week passed in a blur. Khalid measured the days by the number of patients he saw. It seemed safer that way, less stressful to concentrate on the job he had come to do rather than to think about the mess he had made of things with Sam.

There wasn't a moment when he didn't regret that kiss, not a second when he didn't wish it hadn't happened, but there was nothing he could do about it. All he could do was try to put it behind him and hope that Sam would do the same. He certainly didn't relish the thought of her demanding to know why he had kissed her again! Not when he had made such a hash of explaining it the first time. He had come so close to allowing his emotions to take over and the thought made his insides churn. Sam must never guess just how much he had wanted her.

They packed up on the Sunday, ready to move the camp to a fresh site. It was a long and laborious job but if they were to treat as many people as possible, it was essential that they move around. It was the middle of the afternoon by the time everything was loaded onto the trucks and Khalid could tell that everyone was weary. They planned to leave straight after breakfast the following day and travel to the new site while it was still relatively cool. He came to a swift decision, sensing that they all needed a break.

'I don't know about you but I could do with some down time after all that packing. Anyone fancy a barbeque?'

'You mean here?' Peter queried, looking unenthusiastically at the remains of their camp.

'No, out in the desert.' Khalid laughed. 'It's years

since I did anything like that but it should be fun. What do you say?'

'You can count me in,' Jess told him cheerfully. 'So long as I don't have to do the cooking. I'm the world's worst cook even in a kitchen so pity help you if you let me loose with a barbie!'

'Right, you're excused cooking duties,' Khalid told her with a grin. He looked around the group, his heart performing that odd tumbling movement it had started doing lately whenever he looked at Sam. It was an effort not to let her see how on edge he felt. 'What about you, Sam? Are you up for it?'

'Why not?' She gave a little shrug, making it clear that she didn't care one way or the other, and for some reason Khalid felt a tiny bit hurt, not that he showed it, of course.

Everyone else eagerly agreed that it was a great idea so in a very short time everything was organised. They packed what they needed into the four-by-fours and Khalid decided to drive one himself. It was a while since he had driven in the desert at night and it would be good to get in some practice. Jess, Aminah, Peter and Han opted to travel with him, which left Anna, Tom and Sam to go with their driver. Khalid waited while they took their seats, refusing to speculate as to why Sam had chosen not to travel with him. It was obvious why when she wanted to avoid him.

He pushed the thought to the back of his mind as they set off. Although he knew the area quite well, it didn't pay to be too complacent and he needed to concentrate. There was a wadi a few miles away that he had visited several times with his father and he headed in that direction, using the vehicle's on-board navigation system to guide him. The sun was setting now, casting deep shadows across the landscape and making it difficult to pick out familiar landmarks; however, the navigation system helped. Within a very short time they reached their destination only to discover that they weren't the only people who had chosen to spend the evening there. A group of desert tribesmen had set up camp in the wadi. Khalid drew the vehicle to a halt, knowing that it was essential to observe the proprieties.

'I'll just go and introduce myself,' he explained to the others.

'Are you sure they're happy to have visitors?' Jess asked nervously, glancing at the men. Several of them were holding rifles and it was obvious that she found the sight intimidating.

Khalid smiled reassuringly. 'The desert people are very hospitable. They will be insulted if we don't stay. Ignore the guns. It's tradition to be armed when you encounter strangers.'

'Well, if you say so.'

Jess didn't sound convinced but Khalid knew there was no reason to worry. Getting out of the car, he strode over to the leader of the group and introduced himself. It appeared that it was a stag night; the man's son was to be married in a few days' time and the men had come to the wadi to celebrate. They exchanged the usual courtesies and, as he'd expected, they were invited to join them. A fire had already been lit and a whole sheep was roasting on a spit.

Khalid went back and explained all this to the rest of the team, then he and their driver carried over the boxes of supplies they had brought with them so that everyone could share their food. He glanced around, feeling his spirits lift as he watched the members of his party mingling with their hosts. So far they had only come into contact with people who had needed their help and it would be good for them to be able to get a better idea of the nomadic lifestyle. Knowing how people lived was the key to a better understanding.

His gaze alighted on Sam, who was crouched down beside the fire, talking to the youngest member of the party, a boy in his early teens, and he felt his heart ache. Sam fitted in so well here. She seemed to have a genuine rapport with the people as well as an appreciation of the desert. It would be so easy to imagine that she could happily live here but it would be a mistake. A few months coping with this kind of life was one thing but it would be vastly different to live in Azad on a permanent basis and he must never forget that.

Sam accepted the plate of mutton their host offered her with a smile of thanks. Night had fallen now and beyond the circle of light cast by the fire the desert was pitch black. Somewhere in the darkness an animal screamed and she jumped.

'A desert fox out hunting for prey,' a voice said beside her. 'The noise they make is really eerie, isn't it?'

She glanced up when she recognised Khalid's voice and did her best to control the thunderous beating of her heart. He looked so at home in this environment, so *right*, that she felt her senses swirl for a second before she managed to control them. She couldn't afford to be seduced by the romance of the moment. This desert prince wasn't going to sweep her off her feet and have his wicked way with her, if she had any sense!

'It is. Really eerie. It sounded almost like a child

screaming,' she murmured, glad of the darkness because it helped to disguise the colour that flooded her cheeks.

She had never considered herself to be an overly romantic person; she was far too practical. However, there was little doubt that the desert seemed to be casting a spell over her. There was something beguiling about the vastness of the black velvet sky overhead, the brightness of the stars, the scent of meat roasting mingled with the sweetness of incense that stirred her senses. She felt incredibly vulnerable and it was a scary feeling in view of what had happened the other day.

Sam sighed as she bit into the succulent meat. Everything came back to that kiss. It was as though it had imprinted itself into her mind and it was impossible to shift it. Maybe it would have helped if Khalid had explained why it had happened but he seemed to have drawn a line under the event and that was it. Oh, she could try to make him explain but what was the point when he obviously wanted to forget it? The more she probed, the greater the chance that he would realise how much it had affected her, and that was the last thing she needed. She wanted him to believe that she was as indifferent to him as he appeared to be to her.

'This meat's delicious,' she said, changing the subject. 'It tastes miles better than your usual barbeque food.'

'Probably the wood they use for the fire.' He crouched down beside her, taking a piece of meat off his own plate and biting into it.

Sam looked away when she saw his strong white teeth close over the piece of mutton. She didn't need anything else to stir her senses tonight. She just wanted to get through the evening and hope that tomorrow she would be back on a more even keel. Once she was able to focus on work again, it would be that much easier to take control of her emotions. It was just out here, in the desert, with the blackness of the night forming a cocoon of intimacy around them, that it was proving so difficult.

They finished their meal and accepted the cups of coffee that were served at the end. It was thick and black and incredibly sweet but delicious despite all that. Sam put the tiny cup down on the brass tray as someone started to play some music. Leaning back on her elbows, she watched as a couple of the men began to dance. They whirled around, moving faster and faster while the rest of the party clapped and cheered. When one of the men beckoned to Khalid, inviting him to join them, she didn't expect him to comply, but he did.

Joining the group of men, he began to dance, his feet flying as he spun round in time to the music. He possessed a natural grace and Sam found that she couldn't drag her gaze away. When the music finally came to an end, her heart was pounding and her breathing was as laboured as though she had taken part as well. Khalid came over to them, grinning when Anna dryly remarked that he had kept his skills as a dancer very quiet.

'It's been years since I danced like that,' he admitted, sinking down onto the ground. 'I'm afraid I'm rather rusty.'

'You looked pretty good to me,' Anna observed. She glanced at Sam. 'I'd give him a gold star, wouldn't you, Sam?'

'I…ehem… Yes.'

Sam dredged up a smile but it was an effort. This

was yet another side of Khalid that she hadn't known existed and it was worrying to discover how little she really knew about him. Thankfully, Peter provided a welcome distraction when he accepted the men's invitation to join them. His dancing was nowhere near as good as Khalid's, although he gave it his best shot. He was out of breath when he came back.

'Not really my forte,' he gasped, flopping down on the ground.

'Never mind. You can't be good at everything,' Jess assured him.

Sam saw the look that passed between them and bit back a sigh. It was obvious that Jess and Peter were growing very fond of one another and, while she was happy for them, it seemed to highlight her own single status. Her eyes drifted to Khalid, who was speaking to Tom, and she felt her heart ache.

Would she meet someone and fall in love or would her background once again prove to be the sticking point? She had honestly thought that she and Adam could make a go of things but it hadn't worked any more than it had done with Khalid. Maybe he had wanted to protect her, but at the end of the day he must have had concerns about the embarrassment it could have caused his family to have her name linked with theirs. It might be better if she accepted that she would never enjoy the kind of close and loving relationship she had always dreamt about.

They set up camp at the new site the following day. Khalid supervised as the crates containing the more fragile items of equipment were unloaded. They were quicker setting up this time, past experience helping to iron out any problems. By the time lunch was served, everything was ready.

Khalid made his way to the canteen and joined Peter and Han. Once again the women had opted to sit together and he was relieved. Last night had unsettled him even more and he needed time to get himself in hand before he spoke to Sam. They'd been too busy with the move this morning but now that everything was set up, he couldn't avoid her. After all, she was a vital member of the team and it would seem odd if he ignored her.

They were just finishing their coffee when the sound of a helicopter overhead alerted them to the fact that they had visitors. Khalid left the tent, shading his eyes as he watched it set down a short distance away. From its livery, he knew it belonged to the royal flight, although he had no idea who was on board. He smiled in delight when he saw his brother, Shahzad, alighting.

'This is a surprise,' he declared, hurrying forward to greet him. 'Welcome!' His smile widened when he saw his two little nieces being helped out as well. Bending down, he kissed them. 'How did you manage to persuade Papa to bring you to see me?'

'Mama keeps being sick,' six-year-old Janan told him importantly. 'She told Papa that she wanted to be on her own. Didn't she, Izdihar?'

Three-year-old Izdihar nodded, her thumb sliding into her mouth, and Khalid laughed. 'Well, I can understand that. Come. I shall introduce you to all the doctors and nurses then show you where we see all the sick people.'

'And make them better?' Janan put in knowledgeably.

'Hopefully, yes.' Khalid agreed, smiling wryly at his

brother as he led the girls over to where the rest of the team were waiting. He quickly introduced everyone, his heart catching when he saw how gentle Sam was with the children and how they immediately responded to her. When she offered to show them around the camp, they begged their father to let them go with her.

'They will be quite safe with Sam,' Khalid said quietly, when his brother hesitated. 'She won't let any harm come to them.'

'In that case, thank you.' Shahzad bowed to Sam as she took hold of the children's hands. He watched as they skipped along beside her as she led them to the canteen first to get a drink. Turning, he fixed Khalid with a searching look. 'Am I right to think that Sam is the woman you were involved with some years ago?'

'Yes.' Khalid changed the subject. Although he and Shahzad were close, he didn't intend to confide in him. It wouldn't help to lay out all his uncertainties for inspection; it would just confuse the issue even more. 'So, brother, delighted as I am to see you, is this purely a social visit or is there another reason for it?'

'How did you guess?' Shahzad sighed. 'I am worried about Mariam. She is pregnant again, only this time she seems to be experiencing all sorts of problems she never suffered when she was expecting the girls.'

'First of all, congratulations! I know how much you both want another child.' Khalid led the way to the men's tent and offered Shahzad the one and only chair.

'We do. We were thrilled when we discovered she was expecting another child. But she's been so ill— constantly sick and exhausted. I have to confess that I am extremely worried about her.'

'I take it that Mariam has seen her doctor?' Khalid said quietly.

'Yes, several times, but he cannot find anything wrong with her. He keeps insisting that it will pass and that she will feel better in time but she is four months pregnant now and she still doesn't feel right.'

'So what do you intend to do? Seek a second opinion?'

'Yes.' Shahzad sighed. 'However, Mariam feels that it would be unfair to cast any doubt on her doctor's capabilities. You know how quickly rumours spread and it could do him untold harm so she is reluctant to take that route. I certainly don't want her worrying at the moment so I suggested that she seek a second opinion from the obstetrician you have brought with you. If you agree, obviously.'

'Of course. I'm sure that Sam will be only too pleased to help.'

'Ah, so it is the young woman who is looking after Janan and Izdihar,' Shahzad said quietly.

'That's right. Sam very kindly stepped in when the obstetrician who was originally to accompany us had to back out.'

Khalid summoned a smile although he couldn't help feeling uneasy. Introducing Sam to his family was a step he would have preferred not to take, although not for the reasons she would undoubtedly assume. He sighed. Seeing Sam interacting with the people he loved would make it that much harder for him to view her solely as a colleague and that was what he needed to do. Desperately.

'Then can I prevail upon you to ask her if she would be willing to see Mariam? It would be a huge relief to us both to have a second opinion. It would definitely stop Mariam worrying and that is bound to ease the situation.'

How could he refuse? Even though it was the last thing he wanted, Khalid knew that he didn't have a choice. Shahzad's fears for his wife would be all the greater seeing as his own mother had died giving birth to him. It would be unforgiveable to allow Shahzad to suffer any longer if he could do something to help.

'Of course. I shall ask her when she brings the children back.'

'Thank you.'

Shahzad clapped him on the shoulder, looking so relieved that Khalid knew that he had made the right decision. At his suggestion they made their way to Theatre so that his brother could see the equipment he had so generously paid for. There was no sign of Sam and the children and Khalid was glad. He needed to get this into perspective, stop making a mountain out of a very small molehill. So Sam was going be involved with his family for a brief time—so what? It wouldn't change the status quo, wouldn't make him change *his* mind. She could never be part of his life and that was that... only it wasn't that simple, was it? Not simple at all to see her interacting with the people he loved.

Sam returned her young charges to their father, shaking her head when Shahzad asked her if they had been any trouble. 'No trouble at all,' she assured him, and meant it too. The little girls had been a positive delight, eager to see as much as they could of the camp. She laughed when they both clamoured for a kiss. Bending, she kissed their soft little cheeks, feeling a wealth of tenderness fill her. Despite their privileged background, they were lovely children and she had enjoyed spending time with them.

She straightened up, realising that it was time that she got ready for her patients. Clinic was due to begin at three and it was almost that now. She turned to leave then stopped when Khalid appeared.

'May I have a word with you, Sam?' he asked politely.

'Of course.'

Sam followed as he led the way to a spot near to the perimeter of the camp. He paused, staring out across the desert, and she had the distinct impression that he had something on his mind. Turning, he summoned a smile but she could tell how tense he was and reacted instinctively. Whatever he had to say, she had a feeling it wouldn't come easily to him.

'So what is it, Khalid? Is something wrong? Have *I* done something wrong?' she demanded, wanting to get it over as quickly as possible.

'No, of course not.' He drew himself up, his face expressionless as he looked at her. 'Shahzad's wife is expecting another child. Whilst they are both delighted, my brother is extremely worried about Mariam. She isn't at all well and although she has consulted her own doctor, who has told her not to worry, they both feel it would help to have a second opinion.'

'I see.' She shrugged, unsure where this was leading. 'Not a problem, I imagine. You told me that there is a comprehensive health care system in the cities so there must be other obstetricians your sister-in-law can consult.'

'Indeed. However, they are both keen not to cast

any doubts on Mariam's doctor's proficiency.' His eyes met hers. 'In a country as small as Azad, rumours soon abound, which is why Shahzad has asked if you would be willing to examine Mariam. I told him that I would ask you.'

Sam bit her lip, unsure how she felt about the request. In other circumstances, she would have agreed immediately, subject to Mariam's own doctor's approval, of course. However, was it wise to involve herself this way, to get to know Khalid's family when he had gone to such lengths to keep her away from them? He had never introduced her to any members of his family. Although his brother and sister-in-law had visited London several times while they had been seeing one another, Khalid had made no attempt to introduce her to them. Sam had thought it rather strange at the time until she'd realised that he hadn't wanted his family to become involved with a woman like her when it could reflect badly on them. Now she looked him squarely in the eyes.

'Do you honestly believe it's wise to involve me, Khalid? What if someone finds out and decides to dig into my past? No one can claim that I appear to be the ideal candidate to give advice about a royal baby!'

'There is very little chance of anyone finding out, I assure you.' His voice was harsh, edged with an arrogance that immediately put her back up.

'You could be right. After all, you have the money and the power to call the shots, don't you?' She laughed bitterly. 'It all depends what you consider is important. Obviously this is, although our relationship—such as it was—evidently wasn't.'

'That's not fair. It's not even true,' he began, but she didn't allow him to finish. There was no point.

She held up her hand. 'Forget it. It doesn't matter now. If your brother and sister-in-law feel it would help then I shall be happy to give a second opinion, subject to Mariam's own doctor's agreement, obviously.'

'Of course.'

His face closed up, his dark eyes unreadable as he pinned her with a searching look. Sam had no idea what he was looking for and didn't waste time worrying about it either. Turning, she made her way to the clinic and got ready for her first patient. So long as her every waking thought was channelled towards her patients she would survive. And once she left Azad she could get back to normal and carry on with the life she had created for herself.

Tears stung her eyes but she blinked them away. She wouldn't think about how much she would miss Khalid, wouldn't waste time thinking *if only*. Their relationship would never have survived the pressures that would have been put upon it. She knew that even if it hurt.

CHAPTER NINE

KHALID SAW HIS brother and nieces off then went into the clinic. There were already patients waiting to see him so he told Han to fetch in the first one. It was an elderly man who had broken his leg in a fall. Although the fracture had started to heal, it was immediately apparent from the angle of the lower leg that it needed re-setting if it wasn't to cause the old man problems in the future.

Khalid explained what needed to be done to the man and his son, who had accompanied him. It was obvious that they were both unhappy at the thought of him having to break the leg again but he managed to convince them that it would for the best. Their nomadic lifestyle would make it extremely difficult for the father if he was left with a badly deformed limb.

He booked the man in for surgery the following afternoon and made a note to ask Tom to check him over prior to administering the anaesthetic. Once that was done, he worked his way through the rest of his patients, adding a couple more to his list of people requiring surgery. Life in the desert was harsh and accidents occurred frequently so it was little wonder that so many folk required treatment. It confirmed his decision to try to set up a permanent clinic, even though he knew how difficult it would be to get the idea off the ground. Just finding suitably qualified staff willing to work there would be a major undertaking for a start.

'That's me done.' Peter came to join him, perching on the edge of the desk. 'Several more cases of TB, as expected, plus a patient with a rather nasty cough that sounded highly suspicious.' He sighed. 'I've booked him in for a chest X-ray tomorrow, although I already suspect what it's going to show.'

'Cancer is no respecter of circumstances,' Khalid agreed quietly. Out of the corner of his eye, he saw Sam get up and leave her desk. She'd had a busy afternoon as well from the number of files she was carrying, he thought.

She glanced round and he looked away when he felt her gaze land on him. He could see the scorn in her eyes—feel it even!—and it made him feel worse than ever. Why hadn't he explained why he had ended their relationship when he'd had the chance? If he had told her the truth, that it hadn't been the damage it could cause to his family's reputation that had made him do it but the harm it might cause *her*, then maybe she wouldn't be looking at him like that right now.

He started to push back his chair then realised what he was doing. What was the point of raking it all up again? Maybe it would salve his conscience but it wouldn't change things, not really. He and Sam could never be together. She would end up resenting him for taking away everything she held dear: her career and her freedom to be the person she was. Oh, maybe it would work at first but eventually, inevitably, she would come to hate him for ruining her life and he couldn't bear that, couldn't bear to watch her love turn to loathing, not that she gave much sign of loving him these days.

Khalid sank back down onto his seat, turning so that he wouldn't have to watch her leave and be tempted to do something he would only regret. There was no going back and no going forward either. Not for him and Sam.

Sam felt on edge for the rest of the day. Maybe it was that talk she'd had with Khalid earlier but she couldn't seem to settle. Once dinner was over, she returned to the tent and dug out the novel she had been meaning to read for ages only had never found the time. It had received glowing reviews but it failed to hold her attention. She kept thinking about Khalid's request that she should see Mariam, churning it over and searching for a way out, but she couldn't come up with anything plausible. His sister-in-law had asked for her help and how could she refuse when there was no real reason to do so? She was a doctor first and foremost; her patients took priority over her own feelings.

By the time morning dawned, she had accepted the inevitable and just wanted to get it over. When she saw Khalid leaving the canteen, she hurried after him. He was dressed in theatre scrubs, pale blue cotton trousers and a matching top, that made his olive skin appear darker than ever. His body was lithe and muscular beneath the lightweight fabric, the perfectly toned muscles in his chest and abdomen making it clear that he took good care of himself. He had told her once that orthopaedic surgery could be physically demanding and that it required strength as well as skill to put broken bones back together. Keeping himself fit was all part of the job as he saw it and not merely an indulgence. The fact that he looked so good was irrelevant.

'Can I have a word?' she said hurriedly, not wanting to get sidetracked. How Khalid looked wasn't important and she would be well advised to remember that.

'Of course.' He stopped, waiting in silence to hear what she had to say, and Sam felt a ripple of annoyance run through her. Did he need to make it so abundantly clear that he had no interest in her?

'I was wondering if you'd settled on a date for me to see your sister-in-law. The sooner I examine her, the better, from what you told me.'

'Indeed. Shahzad is anxious that Mariam should stop worrying and asked if you would be available this Sunday.'

Sam laughed at the formality of the request. 'Well, I can't think of anything else I'll be doing. Of course, I shall need to check my diary but I don't think I have any dinner engagements or red-carpet functions to attend.'

'Good.' A smile curved his generous mouth, softening his expression in a way that made her pulse leap. 'I wouldn't like it to interfere with your social life, Sam. That would never do.'

'No fear of that, I assure you. My social life, as you call it, doesn't exist.' She gave a little shrug when she saw his brows rise, wishing she hadn't said that. 'Work seems to fill most of my days.'

'I see. So you aren't seeing anyone at the present time?'

'No. I've had my fill of relationships, believe me. I'm happy to be single these days—it's a lot less stressful.'

'But you did get engaged last year,' he said quietly.

He must have seen her surprise. 'Peter told me, that's how I know.'

'Oh, I see.' She shrugged. 'I expect he also told you that it didn't work out and we split up.'

'Indeed. What was the reason for it?'

'We realised that we weren't suited after all.'

She spun round before he could question her further, not wanting to discuss her reasons for ending her engagement with him. She sighed as she made her way to the clinic. She had seen umpteen articles in the newspapers over the years about Khalid, linking him to various beautiful and highly suitable women, so she didn't need to enquire about his love life. There would always be women eager to be seen with Khalid...and much more.

The thought of him sleeping with all those woman was like a dagger being thrust through in her heart and she sucked in her breath. Khalid was a handsome, virile man, and even without the added lure of his wealth and status he would have attracted women by the score. There was no point her wishing that the situation wasn't so because it wouldn't change anything. Khalid was free to sleep with whoever he liked and it had nothing to do with her.

Sunday dawned, the sun rising in a ball of fire above the horizon. Khalid stood at the perimeter of the camp and watched the desert slowly reappear from the nighttime gloom. He hadn't slept. He had simply laid awake waiting for the morning to come. Maybe it was foolish to set such store by what was about to happen but he couldn't help it. Seeing Sam with his brother and sister-in-law wasn't going to be easy. That was the reason why he had shied away from introducing her to them six years ago. He had known that once there was that connection, it would be even harder to draw back. Now, today, it was going to happen and even though there was no reason to view the coming meeting as anything more than a professional obligation, he knew it was going to be difficult.

The sound of a helicopter cut through his musings. His brother had said he would send the helicopter to fetch them early and he had kept his word. Khalid swung round, meaning to go and check if Sam was ready, but she was already crossing the compound. His heart gave a small jolt then started beating faster than normal as he took stock. Her clothes were simple—white cotton jeans teamed with a pale blue shirt with a heavy knit sweater looped around her shoulders for added warmth against the dawn chill—but she still managed to look stunning.

She'd obviously just washed her hair because damp tendrils curled around her face, making his fingers itch to smooth them behind her ears as she stopped beside him. She looked so young and lovely, so fresh and desirable that he was overwhelmed by desire. It took every scrap of control he could muster to look calmly at her when what he really wanted to do was haul her into his arms and kiss her until they were both unable to think clearly.

'I take it that's our taxi,' she said, glancing skywards.

'Yes. Shahzad said he'd make it an early start and it looks like he meant it,' he agreed, relieved to hear that he sounded normal even if he didn't feel it.

'I imagine he's anxious to hear my opinion,' Sam observed, shading her eyes as she watched the helicopter set down a short distance away.

'Indeed.' Khalid glanced at the helicopter, trying not to recall what had happened when the medevac helicopter had collected Jameela and her children. It was pointless going down that route and dangerous too. He didn't intend to kiss Sam again, not if he had any sense. Turning, he forced himself to smile politely at her. 'So, do you have everything you need?'

'I just need to fetch my bag and that's it.'

She didn't return his smile as she made her way over to the clinic and Khalid swallowed his sigh. The days when Sam had smiled at him with true affection in her eyes were long gone and it was stupid to dwell on how much he missed those times. He went and had a word with the pilot instead, checking that his brother was where he had said he would be.

Shahzad and Mariam had a house on the outskirts of Zadra City and spent most of their time there, preferring it to the more formal surroundings of the royal palace. Although they were realistic enough to know that they couldn't ignore their status, they were anxious to ensure that their children grew up in a less rarefied atmosphere and he applauded them for it. It seemed to be paying dividends too because his small nieces were delightfully unspoiled. If he ever had children of his own, he would be more than happy if they turned out as well as the girls had done.

The thought was like a tiny dagger pricking his heart. Khalid tried to put it out of his mind as Sam came back with her case. She climbed on board and got herself settled, placing the bag on the seat next to her. Khalid took the hint and moved further back, not wanting to make an issue of it. So she wanted to sit by herself, so what? It didn't make a scrap of difference to him...only it did if he was honest.

He strapped himself in as the pilot lifted off, wishing that he could feel as indifferent as he was pretending to be. He'd never felt this way before, so edgy and unsure, so uncertain about everything he did. He was used to being in control of himself and his life but it was proving difficult around Sam. She seemed to upset his world, make even the easiest decision far more complicated than it should have been.

He sighed as the helicopter swung round in a slow circle and headed back the way it had come. His life felt very much like this, spinning in circles, and it had to stop. He had to decide what he wanted and go for it without allowing anything to distract him. It was what he had always done in the past, set himself a goal and worked towards it, so it shouldn't be that difficult. All he needed to do was to work out what he wanted to achieve in the next couple of years and not allow anything to throw him off course.

Closing his eyes, Khalid started to work out exactly what he intended to do with his life. Although he had enjoyed working in England, he realised that he wanted to play a bigger part in improving the health of the people in his own country. It would be difficult to set up clinics to provide access to healthcare for the desert people, but it was what he intended to do. Money wasn't an issue, fortunately: his father was generous to a fault and could be relied on to provide the necessary backing. No, it was the logistics of finding suitably qualified staff to run the clinics that would be the biggest problem, but he would find a way round that.

And once that was done then he would have to think

about his own life, and what he wanted from it too, decide if that family he'd thought about so often recently was a possibility. It all depended on him finding the right woman, of course, and that could prove to be the major sticking point. She would have to be very special if he planned to spend the rest of his life with her.

His eyes opened and went immediately to Sam while he felt his heart ache. Despite the number of women he had dated over the years there had only ever been one woman he had wanted that way and that was Sam.

It took less than an hour to reach their destination. The sun was still climbing into the sky when the helicopter touched down, gilding the pale sandstone walls of the buildings with rosy-gold light. Sam picked up her case, nodding her thanks when the pilot helped her to disembark. There was a car standing by to collect them and she followed as Khalid led the way over to it.

He opened the rear door for her, waiting while she slid into the seat. He hadn't said a word on the journey but, then, she hadn't given him a chance to do so. Now she summoned a smile, feeling that it would be easier if she at least attempted to observe the niceties. There was no point making this any more stressful than it was.

'Thank you. It didn't take as long as I thought it would to get here.'

'No?' He gave a small shrug, immediately drawing her attention to the solid width of his shoulders. 'I should have mentioned that Shahzad and Mariam live outside the city. They prefer the more informal atmosphere here to raise the girls. They don't want them to get too spoiled.'

'Well, it seems to have worked. They are lovely children,' Sam said truthfully.

'They are indeed.' He smiled at her with genuine warmth. 'They certainly took a liking to you.'

'That's nice to know.'

Sam returned his smile then made a great production out of fastening her seat belt to avoid looking at him. She let out a sigh as he closed the door and got into the front next to the driver. She had to get a grip, had to stop getting carried away each time Khalid smiled at her. Of course he was pleased that she had praised his nieces. It had been obvious the other day how fond of them he was but it didn't mean anything, not personally. About her. Khalid would have smiled just as warmly at anyone who had complimented the two girls.

It was a little deflating to have to face it but Sam knew that she couldn't allow herself to start believing things that weren't true. She stared out of the window as the driver ferried them to the house, concentrating on what she was seeing. Although it was much smaller than the summer palace where they had spent their first night in Azad it was still an imposing building with several turrets rising into the sky. The driver sounded the horn and the gates were opened then they were inside, drawing up in a small courtyard that was a riot of colour. Sam breathed in deeply as she stepped out of the air-conditioned confines of the car, her brows rising when she recognised the delicate aroma. Turning, she stared in amazement at the masses of plants, scarcely able to believe what she was seeing. Roses? Out here in the desert?

'Mariam planted them. She was brought up in England and roses are her favourite flowers. She insisted on having them in her garden when she and Shahzad had the house built. She tends them almost as lovingly as she tends her children.'

The amusement in Khalid's voice made her smile too. 'Well, they are certainly flourishing. The smell is just gorgeous.'

'It is.' Bending, Khalid plucked a delicate pale pink rose off one of the bushes and handed it to her. 'This is one of my favourites. Smell it.'

Sam buried her nose in the satiny petals and inhaled their scent, feeling the blood start to pound through her veins. It didn't mean anything, she told herself sternly, but there was no escaping the fact that it made her feel all shivery inside to have Khalid present her with the beautiful flower. It was a relief when Shahzad and the girls appeared and she was forced to focus on them rather than on what had happened.

'Welcome, welcome! It is such a pleasure to have you both here in our home.' Shahzad bowed, touching his lips and forehead in the traditional greeting.

'It's a pleasure to be here,' Sam replied, mimicking his actions before turning to greet the children. They both clamoured to be kissed so she bent down and kissed them on their soft little cheeks, laughing when they grabbed hold of her hands and started to drag her towards the door. 'Hey, I'm not here to play. I've come to see your mummy.'

'Mama is still in her room,' Janan informed her. 'She's been sick and Papa told her that she must rest until she feels better.'

'Oh, dear.' Sam glanced at Shahzad and saw the worry in his eyes. She gently untangled herself from the children's grasp and picked up her case. 'I think I'll go and see if there's anything I can do to make her feel more comfortable.'

'You must have something to eat and drink first,' Shahzad demurred, taking his duties as their host very seriously.

'Later, thank you.' Sam smiled at him. 'There will be plenty of time for all that after I've seen your wife.'

'Of course.'

The relief in his voice told its own tale. Sam frowned as he instructed one of the servants to show her the way. It was obvious how worried he was about his wife and she only hoped that she could do something to help.

She followed the young woman inside and along an airy corridor, pausing when the girl indicated that Sam should wait while she knocked on a door. When a voice bade them to enter, she stepped into the room, surprised to discover how modern it was. There was none of the ornate gilding and lavish fabrics that she had expected to see but simple furnishings and fitments in cool neutral colours.

'What a lovely room!' she declared. She smiled at the attractive young woman seated on a daybed in front of the window, taking note of her extreme pallor. It was obvious even from a first glance that Mariam wasn't feeling well and Sam's mind began to race as she ran through a list of possible causes for her continued sickness.

'Thank you. I wanted to create a home that was comfortable for us to live in.' Mariam gave her a sweet smile. 'Whilst I appreciate the beauty of the royal palaces, they are a little too formal for my taste.'

'Well, this is perfect. I'd say you were spot on.' Sam put down her bag and held out her hand. 'Sorry. I should have introduced myself, shouldn't I? I'm Samantha Warren—Sam to my friends so I hope you'll call me that. Your husband told me that you haven't been feeling at all well throughout this pregnancy?'

'No. I haven't. I sailed through my other pregnancies so I can't understand what's wrong this time.' Tears filled Mariam's huge dark eyes. 'I am so afraid that there is something wrong with the baby even though my doctor insists that there is nothing to worry about.'

'It's only natural to worry,' Sam assured her. 'Having sailed through two previous pregnancies, you're bound to feel anxious when this one doesn't seem to be going as you expected. All I can say is that every pregnancy is different and the fact that you aren't blooming this time isn't an indication that there is something wrong with the baby.'

'You honestly believe that?' Mariam said hopefully.

'Oh, yes.' Sam smiled at her. 'I've seen it happen many times, mums who haven't experienced any problems whatsoever during previous pregnancies but who suddenly find themselves feeling dreadful. It's often caused by an imbalance of hormones.

'When you're pregnant, your body produces more of the female sex hormones, oestrogen and progesterone, as well as human placental lactogen and human chorionic gonadotrophin. If the balance isn't right then it affects how you are feeling. The key is to rule out any other potential causes and then simply accept that this time you aren't going to feel on top of the world.' She laughed. 'More often than not that helps to alleviate the problem, funnily enough.'

'Worrying about it makes it worse,' Mariam observed ruefully.

'It can do.' Sam drew up a chair. Opening her case, she took out her sphygmomanometer. 'Now, let's start with the basics, shall we? I'll check your blood pressure then do a urine test. I take it that your own doctor is happy about you seeking a second opinion?' she asked as she wrapped the blood-pressure cuff around Mariam's arm.

'Not exactly happy, no.' Mariam grimaced. 'However, he could hardly refuse.'

'No, I don't suppose so,' Sam agreed wryly. She inflated the cuff, unsurprised when she discovered that Mariam's blood pressure was a little higher than she would have liked it to be. The stress was taking its toll on her and the sooner they sorted out what was wrong, the better.

Mariam provided a urine sample next and Sam tested that, pleased to find that there was no indication that anything was amiss. Her blood-sugar levels were fine and there was no trace of protein in her urine that could be a sign of pre-eclampsia.

'Right, so far so good. I'd like to examine you now if that's all right.'

'Of course.'

Mariam made herself comfortable while Sam carried out a physical examination. She frowned because to her mind Mariam seemed much larger than she would have expected her to be.

'How many weeks are you now?' she asked, gently feeling the position of the baby.

'Twenty.' Mariam grimaced. 'I'm much bigger than I was with either of the girls.'

'But you are certain of your dates?' Sam clarified. 'You're sure that you haven't made a mistake?'

'No.' Mariam flushed. 'I can pinpoint the exact day this baby was conceived during a trip we made to Paris so there's no doubt in my mind about that. Why are you asking? Is something wrong?'

'No. It's just that you're much bigger than I would have expected you to be at this stage.' Sam stepped away from the couch, frowning as she weighed up what she had learned. 'What did your scan show?'

'I haven't had a scan.' Mariam sat up and straightened her dress. 'I didn't have one with either of the girls either. Shahzad and I both agreed when we decided to start a family that we could never abort a child if it was found to be damaged in some way so there was no point.'

'I see.' Sam packed the sphygmomanometer in her case then sat down. She looked intently at Mariam. 'How do you feel about having a scan if it could help to solve the problem of why you have been feeling so ill?'

'You think there's something wrong with the baby!' Mariam exclaimed, pressing her hand to her throat.

'No. What I think...and I may very well be wrong... is that you're expecting more than one baby.' She took hold of Mariam's hand and squeezed it. 'That would account for the extra amniotic fluid you are carrying, not to mention the fact that you feel so sick and exhausted all the time.'

'More than one baby...' Mariam broke off, obviously stunned by the idea.

'It's possible but we shall need to confirm it. And the best way to do that is by having a scan.'

'But surely I should be able to feel if there's more than one baby growing inside me!' Mariam declared, placing her hand on the swell of her stomach.

'Not necessarily, especially if one baby is lying directly behind the other, as I suspect is the case here.' Sam laughed. 'You may find that you are about to get two for the price of one. How would you feel about that?'

'Ecstatic!'

Mariam laughed out loud at the idea. They were both still laughing when the door opened and Shahzad appeared. He looked from one to the other and raised his brows.

'I hope you are going to share the joke with me?'

'I'll leave that to your wife.' Sam stood up. She smiled at Mariam. 'I'll get Khalid to make the arrangements, shall I?'

'Please.' Mariam returned her smile, looking so much better than she had done a short while before that Sam found herself crossing her fingers that her suspicions would prove to be correct.

She left Mariam to break the news to her husband, knowing that they needed to be on their own at this special time. Backtracking along the corridor, she went to find Khalid and discovered that he was in the courtyard, sitting on a stone bench beside the fountain. He looked up when he heard her approaching and she could see the concern in his eyes and was warmed by it. Although he might project an image of being indifferent, he truly cared about his family.

'So, do you know what is wrong with Mariam?' he asked as she sat down beside him.

'I think it's possible that she is expecting more than one baby,' Sam informed him.

'But surely her own consultant should have realised that!' he exclaimed.

'Yes. And he would have done if Mariam hadn't refused to have a scan.' She quickly relayed what Mariam had told her and heard him sigh.

'I had no idea they felt like that. If I had done then I would have urged them to have the scan done before now and save themselves all this worry.'

'It's not your fault,' she assured him. She laid her hand on his arm, feeling her skin tingle when it came into contact with his. She knew she should remove her hand but the need to touch him was just too strong to resist. For some reason she needed to feel close to him at this moment. How strange.

'Maybe not. But if I had spent more time with Shahzad then I might have been privy to his beliefs.' He gave a small shrug, causing the muscles in his forearm to flex beneath her fingers. 'It reinforces the decision I've made to spend more time in Azad. Whilst I have enjoyed working in England and appreciate how much I have learned while I've been there, I need to come back home.'

He looked up and his eyes were very dark as they met hers. 'My future lies here. In Azad.'

CHAPTER TEN

THE SCAN CONFIRMED that Sam's suspicions were correct. Mariam was expecting twins, one baby lying directly behind the other, which was why it had gone undetected for so long. Khalid congratulated his brother, hoping that Shahzad couldn't tell how he really felt. Oh, he was delighted by the news—there was no question about that. However, he couldn't pretend that he didn't feel upset about the way Sam had responded when he had told her of his decision to live in Azad permanently. She hadn't tried to make him reconsider, hadn't said anything really, but what had he expected? That she would beg him to stay in England, stay with her? That was never going to happen.

Once they returned from the hospital, Shahzad announced that they needed to celebrate and set about organising an elaborate dinner for them. Given the choice, Khalid would have preferred to return immediately to their camp but there was no way that he could refuse to join in the celebrations. When Sam protested that she had nothing to wear, Mariam whisked her away with the promise of finding her something suitable so there was no escape on that score. Khalid guessed that Sam was as loath to drag out the visit as he was but she too didn't want to put a damper on the evening.

He used one of the guest rooms to shower and change into some clothes he had left behind the last time he had stayed with his brother. Shahzad was beaming with pride when he tracked him down to the salon, obviously thrilled to bits at the thought of becoming a father again not just once but twice. He handed Khalid a glass of fresh pomegranate juice, raising his own glass aloft to toast the future.

'May we both find everything we are looking for from life.'

Khalid clinked glasses, wishing with all his heart it were that simple. However, what he wanted and what he had to accept were two very different things. He glanced round when he heard footsteps and felt his senses whirl when he saw Sam come into the room. Mariam had kept her word and found Sam something to wear but it was the last thing he had expected to see her dressed in.

In a mesmerised sweep he drank in the picture she made as she stood in the doorway, the azure-blue folds of a traditional Arab dress falling softly around her. She was even wearing a headdress, a lightweight veil trimmed with the same elaborate beading that edged the neckline of her dress. She looked so beautiful that for a moment he couldn't think let alone speak and was grateful for the fact that his brother saved him from standing there looking as though he had been struck dumb.

'You look beautiful, both of you.' Shahzad stepped forward, taking Sam's hand and kissing it.

'Thank you.' Sam smiled but Khalid could tell how tense she was as she came further into the room. She stopped beside the tray of drinks and he hurriedly gathered his wits. It was up to him to make this as stress-free as possible for her. After all, it was just one night, a few short hours to get through before they returned to their camp in the morning. He had endured far worse than this!

'Would you like a drink?' He picked up the jug of pomegranate juice. 'My brother doesn't drink alcohol but this is delicious if you'd like to try it.'

'Thank you.' Sam accepted the glass and took a sip of the ruby-red liquid. 'Mmm, you're right, it *is* delicious.'

'Good.' Khalid topped up his own glass then glanced at Mariam and Shahzad, swallowing a sigh when he realised that they were so wrapped up in their news that they were oblivious to everything else. It was up to him to play the host and it was a job he would have preferred not to do, only good manners dictated otherwise.

'Would you like to take a walk in the rose garden? The scent of the blossoms is stronger at night and I'm sure you'd enjoy it.'

'You don't have to entertain me, Khalid,' Sam said sharply. Her eyes rose to his and he saw the hurt they held and silently cursed himself for making his reluctance so apparent.

'I know I don't.' He touched her hand, unable to lie, even though he knew how dangerous it was to admit the truth. 'I asked you because I can't think of anything I would like more than to enjoy the garden with you, Sam.'

'Oh.'

She didn't say anything else; however, he could tell that she was surprised and wished he had managed to keep his feelings to himself. He led the way, opening the French doors at the far end of the salon that gave direct access to the rose garden. Night had fallen and apart from the light from the torches placed alongside the path, everywhere was dark. It added an air of intimacy, which was heightened by the fact that they had to rely more on their other senses and less on sight.

Khalid breathed in deeply, inhaling the delicate yet potent scent of the roses. Somewhere a frog began to croak, an insistent rhythm that drummed inside his skull and made it difficult to think. His mind seemed to be awash with sensations, with all the things he couldn't afford to feel, but he was powerless to resist their appeal. When Sam stopped and turned to him he acted instinctively, unable to weigh up the dangers of what he was doing when all he was aware of was this need burning inside him.

'Sam.' He said her name so softly that he wondered if he had actually spoken it out loud. Her eyes rose to his and his heart leapt when he saw an answering need reflected in their depths. She didn't try to pull away when he drew her to him, didn't resist in any way. She wanted this kiss as much as he did, needed it just as desperately too.

The thought was the final key that unlocked his restraint. Khalid placed his mouth over hers and shuddered when he felt her immediately respond. When he pulled her to him, holding her so close that he could feel the swell of her breasts pushing against his chest, it felt as though he had come home after a long and tiring journey. *This* was what had been missing from his life, this feeling of completion. With Sam in his arms he felt whole; without her it was as though something vital was missing.

* * *

Sam could feel her heart beating, its rhythm marking time with Khalid's, and shivered. It was almost too much to realise that their bodies were so perfectly attuned. Pressing herself even closer against him, she twined her arms around his neck and drew his head down so she could deepen the kiss, wanting...*needing*...this moment to continue for as long as possible. She wasn't stupid. She knew that it would have to end, but for now it was enough that she could feel his need of her. Maybe they couldn't be together for ever but for this moment Khalid wanted her, *her* and nobody else!

They were both breathing hard when they broke apart, both shaken by the depth of their desire. Khalid cupped her cheek and she could feel his hand trembling and was overwhelmed by tenderness. Even though he projected an image of cool indifference, she knew otherwise. He was neither cool nor indifferent. Not when he held her in his arms and kissed her at least.

'I shouldn't have done that,' he said, his deep voice grating in the silence.

'Maybe not but it's what we both wanted, Khalid.' She tilted her head and looked him in the eyes because she refused to lie. 'If I hadn't wanted you to kiss me I would have stopped you.'

'It can never lead anywhere. You understand that, Sam, don't you?'

'Oh, yes. I'm under no illusions.' She gave a discordant little laugh. 'I'm not the sort of woman a man like you wants in his life. I'm fine for a fling but that's all!'

'That wasn't what I meant!' He caught hold of her by the shoulders, bending so he could look into her eyes, but Sam wasn't about to be persuaded. She needed to face the facts and not be swayed into believing what patently wasn't true.

'If you say so.' She gave a little shrug as she pulled away, deliberately setting some distance between them because she couldn't trust herself. It would be only too easy to allow him to convince her that her past didn't matter but it did. It had mattered six years ago and it still mattered now.

'Ah, so there you are. Mariam sent me to find you. Dinner is ready.'

Sam was glad of the interruption when Shahzad appeared. She could see the curiosity in his eyes as he glanced from her to Khalid. Obviously, he had sensed that something was going on but it wasn't up to her to explain—she would leave that to Khalid. No doubt he would appreciate hearing his brother's opinion, especially if it reinforced his own view, as she suspected it would. Despite how welcoming Shahzad had been, he would be equally loath to allow his family to become involved with someone from her background.

Swinging round, she made her way inside, summoning a smile when she found Mariam waiting for them. Although Mariam still looked a little pale, Sam could tell how much better she was feeling now that her worst fears had been alleviated. 'Feeling better, are you?'

'Much.' Mariam smiled her sweet smile as she came over and kissed Sam on the cheek. 'Thank you so much for persuading me to have that scan. I only wish that I'd agreed to have it done sooner and saved myself and Shahzad all that heartache.'

Sam gave her a hug. 'It's easy to be wise after the event,' she said sympathetically, glancing round when she heard Khalid and his brother come into the room.

Her heart ached as the truth of that statement hit her. She should never have allowed Khalid to kiss her just now, certainly shouldn't have responded the way she had done. Now she not only had to contend with her own emotions but with the knowledge that he still desired her. It would make it that much more difficult to keep him at arm's length as she had to do if she wasn't to find herself right back where she'd been six years ago: her heart broken and her life in tatters.

The thought lay heavily in her heart as she followed Mariam to the dining room. Once again the furniture and fitments were understated and ultra-modern, the only indication of the couple's extreme wealth apparent in the exquisite china and beautiful cut-glass stemware that adorned the table. Candles had been lit and the glow from them should have added to the feeling of celebration, yet Sam found it difficult to get into the right frame of mind. She kept thinking back to what had happened in the rose garden, how Khalid had stated with such certainty that there was no future for them, and it hurt. It really hurt even though she had expected nothing else.

She glanced at him over the rim of her glass, watching how the flickering candlelight highlighted the strong planes of his handsome face. Khalid would never be hers and she would never be his. The future was already mapped out and it wasn't about to change.

Somehow Khalid got through the evening but it was touch and go. He had to force himself to concentrate on the conversation because his mind kept skipping this way and that, always returning to those far-too-brief moments in the rose garden. He knew he should never have kissed Sam, knew that if he could go back in time he would resist temptation somehow, but for some inexplicable reason he didn't regret it. Holding her in his arms, feeling her lips so sweet and responsive under his, was a memory he would cherish. What he *did* regret was the fact that he had hurt her.

The thought plagued him. It was a relief when the evening ended and he could escape to his room. Unlike the royal palaces, his brother had opted for a more relaxed approach when it came to housing his guests. Men and women weren't segregated in separate areas and he discovered that his suite was right next to the one Sam was using. He went in and closed the door, forcing himself to think about nothing more than necessities. They would need to leave extra early the following morning if they weren't to miss the start of clinic...

The sound of the terrace doors being opened in the adjoining suite made his thoughts tail off. He held his breath, his heart jerking painfully when he heard footsteps crossing the terrace. This section of the house overlooked the desert so was Sam taking the chance to enjoy the night-time peace and quiet, hoping that it would soothe her, comfort her, possibly make her feel that bit less hurt?

Knowing that he was responsible for how she felt made him feel worse than ever but there was nothing he could do, no words that he could say that would make the situation better for her. Or for him. If he offered her a future that was linked to his then, inevitably, she would suffer even more, and that was something he couldn't tolerate. He had to protect her, protect himself too because he couldn't bear the thought of suffering the same kind of heartache if he lost her.

'Oh!'

The cry brought him to his feet. Crossing the room, Khalid flung open the terrace doors. Sam was standing at the edge of her terrace, her hand pressed to her throat. Although she had removed the headdress, she was still wearing the dress Mariam had lent her. Even though Khalid was more concerned about what had happened to make her cry out like that, he found himself thinking once again how much it suited her.

'Are you all right?' he demanded, struggling to confine his thoughts to areas where they needed to remain. 'What happened? Why did you cry out like that?'

'It was a lizard. I didn't see it until it ran over my foot.' She gave a little shudder then made a determined effort to collect herself. 'Sorry. I didn't mean to disturb you.'

'It doesn't matter. So long as you're all right, that's the important thing.' He half turned then realised that he couldn't leave it like this. He had to try to repair some of the damage he had caused at the very least. 'About tonight, Sam,' he began, turning back.

'Don't! Please don't apologise. I...I don't think I could bear it.'

Her voice broke as she turned away but not before he had seen the tears that welled into her eyes. Khalid cursed under his breath as he leapt over the ornate iron railing that separated the terraces. Drawing her into his arms, he held her against him, hating himself when he felt the sobs that wracked her slender body. He had done this to her. Him. Nobody else.

'I'm so sorry,' he murmured, stroking her hair. The silky blonde strands twined around his fingers, binding her to him in the sweetest way possible, and his heart ran wild. If he could be granted one wish, it would be to bind her to him for ever, never to let her go, to keep her at his side for eternity. It was at that moment that he finally acknowledged what he had known in his heart for a long time: he loved her. He always would even though he could never have her.

Whether it was that thought, that final uncompromising admission that made him do what he had sworn he must never do, he wasn't sure. But all of a sudden Khalid knew that he had to make love to her, that he couldn't live out the rest of his life without that memory to keep him sane. Tilting her face, he looked deep into her eyes, knowing that he must make it clear what he was asking, offering.

'I want us to make love, Sam, but only if you understand that it can never lead anywhere. You said before that I wouldn't want a woman from your background in my life and it's true, although not for the reasons you believe.' He cupped her face between his hands, wiping away her tears with his thumbs. 'The media interest would be unbearable for you. Your past would be raked up time and time again, every little thing that had happened to your family laid out for public consumption. It wouldn't matter if half of it weren't true—that wouldn't stop them. It would be a nightmare for you.'

'And for you.' She met his gaze, met and held it. 'It wouldn't help you, Khalid, to be linked to a woman like me, would it?' The laugh she gave was filled with such scorn that he flinched. 'When the news first broke you couldn't wait to get rid of me, could you? It must have come as a nasty shock to discover that my mother was just a step away from being a prostitute and that my brother was in prison.'

'It wasn't a shock. I already knew all about your background.'

'You knew! But how could you?'

He heard the disbelief in her voice and realised that he had to explain. 'Because my father's security team had run a background check on you when we first met.' He gave a little shrug. 'They do it whenever I meet anyone new. They checked up on Peter as well.'

'But that's terrible! It's an infringement of a person's rights.'

'I agree, but it's something that happens all the time and not just in countries like Azad. Your own government is very good at checking into the backgrounds of various people,' he added dryly.

She shook her head. 'I still don't think it's right but that's not the point, is it? If you knew about my past then why did you get involved with me? I would have thought you'd have run a mile rather than have your name linked to mine.'

'Why did I get involved with you? Well, that's easy.' He took hold of her hands and held them lightly, willing her to believe him. He wouldn't force her to accept what he had to say; she had to believe it in her own heart for it to mean anything. 'Your past didn't matter to me. The only thing I cared about was you, Sam. *You.* The person you were.'

He took a deep breath but there could be no holding back, no attempt to safeguard his pride at this stage. He had to tell her the truth or be damned.

'It's still the only thing that matters to me. I don't care about anything else. I only care about you and about making sure that you don't get hurt again. That's why I need you to think hard about what I am suggesting. I may want to make love with you, want it more than I've wanted anything in my life, but not if it means that you are going to suffer afterwards.'

CHAPTER ELEVEN

CANDLELIGHT LIT THE ROOM, its soft glow casting shadows over the bed. Sam lay on the cool, silk spread and waited while Khalid closed the shutters. Placing her hand on her heart, she felt it pounding beneath her palm.

She had been here before. Six years ago she had been in this very position, waiting, dreaming, *wanting* to make love with Khalid. The memory of her shock when he had told her that he had changed his mind was still so vivid that she closed her eyes, praying it wouldn't happen a second time. She didn't think she could bear another rejection.

The sound of his footsteps approaching the bed seemed unnaturally loud but Sam didn't open her eyes. She was afraid to do so, afraid to face what might happen a second time. She heard him pause but still she couldn't look at him—she was too scared.

'Sam, look at me.'

His voice was low, filled with understanding, and her lids slowly lifted. He sat down on the side of the bed, lifting her hand and pressing a kiss to her palm. 'Don't be scared. If you've changed your mind then I understand. I don't want you to do anything you might regret.'

Relief poured through her, swamped her. 'I haven't.

Changed my mind, I mean. I was just afraid that you
might have done, like last time...'

She broke off, not wanting to rake over the past at
that moment and spoil it.

'Oh, sweetheart, I'm so sorry. I should have realised.'

He gathered her to him, his lips painting a line of
tender kisses down her cheek. He reached her jaw and
lingered, his mouth resting on the tiny pulse that was
beating there with such frenzy before he straightened.
His voice sounded strained when he continued, hinting
at the effort it had cost him to call a halt, and she felt
reassured. This wasn't going to be a repeat of the last
time. There was no danger of that!

'I haven't changed my mind. If it's what you want
then it's what I want too. Desperately.'

'It is what I want, Khalid. I'm absolutely sure about
that.'

Reaching up, she drew him down towards her, pressing her mouth to his, and heard him sigh. The kiss they
shared was one of tenderness and understanding, of acceptance even, and it helped to dispel the very last of her
fears. Maybe this night had to be a start, a middle and an
end, but it would be worth it to have its memory stored
in her heart. She could take it out whenever she needed
to, remember how it had felt to have Khalid love her.

She closed her eyes, savouring the taste and feel of
his lips as he scattered kisses over her face. He reached
her throat and skated down it, pushing aside the folds
of her dress so he could kiss the upper swell of her
breasts. Mariam's underwear had proved to be far too
large for her so Sam had opted not to wear any that
night. There'd been no real need as the flowing folds
of the gown had protected her modesty. Now there was

very little separating Khalid's seeking mouth from her breasts and that was soon dispensed with.

'You are so beautiful. So perfect...' He couldn't continue because he was too busy lavishing her breasts with kisses to speak.

Sam groaned as he drew her nipple between his lips. Admittedly her experiences of lovemaking were limited, but not once had she felt this need growing stronger and stronger inside her. It was as though it was consuming her totally so that she could no longer think, only feel, but that was probably for the best. She didn't want to think and maybe start having doubts. She wanted this night to be perfect.

His hands returned to the row of tiny buttons down the front of her gown as he worked the rest of them free. Sam heard him suck in his breath as he parted the silky folds of cloth, exposing her naked body to his gaze, and shivered with anticipation. It really was going to happen. Tonight they were finally going to make love.

Khalid stood up and slid off his robe, letting it fall in a heap on the floor. His body was lean and fit, the taut muscles in his chest and shoulders flexing as he lay down beside her on the bed. Sam reached out and ran her hand over the smooth olive-toned skin on his chest, loving the way it slid beneath her palm like the purest silk. He had said that she was beautiful but he was beautiful too in his blatant masculinity.

Her hand glided on, down his chest, over his flat stomach until she reached the thatch of crisp black hair that delineated his masculinity. That he was deeply aroused was obvious and she paused, the colour flooding to her cheeks because all of a sudden she was overcome by shyness. The few times she had made love hadn't prepared her for this. She wasn't sure if she had the experience to make tonight as wonderful for him as she wanted it to be. The thought that she might disappoint him was like a heavy weight suddenly filling her heart.

'What is it? Tell me, my love.' His voice was soft and low, filled with such tenderness that Sam found herself blurting out the truth.

'I'm afraid that you will be disappointed.' She paused then hurried on. 'I...I'm not very experienced when it comes to making love, you see. You...well, you could regret it.'

'Never.' He lifted her hand and kissed her fingers, one by one. His eyes were very dark as they met hers. 'Nothing you do can ever disappoint me, Sam. Remember that.'

Bending, he kissed her on the lips, his mouth gentle at first then quickly becoming more demanding. Sam responded immediately, kissing him back with a hunger that she didn't try to hide. Maybe she lacked his experience but she loved him so much and that would make up for it.

It was the first time she had admitted how she truly felt and it was both exhilarating and terrifying to have to face the fact that she still loved him. Sam drove the thought from her mind. She couldn't deal with it right now, not when Khalid was making her body hum with desire as he stroked and caressed her. Everywhere his hands touched, it felt as though she was on fire, burning up with this insatiable need for him. One caress wasn't enough, neither were a dozen. She wanted more and more, wanted the feelings he was arousing inside her to never end.

'Sam!' He cried out her name, his voice hoarse with passion, and she held him close, feeling her own body grow tense as all the sensations suddenly erupted into one huge conflagration.

Sam closed her eyes, seeing the flames licking behind her lids, *feeling* them pouring through her body. This was how it felt to make love, she thought as she slid over the edge into oblivion. This was how it was meant to be. But even as passion swept her away, she knew that it was only with Khalid that she would experience this depth of feeling, only with him that she would ever know how it really felt to be a woman. It was only Khalid who she would ever love this way.

Soft morning light filtered into the room, chasing away the night's shadows. Khalid lay on his back and watched as the dawn broke. He wished he could stop it happening. Wished he could turn back the clock and keep time in abeyance but he didn't have that power. The minutes would keep ticking past, the hours would keep on stacking up, and a new day would begin.

Last night had been the most wonderful experience he had ever known but it wouldn't last. It couldn't. It couldn't be repeated either. It had been a one-off, a night that he knew would influence his life from now on. Making love with Sam had been everything he had dreamt it would be and so much more. Nothing that happened from here on could match it. Ever.

'What's wrong?'

The gently spoken question alerted him to the fact that Sam was awake. Rolling onto his side, he studied the delicate lines of her face. Her huge grey eyes were still heavy with sleep but he could see remnants of the passion they had shared lingering in their depths. That she had been as moved by the whole experience as he had been wasn't in doubt and he suddenly found himself wishing that it hadn't been so wonderful, so all-consuming for both of them. Maybe it would have been easier to do what needed to be done if they hadn't found such delight in each other's arms.

'Nothing.' He leant forward and kissed her lips, felt her shudder, and drew back. He couldn't afford to make love to her again, couldn't allow temptation to lead him from the path he had to take. For Sam's sake he had to be strong and resist. Tossing back the sheet, he went to get out of bed but she stopped him.

'Don't lie, Khalid. I can tell that something is troubling you.'

He sighed as he sank back onto the mattress and took her in his arms. 'I'm just feeling a little sad because the night has ended. That's all it is.'

'Is it?' She drew back and looked at him. 'It's not because you regret what happened?'

'No!' He pulled her to him, held her close, willed her to believe that regret was the last thing he felt. He didn't regret what they had done; his only regret was that it could never happen again. 'I don't regret it, Sam. How could I when it was everything I had dreamt it would be?'

He kissed her softly, letting his lips linger this time as he didn't have the strength to resist. He could feel her trembling when he raised his head, see the passion that had ignited in her eyes again, and felt his own desire start to flow hotly through his veins. Maybe they couldn't have for ever but they had now and that was something special. Magical.

They made love and once again it was perfect. Each kiss, each caress seemed to take on a depth and meaning he had never experienced before. Khalid's heart was racing, aching, as he drove them both to fresh heights. He had never felt this kind of completion before, never known how it could feel to give and to receive love like this. It was only Sam who could arouse him this way, only Sam he wanted. They were both completely spent when they broke apart, both exhausted by such an outpouring of their passion. When Sam raised his hand and pressed a kiss to his knuckles, he trembled with need, with desire, with love for her.

'I had no idea it could feel like this, Khalid. No matter what happens, I shall never regret what we've done. I want you to know that.'

'I shall never regret it either.' He squeezed her fingers and his heart was heavy as he forced himself to let her go. 'I'd better return to my own room. I wouldn't want to shock the servants.'

'Of course not.' She sat up as he got out of bed, modestly drawing the sheet around her. 'We shall need to leave soon if we don't want to miss the start of clinic.'

'I'll make sure that Shahzad has organised the helicopter as soon as I'm dressed.' He summoned a smile but it wasn't easy as the demands of the day started to press down on him. Last night may have been wonderful but he was all too aware that it was over. It had been a tiny oasis of time, a few precious hours that could never be repeated. From this moment on he would have to get on with his life as Sam would have to get on with hers.

'There will be time for something to eat before we leave,' he said as steadily as he could when it felt as though his heart was in shreds. 'Would you like me to get one of the servants to bring you a tray?'

'If it isn't too much trouble.'

The flatness of her tone told him that she too had realised that this was it, that the night was over and that from this moment on they had to be sensible. Khalid wished he could make the situation easier for her but there was nothing he could do. Despite his joy in their lovemaking, he was still convinced that he had to let her go.

He went back to his room and showered and dressed then went to find his brother. Shahzad was in the rose garden and Khalid could see immediately how much better he looked now that he had stopped worrying about Mariam. How he envied him! Envied him for having found the woman he loved and for being able to share his life with her and their children. Maybe he was being foolish. Maybe there was a way that he and Sam could be together. If she was willing to adapt to life in Azad it could work...

And it could fail miserably too.

'Good morning. And it is a beautiful morning, isn't it?' Shahzad greeted him with undisguised delight and Khalid did his best to shake off the feeling of despondency that threatened to overwhelm him.

'It is indeed.' He dredged up a smile. 'How is Mariam this morning? Feeling better, I hope.'

'Much. Discovering the reason why she has felt so ill lately has improved things a hundredfold. She is thrilled at the thought of having twins, as I am.' Shahzad enveloped him in a brotherly hug. 'Thank you, Khalid, for bringing Sam here. I doubt we would have got to the bottom of the problem if it weren't for her.'

'I'm sure Mariam's own doctor would have realised what was wrong eventually,' he demurred.

'Perhaps and perhaps not.' Shahzad sighed. 'Sometimes our royal status can be a hindrance, can't it? People are less inclined to put forward their opinions and insist on a course of action than they might do otherwise.'

Khalid knew it was true. 'Fortunately Sam doesn't view life that way. She's unimpressed by wealth or status.'

'Which is why you were attracted to her, I imagine.' Shahzad's gaze was searching. 'I expect you knew all about her background before the media latched on to it, but it didn't concern you, did it, brother?'

'No,' Khalid replied truthfully. 'It didn't matter a jot to me.'

'Yet you two split up shortly after the newspapers ran the story?' Shahzad smiled when Khalid looked at him in surprise. 'Oh, yes, I know that you two were seeing one another. There's little that either of us do that doesn't get reported.'

Khalid recognised the truth of that statement. As a member of the Azadian royal family, he should have known that his affairs were being closely monitored. 'Yes, it's true. Sam and I were close at one time. However, after the papers ran that story I knew that we would have to split up. I wasn't concerned about the effect it would have on me—I'm used to being the subject of speculation. However, I realised how hurt and upset she'd have been if her family's shortcomings were continually raked up.'

'I see. And that's why you decided to end your relationship?'

'That plus the fact that I didn't want her to end up

regretting getting involved with me. Sam would have had to give up so much if we had married—her career, her dreams, everything she has worked so hard to achieve. I couldn't do that to her, couldn't take away everything that makes her who she is. She would have ended up resenting me, *blaming* me even, just like my mother ended up blaming our father, and that was a risk I wasn't willing to take.'

He took a deep breath, determinedly ironing any trace of emotion from his voice. 'It's a risk I am still not prepared to take. Once this mission is completed I have no intention of seeing Sam ever again.'

Sam came to an unsteady halt when she heard what Khalid had said. It was no more than she should have expected and yet it hurt unbearably to hear him state it out loud. It made what had happened the previous night seem somehow tawdry. Shameful. Khalid had made love to her and she had truly thought it had meant something to him, but had it? Really?

It was all she could do not to turn tail and scurry back inside but once she did that then it would be even harder to face him in the future. She squared her shoulders, knowing that she had to brazen it out. Khalid had made no promises. On the contrary, he had told her that they didn't have a future. It was her own fault if she had read too much into what had happened last night. It had been sex and that was all. One night of glorious, mind-blowing sex. Most women her age would think nothing of having indulged in such an experience.

'There you are.' She fixed a smile to lips that were inclined to tremble if she let them. However, this new Sam, the one who now understood the joys of sleeping with an experienced partner, wasn't about to show any sign of weakness. 'I was just coming to find you. Are we ready for the off?'

'Just about.' Khalid's tone was cool, the look he gave her equally so, and she was glad that she had managed to keep control of her emotions. He wouldn't thank her for making a scene, certainly not. He turned to his brother. 'Is the helicopter ready to fly us back to camp?'

'Whenever you wish.' Shahzad smiled at them both. 'Mariam will want to see you off, though. I shall go and fetch her.'

He disappeared inside, leaving behind a small silence. Sam wished she could think of something to say but her mind was blank. Had it been purely sex for Khalid? All those magical kisses, those delicately sensual caresses that had turned her bones to liquid fire? Had it been less emotion than experience that had made him seem like the perfect lover?

A sob caught in her throat and she hurriedly turned it into a cough when she felt him look at her. All that was left to her now was pride and if she lost that then heaven knew how she would cope. There was another month to get through, four more weeks of working with Khalid, and it would be unbearable if he suspected how devastated she felt. Maybe he hadn't rejected her last night but she wished he had. It couldn't have felt any worse than this!

Mariam and Shahzad came hurrying out to say their goodbyes. The girls were with them and in the flurry of farewells it was easier to hide her feelings.

'Thank you so much, Sam. To discover I am carrying twins has come as the most wonderful surprise and I am truly grateful to you.' Mariam hugged Sam then smiled at Khalid. 'And thank you for bringing her. Knowing what a doting uncle you are, I'm sure you must be thrilled too, although it's time that you thought about starting a family of your own, isn't it?' She turned to Sam and laughed. 'We're all looking forward to the day when Khalid finally relinquishes his bachelor ways and settles down!'

Sam couldn't think of anything to say. She dredged up a smile, her heart aching at the thought of Khalid marrying and having a family, as indeed he would at some point. It was what was expected of him, after all, that he would find a suitable bride and have children to carry on the royal bloodline. The thought was almost too painful to bear but she had to face facts and not allow herself to imagine that she could fulfil that role. She could never be Khalid's wife and the mother of his children, not someone like her, a Westerner without the right connections.

Her heart was aching as she kissed the children and promised that she would come back and visit them again even though she knew it wasn't going to happen. Once she left Azad, that would be it: she wouldn't return.

The helicopter was waiting for them so they climbed on board. Sam fastened her seat belt, turning to stare out of the window as they lifted off. Tears pricked her eyes as she watched the villa disappear from view. She had discovered the real meaning of what it meant to be a woman in that villa and it was sad to think that she would never go there again but inevitable, given the circumstances. Now she just had to get through the next few weeks and that would be it. She would go back to her own life and put what had happened behind her.

Just for a moment her heart shrank at the thought before she took a deep breath. She had done it before and she could do it again.

CHAPTER TWELVE

THE FOLLOWING MONTH passed in a blur. News of the clinic had spread throughout the desert communities and each time they pitched camp they were inundated with patients. Everyone worked flat out but Khalid was very aware that they were only touching the very tip of the iceberg. There was still so much work to be done, far too much to complete in the time he had allotted for this mission.

It made him see that he needed to instigate the tentative plans he had made to set up a chain of permanent clinics. Between working out the logistics of doing that and seeing patients, he didn't have a minute to himself but he was glad. The less free time he had the better if it meant he didn't keep thinking about Sam and what had happened.

Their final day arrived and everyone was in high spirits as they packed up. Khalid supervised the packing of the more delicate pieces of equipment, which would be needed when his plans reached fruition. Peter offered to help him, an offer he accepted with alacrity. Peter was crucial to his plans and he wanted to have word with him.

'How would you feel about moving out here on a

permanent basis?' he asked, not wasting any time. He helped his friend stow some particularly fragile pieces of technology into one of the crates then looked up. 'I've decided to set up a chain of permanent clinics and I need a director who knows what he's about. Would you be interested?'

'Yes. I would.' Peter's face turned pink with pleasure. 'I was wondering how best to approach you about doing something like that. There's a desperate need for a more permanent source of healthcare out here, isn't there?'

'There is.' Khalid clapped him on the shoulder, unable to hide his delight that Peter was keen to come on board. Normally, he would have opted for a much cooler approach but since *that* night he'd found it far more difficult to hide his feelings. He hastily dismissed the memories that rushed to the forefront of his mind, pictures of Sam's body naked to his gaze and the passion in her eyes. He needed to focus on his plans or he would drive himself mad.

'Obviously it will take some time to get everything organised but I don't want there to be too long of a delay. I'm aiming for three months maximum for the first clinic—would that be too soon for you?'

'Not for me, no. But I may need to convince Jess that it's a good idea.' Peter blushed even more. 'Jess and I... well, we have an understanding, you see. I hope I can persuade her to come with me.'

'So do I. Congratulations! She's a great girl. You couldn't have found anyone better suited to you,' Khalid told him sincerely.

'Thanks.' Peter looked up and grinned. 'Oh, hi there. Has Khalid managed to persuade you to sign up as well?

I hope so. It would be great to have as many of the old team together as possible.'

Khalid glanced round to see who Peter was talking to and felt his heart sink when he saw Sam. By tacit consent they had kept any conversations they'd had confined to work during the past few weeks. He guessed that Sam was as wary as he was of getting into difficult territory. Peter would be mortified if he realised that unwittingly he had taken them down a route neither of them wished to explore.

'I'm not sure what you mean,' Sam replied as she joined them. She looked from Peter to Khalid and raised her brows. 'What's going on?'

'I've decided to make a start on setting up those clinics I was thinking about.' Khalid shrugged, feigning an insouciance he wished he felt. It would have been the icing on the cake if he could have asked Sam to come on board but he didn't dare. It was too risky, too tempting, too *everything*! 'Peter's just agreed to take on the role of director.'

'Really? Congratulations. You couldn't have found anyone better.'

Sam stepped forward and hugged Peter. She looked genuinely delighted but Khalid could see the pain in her eyes and knew that beneath the surface she was mulling it over, assessing why he hadn't offered her a role. He wanted to, wanted it more than anything, but surely she could see how impossible it would be if they had to work together on a long-term basis?

'I would have suggested that you join us but it wouldn't be fair, would it, Sam? Not at this stage in your career. You're in the running for a consultant's post, I believe, and that's more important than anything else.'

'Of course.' She glanced at him and he saw the scorn in her eyes that told him emphatically that she didn't believe him. It stung but there was nothing he could do but stick to his story. 'Anyway, I just wanted to let you know that the clinic is all sorted. Everything's boxed up and clearly labelled so it should be simple enough to unpack whenever you need anything. What time are we leaving?'

'One-thirty.' Khalid checked his watch. There were still four hours to go before the plane was due to take off, more than enough time to get everyone to the airport. He came to a decision, needing to bring things to a swift conclusion when he didn't trust himself not to do something foolish. 'Why don't you and the rest of the women set off now? You can do some shopping at the airport before your flight takes off.'

'Why not indeed?' Sam flicked him an icily polite smile. Her expression warmed up considerably as she turned to Peter. 'It's been great working with you, Peter. Best of luck with the new project.'

They exchanged kisses before she left. Khalid went back to his packing, trying his best to focus on what he was doing, but it was a losing battle. Sam was leaving and he wouldn't see her again. How could he bear it? But how could he not?

The flight to England seemed never-ending. Sam tried to sleep to while away the time but her mind was too busy to relax. Khalid could have stopped her leaving. He could have said something, *anything*, and she would have stayed. Even though it would have raised a lot of eyebrows in such a conservative country as Azad, she would have stayed with him on any terms, but he hadn't said a word, had he? He didn't want her to stay for the simple reason that he didn't want *her*. Not now that he had finally made love to her.

It was a relief to land at Heathrow. In the flurry of farewells nobody noticed her distress and, more importantly, asked her what was wrong. She had been intending to stay overnight in London but she decided to take the next available flight back to Manchester. She wanted to go home to her flat and close the front door so she could lick her wounds in private. That they were wounds she had helped to inflict on herself was something she would have to come to terms with. One thing was certain: she refused to let what had happened ruin her life.

Sam threw herself back into her work with gusto. There'd been several changes while she'd been off, staff had left and new people had been hired so it took her longer than expected to get back into the flow. Added to that, she felt unusually tired but put it down to the fact that she had been working non-stop for months. When her tiredness didn't improve by the time she had been home for six weeks, she started to wonder if she was maybe anaemic and bought herself some iron tablets from the hospital's pharmacy but they didn't improve matters. It was only when she got up one morning and was violently sick that the penny finally dropped with a resounding clang. Was it possible that she was pregnant?

It was too early to go to the shops so Sam went straight into work and took a pregnancy testing kit out of the cupboard. She went into the bathroom and peed on the plastic stick as per instructions then waited for the results. When the word 'PREGNANT' appeared on the screen she groaned out loud. What a fool she was not to have thought of this before. It was her job, so help her; she dealt with pregnant women every day of her working life and understood better than anyone the mechanics of how it happened! Yet she had blithely slept with Khalid without a thought for the consequences. Now she had to decide what to do, although there was no chance of her terminating the pregnancy. She was sure about that.

She placed her hand on her stomach, imagining the tiny life growing inside her, a life that she and Khalid had created. They were both responsible for this child's conception and she had to tell him, no matter how shocked or how angry he was, because he certainly wouldn't have chosen for this to happen, would he? Not a woman from a background like hers carrying his child, a child who had royal blood.

Sam squared her shoulders. Even if he was furious, he still needed to be told, not for his sake or for hers but for the sake of their child. She wasn't going to allow her son or daughter to grow up feeling ashamed, feeling that they had to apologise for their very existence. She knew how that felt and she refused to let her child suffer that kind of heartache. No matter how Khalid felt, this baby would know from the outset who its father was, even if Khalid refused to acknowledge him or her!

Setting in motion his plans for the clinics proved to be easier than Khalid had imagined. His father, King Faisal, proved to be an enthusiastic ally, offering both practical and moral support. His father railroaded the more conservative members of his government and obtained their agreement so that within a remarkably short space of time Khalid was told that he had the go-ahead and that funding would be found to pay for whatever was needed.

Three months later, the first clinic opened. Peter had proved to be invaluable at finding experienced staff to work for them. Although most people were hired on short-term contracts, the excellent pay plus all the other benefits had attracted a lot of interest. Khalid found himself in the enviable position of being able to pick and choose who they hired.

Once the clinic opened, he decided that he could afford to take some time off. He had been working flat out and he needed some down time. It was just the thought of spending his free time thinking about Sam that made him hesitate. He couldn't bear to keep going over and over what had happened when he knew in his heart that he had done the right thing. The only thing. Sam would have wilted and died if she'd had to conform to Azadian standards, even if they were improving.

He decided that he would spend some time endurance riding. He hadn't been able to indulge his interest in the sport for some time. Riders crossed the desert on horseback, setting time limits for the distances they travelled. It was a gruelling and demanding hobby that required a great deal of physical and mental strength from the riders. Although the horses were changed frequently, the riders had to complete the course no matter what. It was almost guaranteed that he wouldn't have time to think about much else, including Sam, hopefully.

He set off at dawn a few days later, accompanied by several friends who also enjoyed the challenges of the sport. They covered a lot of ground and he was delighted with what they had achieved when they stopped for the night. The next leg promised to be the most taxing so they were up before dawn and set off as soon as the sun rose. By mid-morning they were halfway to their destination and on schedule to complete the next leg on time.

It was only when they stopped to change horses that he became aware of a potential problem and his heart sank. The sky was rapidly turning dark, showing all the signs that a major sandstorm was approaching. As they gathered the horses and equipment together and hunkered down to ride out the storm, he found himself thinking about Sam.

Maybe he should have done the same, ridden out any storms that may have occurred in their relationship, fought for that happy ending he wanted so desperately. There were no guarantees in life, apart from the fact that he loved her. He should have fought for what he wanted, he realised. He should have fought for Sam.

The flight to Azad seemed to take for ever. It wasn't a private jet this time but a scheduled flight with all the attendant delays. Sam was exhausted when they finally touched down. She had booked a room at a hotel close to the airport and found a taxi to take her there, aware that this had been the easy bit. She still had to contact Khalid and make arrangements to see him.

Her heart jolted at the thought of his reaction to what she had to tell him but she was determined to do the right thing for this baby. She and Jess had kept in touch so as soon as she got into her hotel room she texted her friend to let her know that she had arrived. Jess had moved out to Azad to be with Peter, although they were observing the proprieties and not actually living together. As Jess had told her, it would make it even more special when they got married, which they planned to do very shortly.

Jess texted her back immediately, offering to meet her for breakfast the following day in the hotel. Whilst two women breakfasting together without a male companion wouldn't raise any eyebrows in the cosmopolitan confines of the hotel, Sam knew that it would be frowned upon outside. The last thing she wanted was to cause a fuss; she had too much else to worry about.

By the time the receptionist phoned to tell her that Jess had arrived the next morning, Sam was all ready. Despite her exhaustion, she hadn't slept and it showed in the dark circles under her eyes. She studied her reflection in the mirror for a moment before practising her smile. She hadn't told Jess why she had come back to Azad. Although she had no intention of keeping it a secret, it didn't seem right to tell anyone about the baby before she told Khalid. She had opted instead for the rather flimsy excuse that she had a few days free and wanted to see how the plans for the clinics were progressing.

Thankfully, Jess seemed to have accepted that but she would soon grow suspicious if Sam appeared with a glum face, hence the smile. However, when she went downstairs and saw Jess waiting for her, it was her friend's expression that worried her most of all. What on earth was wrong with Jess?

'What is it?' Hurrying over, she squeezed Jess's hands. 'It isn't Peter, is it? You two haven't had a row, have you?'

'No. Peter's fine.' Jess gripped Sam's hands and her

face was filled with compassion. 'It's Khalid. I don't know how to tell you this, Sam, but he's missing.'

'Missing. What do you mean?' Sam's heart sank like a stone. She could feel it plummeting all the way down to her feet and was glad that Jess had hold of her because she was afraid that she might keel over.

'Apparently, he was out in the desert with some friends. Endurance riding or some such thing—I dunno 'cos I've never heard of it before. Anyway there was a sandstorm, a really massive one, and one of the men was badly injured. Khalid insisted that it was too dangerous to move him so once they'd dug out the truck, most of the party set off to fetch help. Khalid stayed behind with the injured man and one of the grooms to look after the horses. The rest of the group had taken a GPS reading so they thought it wouldn't be that difficult to find their way back but something must have gone wrong with the GPS.'

Jess gulped. 'To put it bluntly, they can't find Khalid and the other men. They seem to have disappeared off the face of the earth. There are people out searching for them, but although no one has actually come out and said so, it's obvious that they think they're probably dead!'

Khalid tilted the canvas awning to try and deflect the worst of the heat off his friend. It was midday and the temperature was horrendous. Basir was rambling under his breath again and Khalid frowned. There was no doubt that his friend's condition was worsening despite the drugs he had given him to fight off any infection. He desperately needed to get him to hospital so that the displaced fracture to Basir's left femur could be repaired properly. He had done all he could with what limited supplies they'd had with them, but he certainly hadn't been able to do all that was necessary. If help didn't arrive soon, he couldn't guarantee that there would be a happy ending to this story.

Mohammed, the groom, came to tell him about the horses. The man bowed low then explained that they were all well but that water was running short. They had enough to last them another day but after that...well.

Khalid thanked him, trying not let the older man see how worried he was. He checked his watch. It was three days since the rest of the party had left to fetch help so where were they? He could only assume that they had encountered some kind of a problem, although he tried his best not to dwell on the thought. He had to stay positive, believe that help would arrive, believe that they would survive; believe that that he would see Sam again. If he stopped believing, especially that last bit, he would give up.

Closing his eyes, he summoned up her image, unsurprised when within seconds there she was, inside his head. A smile curved his mouth. If the thought of seeing her again wasn't the biggest incentive of all to remain positive, then heaven alone knew what was!

Jess took Sam to see Peter, who was based at the largest of the clinics. It was almost an exact replica of the one Sam had worked in and her heart ached as she recalled everything that had happened during her time there. She pushed the memories aside because she couldn't afford to think about the past. It was the present that mattered and that meant finding Khalid.

Peter greeted her warmly but it was impossible not

to see how worried he was. He sat her down and quietly explained what was happening. There were helicopters out searching for the missing men, plus people on the ground, scouring the desert around where they were believed to have last been seen. It all took time but Khalid would be found, Peter assured her, although Sam suspected that his assurances owed more to wanting to spare her feelings than anything else. They both knew how difficult it would be to find anyone in the vastness of the desert.

The wait was almost unendurable. Sam had nothing to fill the time and spent it worrying. When Jess came racing into the tent to find her, Sam couldn't understand what she was saying at first.

'What is it?' she demanded, leaping to her feet. 'Has something happened?'

'They've found them!' Jess grabbed hold of her and whirled her round in a victory dance. 'They've only gone and found them!'

Sam gazed at her in shock for a second before her vision suddenly blurred. Jess hastily lowered her onto a seat and pushed her head between her knees.

'Sit there while I fetch you some water. You'll feel better in a moment.'

Sam breathed slowly, forcing the faintness away. By the time Jess returned with the water she was able to sit up and take the glass from her. 'Thanks. Sorry about that. It was the shock, I suppose.'

'Just the shock?' Jess gave her an old-fashioned look and it was obvious that she had guessed the real reason for what had happened.

Sam sighed softly. 'OK. Yes, I'm pregnant. And, yes again, Khalid is the baby's father.'

'I thought there must be more to this visit than you were letting on.' Jess sat down beside her and her expression was grave. 'Does he know about the baby?'

'Not yet. That's why I'm here, to tell him.' Sam smiled thinly. 'I'm not expecting him to be pleased but he needs to know.'

'I don't know about him not being pleased. From what Peter's said, I don't think he will be too upset, shall we say. But that's your business, not mine. What I will say, Sam, is that you're doing the right thing, no matter what happens. Khalid needs to know that you're carrying his child. Right. Now let's see about getting you to the hospital. According to Peter, Khalid should be there by now and I'm sure you will want to see him a.s.a.p.'

Sam was grateful for Jess's understanding. Within a very short time everything was organised and Peter had volunteered to drive her into the city. He led the way once they reached the hospital, obviously familiar with the modern, hi-spec building. Khalid had a private suite on the ninth floor and the state-of-the-art lift swiftly conveyed them up there. There was a guard outside but he bowed when he saw Peter and allowed him to knock on the door, which was opened almost immediately by a white-coated manservant. They were ushered into what was obviously a sitting room and offered refreshments, which they both refused. Sam didn't want refreshments: she wanted to see Khalid!

Five minutes later her wish was granted. Sam's breath caught as they were led into a room that contained all the equipment she would have expected to see in a highly equipped hospital unit. Her eyes skated over the familiar monitors and other equipment before coming to rest on the man lying on the bed. There was a tube attached to his arm, undoubtedly feeding him much-needed fluid. After spending so much time out in the desert, he would be dehydrated, although there could be many other things wrong with him as well.

Her gaze moved on, searching for clues as to his condition, but she couldn't see any sign of injury and breathed a little easier. Maybe he wasn't too badly hurt, not so badly hurt that he was in danger at least.

The thought triggered another bout of faintness and she swayed. Peter must have noticed her reaction and unceremoniously bundled her into a chair.

'Sit there and I'll get you some water,' he told her, hurrying over to fill a glass from the carafe standing on the bedside table.

Sam slowly raised her head, her face colouring when she discovered that Khalid was watching her. She thanked Peter for the water and forced herself to sip it slowly and not gulp it down as she felt like doing. Khalid was bound to be surprised to see her but was it only that? Surely it wasn't possible that he had guessed why she had come, like Jess had done?

'So, how are you?' Peter checked the monitors and nodded. 'Your vital signs appear to be normal, if it's any consolation.'

'I'm fine.' Impatience laced Khalid's voice and Sam's skin prickled. She knew what lay behind it, that he had questions he wanted to ask her and didn't welcome the delay. 'My doctor is erring on the side of caution, erring too far in that direction in my opinion. He insisted on the drip and the monitors even though they aren't necessary. I know how I feel and I am perfectly well.'

As though to emphasise the point, he removed a couple of leads, causing the monitor to beep out a noisy warning. Sam breathed in sharply, her head spinning with the sound. The door was flung open and a couple of nurses appeared. They fussed around when they spotted the loosened leads but Khalid shook his head when they tried to re-attach them.

'Leave them,' he ordered regally. 'And while you are here, you can remove the drip as well. It isn't necessary.'

It was obvious that they were unhappy about that idea. The older woman muttered something before they both hurriedly retreated. Sam suspected that they were going to find the doctor and leave the decision to him, not that she blamed them. In their shoes, she would have wanted some backing if she'd been ordered to countermand instructions, even if it was someone of Khalid's standing issuing them.

The thought that he was playing on his royal status to get his own way annoyed her. She glared at him. 'Throwing your toys out of the pram because you can't do what *you* want doesn't exactly show you in a good light, Khalid.'

His head reared up when he heard the scorn in her voice. 'I am a doctor. I know if I'm ill and need all this equipment or not.'

'Perhaps.' She shrugged. 'Although to my mind you aren't in a position to make rational decisions. Not after being out in the sun for so long.'

'You think I am suffering from sunstroke and unable to know my own mind?' he shot back.

'Something like that,' she countered, oddly exhilarated by the spiky exchange. She had spent the past few weeks first brooding about sleeping with him, then missing him, and then worrying about his reaction when she told him she was pregnant. It was a relief to be able to let loose some of the turbulent emotions that filled her.

'Now, now, children. Let's not squabble.' Peter looked from one to the other with undisguised amusement. 'You've both had a shock and my advice is to let things settle before you go tearing strips off each other.' He gave them a moment for that to sink in then went to the door. 'I'm off to find myself a cup of tea. Try to be good while I'm away, won't you?'

Sam watched the door close behind him. Her heart was pounding because she was very aware that now they were alone she would have to tell Khalid why she had come. Maybe she could put it off a while longer but why bother? He had said that he was fine and there was no reason to delay.

'Khalid…'

'I'm sorry, Sam. I have no idea why I behaved that way when I have been longing to see you.' He cut her off but she didn't mind, not when she heard what he said.

'Have you?' she asked huskily.

'Yes. It was the thought of seeing you that kept me going these past few days.' He held out his hand, palm up. 'Seeing you and touching you.'

Sam didn't need to hear anything more. She was across the room in a trice, placing her hand in his and gripping it so tightly that it was a wonder his fingers didn't go numb. 'I've been longing to see you too. See you and…and touch you.'

'My love.'

He pulled her down to him, his mouth claiming hers in a kiss that was an explosion of so many emotions that her heart ran wild. Passion and tenderness, desire and need were all mingled together in one huge surge of feelings that cleared her mind of everything else. It was hard to gather her thoughts when they broke apart but Sam knew that she had to tell him about the baby before they went any further.

'I have something to tell you, Khalid. Something that you may not want to hear but which you need to know. I'm pregnant with your child.'

Khalid felt the world grind to a stop. It was as though it was suddenly teetering on its axis, brought to a halt by the announcement. He stared at Sam, seeing the worry in her eyes as well as the determination. How much courage it must have taken for her to come here and tell him that after the way they had parted, he couldn't imagine, but he was filled to the brim with admiration for her. Filled with that along with so many other emotions he could barely make sense of them all. Then one single thought rose to the surface: She was carrying his child.

'Oh, my sweet!' He pulled her into his arms, held her to his heart and rejoiced. It was something he had longed for yet had never allowed himself to hope it would happen. Now that it had, he knew that he would make it work. Somehow. Some way. *Any way at all!* No matter what problems they encountered, he and Sam would love and care for this precious child. Together.

He kissed her again and it was a kiss that held a promise for the future. Drawing back, he looked deep into her eyes. 'I can't tell you how thrilled I am. It's what I have dreamt about but never thought would happen.' He placed his hand on her stomach, imagining the new life growing inside her womb. 'Having you and a baby was my dearest wish but I was afraid it couldn't be.'

'It was my wish too.' Her tone was flat all of a sudden and it worried him.

'Was? It isn't what you want now?'

'Yes, it's what I want. However, I am realistic enough to know that we can't always have what we want.' She looked round when a knock on the door heralded the return of the nurses. 'We need to talk, Khalid, but we can't do so here. Peter knows where I'm staying—you can get the details from him when you're ready to meet up and discuss where we go from here.'

'I thought that was obvious,' he shot back, unbearably hurt by her attitude. Didn't she want him in her life—was that what she was saying? Had telling him about the baby been purely a token gesture born out of a sense of duty and nothing more? The thought turned his flesh to ice.

'Nothing is obvious in this situation,' she said quietly. 'We just have to do what is right for all of us, and especially what is right for our child.'

She stood up and went to the door, ignoring him when he ordered her to stop. The two nurses, closely followed by his doctor, hurried into the room as Sam left. Khalid allowed them to fuss around him, re-attaching the leads, checking the monitors, performing all the tasks that he would have insisted on in their position. It was less giving in gracefully than lack of interest that made him so compliant. He didn't care what they did; he only cared about Sam and what she was thinking. Feeling. Planning. He couldn't bear the thought that his whole future might lie in her hands and that there was nothing he could do about it!

He took a deep breath after the medics left then calmly detached all the leads once more. Ignoring the monitor, which was beeping like crazy, he got out of bed. He wasn't going to lie here and wait for Sam to reach a decision. No way! He was going to fight for what he wanted. Fight for her and his child and fight tooth and nail too. Sam could find that she had a bigger battle on her hands than she had anticipated but so long as she was happy with the outcome they would both be winners.

CHAPTER THIRTEEN

SAM WENT STRAIGHT to her room after Peter dropped her off at the hotel. Jess had wanted her to go home with her but Sam had refused the well-intentioned offer. She needed to be by herself so she could work out what she should do. It would be so easy to get carried away by Khalid's declarations but deep down she knew it wasn't that simple. Yes, she loved him, and, yes, it appeared that he loved her too; however, she needed to think very carefully about the repercussions it could cause if she agreed to stay with him.

She made herself a cup of coffee and sat by the window to drink it, watching the sunlight reflecting off the modern high-rise towers that comprised this part of the city. Khalid had told her that Azad was changing and it was, but the old values still held firm. How would it affect Khalid if they married and the Azadian people found out about her family? Would it blight him in their eyes, make his position as a member of the ruling family untenable?

He hadn't mentioned marriage, granted, but she knew he would and that was something else she needed to think about. Khalid had a strongly developed sense of honour, so how could she be sure that he wouldn't offer to marry her simply because she was carrying his child? She couldn't bear to think that his life might be blighted because he wanted to do the right thing, couldn't bear to know that his feelings for her weren't as all-encompassing as hers were for him. It would be better for them to part than to live her life knowing that he was with her out of a sense of duty.

Sam's heart was heavy as she stood up and put her cup on the table. She had done what she had set out to do and told Khalid about the baby. There was no reason for her to stay.

As soon as Khalid was dressed, he phoned Peter and asked him where Sam was staying. Once he had the address, he summoned his driver and told the man to take him to her hotel. His impromptu departure from the hospital caused an uproar but he brushed aside the doctor's protests. This was far more important than anything else, far more urgent. Maybe he was mistaken but he had a nasty feeling that if he didn't go and find Sam immediately, she would do something stupid.

He sat on the edge of his seat as the car swept through the busy downtown traffic. When they drew up in the hotel's forecourt he had the door open before his driver could stop the engine. He strode across the foyer and made his way straight to the reception desk. The receptionist blanched when she recognised him but Khalid ignored her discomfort as he demanded to know which room Miss Warren was in. His heart sank when the woman haltingly explained that Miss Warren had checked out and was on her way to the airport.

Khalid returned to his car and told the driver to take him to the airport. Peter had given him Sam's mobile phone number so he tried calling it but it went straight to voice mail. He tried the airlines next and discovered that there was a flight leaving for London in less than an hour's time. He could only assume that she was booked on it.

The drive to the airport seemed never-ending. Khalid could feel his tension mounting as the minutes ticked past. When they finally arrived, he could barely contain himself as he leapt from the car and ran into the terminal. International flights went from Terminal Two so he raced across the concourse, taking the escalator steps two at a time. Sam's flight was boarding and once she got on the plane that would be it; he wouldn't be able to follow her unless he had a ticket…

Cursing his own stupidity, he veered off towards the booking hall. Thankfully, there wasn't a queue and he was able to purchase a first-class ticket for the London flight. A glimpse of his passport immediately afforded him VIP status and he was rushed through the various channels. Five minutes later he was boarding the plane. Now all he had to do was find Sam and talk to her, make her understand that they could work this out.

He grimaced. That was all?

Sam watched as the ground fell away. Tears were stinging her eyes but she blinked them away. She had done the right thing even though it didn't feel like it at this moment. If she had stayed and allowed Khalid to persuade her they could have a future together, she would have regretted it. She loved him too much to risk hurting him. It was better to let him go than live with that constant fear in her mind. She would let him see the baby—there was no question about that. However, she wouldn't tie him to her, wouldn't allow his life to be adversely affected in any way.

The plane levelled off and people started to move about when the seat-belt sign went out. When someone stopped beside her seat, Sam didn't look up, simply assuming that it was a passenger wanting to retrieve something from the overhead locker.

She wasn't prepared in any way when a familiar deep voice said quietly beside her, 'Hello, Sam.'

'Khalid!' Sam's hand flew to her mouth to stifle her gasp as she stared up at him. He smiled thinly but she could see the anger in his eyes and knew that he was less than pleased by her hasty departure.

'The very same. Obviously you didn't expect to see me so soon. I apologise if I've upset your plans.'

'What are you doing here?' she asked, her voice quavering with shock. She took a steadying breath but it didn't help, didn't do anything to quieten her racing heart. Maybe it was foolish but the fact that Khalid had followed her had to mean something, surely?

'You said we needed to talk and I agree with you.' He gave a little shrug. 'I didn't imagine we were going to have that conversation on a plane but needs must.'

Sam glanced along the row of seats and flushed when she realised that they were attracting a great deal of interest. It was obvious that several of the passengers had recognised Khalid and that was simply exacerbating the problem. The thought of them having an in-depth discussion about the baby with all these people listening was more than she could bear.

'This is hardly the best place to talk,' she began but he cut her off.

'I agree. It isn't.' He stepped back, his brows arching

as he nodded to the first-class cabin. 'Come. There's more room up there. We can talk in private.'

'Oh, but I haven't got a ticket for First Class,' she protested, desperately playing for time. It had been such a shock to see Khalid and she needed to work out what she should say to him, muster up all the arguments she could to make him understand that it wasn't possible for them to be together.

'That isn't a problem. I shall take care of it.'

Sam could tell from his tone that he wasn't going to be deterred. He intended to talk to her about the baby and what would happen in the future and nothing she could say would stop him either. She stood up and followed him into the first-class cabin, sitting down where he indicated without a word. There was no point wasting her breath by objecting to his high-handed manner, not when she would need every scrap of breath to put across her reasons for them not being together. She knew Khalid too well to imagine that he would accept her decision without a fight. The thought filled her with dread.

Khalid spoke briefly to the flight attendant then sat down beside her. 'So why did you run off when you knew that we needed to talk?'

'I realised that there wasn't anything else we really needed to say.' She gave a little shrug. 'I'd told you about the baby and that was the main thing.'

'I see. So the fact that we haven't made any decisions about the future isn't important?'

His tone was silky, smooth, but Sam shivered when she heard the underlying thread of steel it held as well. Khalid wasn't going to be fobbed off by half-truths; she would have to be completely honest with him.

'Of course it's important but we need to think about the situation and not rush into something we will regret.'

'And you believe that we will regret making a commitment, regret it if we get married, regret making a life for us and our child?'

It was what she wanted so much but she knew that it could never happen, that the cost was too great. 'I... Yes.' Her voice caught but she forced herself to continue. 'You will regret it, Khalid. I'm certain of that.'

'You are so wrong, so very wrong, my love.' He took her hand and raised it to his lips. 'The only thing I shall ever regret is that I let you go six years ago. I did it with the very best of intentions, because I was afraid of you getting hurt if our relationship became public knowledge, with all the attendant publicity it would have aroused. I was also afraid that you would come to hate me one day for ruining your life.'

'Ruin my life?' she repeated, staring at him in surprise. 'What do you mean by that?'

'That if we had got married and you had moved to Azad to live, your life would have had to change drastically. Although it's easier for women these days than it was when my mother lived there, there are still far too many restrictions on what a woman can do.'

He ran the pad of his thumb over her knuckles and Sam trembled when she felt the light caress. It was all she could do not to tell him that it didn't matter, that she didn't care how her life would be affected, but she knew that she mustn't do that, that she had to listen to what he had to say because it was important to him that she understood.

'What sort of restrictions?' she asked quietly.

'You might not have been able to continue with your

career in medicine, for a start, although, thankfully, that isn't such an issue nowadays. There are far more women doctors working in our hospitals and clinics then there used to be.'

'That's good,' she said softly.

'Yes, it is.' He smiled at her with such tenderness that her breath caught. 'Nevertheless, it will be some time before our women doctors achieve the same degree of equality as their male counterparts. Consultants' posts tend to be offered to men, I'm afraid.'

She gave a tiny shrug. 'It will happen eventually. And let's be realistic. Men tend to get boosted up the career ladder far faster than we women even in the UK.'

'That's true,' he agreed, then sighed. 'However, as the wife of a member of the ruling family, you would be expected to conform to traditional values—home and family first, with your career way down the list of priorities.'

'I understand. Obviously it would take some getting used to but if, as you say, things are changing then it would only be for a limited period, surely?'

'Perhaps. But I know from experience the effect it could have. My mother trained as a barrister but she gave up the law when she married my father. It was fine at first but eventually the fact that she couldn't do the job she loved was too much for her.' He shrugged. 'She and my father divorced when I was in my early teens, not because they didn't love one another but because my mother couldn't cope with life in Azad any longer.'

'How sad. It must have been very difficult for you.' She turned her hand over and squeezed his fingers. 'I can understand how it must have affected you, Khalid, but just because your mother couldn't cope with life in Azad, it doesn't mean that I couldn't cope with it.'

She took a quick breath, knowing that she had to be as honest as he had been. 'No, my biggest fear is the damage it could cause to you and your family if people found out about my background. That's something I couldn't bear. You said that I might come to hate you for ruining my life but it works two ways. You could come to hate me for tarnishing your family's reputation.'

'No. That would never happen.' His fingers closed around hers, holding her fast when she tried to pull away. 'I could never hate you, Sam. Never in a thousand years.' He bent and kissed her, his lips clinging to hers for a mere heartbeat, but she felt the passion they held and shivered. It would be so easy to believe him but she had to be strong and do what was right.

'You can't make promises like that, Khalid. Nobody can.'

'I know how I feel.' He pressed her hand to his chest so she could feel the steady pounding of his heart. 'I know that I could never hate you for any reason. I love you too much, just as I shall love this child we have conceived. That's why I came after you, to make you understand that we need one another.'

'I don't need you, though,' she muttered in a desperate attempt to be sensible.

'Don't you?' He brushed his mouth over hers again then drew back and looked at her. 'Not even a little bit?'

'I... No,' she whispered, trying to stem the shudder that was working its way down her spine.

'Are you sure?' His mouth touched hers once more and lingered so that she could both feel and hear the words. It made it that much harder to stick to what she knew was right. 'Absolutely certain?'

'Yes,' Sam whispered, although she could feel her resolve melting and desperately tried to hold on to what little remained.

'I see.' He sighed throatily as his hand slid up her arm, caressing her skin through the thin fabric of her blouse. 'That's a real shame because I need you. So much. You and our baby. If I'm honest, I can't imagine how I shall live the rest of my life without you both.'

His hand slid up then down, the light pressure of his fingers making her shudder with need, with longing, with far too many things. When he drew her to him and held her against his chest, Sam tried to be strong, tried her best to remember that she mustn't allow this to happen, but her resolve seemed to have disappeared completely. When Khalid tilted her chin and kissed her, she didn't push him away, didn't even attempt to stop what was happening. How could she when it was what she wanted so desperately?

The kiss seemed to last for an eternity and yet at the same time it was over far too quickly. Sam clung to him afterwards, needing the solid support of his body to hold on to as her determination faded into nothing. She loved him so much and if he wanted her to live with him then she would do so and face whatever the future held.

'I love you, my darling.' He stroked her hair, repeating the words in his own tongue, and she sighed softly.

'I love you too. So very much. So much that I can't bear the thought of you getting hurt.'

'As I can't bear the thought of you getting hurt either.' His expression was grave. 'It isn't just the unwelcome attentions of the press you would have to contend with,

Sam, but the vastly different lifestyle you would lead in Azad. Could you bear it, bear to have restrictions placed upon what you do?'

'I don't know,' she said honestly. 'All I can do is give it a go and see what happens.'

'Or I could move to England on a permanent basis.'

'You'd do that?' She drew back and looked at him in surprise.

'Yes.' He smiled. 'If it was a choice between that and losing you then I would do it. Willingly too.'

'I don't know what to say...' She broke off and swallowed, unbearably moved by the offer. 'Thank you so much. I know how you feel about Azad and that you are willing to give up living there for me is more than I could ever hope for.'

'I'd be doing it for us—you, me and our child.' He kissed her hand. 'That would make any sacrifice worthwhile.'

'I feel the same. Maybe it will be very restricting to conform to Azadian mores but I can handle it so long as I have you.'

He sighed. 'I hope that's true. I saw how hard it was for my mother and how frustrated she became at having to adhere to a way of life that was alien to her.'

'But a lot has changed since then, hasn't it? And it's still changing.'

'That's very true.' He smiled. 'Maybe we can help to make those changes happen sooner than they might have done. You will soon charm my fellow countrymen, the way you have charmed me!'

'I doubt that,' she denied, laughing up at him. She sobered abruptly. 'The press will have a field day once the news of our relationship gets out. Are you sure it won't upset you, Khalid?'

'Only if it hurts you.' His gaze was tender. 'I love you, Sam, and I don't care about your background. It's important only in as much as I know how hurt you were when the story was raked up that last time.'

'It did hurt. It hurt to be made to feel that I was somehow to blame for my family's mistakes.' She bit her lip. 'One thing you need to understand, Khalid, is that I love my brother despite what he's done and I refuse to turn my back on him.'

'It's no more than I would have expected.' He kissed her lightly. 'Maybe we can both help him to make a fresh start, if he's willing.'

'That would be wonderful!' She returned his kiss then sat back in her seat. 'I wish we weren't on this plane. It will be ages before we land and we shall have to observe the proprieties.'

'Hmm. No mile-high club for us,' he teased her. He took her hand and held it lightly in his. 'We shall book into one of the airport hotels as soon as we reach London and celebrate our engagement in the appropriate manner. Until then we shall be the very models of decorum. Agreed?'

'Yes. So long as you don't look at me *that* way!'

Khalid laughed as he bent and dropped a kiss on the tip of her nose. The flight attendant stopped by their seats just then and offered them coffee, which they both accepted. Sam drank hers slowly, savouring its richness. It was the best cup of coffee she had ever tasted, although she suspected that it was the thought of what was to happen when they reached London that had enhanced its flavour.

She glanced at Khalid and felt a rush of love consume her when he smiled at her. In that moment, she knew that it was going to be fine, that they would deal with whatever problems they encountered. They loved one another and nothing would stop them being together from this moment on. Happiness filled her as she rested her head against the back of the seat and closed her eyes. She and Khalid had a wonderful future to look forward to with their child.

EPILOGUE

Three years later

'ARE YOU READY, my darling?'

'Almost. I just need to finish brushing Jasmina's hair.' Sam looked up and smiled as Khalid came into the room, thinking that she would never tire of seeing him. She loved him so much and made a point of telling him that each and every day.

They had been married for three glorious years and tonight they were throwing a party to celebrate their third anniversary. She also had something to tell him, news that she knew would thrill him, but she would wait until they were on their own. Now she finished brushing their daughter's hair and gave Jasmina a kiss.

'Go and show Daddy how pretty you look, darling,' she told the little girl.

She watched as Jasmina ran over to Khalid and held up her arms to be picked up. Jasmina had inherited her fair colouring and looked a picture in the pale pink dress that her aunt Mariam had bought for her. Everyone adored her and there was never a shortage of volunteers if Sam needed a babysitter when she was working.

The status of women in Azad had come on in leaps

and bounds, thanks to Khalid's determination to improve matters. Sam had returned to work on a part-time basis when Jasmina was a year old and loved her job at the hospital, working with expectant mothers. Although much had been made of her background when she and Khalid had married, these days it was rarely mentioned. Maybe it was the fact that she and Khalid were so obviously in love but most people ignored the difference in their social standing. Even Khalid's father had accepted her and was proving to be a doting grandparent; Jasmina could twist King Faisal round her dainty little finger by all accounts! Life was working out extremely well and it would only get better after she told Khalid her news.

Suddenly, Sam knew that she couldn't wait a second longer to share it with him. Standing up, she went and kissed him on the cheek. 'I wasn't going to tell you this till later but I can't keep it to myself any longer. I'm pregnant.'

'What?' Khalid stared at her for a moment before his face broke into a delighted smile. Setting Jasmina down, he took Sam into his arms and hugged her. 'When did you find out?'

'This afternoon for certain, although I've had my suspicions for a few days now.' She laughed. 'I wanted to be absolutely sure before I told you.'

'And you are? There's no mistake?'

'Nope! In seven months' time you are going to be a daddy again. What would you like this time, a girl or a boy?'

'I don't care.' He kissed her lingeringly then laughed. 'I don't care what it is. I shall love it with all my heart, just as I love Jasmina and her mother!'

He kissed her again, putting the seal on their happiness. Sam kissed him back, knowing how fortunate she was. Not only had she found the man she loved with all her heart but they had a wonderful future to look forward to together with their family. She couldn't have wished for anything more than what she had.

* * * * *

Snow, sleigh bells and a hint of seduction

Find your perfect Christmas reads at
millsandboon.co.uk/Christmas

MILLS & BOON®

Why shop at millsandboon.co.uk?

Each year, thousands of romance readers find their perfect read at millsandboon.co.uk. That's because we're passionate about bringing you the very best romantic fiction. Here are some of the advantages of shopping at www.millsandboon.co.uk:

Get new books first—you'll be able to buy your favourite books one month before they hit the shops

Get exclusive discounts—you'll also be able to buy our specially created monthly collections, with up to 50% off the RRP

Find your favourite authors—latest news, interviews and new releases for all your favourite authors and series on our website, plus ideas for what to try next

Join in—once you've bought your favourite books, don't forget to register with us to rate, review and join in the discussions

Visit **www.millsandboon.co.uk**
for all this and more today!